Jeffrey Archer is a ma
novels which have all
Penny More, Not a Penn
achieved instant success. Next came
rifying thriller *Shall We Tell the President?*, followed by his triumphant bestseller *Kane and Abel*. His first collection of short stories, *A Quiver Full of Arrows*, came next, and then *The Prodigal Daughter*, the superb sequel to *Kane and Abel*. This was followed by *First Among Equals*, considered by the *Scotsman* to be the finest novel about parliament since Trollope, the thrilling chase story *A Matter of Honour*, his second collection of stories, *A Twist in the Tale*, and the novels *As the Crow Flies* and *Honour Among Thieves*. *Twelve Red Herrings*, his third collection of stories, was followed by the novels *The Fourth Estate* and *The Eleventh Commandment*. A collected edition of his short stories was published in 1997.

Jeffrey Archer was born in 1940 and educated at Wellington School, Somerset and Brasenose College, Oxford. He represented Great Britain in the 100 metres in the early sixties, and entered the House of Commons when he won the by-election at Louth in 1969. He wrote his first novel, *Not a Penny More, Not a Penny Less*, in 1974. From September 1985 to October 1986 he was Deputy Chairman of the Conservative Party, and he was created a Life Peer in the Queen's Birthday Honours of 1992. He lives in Cambridge with his wife and two sons.

By the same author

Novels

NOT A PENNY MORE, NOT A PENNY LESS
SHALL WE TELL THE PRESIDENT?
KANE AND ABEL
THE PRODIGAL DAUGHTER
FIRST AMONG EQUALS
A MATTER OF HONOUR
AS THE CROW FLIES
HONOUR AMONG THIEVES
THE FOURTH ESTATE
THE ELEVENTH COMMANDMENT

Short Stories

A QUIVER FULL OF ARROWS
A TWIST IN THE TALE
TWELVE RED HERRINGS
THE COLLECTED SHORT STORIES

Plays

BEYOND REASONABLE DOUBT
EXCLUSIVE

JEFFREY ARCHER

A QUIVER FULL OF ARROWS

A TWIST IN THE TALE

HarperCollins*Publishers*

This omnibus edition published in 1998 by
HarperCollins*Publishers*

HarperCollins*Publishers*
77–85 Fulham Palace Road,
Hammersmith, London W6 8JB

These novels are entirely works of fiction. The names, characters and incidents portrayed in them are the work of the author's imagination. Any resemblance to actual persons, living or dead, events or localities is entirely coincidental.

ISBN 0 261 67132 4

Printed and bound in Great Britain by
Clays Ltd, St Ives plc

To Robin and Carolyn

Contents

AUTHOR'S NOTE

Of these twelve short stories, eleven are based on known incidents (some embellished with considerable licence). Only one is totally the result of my own imagination.

In the case of 'The Century' I took my theme from three different cricket matches. Lovers of *Wisden* will have to do some considerable delving to uncover them.

'The Luncheon' was inspired by W. Somerset Maugham.

J.A.

The Chinese Statue

THE little Chinese statue was the next item to come under the auctioneer's hammer. Lot 103 caused those quiet murmurings that always precede the sale of a masterpiece. The auctioneer's assistant held up the delicate piece of ivory for the packed audience to admire while the auctioneer glanced around the room to be sure he knew where the serious bidders were seated. I studied my catalogue and read the detailed description of the piece, and what was known of its history.

The statue had been purchased in Ha Li Chuan in 1871 and was referred to as what Sotheby's quaintly described as "the property of a gentleman", usually meaning that some member of the aristocracy did not wish to admit that he was having to sell off one of the family heirlooms. I wondered if that was the case on this occasion and decided to do some research to discover what had caused the little Chinese statue to find its way into the auction rooms on that Thursday morning over one hundred years later.

"Lot No. 103," declared the auctioneer. "What am I bid for this magnificent example of . . . ?"

Sir Alexander Heathcote, as well as being a gentleman, was an exact man. He was exactly six-foot-three and a quarter inches tall, rose at seven o'clock every morning, joined his wife at breakfast to eat one boiled egg cooked for precisely four minutes, two pieces of toast with one spoonful of Cooper's marmalade, and drink one cup of China tea. He would then take a hackney carriage from his home in Cadogan Gardens at exactly eight-twenty and arrive at the Foreign Office at promptly eight-fifty-nine, returning home again on the stroke of six o'clock.

Sir Alexander had been exact from an early age, as became the only son of a general. But unlike his father, he chose to serve his Queen in the diplomatic service, another exacting calling. He progressed from a shared desk at the Foreign Office in Whitehall to third secretary in Calcutta, to second secretary in Vienna, to first secretary in Rome, to Deputy Ambassador in Washington, and finally to minister in Peking. He was delighted when Mr Gladstone invited him to represent the government in China as he had for some considerable time taken more than an amateur interest in the art of the Ming dynasty. This crowning appointment in his distinguished career would afford him what until then he would have considered impossible, an opportunity to observe in their natural habitat some of the great statues, paintings and drawings which he had previously been able to admire only in books.

When Sir Alexander arrived in Peking, after a journey by sea and land that took his party nearly two months, he presented his seals patent to the Empress Tzu-Hsi and a personal letter for her private reading from Queen Victoria. The Empress, dressed from head to toe in white and gold, received her new Ambassador in the throne room of the Imperial Palace. She read the letter from the British monarch while Sir Alexander remained standing to attention. Her Imperial Highness revealed nothing of its contents to the new minister, only wishing him a successful term of office in his appointment. She then moved her lips slightly up at the corners which Sir Alexander judged correctly to mean that the audience had come to an end. As he was conducted back through the great halls of the Imperial Palace by a Mandarin in the long court dress of black and gold, Sir Alexander walked as slowly as possible, taking in the magnificent collection of ivory and jade statues which were scattered casually around the building much in the way Cellini and Michaelangelo today lie stacked against each other in Florence.

As his ministerial appointment was for only three years, Sir Alexander took no leave, but preferred to use his time to put the Embassy behind him and travel on horseback into the outlying districts to learn more about the country and its people. On these trips he was always accompanied by a Mandarin from the palace staff who acted as interpreter and guide.

On one such journey, passing through the muddy streets of a small village with but a few houses called Ha Li Chuan, a distance of some fifty miles from

Peking, Sir Alexander chanced upon an old craftsman's working place. Leaving his servants, the minister dismounted from his horse and entered the ramshackled wooden workshop to admire the delicate pieces of ivory and jade that crammed the shelves from floor to ceiling. Although modern, the pieces were superbly executed by an experienced craftsman and the minister entered the little hut with the thought of acquiring a small memento of his journey. Once in the shop he could hardly move in any direction for fear of knocking something over. The building had not been designed for a six-foot-three and a quarter visitor. Sir Alexander stood still and enthralled, taking in the fine scented jasmine smell that hung in the air.

An old craftsman bustled forward in a long, blue coolie robe and flat black hat to greet him; a jet black plaited pigtail fell down his back. He bowed very low and then looked up at the giant from England. The minister returned the bow while the Mandarin explained who Sir Alexander was and his desire to be allowed to look at the work of the craftsman. The old man was nodding his agreement even before the Mandarin had come to the end of his request. For over an hour the minister sighed and chuckled as he studied many of the pieces with admiration and finally returned to the old man to praise his skill. The craftsman bowed once again, and his shy smile revealed no teeth but only genuine pleasure at Sir Alexander's compliments. Pointing a finger to the back of the shop, he beckoned the two important visitors to follow him. They did so and entered a veritable Aladdin's Cave, with row upon row of beautiful miniature emperors and classical figures. The minister could have happily settled down in the orgy of ivory for at least a week. Sir Alexander and the craftsman chatted away to each other through the interpreter, and the minister's love and knowledge of the Ming dynasty was soon revealed. The little craftsman's face lit up with this discovery and he turned to the Mandarin and in a hushed voice made a request. The Mandarin nodded his agreement and translated.

"I have, Your Excellency, a piece of Ming myself that you might care to see. A statue that has been in my family for over seven generations."

"I should be honoured," said the minister.

"It is I who would be honoured, Your Excellency," said the little man who thereupon scampered out of the back door, nearly falling over a stray dog, and on to an old peasant house a few yards behind the workshop. The minister and the Mandarin remained in the back room, for Sir Alexander knew the old man would never have considered inviting an honoured guest into his humble home until they had known each other for many years, and only then after he had been invited to Sir Alexander's home first. A few minutes passed before the little blue figure came trotting back, pigtail bouncing up and down on his shoulders. He was now clinging on to something that from the very way he held it close to his chest, had to be a treasure. The craftsman passed the piece over for the minister to study. Sir Alexander's mouth opened wide and he could not hide his excitement. The little statue, no more than six inches in height, was of the Emperor Kung and as fine an example of Ming as the minister had seen. Sir Alexander felt confident that the maker was the great Pen Q who had been patronised by the Emperor, so that the date must have been around the turn of the fifteenth century. The statue's only blemish was that the ivory base on which such pieces usually rest was missing, and a small stick protruded from the bottom of the imperial robes; but in the eyes of Sir Alexander nothing could detract from its overall beauty. Although the craftsman's lips did not move, his eyes glowed with the pleasure his guest evinced as he studied the ivory Emperor.

"You think the statue is good?" asked the craftsman through the interpreter.

"It's magnificent," the minister replied. "Quite magnificent."

"My own work is not worthy to stand by its side," added the craftsman humbly.

"No, no," said the minister, though in truth the little craftsman knew the great man was only being kind, for Sir Alexander was holding the ivory statue in a way that already showed the same love as the old man had for the piece.

The minister smiled down at the craftsman as he handed back the Emperor Kung and then he uttered perhaps the only undiplomatic words he had ever spoken in thirty-five years of serving his Queen and country.

"How I wish the piece was mine."

Sir Alexander regretted voicing his thoughts immediately he heard the Mandarin translate them, because he knew only too well the old Chinese tradition that if an honoured guest requests something the giver will grow in the eyes of his fellow men by parting with it.

A sad look came over the face of the little old craftsman as he handed back the figurine to the minister.

"No, no. I was only joking," said Sir Alexander, quickly trying to return the piece to its owner.

"You would dishonour my humble home if you did not take the Emperor, Your Excellency," the old man said anxiously and the Mandarin gravely nodded his agreement.

The minister remained silent for some time. "I have dishonoured my own home, sir," he replied, and looked towards the Mandarin who remained inscrutable.

The little craftsman bowed. "I must fix a base on the statue," he said, "or you will not be able to put the piece on view."

He went to a corner of the room and opened a wooden packing chest that must have housed a hundred bases for his own statues. Rummaging around he picked out a base decorated with small, dark figures that the minister did not care for but which nevertheless made a perfect fit; the old man assured Sir Alexander that although he did not know the base's history, the piece bore the mark of a good craftsman.

The embarrassed minister took the gift and tried hopelessly to thank the little old man. The craftsman once again bowed low as Sir Alexander and the expressionless Mandarin left the little workshop.

As the party travelled back to Peking, the Mandarin observed the terrible state the minister was in, and uncharacteristically spoke first:

"Your Excellency is no doubt aware," he said, "of the old Chinese custom that when a stranger has been generous, you must return the kindness within the calendar year."

Sir Alexander smiled his thanks and thought carefully about the Mandarin's words. Once back in his official residence, he went immediately to the Embassy's extensive library to see if he could discover a realistic value for the little masterpiece. After much diligent research, he came across a drawing of a Ming statue that was almost an exact copy of the one now in his possession and with the help of the Mandarin he was able to assess its true worth, a figure that came to almost three years' emolument for a servant of the Crown. The minister discussed the problem with Lady Heathcote and she left her husband in no doubt as to the course of action he must take.

The following week the minister despatched a letter by private messenger to his bankers, Coutts & Co. in the Strand, London, requesting that they send a large part of his savings to reach him in Peking as quickly as possible. When the funds arrived nine weeks later the minister again approached the Mandarin, who listened to his questions and gave him the details he had asked for seven days later.

The Mandarin had discovered that the little craftsman, Yung Lee, came from the old and trusted family of Yung Shau who had for some five hundred years been craftsmen. Sir Alexander also learned that many of Yung Lee's ancestors had examples of their work in the palaces of the Manchu princes. Yung Lee himself was growing old and wished to retire to the hills above the village where his ancestors had always died. His son was ready to take over the workshop from him and continue the family tradition. The minister thanked the Mandarin for his diligence and had only one more request of him. The Mandarin listened sympathetically to the Ambassador from England and returned to the palace to seek advice.

A few days later the Empress granted Sir Alexander's request.

Almost a year to the day the minister, accompanied by the Mandarin, set out again from Peking for the village of Ha Li Chuan. When Sir Alexander arrived he immediately dismounted from his horse and entered the workshop that he remembered so well, the old man was seated at his bench, his flat hat slightly askew, a piece of uncarved ivory held lovingly between his fingers. He looked up from his work and shuffled towards the minister, not recognising his guest immediately until he could almost touch the foreign giant. Then he bowed low. The minister spoke through the Mandarin:

"I have returned, sir, within the calendar year to repay my debt."

"There was no need, Your Excellency. My family is honoured that the little statue lives in a great Embassy and may one day be admired by the people of your own land."

The minister could think of no words to form an adequate reply and simply requested that the old man should accompany him on a short journey.

The craftsman agreed without question and the three men set out on donkeys towards the north. They travelled for over two hours up a thin winding path into the hills behind the craftsman's workshop, and when they reached the village of Ma Tien they were met by another Mandarin, who bowed low to the minister and requested Sir Alexander and the craftsman to continue their journey with him on foot. They walked in silence to the far side of the village and only stopped when they had reached a hollow in the hill from which there was a magnificent view of the valley all the way down to Ha Li Chuan. In the hollow stood a newly completed small white house of the most perfect proportions. Two stone lion dogs, tongues hanging over their lips, guarded the front entrance. The little old craftsman who had not spoken since he had left his workshop remained mystified by the purpose of the journey until the minister turned to him and offered:

"A small, inadequate gift and my feeble attempt to repay you in kind."

The craftsman fell to his knees and begged forgiveness of the Mandarin as he knew it was forbidden for an artisan to accept gifts from a foreigner. The Mandarin raised the frightened blue figure from the ground, explaining to his countryman that the Empress herself had sanctioned the minister's request. A smile of joy came over the face of the craftsman and he slowly walked up to the doorway of the beautiful little house unable to resist running his hand over the carved lion dogs. The three travellers then spent over an hour admiring the little house before returning in silent mutual happiness back to the workshop in Ha Li Chuan. The two men thus parted, honour satisfied, and Sir Alexander rode to his Embassy that night content that his actions had met with the approval of the Mandarin as well as Lady Heathcote.

The minister completed his tour of duty in Peking, and the Empress awarded him the Silver Star of China and a grateful Queen added the KCVO to his already long list of decorations. After a few weeks back at the Foreign Office clearing the China desk, Sir Alexander retired to his native Yorkshire, the only English county whose inhabitants still hope to be born and die in the same place – not unlike the Chinese.

Sir Alexander spent his final years in the home of his late father with his wife and the little Ming Emperor. The statue occupied the centre of the mantelpiece in the drawing room for all to see and admire.

Being an exact man, Sir Alexander wrote a long and detailed will in which he left precise instructions for the disposal of his estate, including what was to happen to the little statue after his death. He bequeathed the Emperor Kung to his first son requesting that he do the same, in order that the statue might always pass to the first son, or a daughter if the direct male line faltered. He also made a provision that the statue was never to be disposed of, unless the family's honour was at stake. Sir Alexander Heathcote died at the stroke of midnight on his seventieth year.

* * *

His first-born, Major James Heathcote, was serving his Queen in the Boer War at the time he came into possession of the Ming Emperor. The Major was a fighting man, commissioned with the Duke of Wellington's Regiment, and although he had little interest in culture even he could see the family heirloom was no ordinary treasure, so he loaned the statue to the regimental mess at Halifax in order that the Emperor could be displayed in the dining room for his brother officers to appreciate.

When James Heathcote became Colonel of the Dukes, the Emperor stood proudly on the table alongside the trophies won at Waterloo and Sebastopol in the Crimea and Madrid. And there the Ming Statue remained until the colonel's retirement to his father's house in Yorkshire, when the Emperor returned once again to the drawing room mantelpiece. The colonel was not a man to disobey his late father, even in death, and he left clear instructions that the heirloom must always be passed on to the first-born of the Heathcotes unless the family honour was in jeopardy. Colonel James Heathcote MC did not die a soldier's death; he simply fell asleep one night by the fire, the *Yorkshire Post* on his lap.

The colonel's first-born, the Reverend Alexander Heathcote, was at the time presiding over a small flock in the parish of Much Hadham in Hertfordshire. After burying his father with military honours, he placed the little Ming Emperor on the mantelpiece of the vicarage. Few members of the Mothers' Union appreciated the masterpiece but one or two old ladies were heard to remark on its delicate carving. And it was not until the Reverend became the Right Reverend, and the little statue found its way into the Bishop's palace, that the Emperor attracted the admiration he deserved. Many of those who visited the palace and heard the story of how the Bishop's grandfather had acquired the Ming statue were fascinated to learn of the disparity between the magnificent statue and its base. It always made a good after-dinner story.

God takes even his own ambassadors, but He did not do so before allowing Bishop Heathcote to complete a will leaving the statue to his son, with his grandfather's exact instructions carefully repeated. The Bishop's son, Captain James Heathcote, was a serving officer in his grandfather's regiment, so the Ming statue returned to the mess table in Halifax. During the Emperor's absence, the regimental trophies had been augmented by those struck for Ypres, the Marne and Verdun. The regiment was once again at war with Germany, and young Captain James Heathcote was killed on the beaches of Dunkirk and died intestate. Thereafter English law, the known wishes of his great-grandfather and common sense prevailed, and the little Emperor came into the possession of the captain's two-year-old son.

Alex Heathcote was, alas, not of the mettle of his doughty ancestors and he grew up feeling no desire to serve anyone other than himself. When Captain James had been so tragically killed, Alexander's mother lavished everything on the boy that her meagre income would allow. It didn't help, and it was not entirely young Alex's fault that he grew up to be, in the words of his grandmother, a selfish, spoiled little brat.

When Alex left school, only a short time before he would have been expelled, he found he could never hold down a job for more than a few weeks. It always seemed necessary for him to spend a little more than he, and finally his mother, could cope with. The good lady, deciding she could take no more of this life, departed it, to join all the other Heathcotes, not in Yorkshire, but in heaven.

In the swinging sixties, when casinos opened in Britain, young Alex was convinced that he had found the ideal way of earning a living without actually having to do any work. He developed a system for playing roulette with which it was impossible to lose. He did lose, so he refined the system and promptly lost more; he refined the system once again which resulted in him having to borrow to cover his losses. Why not? If the worst came to the worst, he told himself, he could always dispose of the little Ming Emperor.

The worst did come to the worst, as each one of Alex's newly refined systems took him progressively into greater debt until the casinos began to press him for payment. When finally, one Monday morning, Alex received an unsolicited call from two gentlemen who seemed determined to collect some eight thousand pounds he owed their masters, and hinted at bodily harm if the matter was not dealt with within fourteen days, Alex caved in. After all, his great-great-grandfather's instructions had been exact: the Ming statue was to be sold if the family honour was ever at stake.

Alex took the little Emperor off the mantelpiece

in his Cadogan Gardens flat and stared down at its delicate handiwork, at least having the grace to feel a little sad at the loss of the family heirloom. He then drove to Bond Street and delivered the masterpiece to Sotheby's, giving instructions that the Emperor should be put up for auction.

The head of the Oriental department, a pale, thin man, appeared at the front desk to discuss the masterpiece with Alex, looking not unlike the Ming statue he was holding so lovingly in his hands.

"It will take a few days to estimate the true value of the piece," he purred, "but I feel confident on a cursory glance that the statue is as fine an example of Pen Q as we have ever had under the hammer."

"That's no problem," replied Alex, "as long as you can let me know what it's worth within fourteen days."

"Oh, certainly," replied the expert. "I feel sure I could give you a floor price by Friday."

"Couldn't be better," said Alex.

During that week he contacted all his creditors and without exception they were prepared to wait and learn the appraisal of the expert. Alex duly returned to Bond Street on the Friday with a large smile on his face. He knew what his great-great-grandfather had paid for the piece and felt sure that the statue must be worth more than ten thousand pounds. A sum that would not only yield him enough to cover all his debts but leave him a little over to try out his new refined, refined system on the roulette table. As he climbed the steps of Sotheby's, Alex silently thanked his great-great-grandfather. He asked the girl on reception if he could speak to the head of the Oriental department. She picked up an internal phone and the expert appeared a few moments later at the front desk with a sombre look on his face. Alex's heart sank as he listened to his words: "A nice little piece, your Emperor, but unfortunately a fake, probably about two hundred, two hundred and fifty years old but only a copy of the original, I'm afraid. Copies were often made because . . ."

"How much is it worth?" interrupted an anxious Alex.

"Seven hundred pounds, eight hundred at the most."

Enough to buy a gun and some bullets, thought Alex sardonically as he turned and started to walk away.

"I wonder, sir . . ." continued the expert.

"Yes, yes, sell the bloody thing," said Alex, without bothering to look back.

"And what do you want me to do with the base?"

"The base?" repeated Alex, turning round to face the Orientalist.

"Yes, the base. It's quite magnificent, fifteenth century, undoubtedly a work of genius, I can't imagine how . . ."

"Lot No. 103," announced the auctioneer. "What am I bid for this magnificent example of . . . ?"

The expert turned out to be right in his assessment. At the auction at Sotheby's that Thursday morning I obtained the little Emperor for seven hundred and twenty guineas. And the base? That was acquired by an American gentleman of not unknown parentage for twenty-two thousand guineas.

The Luncheon

SHE waved at me across a crowded room of the St Regis Hotel in New York. I waved back realising I knew the face but I was unable to place it. She squeezed past waiters and guests and had reached me before I had a chance to ask anyone who she was. I racked that section of my brain which is meant to store people, but it transmitted no reply. I realised I would have to resort to the old party trick of carefully worded questions until her answers jogged my memory.

"How *are* you, darling?" she cried, and threw her arms around me, an opening that didn't help as we were at a Literary Guild cocktail party, and anyone will throw their arms around you on such occasions, even the directors of the Book-of-the-Month Club. From her accent she was clearly American and looked to be approaching forty, but thanks to the genius of modern make-up might even have overtaken it. She wore a long white cocktail dress and her blonde hair was done up in one of those buns that looks like a cottage loaf. The overall effect made her appear somewhat like a chess queen. Not that the cottage loaf helped because she might have had dark hair flowing to her shoulders when we last met. I do wish women would realise that when they change their hair style they often achieve exactly what they set out to do: look completely different to any unsuspecting male.

"I'm well, thank you," I said to the white queen. "And you?" I inquired as my opening gambit.

"I'm just fine, darling," she replied, taking a glass of champagne from a passing waiter.

"And how's the family?" I asked, not sure if she even had one.

"They're all well," she replied. No help there. "And how is Louise?" she inquired.

"Blooming," I said. So she knew my wife. But then not necessarily, I thought. Most American women are experts at remembering the names of men's wives. They have to be, when on the New York circuit they change so often it becomes a greater challenge than *The Times* crossword.

"Have you been to London lately?" I roared above the babble. A brave question, as she might never have been to Europe.

"Only once since we had lunch together." She looked at me quizzically. "You don't remember who I am, do you?" she asked as she devoured a cocktail sausage.

I smiled.

"Don't be silly, Susan," I said. "How could I ever forget?"

She smiled.

I confess that I remembered the white queen's

name in the nick of time. Although I still had only vague recollections of the lady, I certainly would never forget the lunch.

I had just had my first book published and the critics on both sides of the Atlantic had been complimentary, even if the cheques from my publishers were less so. My agent had told me on several occasions that I shouldn't write if I wanted to make money. This created a dilemma because I couldn't see how to make money if I didn't write.

It was around this time that the lady, who was now facing me and chattering on oblivious to my silence, telephoned from New York to heap lavish praise on my novel. There is no writer who does not enjoy receiving such calls, although I confess to having been less than captivated by an eleven-year-old girl who called me collect from California to say she had found a spelling mistake on page forty-seven and warned me she would ring again if she discovered another. However, this particular lady might have ended her transatlantic congratulations with nothing more than goodbye if she had not dropped her own name. It was one of those names that can, on the spur of the moment, always book a table at a chic restaurant or a seat at the opera which mere mortals like myself would have found impossible to achieve given a month's notice. To be fair, it was her husband's name that had achieved the reputation, as one of the world's most distinguished film producers.

"When I'm next in London you must have lunch with me," came crackling down the phone.

"No," said I gallantly, "you must have lunch with *me*."

"How perfectly charming you English always are," she said.

I have often wondered how much American women get away with when they say those few words to an Englishman. Nevertheless, the wife of an Oscar-winning producer does not phone one every day.

"I promise to call you when I'm next in London," she said.

And indeed she did, for almost six months to the day she telephoned again, this time from the Connaught Hotel to declare how much she was looking forward to our meeting.

"Where would you like to have lunch?" I said, realising a second too late, when she replied with the name of one of the most exclusive restaurants in town, that I should have made sure it was I who chose the venue. I was glad she couldn't see my forlorn face as she added with unabashed liberation:

"Monday, one o'clock. Leave the booking to me – I'm known there."

On the day in question I donned my one respectable suit, a new shirt which I had been saving for a special occasion since Christmas, and the only tie that looked as if it hadn't previously been used to hold up my trousers. I then strolled over to my bank and asked for a statement of my current account. The teller handed me a long piece of paper unworthy of its amount. I studied the figure as one who has to take a major financial decision. The bottom line stated in black lettering that I was in credit to the sum of thirty-seven pounds and sixty-three pence. I wrote out a cheque for thirty-seven pounds. I feel that a gentleman should always leave his account in credit, and I might add it was a belief that my bank manager shared with me. I then walked up to Mayfair for my luncheon date.

As I entered the restaurant I observed too many waiters and plush seats for my liking. You can't eat either, but you can be charged for them. At a corner table for two sat a woman who, although not young, was elegant. She wore a blouse of powder blue crêpe-de-chine, and her blonde hair was rolled away from her face in a style that reminded me of the war years, and had once again become fashionable. It was clearly my transatlantic admirer, and she greeted me in the same "I've known you all my life" fashion as she was to do at the Literary Guild cocktail party years later. Although she had a drink in front of her I didn't order an apéritif, explaining that I never drank before lunch – and would like to have added, "but as soon as your husband makes a film of my novel, I will."

She launched immediately into the latest Hollywood gossip, not so much dropping names as reciting them, while I ate my way through the crisps from the bowl in front of me. A few minutes later a waiter materialised by the table and presented us with two large embossed leather menus, considerably better bound than my novel. The place positively reeked of unnecessary expense. I opened the menu and studied the first chapter with horror; it was eminently putdownable. I had no idea that simple food obtained from Covent Garden that morning could cost quite so much by merely being transported to Mayfair. I could have bought her the same dishes for a quarter of the price at my favourite bistro, a mere one hundred yards away, and to add to my discomfort I observed that it was one of those restaurants where the guest's menu made no mention of the prices. I settled down to study the long list of French dishes which only served to remind me that I hadn't eaten well for over a month, a state of affairs that was about to be prolonged by a further day. I remembered my bank balance and morosely reflected that I would probably have to wait until my agent sold the Icelandic rights of my novel before I could afford a square meal again.

"What would you like?" I said gallantly.

"I always enjoy a light lunch," she volunteered. I sighed with premature relief, only to find that light did not necessarily mean "inexpensive".

She smiled sweetly up at the waiter, who looked as if *he* wouldn't be wondering where his next meal might be coming from, and ordered just a sliver of smoked salmon, followed by two tiny tender lamb cutlets. Then she hesitated, but only for a moment, before adding "and a side salad".

I studied the menu with some caution, running my finger down the prices, not the dishes.

"I also eat lightly at lunch," I said mendaciously. "The chef's salad will be quite enough for me." The waiter was obviously affronted but left peaceably.

She chatted of Coppola and Preminger, of Al Pacino and Robert Redford, and of Greta Garbo as if she saw her all the time. She was kind enough to stop for a moment and ask what I was working on at present. I would have liked to have replied – on how I was going to explain to my wife that I only have sixty-three pence left in the bank; whereas I actually discussed my ideas for another novel. She seemed impressed, but still made no reference to her husband. Should I mention him? No. Mustn't sound pushy, or as though I needed the money.

The food arrived, or that is to say her smoked salmon did, and I sat silently watching her eat my bank account while I nibbled a roll. I looked up only to discover a wine waiter hovering by my side.

"Would you care for some wine?" said I, recklessly.

"No, I don't think so," she said. I smiled a little too soon: "Well, perhaps a little something white and dry."

The wine waiter handed over a second leather-bound book, this time with golden grapes embossed on the cover. I searched down the pages for half bottles, explaining to my guest that I never drank at lunch. I chose the cheapest. The wine waiter reappeared a moment later with a large silver salver full of ice in which the half bottle looked drowned, and, like me, completely out of its depth. A junior waiter cleared away the empty plate while another wheeled a large trolley to the side of our table and served the lamb cutlets and the chef's salad. At the same time a third waiter made up an exquisite side salad for my guest which ended up bigger than my complete order. I didn't feel I could ask her to swap.

To be fair, the chef's salad was superb – although I confess it was hard to appreciate such food fully while trying to work out a plot that would be convincing if I found the bill came to over thirty-seven pounds.

"How silly of me to ask for white wine with lamb," she said, having nearly finished the half bottle. I ordered a half bottle of the house red without calling for the wine list.

She finished the white wine and then launched into the theatre, music and other authors. All those who were still alive she seemed to know and those who were dead she hadn't read. I might have enjoyed the performance if it hadn't been for the fear of wondering if I would be able to afford it when the curtain came down. When the waiter cleared away the empty dishes he asked my guest if she would care for anything else.

"No, thank you," she said – I nearly applauded. "Unless you have one of your famous apple surprises."

"I fear the last one may have gone, madam, but I'll go and see."

Don't hurry, I wanted to say, but instead I just smiled as the rope tightened around my neck. A few moments later the waiter strode back in triumph weaving between the tables holding the apple surprise, in the palm of his hand, high above his head. I prayed to Newton that the apple would obey his law. It didn't.

"The last one, madam."

"Oh, what luck," she declared.

"Oh, what luck," I repeated, unable to face the menu and discover the price. I was now attempting some mental arithmetic as I realised it was going to be a close run thing.

"Anything else, madam?" the ingratiating waiter inquired.

I took a deep breath.

"Just coffee," she said.

"And for you, Sir?"

"No, no, not for me." He left us. I couldn't think of an explanation for why I didn't drink coffee.

She then produced from the large Gucci bag by her side a copy of my novel, which I signed with a flourish, hoping the head waiter would see me and feel I was the sort of man who should be allowed to sign the bill as well, but he resolutely remained at the far end of the room while I wrote the words "An unforgettable meeting" and appended my signature.

While the dear lady was drinking her coffee I picked at another roll and called for the bill, not because I was in any particular hurry, but like a guilty defendant at the Old Bailey I preferred to wait no longer for the judge's sentence. A man in a smart green uniform, whom I had never seen before appeared carrying a silver tray with a folded piece of paper on it looking not unlike my bank statement. I pushed back the edge of the check slowly and read the figure: thirty-six pounds and forty pence. I casually put my hand into my inside pocket and withdrew my life's possessions and then placed the crisp new notes on the silver tray. They were whisked away. The man in the green uniform returned a few moments later with my sixty pence change, which I pocketed as it was the only way I was going to get a bus home. The waiter gave me a look that would have undoubtedly won him a character part in any film produced by the lady's distinguished husband.

My guest rose and walked across the restaurant, waving at, and occasionally kissing people that I had previously only seen in glossy magazines. When she reached the door she stopped to retrieve her coat, a mink. I helped her on with the fur, again failing to leave a tip. As we stood on the Curzon Street pavement, a dark blue Rolls-Royce drew up beside us and a liveried chauffeur leaped out and opened the rear door. She climbed in.

"Goodbye, darling," she said, as the electric window slid down. "Thank you for such a lovely lunch."

"Goodbye," I said, and summoning up my courage added: "I do hope when you are next in town I shall have the opportunity of meeting your distinguished husband."

"Oh, darling, didn't you know?" she said as she looked out from the Rolls-Royce.

"Know what?"

"We were divorced ages ago."

"Divorced?" said I.

"Oh, yes," she said gaily, "I haven't spoken to him for years."

I just stood there looking helpless.

"Oh, don't worry yourself on my account," she said. "He's no loss. In any case I have recently married again" – another film producer, I prayed – "In fact, I quite expected to bump into my husband today – you see, he owns the restaurant."

Without another word the electric window purred up and the Rolls-Royce glided effortlessly out of sight leaving me to walk to the nearest bus stop.

* * *

As I stood surrounded by Literary Guild guests, staring at the white queen with the cottage loaf bun, I could still see her drifting away in that blue Rolls-Royce. I tried to concentrate on her words.

"I knew you wouldn't forget me, darling," she was saying. "After all, I did take you to lunch, didn't I?"

The Coup

THE blue and silver 707 jet, displaying a large "P" on its tail plane, taxied to a halt at the north end of Lagos International Airport. A fleet of six black Mercedes drove up to the side of the aircraft and waited in a line resembling a land-bound crocodile. Six sweating, uniformed drivers leaped out and stood to attention. When the driver of the front car opened his rear door, Colonel Usman of the Federal Guard stepped out, and walked quickly to the bottom of the passenger steps which had been hurriedly pushed into place by four of the airport staff.

The front section cabin door swung back and the colonel stared up into the gap, to see, framed against the dark interior of the cabin, a slim, attractive hostess dressed in a blue suit with silver piping. On her jacket lapel was a large "P". She turned and nodded in the direction of the cabin. A few seconds later, an immaculately dressed tall man with thick black hair and deep brown eyes replaced her in the doorway. The man had an air of effortless style about him which self-made millionaires would have paid a considerable part of their fortune to possess. The colonel saluted as Senhor Eduardo Francisco de Silveira, head of the Prentino empire gave a curt nod.

De Silveira emerged from the coolness of his air-conditioned 707 into the burning Nigerian sun without showing the slightest sign of discomfort. The colonel guided the tall, elegant Brazilian, who was accompanied only by his private secretary, to the front Mercedes while the rest of the Prentino staff filed down the back stairway of the aircraft and filled the other five cars. The driver, a corporal who had been detailed to be available night and day for the honoured guest, opened the rear door of the front car and saluted. Eduardo de Silveira showed no sign of acknowledgment. The corporal smiled nervously, revealing the largest set of white teeth the Brazilian had ever seen.

"Welcome to Lagos," the corporal volunteered. "Hope you make very big deal while you are in Nigeria."

Eduardo did not comment as he settled back into his seat and stared out of the tinted window to watch some passengers of a British Airways 707 that had landed just before him form a long queue on the hot tarmac as they waited patiently to clear customs. The driver put the car into first gear and the black crocodile proceeded on its journey. Colonel Usman who was now in the front seat beside the corporal, soon discovered that the Brazilian guest did not care for small talk, and the secretary who was seated by his employer's side never once opened his mouth. The colonel, used to doing things by example, remained silent, leaving de Silveira to consider his plan of campaign.

Eduardo Francisco de Silveira had been born in the small village of Rebeti, a hundred miles north of Rio de Janeiro, heir to one of the two most powerful family fortunes in Brazil. He had been educated privately in Switzerland before attending the University of California in Los Angeles. He went on to complete his education at the Harvard Business School. After Harvard he returned from America to work in Brazil where he started neither at the top nor the bottom of the firm but in the middle, managing his family's mining interests in Minas Gerais. He quickly worked his way to the top, even faster than his father had planned, but then the boy turned out to be not so much a chip as a chunk off the old block. At twenty-nine he married Maria, eldest daughter of his father's closest friend, and when twelve years later his father died Eduardo succeeded to the Prentino throne. There were seven sons in all: the second son, Alfredo, was now in charge of banking; João ran shipping; Carlos organised construction; Manoel arranged food and supplies; Jaime managed the family newspapers, and little Antonio, the last – and certainly the least – ran the family farms. All the brothers reported to Eduardo before making any major decision, for he was still chairman of the largest private company in Brazil, despite the boastful claims of his old family enemy, Manuel Rodrigues.

When General Castelo Branco's military regime overthrew the civilian government in 1964 the generals agreed that they could not kill off all the de

Silveiras or the Rodrigues so they had better learn to live with the two rival families. The de Silveiras for their part had always had enough sense never to involve themselves in politics other than by making payments to every government official, military or civilian, according to his rank. This ensured that the Prentino empire grew alongside whatever faction came to power. One of the reasons Eduardo de Silveira had allocated three days in his crowded schedule for a visit to Lagos was that the Nigerian system of government seemed to resemble so closely that of Brazil, and at least on this project he had cut the ground from under Manuel Rodrigues' feet which would more than make up for losing the Rio airport tender to him. Eduardo smiled at the thought of Rodrigues not realising that he was in Nigeria to close a deal that could make him twice the size of his rival.

As the black Mercedes moved slowly through the teeming noisy streets paying no attention to traffic lights, red or green, Eduardo thought back to his first meeting with General Mohammed, the Nigerian Head of State, on the occasion of the President's official visit to Brazil. Speaking at the dinner given in General Mohammed's honour, President Ernesto Geisel declared a hope that the two countries would move towards closer co-operation in politics and commerce. Eduardo agreed with his unelected leader and was happy to leave the politics to the President if he allowed him to get on with the commerce. General Mohammed made his reply, on behalf of the guests, in an English accent that normally would only be associated with Oxford.

The general talked at length of the project that was most dear to his heart, the building of a new Nigerian capital in Abuja, a city which he considered might even rival Brasilia. After the speeches were over, the general took de Silveira on one side and spoke in greater detail of the Abuja city project asking him if he might consider a private tender. Eduardo smiled and only wished that his enemy, Rodrigues, could hear the intimate conversation he was having with the Nigerian Head of State.

Eduardo studied carefully the outline proposal sent to him a week later, after the general had returned to Nigeria, and agreed to his first request by despatching a research team of seven men to fly to Lagos and complete a feasibility study on Abuja.

One month later, the team's dctailed report was in de Silveira's hands. Eduardo came to the conclusion that the potential profitability of the project was worthy of a full proposal to the Nigerian government. He contacted General Mohammed personally to find that he was in full agreement and authorised the go-ahead. This time twenty-three men were despatched to Lagos and three months and one hundred and seventy pages later, Eduardo signed and sealed the proposal designated as, "A New Capital for Nigeria". He made only one alteration to the final document. The cover of the proposal was in blue and silver with the Prentino logo in the centre: Eduardo had that changed to green and white, the national colours of Nigeria, with the national emblem of an eagle astride two horses: he realised it was the little things that impressed generals and often tipped the scales. He sent ten copies of the feasibility study to Nigeria's Head of State with an invoice for one million dollars.

When General Mohammed had studied the proposal he invited Eduardo de Silveira to visit Nigeria as his guest, in order to discuss the next stage of the project. De Silveira telexed back, provisionally accepting the invitation, and pointing out politely but firmly that he had not yet received reimbursement for the one million dollars spent on the initial feasibility study. The money was telexed by return from the Central Bank of Nigeria and de Silveira managed to find four consecutive days in his diary for "The New Federal Capital project": his schedule demanded that he arrived in Lagos on a Monday morning because he had to be in Paris at the latest by the Thursday night.

While these thoughts were going through Eduardo's mind, the Mercedes drew up outside Dodan Barracks. The iron gates swung open and a full armed guard gave the general salute, an honour normally afforded only to a visiting Head of State. The black Mercedes drove slowly through the gates and came to a halt outside the President's private residence. A brigadier waited on the steps to escort de Silveira through to the President.

The two men had lunch together in a small room that closely resembled a British officers' mess. The meal consisted of a steak, that would not have been acceptable to any South American cowhand surrounded by vegetables that reminded Eduardo of his schooldays. Still, Eduardo had never yet met a soldier who understood that a good chef was every bit as important as a good batman. During the lunch they talked in overall terms about the problems of building a whole new city in the middle of an equatorial jungle.

The provisional estimate of the cost of the project had been one thousand million dollars but de Silveira warned the President that the final outcome might well end up nearer three thousand million dollars the President's jaw dropped slightly. De Silveira had to admit that the project would be the most ambitious that Prentino International had ever tackled, but he was quick to point out to the President that the same would be true of any construction company in the world.

De Silveira, not a man to play his best card early, waited until the coffee to slip into the conversation that he had just been awarded, against heavy opposition (that had included Rodrigues), the contract to build an eight-lane highway through the Amazonian jungle, which would eventually link up with the Pan-American highway, a contract second in size only to the one they were now contemplating in Nigeria. The President was impressed and inquired if the venture would not prevent de Silveira involving himself in the new capital project.

"I'll know the answer to that question in three days' time," replied the Brazilian, and undertook to have a further discussion with the Head of State at the end of his visit when he would let him know if he was prepared to continue with the scheme.

After lunch Eduardo was driven to the Federal Palace Hotel where the entire sixth floor had been placed at his disposal. Several complaining guests who had come to Nigeria to close deals involving mere millions had been asked to vacate their rooms at short notice to make way for de Silveira and his staff. Eduardo knew nothing of these goings on, as there was always a room available for him wherever he arrived in the world.

The six Mercedes drew up outside the hotel and the colonel guided his charge through the swing doors and past reception. Eduardo had not checked himself into a hotel for the past fourteen years except on those occasions when he chose to register under an assumed name, not wanting anyone to know the identity of the woman he was with.

The chairman of Prentino International walked down the centre of the hotel's main corridor and stepped into a waiting lift. His legs went weak and he suddenly felt sick. In the corner of the lift stood a stubby, balding, overweight man, who was dressed in a pair of old jeans and a tee-shirt, his mouth continually opening and closing as he chewed gum. The two men stood as far apart as possible, neither showing any sign of recognition. The lift stopped at the fifth floor and Manuel Rodrigues, chairman of Rodrigues International SA, stepped out, leaving behind him the man who had been his bitter rival for thirty years.

Eduardo held on to the rail in the lift to steady himself as he still felt dizzy. How he despised that uneducated self-made upstart whose family of four half-brothers, all by different fathers, claimed they now ran the largest construction company in Brazil. Both men were as interested in the other's failure as they were in their own success.

Eduardo was somewhat puzzled to know what Rodrigues could possibly be doing in Lagos as he felt certain that his rival had not come into contact with the Nigerian president. After all, Eduardo had never collected the rent on a small house in Rio that was occupied by the mistress of a very senior official in the government's protocol department. And the man's only task was to be certain that Rodrigues was never invited to any function attended by a visiting dignitary when in Brazil. The continual absence of Rodrigues from these state occasions ensured the absent-mindedness of Eduardo's rent collector in Rio.

Eduardo would never have admitted to anyone that Rodrigues' presence worried him, but he nevertheless resolved to find out immediately what had brought his old enemy to Nigeria. Once he reached his suite de Silveira instructed his private secretary to check what Manuel Rodrigues was up to. Eduardo was prepared to return to Brazil immediately if Rodrigues turned out to be involved in any way with the new capital project, while one young lady in Rio would suddenly find herself looking for alternative accommodation.

Within an hour, his private secretary returned with the information that his chairman had requested. Rodrigues, he had discovered, was in Nigeria to tender for the contract to construct a new port in Lagos and was apparently not involved in any way with the new capital, and in fact was still trying to arrange a meeting with the President.

"Which minister is in charge of the ports and when am I due to see him?" asked de Silveira.

The secretary delved into his appointments file. "The Minister of Transport," the secretary said. "You have an appointment with him at nine o'clock on Thursday morning." The Nigerian Civil Service had mapped out a four-day schedule of meetings for de Silveira that included every cabinet minister involved in the new city project. "It's the last meeting before your final discussion with the President. You then fly on to Paris."

"Excellent. Remind me of this conversation five minutes before I see the minister and again when I talk to the President."

The secretary made a note in the file and left.

Eduardo sat alone in his suite, going over the reports on the new capital project submitted by his experts. Some of his team were already showing signs of nervousness. One particular anxiety that always came up with a large construction contract was the principal's ability to pay, and pay on time. Failure to do so was the quickest route to bankruptcy, but since the discovery of oil in Nigeria there seemed to be no shortage of income and certainly no shortage of people willing to spend that money on behalf of the government. These anxieties did not worry de Silveira as he always insisted on a substantial payment in advance; otherwise he wouldn't move himself or his vast staff one centimetre out of Brazil. However, the massive scope of this particular contract made the circumstances somewhat unusual. Eduardo realised that it would be most damaging to his international reputation if he started the assignment and then was seen not to complete it. He re-read the reports over a quiet dinner in his room and retired to bed early, having wasted an hour in vainly trying to place a call through to his wife.

De Silveira's first appointment the next morning was with the Governor of the Central Bank of Nigeria. Eduardo wore a newly-pressed suit, fresh shirt, and highly polished shoes: for four days no one would see him in the same clothes. At eight-forty-five there was a quiet knock on the door of his suite and the secretary opened it to find Colonel Usman standing to attention, waiting to escort Eduardo to the bank. As they were leaving the hotel Eduardo again saw Manuel Rodrigues, wearing the same pair of jeans, the same crumpled tee-shirt, and probably chewing the same gum as he stepped into a BMW in front of him. De Silveira only stopped scowling at the disappearing BMW when he remembered his Thursday morning appointment with the minister in charge of ports, followed by a meeting with the President.

The Governor of the Central Bank of Nigeria was in the habit of proposing how payment schedules would be met and completion orders would be guaranteed. He had never been told by anyone that if the payment was seven days overdue he could consider the contract null and void, and they could take it or leave it. The minister would have made some comment if Abuja had not been the President's pet project. That position established, de Silveira went on to check the bank's reserves, long-term deposits, overseas commitments, and estimated oil revenues for the next five years. He left the Governor in what could only be described as a jelly-like state. Glistening and wobbling. Eduardo's next appointment was an unavoidable courtesy call on the Brazilian Ambassador for lunch. He hated these functions as he believed embassies to be fit only for cocktail parties and discussion of out-of-date trivia, neither of which he cared for. The food in such establishments was invariably bad and the company worse. It turned out to be no different on this occasion and the only profit (Eduardo considered everything in terms of profit and loss) to be derived from the encounter was the information that Manuel Rodrigues was on a short list of three for the building of the new port in Lagos, and was expecting to have an audience with the President on Friday if he was awarded the contract. By Thursday morning that will be a short list of two and there will be no meeting with the President, de Silveira promised himself, and considered that was the most he was likely to gain from the lunch until the Ambassador added:

"Rodrigues seems most keen on you being awarded the new city contract at Abuja. He's singing your praises to every minister he meets. Funny," the Ambassador continued, "I always thought you two didn't see eye to eye."

Eduardo made no reply as he tried to fathom out what trick Rodrigues could be up to by promoting his cause.

Eduardo spent the afternoon with the Minister of Finance and confirmed the provisional arrangements he had made with the Governor of the bank. The Minister of Finance had been forewarned by the Governor what he was to expect from an encounter with Eduardo de Silveira and that he was not to be taken aback by the Brazilian's curt demands. De Silveira, aware that this warning would have taken place, let the poor man bargain a little and even gave way on a few minor points that he would be able to tell the President about at the next meeting of the Supreme Military Council. Eduardo left the smiling minister believing that he had scored a point or two against the formidable South American.

That evening, Eduardo dined privately with his senior advisers who themselves were already dealing with the ministers' officials. Each was now coming up with daily reports about the problems that would have to be faced if they worked in Nigeria. His chief engineer was quick to emphasise that skilled labour could not be hired at any price as the Germans had already cornered the market for their extensive road projects. The financial advisers also presented a gloomy report, of international companies waiting six months or more for their cheques to be cleared by the central bank. Eduardo made notes on the views they expressed but never ventured an opinion himself. His staff left him a little after eleven and he decided to take a stroll around the hotel grounds before retiring to bed. On his walk through the luxuriant tropical gardens he only just avoided a face-to-face confrontation with Manuel Rodrigues by darting behind a large Iroko plant. The little man passed by champing away at his gum, oblivious to Eduardo's baleful glare. Eduardo informed a chattering grey parrot of his most secret thoughts: by Thursday afternoon, Rodrigues, you will be on your way back to Brazil with a suitcase full of plans that can be filed under "abortive projects". The parrot cocked his head and screeched at him as if he had been let in on his secret. Eduardo allowed himself a smile and returned to his room.

Colonel Usman arrived on the dot of eight-forty-five again the next day and Eduardo spent the morning with the Minister of Supplies and Co-operatives – or lack of them, as he commented to his private secretary afterwards. The afternoon was spent with the Minister of Labour checking over the availability of unskilled workers and the total lack of skilled operatives. Eduardo was fast reaching the conclusion that, despite the professed optimism of the ministers concerned, this was going to be the toughest contract he had ever tackled. There was more to be lost than money if the whole international business world stood watching him fall flat on his face. In the evening his staff reported to him once again, having solved a few old problems and unearthed some new ones. Tentatively, they had come to the conclusion that if the present regime stayed in power, there need be no serious concern over payment, as the President had earmarked the new city as a priority project. They had even heard a rumour that the army would be willing to lend-lease part of the Service Corps if there turned out to be a shortage of skilled labour. Eduardo made a note to have this point confirmed in writing by the Head of State during their final meeting the next day. But the labour problem was not what was occupying Eduardo's thoughts as he put on his silk pyjamas that night. He was chuckling at the idea of Manuel Rodrigues' imminent and sudden departure for Brazil. Eduardo slept well.

He rose with renewed vigour the next morning, showered and put on a fresh suit. The four days were turning out to be well worth while and a single stone might yet kill two birds. By eight-forty-five, he was waiting impatiently for the previously punctual colonel. The colonel did not show up at eight-forty-five and had still not appeared when the clock on his mantelpiece struck nine. De Silveira sent his private secretary off to find out where he was while he paced angrily backwards and forwards through the hotel suite. His secretary returned a few minutes later in a panic with the information that the hotel was surrounded by armed guards. Eduardo did not panic. He had been through eight coups in his life from which he had learnt one golden rule: the new regime never kills visiting foreigners as it needs their money every bit as much as the last government. Eduardo picked up the telephone but no one answered him so he switched on the radio. A tape recording was playing:

"This is Radio Nigeria, this is Radio Nigeria. There has been a coup. General Mohammed has been overthrown and Lieutenant Colonel Dimka has assumed leadership of the new revolutionary government. Do not be afraid; remain at home and everything will be back to normal in a few hours.

This is Radio Nigeria, this is Radio Nigeria. There has been a . . ."

Eduardo switched off the radio as two thoughts flashed through his mind. Coups always held up everything and caused chaos, so undoubtedly he had wasted the four days. But worse, would it now be possible for him even to get out of Nigeria and carry on his normal business with the rest of the world?

By lunchtime, the radio was playing martial music interspersed with the tape recorded message he now knew off by heart. Eduardo detailed all his staff to find out anything they could and to report back to him direct. They all returned with the same story; that it was impossible to get past the soldiers surrounding the hotel so no new information could be unearthed. Eduardo swore for the first time in months. To add to his inconvenience, the hotel manager rang through to say that regretfully Mr de Silveira would have to eat in the main dining room as there would be no room service until further notice. Eduardo went down to the dining room somewhat reluctantly only to discover that the head waiter showed no interest in who he was and placed him unceremoniously at a small table already occupied by three Italians. Manuel Rodrigues was seated only two tables away: Eduardo stiffened at the thought of the other man enjoying his discomfiture and then remembered it was that morning he was supposed to have seen the Minister of Ports. He ate his meal quickly despite being served slowly and when the Italians tried to make conversation with him he waved them away with his hand, feigning lack of understanding, despite the fact that he spoke their language fluently. As soon as he had finished the second course he returned to his room. His staff had only gossip to pass on and they had been unable to make contact with the Brazilian Embassy to lodge an official protest. "A lot of good an official protest will do us," said Eduardo, slumping down in his chair. "Who do you send it to, the new regime or the old one?"

He sat alone in his room for the rest of the day, interrupted only by what he thought was the sound of gunfire in the distance. He read the New Federal Capital project proposal and his advisers' reports for a third time.

The next morning Eduardo, dressed in the same suit as he had worn on the day of his arrival, was greeted by his secretary with the news that the coup had been crushed; after fierce street fighting, he informed his unusually attentive chairman, the old regime had regained power but not without losses; among those killed in the uprising had been General Mohammed, the Head of State. The secretary's news was officially confirmed on Radio Nigeria later that morning. The ringleader of the abortive coup had been one Lieutenant Colonel Dimka: Dimka, along with one or two junior officers, had escaped, and the government had ordered a dusk to dawn curfew until the evil criminals were apprehended.

Pull off a coup and you're a national hero, fail and you're an evil criminal; in business it's the same difference between bankruptcy and making a fortune, considered Eduardo as he listened to the news report. He was beginning to form plans in his mind for an early departure from Nigeria when the newscaster made an announcement that chilled him to the very marrow.

"While Lieutenant Colonel Dimka and his accomplices remain on the run, airports throughout the country will be closed until further notice."

When the newscaster had finished his report, martial music was played in memory of the late General Mohammed.

Eduardo went downstairs in a flaming temper. The hotel was still surrounded by armed guards. He stared at the fleet of six empty Mercedes which was parked only ten yards beyond the soldiers' rifles. He marched back into the foyer, irritated by the babble of different tongues coming at him from every direction. Eduardo looked around him: it was obvious that many people had been stranded in the hotel overnight and had ended up sleeping in the lounge or the bar. He checked the paperback rack in the lobby for something to read but there were only four copies left of a tourist guide to Lagos; everything had been sold. Authors who had not been read for years were now changing hands at a premium. Eduardo returned to his room which was fast assuming the character of a prison, and baulked at reading the New Federal Capital project for a fourth time. He tried again to make contact with the Brazilian Ambassador to discover if he could obtain special permission to leave the country as he had his own aircraft. No one answered the Embassy phone. He went down for an early lunch only to find the dining room was once again packed to capacity.

Eduardo was placed at a table with some Germans who were worrying about a contract that had been signed by the government the previous week, before the abortive coup. They were wondering if it would still be honoured. Manuel Rodrigues entered the room a few minutes later and was placed at the next table.

During the afternoon, de Silveira ruefully examined his schedule for the next seven days. He had been due in Paris that morning to see the Minister of the Interior, and from there should have flown on to London to confer with the chairman of the Steel Board. His calendar was fully booked for the next ninety-two days until his family holiday in May. "I'm having this year's holiday in Nigeria," he commented wryly to an assistant.

What annoyed Eduardo most about the coup was the lack of communication it afforded with the outside world. He wondered what was going on in Brazil and he hated not being able to telephone or telex Paris or London to explain his absence personally. He listened addictively to Radio Nigeria on the hour every hour for any new scrap of information. At five o'clock, he learned that the Supreme Military Council had elected a new President who would address the nation on television and radio at nine o'clock that night.

Eduardo de Silveira switched on the television at eight-forty-five; normally an assistant would have put it on for him at one minute to nine. He sat watching a Nigerian lady giving a talk on dressmaking, followed by the weather forecast man who supplied Eduardo with the revealing information that the temperature would continue to be hot for the next month. Eduardo's knee was twitching up and down nervously as he waited for the address by the new President. At nine o'clock, after the national anthem had been played, the new Head of State, General Obasanjo, appeared on the screen in full dress uniform. He spoke first of the tragic death and sad loss for the nation of the late President, and went on to say that his government would continue to work in the best interest of Nigeria. He looked ill at ease as he apologised to all foreign visitors who were inconvenienced by the attempted coup but went on to make it clear that the dusk to dawn curfew would continue until the rebel leaders were tracked down and brought to justice. He confirmed that, all airports would remain closed until Lieutenant Colonel Dimka was in safe custody. The new President ended his statement by saying that all other forms of communication would be opened up again as soon as possible. The national anthem was played for a second time, while Eduardo thought of the millions of dollars that might be lost to him by his incarceration in that hotel room, while his private plane sat idly on the tarmac only a few miles away. One of his senior managers opened a book as to how long it would take for the authorities to capture Lieutenant Colonel Dimka; he did not tell de Silveira how short the odds were on a month.

Eduardo went down to the dining room in the suit he had worn the day before. A junior waiter placed him at a table with some Frenchmen who had been hoping to win a contract to drill bore holes in the Niger state. Again Eduardo waved a languid hand when they tried to include him in their conversation. At that very moment he was meant to be with the French Minister of the Interior, not with some French hole-borers. He tried to concentrate on his watered-down soup, wondering how much longer it would be before it would be just water. The head waiter appeared by his side, gesturing to the one remaining seat at the table, in which he placed Manuel Rodrigues. Still neither man gave any sign of recognising the other. Eduardo debated with himself whether he should leave the table or carry on as if his oldest rival was still in Brazil. He decided the latter was more dignified. The Frenchmen began an argument among themselves as to when they would be able to get out of Lagos. One of them declared emphatically that he had heard on the highest authority that the government intended to track down every last one of those involved in the coup before they opened the airports and that might take up to a month.

"What?" said the two Brazilians together, in English.

"I can't stay here for a month," said Eduardo.

"Neither can I," said Manuel Rodrigues.

"You'll have to, at least until Dimka is captured," said one of the Frenchmen, breaking into English. "So you must both relax yourselves, yes?"

The two Brazilians continued their meal in silence. When Eduardo had finished he rose from the table and without looking directly at Rodrigues said goodnight in Portuguese. The old rival inclined his head in reply to the salutation.

The next day brought forth no new information. The hotel remained surrounded with soldiers and by the evening Eduardo had lost his temper with every member of staff with whom he had come into contact. He went down to dinner on his own and as he entered the dining room he saw Manuel Rodrigues sitting alone at a table in the corner. Rodrigues looked up, seemed to hesitate for a moment, and then beckoned to Eduardo. Eduardo himself hesitated before walking slowly towards Rodrigues and taking the seat opposite him. Rodrigues poured him a glass of wine. Eduardo, who rarely drank, drank it. Their conversation was stilted to begin with, but as both men consumed more wine so they each began to relax in the other's company. By the time coffee had arrived, Manuel was telling Eduardo what he could do with this god-forsaken country.

"You will not stay on, if you are awarded the ports contract?" inquired Eduardo.

"Not a hope," said Rodrigues, who showed no surprise that de Silveira knew of his interest in the ports contract. "I withdrew from the short list the day before the coup. I had intended to fly back to Brazil that Thursday morning."

"Can you say why you withdrew?"

"Labour problems mainly, and then the congestion of the ports."

"I am not sure I understand," said Eduardo, understanding full well but curious to learn if Rodrigues had picked up some tiny detail his own staff had missed.

Manuel Rodrigues paused to ingest the fact that the man he had viewed as his most dangerous enemy for over thirty years was now listening to his own inside information. He considered the situation for a moment while he sipped his coffee. Eduardo didn't speak.

"To begin with, there's a terrible shortage of skilled labour, and on top of that there's this mad quota system."

"Quota system?" said Eduardo innocently.

"The percentage of people from the contractor's country which the government will allow to work in Nigeria."

"Why should that be a problem?" said Eduardo, leaning forward.

"By law, you have to employ at a ratio of fifty nationals to one foreigner so I could only have brought over twenty-five of my top men to organise a fifty million dollar contract, and I'd have had to make do with Nigerians at every other level. The government are cutting their own throats with the wretched system; they can't expect unskilled men, black or white, to become experienced engineers overnight. It's all to do with their national pride. Someone must tell them they can't afford that sort of pride if they want to complete the job at a sensible price. That path is the surest route to bankruptcy. On top of that, the Germans have already rounded up all the best skilled labour for their road projects."

"But surely," said Eduardo, "you charge according to the rules, however stupid, thus covering all eventualities, and as long as you're certain that payment is guaranteed . . ."

Manuel raised his hand to stop Eduardo's flow:

"That's another problem. You can't be certain. The government reneged on a major steel contract only last month. In so doing," he explained, "they had bankrupted a distinguished international company. So they are perfectly capable of trying the same trick with me. And if they don't pay up, who do you sue? The Supreme Military Council?"

"And the ports problem?"

"The port is totally congested. There are one hundred and seventy ships desperate to unload their cargo with a waiting time of anything up to six months. On top of that, there is a demurrage charge of five thousand dollars a day and only perishable foods are given any priority."

"But there's always a way round that sort of problem," said Eduardo, rubbing a thumb twice across the top of his fingers.

"Bribery? It doesn't work, Eduardo. How can you possibly jump the queue when all one hundred and seventy ships have already bribed the harbour master? And don't imagine that fixing the rent on a flat for one of his mistresses would help either," said Rodrigues grinning. "With that man you will have to supply the mistress as well."

Eduardo held his breath but said nothing.

"Come to think of it," continued Rodrigues, "if the situation becomes any worse, the harbour master will be the one man in the country who is richer than you."

Eduardo laughed for the first time in three days.

"I tell you, Eduardo, we could make a bigger profit building a salt mine in Siberia."

Eduardo laughed again and some of the Prentino

and Rodrigues staff dining at other tables stared in disbelief at their masters.

"You were in for the big one, the new city of Abuja?" said Manuel.

"That's right," admitted Eduardo.

"I have done everything in my power to make sure you were awarded that contract," said the other quietly.

"What?" said Eduardo in disbelief. "Why?"

"I thought Abuja would give the Prentino empire more headaches than even you could cope with, Eduardo, and that might possibly leave the field wide open for me at home. Think about it. Every time there's a cutback in Nigeria, what will be the first head to roll off the chopping block? 'The unnecessary city' as the locals all call it."

"The unnecessary city?" repeated Eduardo.

"Yes, and it doesn't help when you say you won't move without advance payment. You know as well as I do, you will need one hundred of your best men here full time to organise such a massive enterprise. They'll need feeding, salaries, housing, perhaps even a school and a hospital. Once they were settled down here, you can't just pull them off the job every two weeks because the government is running late clearing the cheques. It's not practical and you know it" Rodrigues poured Eduardo de Silveira another glass of wine.

"I had already taken that into consideration," Eduardo said as he sipped the wine, "but I thought that with the support of the Head of State."

"The late Head of State –"

"I take your point, Manuel."

"Maybe the next Head of State will also back you, but what about the one after that? Nigeria has had three coups in the past three years."

Eduardo remained silent for a moment.

"Do you play backgammon?"

"Yes. Why do you ask?"

"I must make *some* money while I'm here." Manual laughed.

"Why don't you come to my room," continued de Silveira. "Though I must warn you I always manage to beat my staff."

"Perhaps they always manage to lose," said Manuel, as he rose and grabbed the half empty bottle of wine by its neck. Both men were laughing as they left the dining room.

After that, the two chairmen had lunch and dinner together every day. Within a week, their staff were eating at the same tables. Eduardo could be seen in the dining room without a tie while Manuel wore a shirt for the first time in years. By the end of a fortnight, the two rivals had played each other at table tennis, backgammon and bridge with the stakes set at one hundred dollars a point. At the end of each day Eduardo always seemed to end up owing Manuel about a million dollars which Manuel happily traded for the best bottle of wine left in the hotel's cellar.

Although Lieutenant Colonel Dimka had been sighted by about forty thousand Nigerians in about as many different places, he still remained resolutely uncaptured. As the new President had insisted, airports remained closed but communications were opened which at least allowed Eduardo to telephone and telex Brazil. His brothers and wife were sending replies by the hour, imploring Eduardo to return home at any cost: decisions on major contracts throughout the world were being held up by his absence. But Eduardo's message back to Brazil was always the same: as long as Dimka is on the loose, the airports will remain closed.

It was on a Tuesday night during dinner that Eduardo took the trouble to explain to Manuel why Brazil had lost the World Cup. Manuel dismissed Eduardo's outrageous claims as ill-informed and prejudiced. It was the only subject on which they hadn't agreed in the past three weeks.

"I blame the whole fiasco on Zagalo," said Eduardo.

"No, no, you cannot blame the manager," said Manuel. "The fault lies with our stupid selectors who know even less about football than you do. They should never have dropped Leao from goal and in any case we should have learned from the Argentinian defeat last year that our methods are now out of date. You must attack, attack, if you want to score goals."

"Rubbish. We still have the surest defence in the world."

"Which means the best result you can hope for is a 0–0 draw."

"Never . . ." began Eduardo.

"Excuse me, sir." Eduardo looked up to see his private secretary standing by his side looking anxiously down at him.

"Yes, what's the problem?"

"An urgent telex from Brazil, sir."

Eduardo read the first paragraph and then asked Manuel if he would be kind enough to excuse him for a few minutes. The latter nodded politely. Eduardo left the table and as he marched through the dining room seventeen other guests left unfinished meals and followed him quickly to his suite on the top floor, where the rest of his staff were already assembled. He sat down in the corner of the room on his own. No one spoke as he read through the telex carefully, suddenly realising how many days he had been imprisoned in Lagos.

The telex was from his brother Carlos and the contents concerned the Pan-American road project, an eight-lane highway that would stretch from Brazil to Mexico. Prentinos had tendered for the section that ran through the middle of the Amazon jungle and had to have the bank guarantees signed and certified by midday tomorrow; Tuesday. But Eduardo had quite forgotten which Tuesday it was and the document he was committed to sign by the following day's deadline.

"What's the problem?" Eduardo asked his private secretary. "The Banco do Brasil have already agreed with Alfredo to act as guarantors. What's stopping Carlos signing the agreement in my absence?"

"The Mexicans are now demanding that responsibility for the contract be shared because of the insurance problems: Lloyd's of London will not cover the entire risk if only one company is involved. The details are all on page seven of the telex."

Eduardo flicked quickly through the pages. He read that his brothers had already tried to put pressure on Lloyd's, but to no avail. That's like trying to bribe a maiden aunt into taking part in a public orgy, thought Eduardo, and he would have told them as much if he had been back in Brazil. The Mexican Government was therefore insisting that the contract be shared with an international construction company acceptable to Lloyd's if the legal documents were to be signed by the midday deadline the following day.

"Stay put," said Eduardo to his staff, and he returned to the dining room alone, trailing the long telex behind him. Rodrigues watched him as he scurried back to their table.

"You look like a man with a problem."

"I am," said Eduardo. "Read that."

Manuel's experienced eye ran down the telex, picking out the salient points. He had tendered for the Amazon road project himself and could still recall the details. At Eduardo's insistence, he re-read page seven.

"Mexican bandits," he said as he returned the telex to Eduardo. "Who do they think they are, telling Eduardo de Silveira how he must conduct his business. Telex them back immediately and inform them you're chairman of the greatest construction company in the world and they can roast in hell before you will agree to their pathetic terms. You know it's far too late for them to go out to tender again with every other section of the highway ready to begin work. They would lose millions. Call their bluff, Eduardo."

"I think you may be right, Manuel, but any hold-up now can only waste my time and money, so I intend to agree to their demand and look for a partner."

"You'll never find one at such short notice."

"I will."

"Who?"

Eduardo de Silveira hesitated only for a second. "You, Manuel. I want to offer Rodrigues International SA fifty per cent of the Amazon road contract."

Manuel Rodrigues looked up at Eduardo. It was the first time that he had not anticipated his old rival's next move. "I suppose it might help cover the millions you owe me in table tennis debts."

The two men laughed, then Rodrigues stood up and they shook hands gravely. De Silveira left the dining room on the run and wrote out a telex for his manager to transmit.

"Sign, accept terms, fifty per cent partner will be Rodrigues International Construction SA, Brazil."

"If I telex that message, sir, you do realise that it's legally binding?"

"Send it," said Eduardo.

Eduardo returned once again to the dining room where Manuel had ordered the finest bottle of champagne in the hotel. Just as they were calling for a second bottle, and singing a spirited version of *Esta Cheganda a hora*, Eduardo's private secretary appeared by his side again, this time with two telexes, one from the President of the Banco do Brasil and a second from his brother Carlos. Both wanted confirmation of the agreed partner for the Amazon road project. Eduardo uncorked the second bottle of champagne without looking up at his private secretary.

"Confirm Rodrigues International Construction to the President of the bank and my brother," he said as he filled Manuel's empty glass. "And don't bother me again tonight."

"Yes, sir," said the private secretary and left without another word.

Neither man could recall what time he climbed into bed that night but de Silveira was abruptly awakened from a deep sleep by his secretary early the next morning. Eduardo took a few minutes to digest the news. Lieutenant Colonel Dimka had been caught in Kano at three o'clock that morning, and all the airports were now open again. Eduardo picked up the phone and dialled three digits.

"Manuel, you've heard the news? . . . Good . . . Then you must fly back with me in my 707 or it may be days before you get out . . . One hour's time in the lobby . . . See you then."

At eight-forty-five there was a quiet knock on the door and Eduardo's secretary opened it to find Colonel Usman standing to attention, just as he had done in the days before the coup. He held a note in his hand. Eduardo tore open the envelope to find an invitation to lunch that day with the new Head of State, General Obasanjo.

"Please convey my apologies to your President," said Eduardo, "and be kind enough to explain that

I have pressing commitments to attend to in my own country."

The colonel retired reluctantly. Eduardo dressed in the suit, shirt and tie he had worn on his first day in Nigeria and took the lift downstairs to the lobby where he joined Manuel who was once more wearing jeans and a tee-shirt. The two chairmen left the hotel and climbed into the back of the leading Mercedes and the motorcade of six began its journey to the airport. The colonel, who now sat in front with the driver, did not venture to speak to either of the distinguished Brazilians for the entire journey. The two men, he would be able to tell the new President later, seemed to be preoccupied with a discussion on an Amazon road project and how the responsibility should be divided between their two companies.

Customs were bypassed as neither man had anything they wanted to take out of the country other than themselves, and the fleet of cars came to a halt at the side of Eduardo's blue and silver 707. The staff of both companies climbed aboard the rear section of the aircraft, also engrossed in discussion on the Amazon road project.

A corporal jumped out of the lead car and opened the back door, to allow the two chairmen to walk straight up the steps and board the front section of the aircraft.

As Eduardo stepped out of the Mercedes, the Nigerian driver saluted smartly. "Goodbye, sir," he said, revealing the large set of white teeth once again.

Eduardo said nothing.

"I hope," said the corporal politely, "you made very big deal while you were in Nigeria."

The First Miracle

TOMORROW it would be 1 AD, but nobody had told him.

If anyone had, he wouldn't have understood because he thought that it was the forty-third year in the reign of the Emperor, and in any case, he had other things on his mind. His mother was still cross with him and he had to admit that he'd been naughty that day, even by the standards of a normal thirteen-year-old. He hadn't meant to drop the pitcher when she had sent him to the well for water. He tried to explain to his mother that it wasn't his fault that he had tripped over a stone; and that at least was true. What he hadn't told her was that he was chasing a stray dog at the time. And then there was that pomegranate; how was he meant to know that it was the last one, and that his father had taken a liking to them? The boy was now dreading his father's return and the possibility that he might be given another thrashing. He could still remember the last one when he hadn't been able to sit down for two days without feeling the pain, and the thin red scars didn't completely disappear for over three weeks.

He sat on the window ledge in a shaded corner of his room trying to think of some way he could redeem himself in his mother's eyes, now that she had thrown him out of the kitchen. Go outside and play, she had insisted, after he had spilt some cooking oil on his tunic. But that wasn't much fun as he was only allowed to play by himself. His father had forbidden him to mix with the local boys. How he hated this country; if only he were back home with his friends, there would be so much to do. Still, only another three weeks and he could . . . The door swung open and his mother came into the room. She was dressed in the thin black garments so favoured by locals: they kept her cool, she had explained to the boy's father. He had grunted his disapproval so she always changed back into imperial dress before he returned in the evening.

"Ah, there you are," she said, addressing the crouched figure of her son.

"Yes, Mother."

"Daydreaming as usual. Well, wake up because I need you to go into the village and fetch some food for me."

"Yes, Mother, I'll go at once," the boy said as he jumped off the window ledge.

"Well, at least wait until you've heard what I want."

"Sorry, Mother."

"Now listen, and listen carefully." She started counting on her fingers as she spoke. "I need a chicken, some raisins, figs, dates and . . . ah yes, two pomegranates."

The boy's face reddened at the mention of the pomegranates and he stared down at the stone floor, hoping she might have forgotten. His mother put her hand into the leather purse that hung from her waist and removed two small coins, but before she handed them over she made her son repeat the instructions.

"One chicken, raisins, figs, dates, and two pomegranates," he recited, as he might the modern poet, Virgil.

"And be sure to see they give you the correct change," she added. "Never forget the locals are all thieves."

"Yes, Mother . . ." For a moment the boy hesitated.

"If you remember everything and bring back the right amount of money, I might forget to tell your father about the broken pitcher and the pomegranate."

The boy smiled, pocketed the two small silver coins in his tunic, and ran out of the house into the compound. The guard who stood on duty at the gate removed the great wedge of wood which allowed the massive door to swing open. The boy jumped through the hole in the gate and grinned back at the guard.

"Been in more trouble again today?" the guard shouted after him.

"No, not this time," the boy replied. "I'm about to be saved."

He waved farewell to the guard and started to walk briskly towards the village while humming a tune that reminded him of home. He kept to the centre of the dusty winding path that the locals had the nerve to call a road. He seemed to spend half his time removing little stones from his sandals. If his father had been posted here for any length of time he would have made some changes; then they would have had a real road, straight and wide enough to take a chariot. But not before his mother had sorted out the serving girls. Not one of them knew how to lay a table or even prepare food so that it was at least clean. For the first time in his life he had seen his mother in a kitchen, and he felt sure it would be the last, as they would all be returning home now that his father was coming to the end of his assignment.

The evening sun shone down on him as he walked; it was a very large red sun, the same red as his father's tunic. The heat it gave out made him sweat and long for something to drink. Perhaps there would be enough money left over to buy himself a pomegranate. He couldn't wait to take one home and show his friends how large they were in this barbaric land. Marcus, his best friend, would undoubtedly have seen one as big because his father had commanded a whole army in these parts, but the rest of the class would still be impressed.

The village to which his mother had sent him was only two miles from the compound and the dusty path ran alongside a hill overlooking a large valley. The road was already crowded with travellers who would be seeking shelter in the village. All of them had come down from the hills at the express orders of his father, whose authority had been vested in him by the Emperor himself. Once he was sixteen, he too would serve the Emperor. His friend Marcus wanted to be a soldier and conquer the rest of the world. But he was more interested in the law and teaching his country's customs to the heathens in strange lands.

Marcus had said, "I'll conquer them and then you can govern them."

A sensible division between brains and brawn he had told his friend, who didn't seem impressed and had ducked him in the nearest bath.

The boy quickened his pace as he knew he had to be back in the compound before the sun disappeared behind the hills. His father had told him many times that he must always be locked safely inside before sunset. He was aware that his father was not a popular man with the locals, and he had warned his son that he would always be safe while it was light as no one would dare to harm him while others could watch what was going on, but once it was dark anything could happen. One thing he knew for certain: when he grew up he wasn't going to be a tax collector or work in the census office.

When he reached the village he found the narrow twisting lanes that ran between the little white houses swarming with people who had come from all the neighbouring lands to obey his father's order and be registered for the census, in order that they might be taxed. The boy dismissed the plebs from his mind. (It was Marcus who had taught him to refer to all foreigners as plebs.) When he entered the market place he also dismissed Marcus from his mind and began to concentrate on the supplies his mother wanted. He mustn't make any mistakes this time or he would undoubtedly end up with that thrashing from his father. He ran nimbly between the stalls, checking the food carefully. Some of the local people stared at the fair-skinned boy with the curly brown hair and the straight, firm nose. He displayed no imperfections or disease like the majority of them. Others turned their eyes away from him; after all, he had come from the land of the natural rulers. These thoughts did not pass through his mind. All the boy noticed was that their native skins were parched and lined from too much sun. He knew that too much sun was bad for you: it made you old before your time, his tutor had warned him.

At the end stall, the boy watched an old woman haggling over an unusually plump live chicken and as he marched towards her she ran away in fright, leaving the fowl behind her. He stared at the stallkeeper and refused to bargain with the peasant. It was beneath his dignity. He pointed to the chicken and gave the man one denarius. The man bit the round silver coin and looked at the head of Augustus Caesar, ruler of half the world. (When his tutor had told him, during a history lesson, about the Emperor's achievements, he remembered thinking, I hope Caesar doesn't conquer the whole world before I have a chance to join in.) The stallkeeper was still staring at the silver coin.

"Come on, come on, I haven't got all day," said the boy sounding like his father.

The local did not reply because he couldn't understand what the boy was saying. All he knew for certain was that it would be unwise for him to annoy the invader. The stallkeeper held the chicken firmly by the neck and taking a knife from his belt cut its head off in one movement and passed the dead fowl over to the boy. He then handed back some of his local coins, which had stamped on them the image of a man the boy's father described as "that useless Herod". The boy kept his hand held out, palm open, and the local placed bronze talents into it until he had no more. The boy left him talentless and moved to another stall, this time pointing to bags containing raisins, figs and dates. The new stallkeeper made a measure of each for which he received five of the useless Herod coins. The man was about to protest about the barter but the boy stared at him fixedly in the eyes, the way he had seen his father do so often. The stallkeeper backed away and only bowed his head.

Now, what else did his mother want? He racked his brains. A chicken, raisins, dates, figs and . . . of course, two pomegranates. He searched among the fresh-fruit stalls and picked out three pomegranates, and breaking one open, began to eat it, spitting out the pips on the ground in front of him. He paid the stallkeeper with the two remaining bronze talents, feeling pleased that he had carried out his mother's wishes while still being able to return home with one of the silver denarii. Even his father would be impressed by that. He finished the pomegranate and, with his arms laden, headed slowly out of the market back towards the compound, trying to avoid the stray dogs that continually got under his feet.

They barked and sometimes snapped at his ankles: they did not know who he was.

When the boy reached the edge of the village he noticed the sun was already disappearing behind the highest hill, so he quickened his pace, remembering his father's words about being home before dusk. As he walked down the stony path, those still on the way towards the village kept a respectful distance, leaving him a clear vision as far as the eye could see, which wasn't all that far as he was carrying so much in his arms. But one sight he did notice a little way ahead of him was a man with a beard – a dirty, lazy habit his father had told him – wearing the ragged dress that signified that he was of the tribe of Jacob, tugging a reluctant donkey which in turn was carrying a very fat woman. The woman was, as their custom demanded, covered from head to toe in black. The boy was about to order them out of his path when the man left the donkey on the side of the road and went into a house which from its sign, claimed to be an inn.

Such a building in his own land would never have passed the scrutiny of the local councillors as a place fit for paying travellers to dwell in. But the boy realised that this particular week to find even a mat to lay one's head on might be considered a luxury. He watched the bearded man reappear through the door with a forlorn look on his tired face. There was clearly no room at the inn.

The boy could have told him that before he went in, and wondered what the man would do next, as it was the last dwelling house on the road. Not that he was really interested; they could both sleep in the hills for all he cared. It was about all they looked fit for. The man with the beard was telling the woman something and pointing behind the inn, and without another word he led the donkey off in the direction he had been indicating. The boy wondered what could possibly be at the back of the inn and, his curiosity roused, followed them. As he came to the corner of the building, he saw the man was coaxing the donkey through an open door of what looked like a barn. The boy followed the strange trio and watched them through the crack left by the open door. The barn was covered in dirty straw and full of chickens, sheep and oxen, and smelled to the boy like the sewers they built in the side streets back home. He began to feel sick. The man was clearing away some of the worst of the straw from the centre of the barn, trying to make a clean patch for them to rest on – a near hopeless task, thought the boy. When the man had done as best he could he lifted the fat woman down from the donkey and placed her gently in the straw. Then he left her and went over to a trough on the other side of the barn where one of the oxen was drinking. He cupped his fingers together, put them in the trough and filling his hands with water, returned to the fat woman.

The boy was beginning to get bored and was about to leave when the woman leaned forward to drink from the man's hands. The shawl fell from her head and he saw her face for the first time.

He stood transfixed, staring at her. He had never seen anything more beautiful. Unlike the common members of her tribe, the woman's skin was translucent in quality, and her eyes shone, but what most struck the boy was her manner and presence. Never had he felt so much in awe, even remembering his one visit to the Senate House to hear a declamation from Augustus Caesar.

For a moment he remained mesmerised, but then he knew what he must do. He walked through the open door towards the woman, fell on his knees before her and offered the chicken. She smiled and he gave her the pomegranates and she smiled again. He then dropped the rest of the food in front of her, but she remained silent. The man with the beard was returning with more water, and when he saw the young foreigner he fell on his knees spilling the water onto the straw and then covered his face. The boy stayed on his knees for some time before he rose, and walked slowly towards the barn door. When he reached the opening, he turned back and stared once more into the face of the beautiful woman. She still did not speak.

The young Roman hesitated only for a second, and then bowed his head.

It was already dusk when he ran back out on to the winding path to resume his journey home, but he was not afraid. Rather he felt he had done something good and therefore no harm could come to him. He looked up into the sky and saw directly above him the first star, shining so brightly in the east that he wondered why he could see no others. His father had told him that different stars were visible in different lands, so he dismissed the puzzle from his mind, replacing it with the anxiety of not being home before dark. The road in front of him was now empty so he was able to walk quickly towards the compound, and was not all that far from safety when he first heard the singing and shouting. He turned quickly to see where the danger was coming from, staring up into the hills above him. To begin with, he couldn't make sense of what he saw. Then his eyes focused in disbelief on one particular field in which the shepherds were leaping up and down, singing, shouting and clapping their hands. The boy noticed that all the sheep were safely penned in a corner of the field for the night, so they had nothing to fear. He had been told by Marcus that sometimes the shepherds in this land would make a lot of noise at night because they believed it kept away the evil spirits. How could anyone be that stupid, the boy wondered, when there was a flash of lightning across the sky and the field was suddenly ablaze with light. The shepherds fell to their knees, silent, staring up into the sky for several minutes as though they were listening intently to something. Then all was darkness again.

The boy started running towards the compound as fast as his legs could carry him; he wanted to be inside and hear the safety of the great gate close behind him and watch the centurion put the wooden wedge firmly back in its place. He would have run all the way had he not seen something in front of him that brought him to a sudden halt. His father had taught him never to show any fear when facing danger. The boy caught his breath in case it would make them think that he was frightened. He was frightened, but he marched proudly on, determined he would never be forced off the road. When they did meet face to face, he was amazed.

Before him stood three camels and astride the beasts three men, who stared down at him. The first was clad in gold and with one arm protected something hidden beneath his cloak. By his side hung a large sword, its sheath covered in all manner of rare stones, some of which the boy could not even name. The second was dressed in white and held a silver casket to his breast, while the third wore red and carried a large wooden box. The man robed in gold put up his hand and addressed the boy in a strange tongue which he had never heard uttered before, even by his tutor. The second man tried Hebrew but to no avail and the third yet another tongue without eliciting any response from the boy.

The boy folded his arms across his chest and told them who he was, where he was going, and asked where they might be bound. He hoped his piping voice did not reveal his fear. The one robed in gold replied first and questioned the boy in his own tongue.

"Where is he that is born King of the Jews? For we have seen his star in the east, and are come to worship him."

"King Herod lives beyond the . . ."

"We speak not of King Herod," said the second man, "for he is but a king of men as we are."

"We speak," said the third, "of the King of Kings and are come to offer him gifts of gold, frankincense and myrrh."

"I know nothing of the King of Kings," said the boy, now gaining in confidence. "I recognise only Augustus Caesar, Emperor of the known world."

The man robed in gold shook his head and, pointing to the sky, inquired of the boy: "You observe that bright star in the east. What is the name of the village on which it shines?"

The boy looked up at the star, and indeed the village below was clearer to the eye than it had been in sunlight.

"But that's only Bethlehem," said the boy, laughing. "You will find no King of Kings there."

"Even there we shall find him," said the second king, "for did not Herod's chief priest tell us:

> And thou Bethlehem, in the land of Judah,
> Art not least among the princes of Judah,
> For out of thee shall come a Governor
> That shall rule my people Israel."

"It cannot be," said the boy now almost shouting at them. "Augustus Caesar rules Israel and all the known world."

But the three robed men did not heed his words and left him to ride on towards Bethlehem.

Mystified the boy set out on the last part of his journey home. Although the sky had become pitch black, whenever he turned his eyes towards Bethlehem the village was still clearly visible in the brilliant starlight. Once again he started running towards the compound, relieved to see its outline rising up in front of him. When he reached the great wooden gate, he banged loudly and repeatedly until a centurion, sword drawn, holding a flaming torch, came out to find out who it was that disturbed his watch. When he saw the boy, he frowned.

"Your father is very angry. He returned at sunset

and is about to send out a search party for you."

The boy darted past the centurion and ran all the way to his family's quarters, where he found his father addressing a sergeant of the guard. His mother was standing by his side, weeping.

The father turned when he saw his son and shouted: "Where have you been?"

"To Bethlehem."

"Yes, I know that, but whatever possessed you to return so late? Have I not told you countless times never to be out of the compound after dark? Come to my study at once."

The boy looked helplessly towards his mother, who was still crying, but not out of relief, and turned to follow his father into the study. The guard sergeant winked at him as he passed by but the boy knew nothing could save him now. His father strode ahead of him into the study and sat on a leather stool by his table. His mother followed and stood silently by the door.

"Now tell me exactly where you have been and why you took so long to return, and be sure to tell me the truth."

The boy stood in front of his father and told him everything that had come to pass. He started with how he had gone to the village and taken great care in choosing the food and in so doing had saved half the money his mother had given him. How on the way back he had seen a fat lady on a donkey unable to find a place at the inn and then he explained why he had given her the food. He went on to describe how the shepherds had shouted and beat their breasts until there was a great light in the sky at which they had all fallen silent on their knees, and then finally how he had met the three robed men who were searching for the King of Kings.

The father grew angry at his son's words.

"What a story you tell," he shouted. "Do tell me more. Did you find this King of Kings?"

"No, Sir. I did not," he replied, as he watched his father rise and start pacing around the room.

"Perhaps there is a more simple explanation as to why your face and fingers are stained red with pomegranate juice," he suggested.

"No, Father. I did buy an extra pomegranate but even after I had bought all the food, I still managed to save one silver denarius."

The boy handed the coin over to his mother believing it would confirm his story. But the sight of the piece of silver only made his father more angry. He stopped pacing and stared down into the eyes of his son.

"You have spent the other denarius on yourself and now you have nothing to show for it?"

"That's not true, Father, I . . ."

"Then I will allow you one more chance to tell me the truth," said his father as he sat back down. "Fail me, boy, and I shall give you a thrashing that you will never forget for the rest of your life."

"I have already told you the truth, Father."

"Listen to me carefully, my son. We were born Romans, born to rule the world because our laws and customs are tried and trusted and have always been based firmly on absolute honesty. Romans never lie; it remains our strength and the weakness of our enemies. That is why we rule while others are ruled and as long as that is so the Roman Empire will never fall. Do you understand what I am saying, my boy?"

"Yes, Father, I understand."

"Then you'll also understand why it is imperative to tell the truth."

"But I have not lied, Father."

"Then there is no hope for you," said the man angrily. "And you leave me only one way to deal with this matter."

The boy's mother wanted to come to her son's aid, but knew any protest would be useless. The father rose from his chair and removed the leather belt from around his waist and folded it double, leaving the heavy brass studs on the outside. He then ordered his son to touch his toes. The young boy obeyed without hesitation and the father raised the leather strap above his head and brought it down on the child with all his strength. The boy never flinched or murmured, while his mother turned away from the sight, and wept. After the father had administered the twelfth stroke he ordered his son to go to his room. The boy left without a word and his mother followed and watched him climb the stairs. She then hurried away to the kitchen and gathered together some olive oil and ointments which she hoped would soothe the pain of her son's wounds. She carried the little jars up to his room, where she found him already in bed. She went over to his side and pulled the sheet back. He turned on to his chest while she prepared the oils. Then she removed his night tunic gently for fear of adding to his pain. Having done so, she stared down at his body in disbelief.

The boy's skin was unmarked.

She ran her fingers gently over her son's unblemished body and found it to be as smooth as if he had just bathed. She turned him over, but there was not a mark on him anywhere. Quickly she covered him with the sheet.

"Say nothing of this to your father, and remove the memory of it from your mind forever, because the very telling of it will only make him more angry."

"Yes, Mother."

The mother leaned over and blew out the candle by the side of the bed, gathered up the unused oils and tiptoed to the door. At the threshold, she turned in the dim light to look back at her son and said:

"Now I know you were telling the truth, Pontius."

The Perfect Gentleman

I would never have met Edward Shrimpton if he hadn't needed a towel. He stood naked by my side staring down at a bench in front of him, muttering, "I could have sworn I left the damn thing there."

I had just come out of the sauna, swathed in towels, so I took one off my shoulder and passed it to him. He thanked me and put out his hand.

"Edward Shrimpton," he said smiling. I took his hand and wondered what we must have looked like standing there in the gymnasium locker room of the Metropolitan Club in the early evening, two grown men shaking hands in the nude.

"I don't remember seeing you in the club before," he added.

"No, I'm an overseas member."

"Ah, from England. What brings you to New York?"

"I'm pursuing an American novelist whom my company would like to publish in England."

"And are you having any success?"

"Yes, I think I'll close the deal this week – as long

as the agent stops trying to convince me that his author is a cross between Tolstoy and Dickens and should be paid accordingly."

"Neither was paid particularly well, if I remember correctly," offered Edward Shrimpton as he energetically rubbed the towel up and down his back.

"A fact I pointed out to the agent at the time who only countered by reminding me that it was my House who had published Dickens originally."

"I suggest," said Edward Shrimpton, "that you *remind* him that the end result turned out to be successful for all concerned."

"I did, but I fear this agent is more interested in 'up front' than posterity."

"As a banker that's a sentiment of which I could hardly disprove as: the one thing we have in common with publishers is that our clients are always trying to tell us a good tale."

"Perhaps you should sit down and write one of them for me?" I said politely.

"Heaven forbid, you must be sick of being told that there's a book in every one of us so I hasten to assure you that there isn't one in me."

I laughed, as I found it refreshing not to be informed by a new acquaintance that his memoirs, if only he could find the time to write them, would overnight, be one of the world's best sellers.

"Perhaps there's a story in you, but you're just not aware of it." I suggested.

"If that's the case, I'm afraid it's passed me by."

Mr Shrimpton re-emerged from behind the row of little tin cubicles and handed me back my towel. He was now fully dressed and stood, I would have guessed, a shade under six feet. He wore a Wall Street banker's pinstripe suit and, although he was nearly bald, he had a remarkable physique for a man who must have been well into his sixties. Only his thick white moustache gave away his true age, and would have been more in keeping with a retired English colonel than a New York banker.

"Are you going to be in New York long?" he inquired, as he took a small leather case from his inside pocket and removed a pair of half-moon spectacles and placed them on the end of his nose.

"Just for the week."

"I don't suppose you're free for lunch tomorrow, by any chance?" he inquired, peering over the top of his glasses.

"Yes, I am. I certainly can't face another meal with that agent."

"Good, good, then why don't you join me and I can follow the continuing drama of capturing the elusive American Author?"

"And perhaps I'll discover there is a story in you after all."

"Not a hope," he said, "you would be backing a loser if you depend on that," and once again he offered his hand. "One o'clock, members' dining room suit you?"

"One o'clock, members' dining room." I repeated.

As he left the locker room I walked over to the mirror and straightened my tie. I was dining that night with Eric McKenzie, a publishing friend, who had originally proposed me for membership of the club. To be accurate, Eric McKenzie was a friend of my father rather than myself. They had met just before the war while on holiday in Portugal and when I was elected to the club, soon after my father's retirement, Eric took it upon himself to have dinner with me whenever I was in New York. One's parents' generation never see one as anything but a child who will always be in need of constant care and attention. As he was a contemporary of my father, Eric must have been nearly seventy and, although hard of hearing and slightly bent, he was always amusing and good company, even if he did continually ask me if I was aware that his grandfather was Scottish.

As I strapped on my watch, I checked that he was due to arrive in a few minutes. I put on my jacket and strolled out into the hall to find that he was already there, waiting for me. Eric was killing time by reading the out-of-date club notices. Americans, I have observed, can always be relied upon to arrive early or late; never on time. I stood staring at the stooping man, whose hair but for a few strands had now turned silver. His three-piece suit had a button missing on the jacket which reminded me that his wife had died last year. After another thrust-out hand and exchange of welcomes, we took the lift to the second floor and walked to the dining room.

The members' dining room at the Metropolitan differs little from any other men's club. It has a fair sprinkling of old leather chairs, old carpets, old portraits and old members. A waiter guided us to a corner table which overlooked Central Park. We ordered, and then settled back to discuss all the subjects I found I usually cover with an acquaintance I only have the chance to catch up with a couple of times a year – our families, children, mutual friends, work; baseball and cricket. By the time we had reached cricket we had also reached coffee, so we strolled down to the far end of the room and made ourselves comfortable in two well-worn leather chairs. When the coffee arrived I ordered two brandies and watched Eric unwrap a large Cuban cigar. Although they displayed a West Indian band on the outside, I knew they were Cuban because I had picked them up for him from a tobacconist in St James's, Piccadilly, which specialises in changing the labels for its American customers. I have often thought that they must be the only shop in the world that changes labels with the sole purpose of making a superior product appear inferior. I am certain my wine merchant does it the other way round.

While Eric was attempting to light the cigar, my eyes wandered to a board on the wall. To be more accurate it was a highly polished wooden plaque with oblique golden lettering painted on it, honouring those men who over the years had won the club's Backgammon Championship. I glanced idly down the list, not expecting to see anybody with whom I would be familiar, when I was brought up by the name of Edward Shrimpton. Once in the late thirties he had been the runner-up.

"That's interesting," I said.

"What is?" asked Eric, now wreathed in enough smoke to have puffed himself out of Grand Central Station.

"Edward Shrimpton was runner-up in the club's Backgammon Championship in the late thirties. I'm having lunch with him tomorrow."

"I didn't realise you knew him."

"I didn't until this afternoon," I said, and then explained how we had met.

Eric laughed and turned to stare up at the board. Then he added, rather mysteriously: "That's a night I'm never likely to forget."

"Why?" I asked.

Eric hesitated, and looked uncertain of himself before continuing: "Too much water has passed under the bridge for anyone to care now." He paused again, as a hot piece of ash fell to the floor and added to the burn marks that made their own private pattern in the carpet. "Just before the war Edward Shrimpton was among the best half dozen backgammon players in the world. In fact, it must have been around that time he won the unofficial world championship in Monte Carlo."

"And he couldn't win the club championship?"

"Couldn't would be the wrong word, dear boy. 'Didn't' might be more accurate." Eric lapsed into another preoccupied silence.

"Are you going to explain?" I asked, hoping he would continue, "or am I to be left like a child who wants to know who killed Cock Robin?"

"All in good time, but first allow me to get this damn cigar started."

I remained silent and four matches later, he said "Before I begin, take a look at the man sitting over there in the corner with the young blonde."

I turned and glanced back towards the dining room area, and saw a man attacking a porterhouse steak. He looked about the same age as Eric and wore a smart new suit that was unable to disguise that he had a weight problem: only his tailor could have smiled at him with any pleasure. He was seated opposite a slight, not unattractive strawberry blonde of half his age who could have trodden on a beetle and failed to crush it.

"What an unlikely pair. Who are they?"

"Harry Newman and his fourth wife. They're always the same. The wives I mean – blonde hair, blue eyes, ninety pounds, and dumb. I can never understand why any man gets divorced only to marry a carbon copy of the original."

"Where does Edward Shrimpton fit into the jig-saw?" I asked, trying to guide Eric back on to the subject.

"Patience, patience," said my host, as he relit his cigar for the second time. "At your age you've far more time to waste than I have."

I laughed and picked up the cognac nearest to me and swirled the brandy around in my cupped hands.

"Harry Newman," continued Eric, now almost hidden in smoke, "was the fellow who beat Edward Shrimpton in the final of the club championship that year, although in truth he was never in the same class as Edward."

"Do explain," I said, as I looked up at the board to check that it was Newman's name that preceded Edward Shrimpton's.

"Well," said Eric, "after the semi-final, which

Edward had won with consummate ease, we all assumed the final would only be a formality. Harry had always been a good player, but as I had been the one to lose to him in the semi-finals, I knew he couldn't hope to survive a contest with Edward Shrimpton. The club final is won by the first man to twenty-one points, and if I had been asked for an opinion at the time I would have reckoned the result would end up around 21–5 in Edward's favour. Damn cigar," he said, and lit it for a fourth time. Once again I waited impatiently.

"The final is always held on a Saturday night, and poor Harry over there," said Eric, pointing his cigar towards the far corner of the room while depositing some more ash on the floor, "who all of us thought was doing rather well in the insurance business, had a bankruptcy notice served on him the Monday morning before the final – I might add through no fault of his own. His partner had cashed in his stock without Harry's knowledge, disappeared, and left him with all the bills to pick up. Everyone in the club was sympathetic.

"On the Thursday the press got hold of the story, and for good measure they added that Harry's wife had run off with the partner. Harry didn't show his head in the club all week, and some of us wondered if he would scratch from the final and let Edward win by default as the result was such a foregone conclusion anyway. But the Games Committee received no communication from Harry to suggest the contest was off so they proceeded as though nothing had happened. On the night of the final, I dined with Edward Shrimpton here in the club. He was in fine form. He ate very little and drank nothing but a glass of water. If you had asked me then I wouldn't have put a penny on Harry Newman even if the odds had been ten to one.

"We all dined upstairs on the third floor, as the Committee had cleared this room so that they could seat sixty in a square around the board. The final was due to start at nine o'clock. By twenty to nine there wasn't a seat left in the place, and members were already standing two deep behind the square: it wasn't every day we had the chance to see a world champion in action. By five to nine, Harry still hadn't turned up and some of the members were beginning to get a little restless. As nine o'clock chimed, the referee went over to Edward and had a word with him. I saw Edward shake his head in disagreement and walk away. Just at the point, when I thought the referee would have to be firm and award the match to Edward, Harry strolled in looking very dapper adorned in a dinner jacket several sizes smaller than the suit he is wearing tonight. Edward went straight up to him, shook him warmly by the hand and together they walked into the centre of the room. Even with the throw of the first dice there was a tension about that match. Members were waiting to see how Harry would fare in the opening game."

The intermittent cigar went out again. I leaned over and struck a match for him.

"Thank you, dear boy. Now, where was I? Oh, yes, the first game. Well, Edward only just won the first game and I wondered if he wasn't concentrating or if perhaps he had become a little too relaxed while waiting for his opponent. In the second game the dice ran well for Harry and he won fairly easily. From that moment on it became a finely fought battle, and by the time the score had reached 11–9 in Edward's favour the tension in the room was quite electric. By the ninth game I began watching more carefully and noticed that Edward allowed himself to be drawn into a back game, a small error in judgment that only a seasoned player would have spotted. I wondered how many more subtle errors had already passed that I hadn't observed. Harry went on to win the ninth making the score 18–17 in his favour. I watched even more diligently as Edward did just enough to win the tenth game and, with a rash double, just enough to lose the eleventh, bring the score to 20 all, so that everything would depend on the final game. I swear that nobody had left the room that evening, and not one back remained against a chair; some members were even hanging on to the window ledges. The room was now full of drink and thick with cigar smoke, and yet when Harry picked up the dice cup for the last game you could hear the little squares of ivory rattle before they hit the board. The dice ran well for Harry in that final game and Edward only made one small error early on that I was able to pick up; but it was enough to give Harry game, match and championship. After the last throw of the dice everyone in that room, including Edward, gave the new champion a standing ovation."

"Had many other members worked out what had really happened that night?"

"No, I don't think so," said Eric. "And certainly

Harry Newman hadn't. The talk afterwards was that Harry had never played a better game in his life and what a worthy champion he was, all the more for the difficulties he laboured under."

"Did Edward have anything to say?"

"Toughest match he'd been in since Monte Carlo and only hoped he would be given the chance to avenge the defeat next year."

"But he wasn't," I said, looking up again at the board. "He never won the club championship."

"That's right. After Roosevelt had insisted we help you guys out in England, the club didn't hold the competition again until 1946, and by then Edward had been to war and had lost all interest in the game."

"And Harry?"

"Oh, Harry. Harry never looked back after that; must have made a dozen deals in the club that night. Within a year he was on top again and even found himself another cute little blonde."

"What does Edward say about the result now, thirty years later?"

"Do you know that remains a mystery to this day. I have never heard him mention the game once in all that time."

Eric's cigar had come to the end of its working life and he stubbed the remains out in an ashless ashtray. It obviously acted as a signal to remind him that it was time to go home. He rose a little unsteadily and I walked down with him to the front door.

"Goodbye my boy," he said, "do give Edward my best wishes when you have lunch with him tomorrow. And remember not to play him at backgammon. He'd still kill you."

The next day I arrived in the front hall a few minutes before our appointed time, not sure if Edward Shrimpton would fall into the category of early or late Americans. As the clock struck one, he walked through the door: there has to be an exception to every rule. We agreed to go straight up to lunch since he had to be back in Wall Street for a two-thirty appointment. We stepped into the packed lift, and I pressed the No. 3 button. The doors closed like a tired concertina and the slowest lift in America made its way towards the second floor.

As we entered the dining room, I was amused to see Harry Newman was already there, attacking another steak, while the little blonde lady was nibbling a salad. He waved expansively at Edward Shrimpton, who returned the gesture with a friendly nod. We sat down at a table in the centre of the room and studied the menu. Steak and kidney pie was the dish of the day, which was probably the case in half the mens' clubs in the world. Edward wrote down our orders in a neat and legible hand on the little white slip provided by the waiter.

Edward asked me about the author I was chasing and made some penetrating comments about her earlier work, to which I responded as best I could while trying to think of a plot to make him discuss the pre-war backgammon championship, which I considered would make a far better story than anything she had ever written. But he never talked about himself once during the meal, so I despaired.

Finally, staring up at the plaque on the wall, I said clumsily:

"I see you were runner-up in the club backgammon championship just before the war. You must have been a fine player."

"No, not really," he replied. "Not many people bothered about the game in those days. There is a different attitude today with all the youngsters taking it so seriously."

"What about the champion?" I said, pushing my luck.

"Harry Newman? – He was an outstanding player, and particularly good under pressure. He's the gentleman who greeted us when we came in. That's him sitting over there in the corner with his wife."

I looked obediently towards Mr Newman's table but my host added nothing more so I gave up. We ordered coffee and that would have been the end of Edward's story if Harry Newman and his wife had not headed straight for us after they had finished their lunch. Edward was on his feet long before I was, despite my twenty-year advantage. Harry Newman looked even bigger standing up, and his little blonde wife looked more like the dessert than his spouse.

"Ed," he boomed, "how are you?"

"I'm well, thank you, Harry," Edward replied. "May I introduce my guest?"

"Nice to know you," he said. "Rusty, I've always wanted you to meet Ed Shrimpton because I've talked to you about him so often in the past."

"Have you, Harry?" she squeaked.

"Of course. You remember, honey. Ed is up there on the backgammon honours board," he said, pointing a stubby finger towards the plaque. "With only one name in front of him and that's mine. And Ed was the world champion at the time. Isn't that right, Ed?"

"That's right, Harry."

"So I suppose I really should have been the world champion that year, wouldn't you say?"

"I couldn't quarrel with that conclusion," replied Edward.

"On the big day, Rusty, when it really mattered, and the pressure was on, I beat him fair and square."

I stood in silent disbelief as Edward Shrimpton still volunteered no disagreement.

"We must play again for old times' sake, Ed," the fat man continued. "It would be fun to see if you could beat me now. Mind you, I'm a bit rusty nowadays, Rusty." He laughed loudly at his own joke but his spouse's face remained blank. I wondered how long it would be before there was a fifth Mrs Newman.

"It's been great to see you again, Ed. Take care of yourself."

"Thank you Harry," said Edward.

We both sat down again as Newman and his wife left the dining room. Our coffee was now cold so we ordered a fresh pot. The room was almost empty and when I had poured two cups for us Edward leaned over to me conspiratorially and whispered: "Now there's a hell of a story for a publisher like you," he said. "I mean the real truth about Harry Newman."

My ears pricked up as I anticipated his version of the story of what had actually happened on the night of that pre-war backgammon championship over thirty years before.

"Really?" I said, innocently.

"Oh, yes," said Edward. "It was not as simple as you might think. Just before the war Harry was let down very badly by his business partner who not only stole his money, but for good measure his wife as well. The very week that he was at his lowest he won the club backgammon championship, put all his troubles behind him and, against the odds, made a brilliant come-back. You know, he's worth a fortune today. Now, wouldn't you agree that that would make one hell of a story?"

One-Night Stand

THE two men had first met at the age of five when they were placed side by side at school, for no more compelling reason than that their names, Thompson and Townsend, came one after each other on the class register. They soon became best friends, a tie which at that age is more binding than any marriage. After passing their eleven-plus examination they proceeded to the local grammar school with no Timpsons, Tooleys or Tomlinsons to divide them and, having completed seven years in that academic institution, reached an age when one either has to go to work or to university. They opted for the latter on the grounds that work should be put off until the last possible moment. Happily, they both possessed enough brains and native wit to earn themselves places at Durham University to read English.

Undergraduate life turned out to be as sociable as primary school. They both enjoyed English, tennis, cricket, good food and girls. Luckily, in the last of these predilections they differed only on points of detail. Michael, who was six-foot-two, willowy with dark curly hair, preferred tall, bosomy blondes with blue eyes and long legs. Adrian, a stocky man of five-foot-ten, with straight, sandy hair always fell for small, slim, dark-haired, dark-eyed girls. So whenever Adrian came across a girl that Michael took an interest in or vice versa, whether she was an undergraduate or barmaid, the one would happily exaggerate their friend's virtues. Thus they spent three idyllic years in unison at Durham, gaining considerably more than a Bachelor of Arts degree. As neither of them had impressed the examiners enough to waste a further two years expounding their theories for a Ph.D they could no longer avoid the real world.

Twin Dick Whittingtons, they set off for London, where Michael joined the BBC as a trainee while Adrian was signed up by Benton & Bowles, the international advertising agency, as an accounts assistant. They acquired a small flat in the Earl's Court Road which they painted orange and brown, and proceeded to live the life of two young blades, for that is undoubtedly how they saw themselves.

Both men spent a further five years in this blissful bachelor state until they each fell for a girl who fulfilled their particular requirements. They were married within weeks of each other; Michael to a tall, blue-eyed blonde whom he met while playing tennis at the Hurlingham Club: Adrian to a slim, dark-eyed, dark-haired executive in charge of the Kellogg's Cornflakes account. Both officiated as the other's best man and each proceeded to sire three children at yearly intervals, and in that again they differed, but as before only on points of detail,

Michael having two sons and a daughter, Adrian two daughters and a son. Each became godfather to the other's first-born son.

Marriage hardly separated them in anything as they continued to follow much of their old routine, playing cricket together at weekends in the summer and football in the winter, not to mention regular luncheons during the week.

After the celebration of his tenth wedding anniversary, Michael, now a senior producer with Thames Television, admitted rather coyly to Adrian that he had had his first affair: he had been unable to resist a tall, well-built blonde from the typing pool who was offering more than shorthand at seventy words a minute. Only a few weeks later, Adrian, now a senior account manager with Pearl and Dean, also went under, selecting a journalist from Fleet Street who was seeking some inside information on one of the companies he represented. She became a tax-deductible item. After that, the two men quickly fell back into their old routine. Any help they could give each other was provided unstintingly, creating no conflict of interests because of their different tastes. Their married lives were not suffering – or so they convinced each other – and at thirty-five, having come through the swinging sixties unscathed, they began to make the most of the seventies.

Early in that decade, Thames Television decided to send Michael off to America to edit an ABC film about living in New York, for consumption by British viewers. Adrian, who had always wanted to see the eastern seaboard, did not find it hard to arrange a trip at the same time as he claimed it was necessary for him to carry out some more than usually spurious research for an Anglo-American tobacco company. The two men enjoyed a lively week together in New York, the highlight of which was a party held by ABC on the final evening to view the edited edition of Michael's film on New York, "An Englishman's View of the Big Apple".

When Michael and Adrian arrived at the ABC studios they found the party was already well under way, and both entered the room together, looking forward to a few drinks and an early night before their journey back to England the next day.

They spotted her at exactly the same moment.

She was of medium height and build, with soft green eyes and auburn hair – a striking combination of both men's fantasies. Without another thought each knew exactly where he desired to end up that particular night and, two minds with but a single idea, they advanced purposefully upon her.

"Hello, my name is Michael Thompson."

"Hello," she replied. "I'm Debbie Kendall."

"And I'm Adrian Townsend."

She offered her hand and both tried to grab it. When the party had come to an end, they had, between them, discovered that Debbie Kendall was an ABC floor producer on the evening news spot. She was divorced and had two children who lived with her in New York. But neither of them was any nearer to impressing her, if only because each worked so hard to outdo the other; they both showed off abominably and even squabbled over fetching their new companion her food and drink. In the other's absence they found themselves running down their closest friend in a subtle but damning way.

"Adrian's a nice chap if it wasn't for his drinking," said Michael.

"Super fellow Michael, such a lovely wife and you should see his three adorable children," added Adrian.

They both escorted Debbie home and reluctantly left her on the doorstep of her 68th Street apartment. She kissed the two of them perfunctorily on the cheek, thanked them and said goodnight. They walked back to their hotel in silence.

When they reached their room on the nineteenth floor of the Plaza, it was Michael who spoke first.

"I'm sorry," he said. "I made a bloody fool of myself."

"I was every bit as bad," said Adrian, "we shouldn't fight over a woman. We never have done in the past."

"Agreed," said Michael. "So why not an honourable compromise?"

"What do you suggest?"

"As we both return to London tomorrow morning, let's agree whichever one of us comes back first . . ."

"Perfect," said Adrian and they shook hands to seal the bargain, as if they were both back at school playing a cricket match, and had to decide on who should bat first. The deal made, they climbed into their respective beds, and slept soundly.

* * *

Once back in London both men did everything in their power to find an excuse for returning to New York. Neither contacted Debbie Kendall by phone or letter as it would have broken their gentleman's agreement, but when the weeks grew to be months both became despondent and it seemed that neither was going to be given the opportunity to return. Then Adrian was invited to Los Angeles to address a Media Conference. He remained unbearably smug about the whole trip, confident he would be able to drop into New York on the way to London. It was Michael who discovered that British Airways were offering cheap tickets for wives who accompanied their husbands on a business trip: Adrian was therefore unable to return via New York. Michael breathed a sigh of relief which turned to triumph when he was selected to go to Washington and cover the president's Address to Congress. He suggested to the head of Outside Broadcasts that it would be wise to drop into New York on the way home and strengthen the contacts he had previously made with ABC. The head of Outside Broadcasts agreed, but told Michael he must be back the following day to cover the opening of Parliament.

Adrian phoned up Michael's wife and briefed her on cheap trips to the States when accompanying your husband. "How kind of you to be so thoughtful Adrian but alas my school never allows time off during term, and in any case," she added, "I have a dreadful fear of flying."

Michael was very understanding about his wife's phobia and went off to book a single ticket.

* * *

Michael flew into Washington on the following Monday and called Debbie Kendall from his hotel room, wondering if she would even remember the two vainglorious Englishmen she had briefly met some months before, and if she did whether she would also recall which one he was. He dialled nervously and listened to the ringing tone. Was she in, was she even in New York? At last a click and a soft voice said hello.

"Hello, Debbie, it's Michael Thompson."

"Hello, Michael. What a nice surprise. Are you in New York?"

"No, Washington, but I'm thinking of flying up. You wouldn't be free for dinner on Thursday by any chance?"

"Let me just check my diary."

Michael held his breath as he waited. It seemed like hours.

"Yes, that seems to be fine."

"Fantastic. Shall I pick you up around eight?"

"Yes, thank you, Michael. I'll look forward to seeing you then."

Heartened by this early success Michael immediately penned a telegram of commiseration to Adrian on his sad loss. Adrian didn't reply.

Michael took the shuttle up to New York on the Thursday afternoon as soon as he had finished editing the President's speech for the London office. After settling into another hotel room – this time insisting on a double bed just in case Debbie's children were at home – he had a long bath and a slow shave, cutting himself twice and slapping on a little too much aftershave. He rummaged around for his most telling tie, shirt and suit, and after he had finished dressing he studied himself in the mirror, carefully combing his freshly washed hair to make the long thin strands appear casual as well as cover the parts where his hair was beginning to recede. After a final check, he was able to convince himself that he looked less than his thirty-eight years. Michael then took the lift down to the ground floor, and stepping out of the Plaza on to a neon-lit Fifth Avenue he headed jauntily towards 68th Street. En route, he acquired a dozen roses from a little shop at the corner of 65th Street and Madison Avenue and, humming to himself, proceeded confidently. He arrived at the front door of Debbie Kendall's little brownstone at eight-five.

When Debbie opened the door, Michael thought she looked even more beautiful than he had remembered. She was wearing a long blue dress with a frilly white silk collar and cuffs that covered every part of her body from neck to ankles and yet she could not have been more desirable. She wore almost no make-up except a touch of lipstick that Michael already had plans to remove. Her green eyes sparkled.

"Say something," she said smiling.

"You look quite stunning, Debbie," was all he could think of as he handed her the roses.

"How sweet of you," she replied and invited him in.

Michael followed her into the kitchen where she hammered the long stems and arranged the flowers in a porcelain vase. She then led him into the living room, where she placed the roses on an oval table beside a photograph of two small boys.

"Have we time for a drink?"

"Sure. I've booked a table at Elaine's for eight-thirty."

"My favourite restaurant," she said, with a smile that revealed a small dimple on her cheek. Without asking, Debbie poured two whiskies and handed one of them to Michael.

What a good memory she has, he thought, as he nervously kept picking up and putting down his glass, like a teenager on his first date. When Michael had eventually finished his drink, Debbie suggested that they should leave.

"Elaine wouldn't keep a table free for one minute, even if you were Henry Kissinger."

Michael laughed, and helped her on with her coat. As she unlatched the door, he realised there was no baby-sitter or sound of children. They must be staying with their father, he thought. Once on the street, he hailed a cab and directed the driver to 87th and 2nd. Michael had never been to Elaine's before. The restaurant had been recommended by a friend from ABC who had assured him: "That joint will give you more than half a chance."

As they entered the crowded room and waited by the bar for the Maître d', Michael could see it was the type of place that was frequented by the rich and famous and wondered if his pocket could stand the expense and, more importantly, whether such an outlay would turn out to be a worthwhile investment.

A waiter guided them to a small table at the back of the room, where they both had another whisky while they studied the menu. When the waiter returned to take their order, Debbie wanted no first course, just the veal piccate, so Michael ordered the same for himself. She refused the addition of garlic butter. Michael allowed his expectations to rise slightly.

"How's Adrian?" she asked.

"Oh, as well as can be expected," Michael replied. "He sends you his love, of course." He emphasised the word love.

"How kind of him to remember me, and please return mine. What brings you to New York this time, Michael? Another film?"

"No. New York may well have become everybody's second city, but this time I only came to see you."

"To see me?"

"Yes, I had a tape to edit while I was in Washington, but I always knew I could be through with that by lunch today so I hoped you would be free to spend an evening with me."

"I'm flattered."

"You shouldn't be."

She smiled. The veal arrived.

"Looks good," said Michael.

"Tastes good, too," said Debbie. "When do you fly home?"

"Tomorrow morning, eleven o'clock flight, I'm afraid."

"Not left yourself time to do much in New York."

"I only came up to see you," Michael repeated. Debbie continued eating her veal. "Why would any man want to divorce you, Debbie?"

"Oh, nothing very original, I'm afraid. He fell in

love with a twenty-two year old blonde and left his thirty-two year old wife."

"Silly man. He should have had an affair with the twenty-two year old blonde and remained faithful to his thirty-two year old wife."

"Isn't that a contradiction in terms?"

"Oh, no, I don't think so. I've never thought it unnatural to desire someone else. After all, it's a long life to go through and be expected never to want another woman."

"I'm not so sure I agree with you," said Debbie thoughtfully. "I would like to have remained faithful to one man."

Oh hell, thought Michael, not a very auspicious philosophy.

"Do you miss him?" he tried again.

"Yes, sometimes. It's true what they say in the glossy menopause magazines, one can be very lonely when you suddenly find yourself on your own."

That sounds more promising, thought Michael, and he heard himself saying: "Yes, I can understand that, but someone like you shouldn't have to stay on your own for very long."

Debbie made no reply.

Michael refilled her glass of wine nearly to the brim, hoping he could order a second bottle before she finished her veal.

"Are you trying to get me drunk, Michael?"

"If you think it will help," he replied laughing.

Debbie didn't laugh. Michael tried again.

"Been to the theatre lately?"

"Yes, I went to *Evita* last week. I loved it" – wonder who took you, thought Michael – "but my mother fell asleep in the middle of the second act. I think I shall have to go and see it on my own a second time."

"I only wish I was staying long enough to take you."

"That would be fun," she said.

"Whereas I shall have to be satisfied with seeing the show in London."

"With your wife."

"Another bottle of wine please, waiter."

"No more for me, Michael, really."

"Well, you can help me out a little." The waiter faded away. "Do you get to England at all yourself?" asked Michael.

"No, I've only been once when Roger, my ex, took the whole family. I loved the country. It fulfilled every one of my hopes but I'm afraid we did what all Americans are expected to do. The Tower of London, Buckingham Palace, followed by Oxford and Stratford, before flying on to Paris."

"A sad way to see England; there's so much more I could have shown you."

"I suspect when the English come to America they don't see much outside of New York, Washington, Los Angeles, and perhaps San Francisco."

"I agree," said Michael, not wanting to disagree. The waiter cleared away their empty plates.

"Can I tempt you with a dessert, Debbie?"

"No, no, I'm trying to lose some weight." Michael slipped a hand gently around her waist. "You don't need to," he said. "You feel just perfect."

She laughed. He smiled.

"Nevertheless, I'll stick to coffee, please."

"A little brandy?"

"No, thank you, just coffee."

"Black?"

"Black."

"Coffee for two, please," Michael said to the hovering waiter.

"I wish I had taken you somewhere a little quieter and less ostentatious," he said, turning back to Debbie.

"Why?"

Michael took her hand. It felt cold. "I would like to have said things to you that shouldn't be listened to by people on the next table."

"I don't think anyone would be shocked by what they overheard at Elaine's, Michael."

"Very well then. Do you believe in love at first sight?"

"No, but I think it's possible to be physically attracted to a person on first meeting them."

"Well I must confess, I was to you."

Again she made no reply.

The coffee arrived and Debbie released her hand to take a sip. Michael followed suit.

"There were one hundred and fifty women in that room the night we met, Debbie, and my eyes never left you once."

"Even during the film?"

"I'd seen the damn thing a hundred times. I feared I might never see you again."

"I'm touched."

"Why should you be? It must be happening to you all the time."

"Now and then," she said. "But I haven't taken

anyone too seriously since my husband left me."

"I'm sorry."

"No need. It's just not that easy to get over someone you've lived with for ten years. I doubt if many divorcees are quite that willing to jump into bed with the first man who comes along as all the latest films suggest."

Michael took her hand again, hoping fervently he did not fall into that category.

"It's been such a lovely evening. Why don't we stroll down to the Carlyle and listen to Bobby Short?" Michael's ABC friend had recommended the move if he felt he was still in with a chance.

"Yes, I'd enjoy that," said Debbie.

Michael called for the bill – eighty-seven dollars. Had it been his wife sitting on the other side of the table he would have checked each item carefully, but not on this occasion. He just left five twenty dollar bills on a side plate and didn't wait for the change. As they stepped out on to 2nd Avenue, he took Debbie's hand and together they started walking downtown. On Madison Avenue they stopped in front of shop windows and he bought her a fur coat, a Cartier watch and a Balenciaga dress. Debbie thought it was lucky that all the stores were closed.

They arrived at the Carlyle just in time for the eleven o'clock show. A waiter, flashing a pen torch, guided them through the little dark room on the ground floor to a table in the corner. Michael ordered a bottle of champagne as Bobby Short struck up a chord and drawled out the words: "Georgia, Georgia, oh, my sweet . . ." Michael, now unable to speak to Debbie above the noise of the band, satisfied himself with holding her hand and when the entertainer sang, "This time we almost made the pieces fit, didn't we, gal?" he leaned over and kissed her on the cheek. She turned and smiled – was it faintly conspiratorial, or was he just wishful thinking? – and then she sipped her champagne. On the dot of twelve, Bobby Short shut the piano lid and said, "Goodnight, my friends, the time has come for all you good people to go to bed – and some of you naughty ones too." Michael laughed a little too loud but was pleased that Debbie laughed as well.

They strolled down Madison Avenue to 68th Street chatting about inconsequential affairs, while Michael's thoughts were of only one affair. When they arrived at her 68th Street apartment, she took out her latch key.

"Would you like a nightcap?" she asked without any suggestive intonation.

"No more drink, thank you, Debbie, but I would certainly appreciate a coffee."

She led him into the living room.

"The flowers have lasted well," she teased, and left him to make the coffee. Michael amused himself by flicking through an old copy of *Time* magazine, looking at the pictures, not taking in the words. She returned after a few minutes with a coffee pot and two small cups on a lacquered tray. She poured the coffee, black again, and then sat down next to Michael on the couch, drawing one leg underneath her while turning slightly towards him. Michael downed his coffee in two gulps, scalding his mouth slightly. Then, putting down his cup, he leaned over and kissed her on the mouth. She was still clutching on to her coffee cup. Her eyes opened briefly as she manoeuvred the cup on to a side table. After another long kiss she broke away from him.

"I ought to make an early start in the morning."

"So should I," said Michael, "but I am more worried about not seeing you again for a long time."

"What a nice thing to say," Debbie replied.

"No, I just care," he said, before kissing her again.

This time she responded; he slipped one hand on to her breast while the other one began to undo the row of little buttons down the back of her dress. She broke away again.

"Don't let's do anything we'll regret."

"I know we won't regret it," said Michael.

He then kissed her on the neck and shoulders, slipping her dress off as he moved deftly down her body to her breast, delighted to find she wasn't wearing a bra.

"Shall we go upstairs, Debbie? I'm too old to make love on the sofa."

Without speaking, she rose and led him by the hand to her bedroom which smelled faintly and deliciously of the scent she herself was wearing.

She switched on a small bedside light and took off the rest of her clothes, letting them fall where she stood. Michael never once took his eyes off her body as he undressed clumsily on the other side of the bed. He slipped under the sheets and quickly joined her. When they had finished making love, an experience he hadn't enjoyed as much for a long time, he lay there pondering on the fact that she had succumbed at all, especially on their first date.

They lay silently in each other's arms before making love for a second time, which was every bit as delightful as the first. Michael then fell into a deep sleep.

He woke first the next morning and stared across at the beautiful woman who lay by his side. The digital clock on the bedside table showed seven-o-three. He touched her forehead lightly with his lips and began to stroke her hair. She woke lazily and smiled up at him. Then they made morning love, slowly, gently, but every bit as pleasing as the night before. He didn't speak as she slipped out of bed and ran a bath for him before going to the kitchen to prepare breakfast. Michael relaxed in the hot bath crooning a Bobby Short number at the top of his voice. How he wished that Adrian could see him now. He dried himself and dressed before joining Debbie in the smart little kitchen where they shared breakfast together. Eggs, bacon, toast, English marmalade, and steaming black coffee. Debbie then had a bath and dressed while Michael read the *New York Times*. When she reappeared in the living room wearing a smart coral dress, he was sorry to be leaving so soon.

"We must leave now, or you'll miss your flight."

Michael rose reluctantly and Debbie drove him back to his hotel, where he quickly threw his clothes into a suitcase, settled the bill for his unslept-in double bed and joined her back in the car. On the journey to the airport they chatted about the coming elections and pumpkin pie almost as if they had been married for years or were both avoiding admitting the previous night had ever happened.

Debbie dropped Michael in front of the Pan Am building and put the car in the parking lot before joining him at the check-in counter. They waited for his flight to be called.

"Pan American announces the departure of their Flight Number 006 to London Heathrow. Will all passengers please proceed with their boarding passes to Gate Number Nine?"

When they reached the "passengers-only" barrier, Michael took Debbie briefly in his arms. "Thank you for a memorable evening," he said.

"No, it is I who must thank you, Michael," she replied as she kissed him on the cheek.

"I must confess I hadn't thought it would end up quite like that," he said.

"Why not?" she asked.

"Not easy to explain," he replied, searching for words that would flatter and not embarrass. "Let's say I was surprised that . . ."

"You were surprised that we ended up in bed together on our first night? You shouldn't be."

"I shouldn't?"

"No, there's a simple enough explanation. My friends all told me when I got divorced to find myself a man and have a one-night stand. The idea sounded fun but I didn't like the thought of the men in New York thinking I was easy." She touched him gently on the side of his face. "So when I met you and Adrian, both safely living over three thousand miles away, I thought to myself 'whichever one of you comes back first ' . . ."

The Century

"LIFE is a game", said A. T. Pierson, thus immortalising himself without actually having to do any real work. Though E. M. Forster showed more insight when he wrote "Fate is the Umpire, and Hope is the Ball, which is why I will never score a century at Lord's."

When I was a freshman at University, my room mate invited me to have dinner in a sporting club to which he belonged called Vincent's. Such institutions do not differ greatly around the Western world. They are always brimful of outrageously fit, healthy young animals, whose sole purpose in life seems to be to challenge the opposition of some neighbouring institution to ridiculous feats of physical strength. My host's main rivals, he told me with undergraduate fervour, came from a high-thinking, plain-living establishment which had dozed the unworldly centuries away in the flat, dull, fen country of England, cartographically described on the map as Cambridge. Now the ultimate ambition of men such as my host was simple enough: in whichever sport they aspired to beat the "Tabs" the select few were rewarded with a Blue. As there is no other way of gaining this distinction at either Oxford or Cambridge, every place in the team is contested for with considerable zeal. A man may be selected and indeed play in every other match of the season for the University, even go on to represent his country, but if he does not play in the Oxford and Cambridge match, he cannot describe himself as a Blue.

My story concerns a delightful character I met that evening when I dined as a guest at Vincent's. The undergraduate to whom I refer was in his final year. He came from that part of the world that we still dared to describe in those days (without a great deal of thought) as the colonies. He was an Indian by birth, and the son of a man whose name in England was a household word, if not a legend, for he had captained Oxford and India at cricket, which meant that outside of the British Commonwealth he was about as well known as Babe Ruth is to the English. The young man's father had added to his fame by scoring a century at Lord's when captaining the University cricket side against Cambridge. In fact, when he went on to captain India against England he used to take pride in wearing his cream sweater with the wide dark blue band around the neck and waist. The son, experts predicted, would carry on in the family tradition. He was in much the same mould as his father, tall and rangy with jet-black hair, and as a cricketer, a fine right-handed batsman and a useful left-arm spin bowler. (Those of you who have never been able to comprehend the

English language let alone the game of cricket might well be tempted to ask why not a fine right-arm batsman and a useful left-handed spin bowler. The English, however, always cover such silly questions with the words: Tradition, dear boy, tradition.)

The young Indian undergraduate, like his father, had come up to Oxford with considerably more interest in defeating Cambridge than the examiners. As a freshman, he had played against most of the English county sides, notching up a century against three of them, and on one occasion taking five wickets in an innings. A week before the big match against Cambridge, the skipper informed him that he had won his Blue and that the names of the chosen eleven would be officially announced in *The Times* the following day. The young man telegraphed his father in Calcutta with the news, and then went off for a celebratory dinner at Vincent's. He entered the Club's dining room in high spirits to the traditional round of applause afforded to a new Blue, and as he was about to take a seat he observed the boat crew, all nine of them, around a circular table at the far end of the room. He walked across to the captain of boats and remarked: "I thought you chaps sat one behind each other."

Within seconds, four thirteen-stone men were sitting on the new Blue while the cox poured a jug of cold water over his head.

"If you fail to score a century", said one oar, "we'll use hot water next time." When the four oars had returned to their table, the cricketer rose slowly, straightened his tie in mock indignation, and as he passed the crews' table, patted the five-foot one inch, 102-pound cox on the head and said, "Even losing teams should have a mascot."

This time they only laughed but it was in the very act of patting the cox on the head that he first noticed his thumb felt a little bruised and he commented on the fact to the wicket-keeper who had joined him for dinner. A large entrecôte steak arrived and he found as he picked up his knife that he was unable to grip the handle properly. He tried to put the inconvenience out of his mind, assuming all would be well by the following morning. But the next day he woke in considerable pain and found to his dismay that the thumb was not only black but also badly swollen. After reporting the news to his captain he took the first available train to London for a consultation with a Harley Street specialist. As the carriage rattled through Berkshire, he read in *The Times* that he had been awarded his Blue.

The specialist studied the offending thumb for some considerable time and expressed his doubt that the young man would be able to hold a ball, let alone a bat, for at least a fortnight. The prognosis turned out to be accurate and our hero sat disconsolate in the stand at Lord's, watching Oxford lose the match and the twelfth man gain his Blue. His father, who had flown over from Calcutta especially for the encounter, offered his condolences, pointing out that he still had two years left in which to gain the honour.

As his second Trinity term approached, even the young man forgot his disappointment and in the opening match of the season against Somerset scored a memorable century, full of cuts and drives that reminded *aficionados* of his father. The son had been made Secretary of cricket in the closed season as it was universally acknowledged that only bad luck and the boat crew had stopped him from reaping his just reward as a freshman. Once again, he played in every fixture before the needle match, but in the last four games against county teams he failed to score more than a dozen runs and did not take a single wicket, while his immediate rivals excelled themselves. He was going through a lean patch, and was the first to agree with his captain that with so much talent around that year he should not be risked against Cambridge. Once again he watched Oxford lose the Blues match and his opposite number the Cambridge Secretary, Robin Oakley, score a faultless century. A man well into his sixties sporting an MCC tie came up to the young Indian during the game, patted him on the shoulder, and remarked that he would never forget the day his father had scored a hundred against Cambridge: it didn't help.

When the cricketer returned for his final year, he was surprised and delighted to be selected by his fellow teammates to be captain, an honour never previously afforded to a man who had not been awarded the coveted Blue. His peers recognised his outstanding work as Secretary and knew if he could reproduce the form of his freshman year he would undoubtedly not only win a Blue but go on to represent his country.

The tradition at Oxford is that in a man's final year he does not play cricket until he has sat Schools, which leaves him enough time to play in the last three county matches before the Varsity match. But as the new captain had no interest in graduating, he by-passed tradition and played cricket from the opening day of the summer season. His touch never failed him for he batted magnificently and on those rare occasions when he did have an off-day with the bat, he bowled superbly. During the term he led Oxford to victory over three county sides, and his team looked well set for their revenge in the Varsity match.

As the day of the match drew nearer, the cricket correspondent of *The Times* wrote that anyone who had seen him bat this season felt sure that the young Indian would follow his father into the record books by scoring a century against Cambridge: but the correspondent did add that he might be vulnerable against the early attack of Bill Potter, the Cambridge fast bowler.

Everyone wanted the Oxford captain to succeed, for he was one of those rare and gifted men whose charm creates no enemies.

When he announced his Blues team to the press, he did not send a telegram to his father for fear that the news might bring bad luck, and for good measure he did not speak to any member of the boat crew for the entire week leading up to the match. The night before the final encounter he retired to bed at seven although he did not sleep.

On the first morning of the three-day match, the sun shone brightly in an almost cloudless sky and by eleven o'clock a fair sized crowd were already in their seats. The two captains in open necked white shirts, spotless white pressed trousers and freshly creamed white boots came out to study the pitch before they tossed. Robin Oakley of Cambridge won and elected to bat.

By lunch on the first day Cambridge had scored seventy-nine for three and in the early afternoon, when his fast bowlers were tired from their second spell and had not managed an early breakthrough, the captain put himself on. When he was straight, the ball didn't reach a full length, and when he bowled a full length, he was never straight; he quickly took himself off. His less established bowlers managed the necessary breakthrough and Cambridge were all out an hour after tea for 208.

The Oxford openers took the crease at ten to six; forty minutes to see through before close of play on the first day. The captain sat padded up on the pavilion balcony, waiting to be called upon only if a wicket fell. His instructions had been clear: no heroics, bat out the forty minutes so that Oxford could start afresh the next morning with all ten wickets intact. With only one over left before the close of play, the young freshman opener had his middle stump removed by Bill Potter, the Cambridge fast bowler. Oxford were eleven for one. The captain came to the crease with only four balls left to face before the clock would show six-thirty. He took his usual guard, middle and leg, and prepared himself to face the fastest man in the Cambridge side. Potter's first delivery came rocketing down and was just short of a length, moving away outside the off stump. The ball nicked the corner of the bat – or was it pad? – and carried to first slip, who dived to his right and took the catch low down. Eleven Cambridge men screamed "Howzat". Was the captain going to be out – for a duck? Without waiting for the umpire's decision he turned and walked back to the pavilion, allowing no expression to appear on his face though he continually hit the side of his pad with his bat. As he climbed the steps he saw his father, sitting on his own in the members' enclosure. He walked on through the Long Room, to cries of "Bad luck, old fellow" from men holding slopping pints of beer, and "Better luck in the second innings" from large-bellied old Blues.

The next day, Oxford kept their heads down and put together a total of 181 runs, leaving themselves only a twenty-seven run deficit. When Cambridge batted for a second time they pressed home their slight advantage and the captain's bowling figures ended up as eleven overs, no maidens, no wickets, forty-two runs. He took his team off the field at the end of play on the second day with Cambridge standing at 167 for seven, Robin Oakley the Cambridge captain having notched up a respectable sixty-three not out, and he looked well set for a century.

On the morning of the third day, the Oxford quickies removed the last three Cambridge wickets for nineteen runs in forty minutes and Robin Oakley ran out of partners, and left the field with eighty-nine not out. The Oxford captain was the first to commiserate with him. "At least you notched a hundred last year," he added.

"True," replied Oakley, "so perhaps it's your turn this year. But not if I've got anything to do with it!"

The Oxford captain smiled at the thought of scoring a century when his team only needed 214 runs at a little under a run a minute to win the match.

The two Oxford opening batsmen began their innings just before midday and remained together until the last over before lunch when the freshman was once again clean bowled by Cambridge's ace fast bowler, Bill Potter. The captain sat on the balcony nervously, padded up and ready. He looked down on the bald head of his father, who was chatting to a former captain of England. Both men had scored centuries in the Varsity match. The captain pulled on his gloves and walked slowly down the pavilion steps, trying to look casual; he had never felt more nervous in his life. As he passed his father, the older man turned his sun-burned face towards his only child and smiled. The crowd warmly applauded the captain all the way to the crease. He took guard, middle and leg again, and prepared to face the attack. The eager Potter who had despatched the captain so brusquely in the first innings came thundering down towards him hoping to be the cause of a pair. He delivered a magnificent first ball that swung in from his legs and beat the captain all ends up, hitting him with a thud on the front pad.

"Howzat?" screamed Potter and the entire Cambridge side as they leaped in the air.

The captain looked up apprehensively at the umpire who took his hands out of his pockets and moved a pebble from one palm to the other to remind him that another ball had been bowled. But he affected no interest in the appeal. A sigh of relief went up from the members in the pavilion. The captain managed to see through the rest of the over and returned to lunch nought not out, with his side twenty-four for one.

After lunch Potter returned to the attack. He rubbed the leather ball on his red-stained flannels and hurled himself forward, looking even fiercer than he had at start of play. He released his missile with every ounce of venom he possessed, but in so doing he tried a little too hard and the delivery was badly short. The captain leaned back and hooked the ball to the Tavern boundary for four, and from that moment he never looked as if anyone would prise him from the crease. He reached his fifty in seventy-one minutes, and at ten past four the Oxford team came into tea with the score at 171 for five and the skipper on eighty-two not out. The young man did not look at his father as he climbed the steps of the pavilion. He needed another eighteen runs before he could do that and by then his team would be safe. He ate and drank nothing at tea, and spoke to no one.

After twenty minutes a bell rang and the eleven Cambridge men returned to the field. A minute later, the captain and his partner walked back out to the crease, their open white shirts flapping in the breeze. Two hours left for the century and victory. The captain's partner only lasted another five balls and the captain himself seemed to have lost that natural flow he had possessed before tea, struggling into the nineties with ones and twos. The light was getting bad and it took him a full thirty minutes to reach ninety-nine, by which time he had lost another partner: 194 for seven. He remained on ninety-nine for twelve minutes, when Robin Oakley the Cambridge captain took the new ball and brought his ace speed man back into the attack.

Then there occurred one of the most amazing incidents I have ever witnessed in a cricket match. Robin Oakley set an attacking field for the new ball – three slips, a gully, cover point, mid off, mid on, mid wicket and a short square leg, a truly vicious circle. He then tossed the ball to Potter who knew this would be his last chance to capture the Oxford captain's wicket and save the match; once he had scored the century he would surely knock off the rest of the runs in a matter of minutes. The sky was becoming bleak as a bank of dark clouds passed over the ground, but this was no time to leave the field for bad light. Potter shone the new ball once more on his white trousers and thundered up to hurl a delivery that the captain jabbed at and missed. One or two fielders raised their hands without appealing. Potter returned to his mark, shining the ball with even more relish and left a red blood-like stain down the side of his thigh. The second ball, a yorker, beat the captain completely and must have missed the off stump by about an inch; there was a general sigh around the ground. The third ball hit the captain on the middle of the pad and the eleven Cambridge men threw their arms in the air and screamed for leg before wicket but the umpire was not moved.

The captain jabbed at the fourth ball and it carried tentatively to mid on, where Robin Oakley had placed himself a mere twenty yards in front of the bat, watching his adversary in disbelief as he set off for a run he could never hope to complete. His batting partner remained firmly in his crease, incredulous: one didn't run when the ball was hit to mid on unless it was the last delivery of the match.

The captain of Oxford, now stranded fifteen yards from safety, turned and looked at the captain of Cambridge, who held the ball in his hand. Robin Oakley was about to toss the ball to the wicket-keeper who in turn was waiting to remove the bails and send the Oxford captain back to the pavilion, run out for ninety-nine, but Oakley hesitated and, for several seconds the two gladiators stared at each other and then the Cambridge captain placed the ball in his pocket. The Oxford captain walked slowly back to his crease while the crowd remained silent in disbelief. Robin Oakley tossed the ball to Potter who thundered down to deliver the fifth ball, which was short, and the Oxford captain effortlessly placed it through the covers for four runs. The crowd rose as one and old friends in the pavilion thumped the father's back.

He smiled for a second time.

Potter was now advancing with his final effort and, exhausted, he delivered another short ball which should have been despatched to the boundary with ease but the Oxford captain took one pace backwards and hit his own stumps. He was out, hit wicket, bowled Potter for 103. The crowd rose for a second time as he walked back to the pavilion and grown men who had been decorated in two wars had tears in their eyes. Seven minutes later, everyone left the field, drenched by a thunderstorm.

The match ended in a draw.

Broken Routine

SEPTIMUS Horatio Cornwallis did not live up to his name. With such a name he should have been a cabinet minister, an admiral, or at least a rural dean. In fact, Septimus Horatio Cornwallis was a claims adjuster at the head office of the Prudential Assurance Company Limited, 172 Holborn Bars, London EC1.

Septimus's names could be blamed on his father, who had a small knowledge of Nelson, on his mother who was superstitious, and on his great-great-great-grandfather who was alleged to have been a second cousin of the illustrious Governor-General of India. On leaving school Septimus, a thin, anaemic young man prematurely balding, joined the Prudential Assurance Company; his careers master having told him that it was an ideal opening for a young man with his qualifications. Some time later, when Septimus reflected on the advice, it worried him, because even he realised that he had no qualifications. Despite this set-back, Septimus rose slowly over the years from office boy to claims adjuster (not so much climbing the ladder as resting upon each rung for some considerable time), which afforded him the grandiose title of assistant deputy manager (claims department).

Septimus spent his day in a glass cubicle on the sixth floor, adjusting claims and recommending payments of anything up to one million pounds. He felt if he kept his nose clean (one of Septimus's favourite expressions), he would, after another twenty years, become a manager (claims department) and have walls around him that you couldn't see through and a carpet that wasn't laid in small squares of slightly differing shades of green. He might even become one of those signatures on the million pound cheques.

Septimus resided in Sevenoaks with his wife, Norma, and his two children, Winston and Elizabeth, who attended the local comprehensive school. They would have gone to the grammar school, he regularly informed his colleagues, but the Labour government had stopped all that.

Septimus operated his daily life by means of a set of invariant sub-routines, like a primitive microprocessor, while he supposed himself to be a great follower of tradition and discipline. For if he was nothing, he was at least a creature of habit. Had, for some unexplicable reason, the KGB wanted to assassinate Septimus, all they would have had to do was put him under surveillance for seven days and they would have known his every movement throughout the working year.

Septimus rose every morning at seven-fifteen and donned one of his two pin-head patterned dark suits. He left his home at 47 Palmerston Drive at seven-fifty-five, having consumed his invariable breakfast of one soft-boiled egg, two pieces of toast, and two cups of tea. On arriving at Platform One of Sevenoaks station he would purchase a copy of the *Daily Express* before boarding the eight-twenty-seven to Cannon Street. During the journey Septimus would read his newspaper and smoke two cigarettes, arriving at Cannon Street at nine-seven. He would then walk to the office, and be sitting at his desk in his glass cubicle on the sixth floor, confronting the first claim to be adjusted, by nine-thirty. He took his coffee break at eleven, allowing himself the luxury of two more cigarettes, when once again he would regale his colleagues with the imagined achievements of his children. At eleven-fifteen he returned to work.

At one o'clock he would leave the Great Gothic Cathedral (another of his expressions) for one hour, which he passed at a pub called The Havelock where he would drink a half-pint of Carlsberg lager with a dash of lime, and eat the dish of the day. After he finished his lunch, he would once again smoke two cigarettes. At one-fifty-five he returned to the insurance records until the fifteen minute tea break at four o'clock which was another ritual occasion for two more cigarettes. On the dot of five-thirty, Septimus would pick up his umbrella and reinforced steel briefcase with the initials S.H.C. in silver on the side and leave, double locking his glass cubicle. As he walked through the typing pool, he would announce with a mechanical jauntiness "See you same time tomorrow, girls", hum a few bars from *The Sound of Music* in the descending lift, and then walk out into the torrent of office workers surging down High Holborn. He would stride purposefully towards Cannon Street station, umbrella tapping away on the pavement while he rubbed shoulders with bankers, shippers, oil men, and brokers, not discontent to think himself part of the great City of London.

Once he reached the station, Septimus would purchase a copy of the *Evening Standard* and a packet of ten Benson & Hedges cigarettes from Smith's bookstall, placing both on the top of his Prudential documents already in the briefcase. He would board the fourth carriage of the train on Platform Five at five-fifty, and secure his favoured window seat in a closed compartment facing the engine, next to the balding gentleman with the inevitable *Financial Times*, and opposite the smartly dressed secretary who read long romantic novels to somewhere beyond Sevenoaks. Before sitting down he would extract the *Evening Standard* and the new packet of Benson & Hedges from his briefcase, put them both on the armrest of his seat, and place the briefcase and his rolled umbrella on the rack above him. Once settled, he would open the packet of cigarettes and smoke the first of the two which were allocated for the journey while reading the *Evening Standard*. This would leave him eight to be smoked before catching the five-fifty the following evening.

As the train pulled into Sevenoaks station, he would mumble goodnight to his fellow passengers (the only word he ever spoke during the entire journey) and leave, making his way straight to the semi-detached at 47 Palmerston Drive, arriving at the front door a little before six-forty-five. Between six-forty-five and seven-thirty he would finish reading his paper or check over his children's homework with a tut-tut when he spotted a mistake, or a sigh when he couldn't fathom the new maths. At seven-thirty his "good lady" (another of his favoured expressions) would place on the kitchen table in front of him the *Woman's Own* dish of the day or his favourite dinner of three fish fingers, peas and chips. He would then say "If God had meant fish to have fingers, he would have given them hands," laugh, and cover the oblong fish with tomato sauce, consuming the meal to the accompaniment of his wife's recital of the day's events. At nine, he watched the real news on BBC 1 (he never watched ITV) and at ten-thirty he retired to bed.

This routine was adhered to year in year out with breaks only for holidays, for which Septimus naturally also had a routine. Alternate Christmases were spent with Norma's parents in Watford and the ones in between with Septimus's sister and brother-in-law in Epsom, while in the summer, their high spot of the year, the family took a package holiday for two weeks in the Olympic Hotel, Corfu.

Septimus not only liked his life-style, but was distressed if for any reason his routine met with the slightest interference. This humdrum existence seemed certain to last him from womb to tomb, for Septimus was not the stuff on which authors base two hundred thousand word sagas. Nevertheless there was one occasion when Septimus's routine was not merely interfered with, but frankly, shattered.

* * *

One evening at five-twenty-seven, when Septimus was closing the file on the last claim for the day, his immediate superior, the Deputy Manager, called him in for a consultation. Owing to this gross lack of consideration, Septimus did not manage to get away from the office until a few minutes after six. Although everyone had left the typing pool, still he saluted the empty desks and silent typewriters with the invariable "See you same time tomorrow, girls," and hummed a few bars of *Edelweiss* to the descending lift. As he stepped out of the Great Gothic Cathedral it started to rain. Septimus reluctantly undid his neatly rolled umbrella, and putting it up dashed through the puddles, hoping that he would be in time to catch the six-thirty-two. On arrival at Cannon Street, he queued for his paper and cigarettes and put them in his briefcase before rushing on to Platform Five. To add to his annoyance, the loudspeaker was announcing with perfunctory apology that three trains had already been taken off that evening because of a go slow.

Septimus eventually fought his way through the dripping, bustling crowds to the sixth carriage of a train that was not scheduled on any timetable. He discovered that it was filled with people he had never seen before and, worse, almost every seat was already occupied. In fact, the only place he could find to sit was in the middle of the train with his back to the engine. He threw his briefcase and creased umbrella onto the rack above him and reluctantly squeezed himself into the seat, before looking around the carriage. There was not a familiar face among the other six occupants. A woman with three children more than filled the seat opposite him, while an elderly man was sleeping soundly on his left. On the other side of him, leaning over and looking out of the window, was a young man of about twenty.

When Septimus first laid eyes on the boy he couldn't believe what he saw. The youth was clad in a black leather jacket and skin-tight jeans and was whistling to himself. His dark, creamed hair was combed up at the front and down at the sides, while the only two colours of the young man's outfit that matched were his jacket and fingernails. But worst of all to one of Septimus's sensitive nature was the slogan printed in boot studs on the back of his jacket. "Heil Hitler" it declared unashamedly over a white-painted Nazi sign and, as if that were not enough, below the swastika in gold shone the words: "Up yours". What was the country coming to? thought Septimus. They ought to bring back National Service for delinquents like that. Septimus himself, had not been eligible for National Service on account of his flat feet.

Septimus decided to ignore the creature, and picking up the packet of Benson & Hedges on the armrest by his side, lit one and began to read the *Evening Standard*. He then replaced the packet of cigarettes on the armrest, as he always did, knowing he would smoke one more before reaching Sevenoaks. When the train eventually moved out of Cannon Street the darkly clad youth turned towards Septimus and, glaring at him, picked up the packet of cigarettes, took one, lit it, and started to puff away. Septimus could not believe what was happening. He was about to protest when he realised that none of his regulars was in the carriage to back him up. He considered the situation for a moment and decided that Discretion was the better part of Valour. (Yet another of the sayings of Septimus.)

When the train stopped at Petts Wood, Septimus put down the newspaper although he had scarcely read a word and as he nearly always did, took his second cigarette. He lit it, inhaled, and was about to retrieve the *Evening Standard* when the youth grabbed at the corner, and they ended up with half the paper each. This time Septimus did look around the carriage for support. The children opposite started giggling, while their mother consciously averted her eyes from what was taking place, obviously not wanting to become involved; the old man on Septimus's left was now snoring. Septimus was about to secure the packet of cigarettes by putting them in his pocket when the youth pounced on them, removed another and lit it, inhaled deeply, and then blew the smoke quite deliberately across Septimus's face before placing the cigarettes back on the armrest. Septimus's answering glare expressed as much malevolence as he was able to project through the grey haze. Grinding his teeth in fury, he returned to the *Evening Standard*, only to discover that he had ended up with situations vacant, used cars and sports sections, subjects in which he had absolutely no interest. His one compensation, however, was his certainty that sport was the only section the oik really wanted. Septimus was now, in any case, incapable of reading the paper, trembling as he was with the outrages perpetrated by his neighbour.

His thoughts were now turning to revenge and gradually a plan began to form in his mind with which he was confident the youth would be left in no doubt that virtue can sometimes be more than its own reward. (A variation on a saying of Septimus.) He smiled thinly and, breaking his routine, he took a third cigarette and defiantly placed the packet back on the armrest. The youth stubbed out his own cigarette and, as if taking up the challenge, picked up the packet, removed another one and lit it. Septimus was by no means beaten; he puffed his way quickly through the weed, stubbed it out, a quarter unsmoked, took a fourth and lit it immediately. The race was on for there were now only two cigarettes left. But Septimus, despite a great deal of puffing and coughing, managed to finish his fourth cigarette ahead of the youth. He leaned across the leather jacket and stubbed his cigarette out in the window ashtray. The carriage was now fillcd with smoke, but the youth was still puffing as fast as he could. The children opposite were coughing and the woman was waving her arms around like a windmill. Septimus ignored her and kept his eye on the packet of cigarettes while pretending to read about Arsenal's chances in the FA cup.

Septimus then recalled Montgomery's maxim that surprise and timing in the final analysis are the weapons of victory. As the youth finished his fourth cigarette and was stubbing it out the train pulled slowly into Sevenoaks station. The youth's hand was raised, but Septimus was quicker. He had anticipated the enemy's next move, and now seized the cigarette packet. He took out the ninth cigarette and, placing it between his lips, lit it slowly and luxuriously, inhaling as deeply as he could before blowing the smoke out straight into the face of the enemy. The youth stared up at him in dismay. Septimus then removed the last cigarette from the packet and crumpled the tobacco into shreds between his first finger and thumb, allowing the little flakes to fall back into the empty packet. Then he closed the packet neatly, and with a flourish replaced the little gold box on the armrest. In the same movement he picked up from his vacant seat the sports section of the *Evening Standard*, tore the paper in half, in quarters, in eighths and finally in sixteenths, placing the little squares in a neat pile on the youth's lap.

The train came to a halt at Sevenoaks. A triumphant Septimus, having struck his blow for the silent majority, retrieved his umbrella and briefcase from the rack above him and turned to leave.

As he picked up his briefcase it knocked the armrest in front of him and the lid sprang open. Everyone in the carriage stared at its contents. For there, on top of his Prudential documents, was a neatly folded copy of the *Evening Standard* and an unopened packet of ten Benson & Hedges cigarettes.

Henry's Hiccup

WHEN the Grand Pasha's first son was born in 1900 (he had sired twelve daughters by six wives) he named the boy Henry after his favourite king of England. Henry entered this world with more money than even the most blasé tax collector could imagine and therefore seemed destined to live a life of idle ease.

The Grand Pasha who ruled over ten thousand families, was of the opinion that in time there would be only five kings left in the world – the kings of spades, hearts, diamonds, clubs, and England. With this conviction in mind, he decided that Henry should be educated by the British. The boy was therefore despatched from his native Cairo at the age of eight to embark upon a formal education, young enough to retain only vague recollections of the noise, the heat, and the dirt of his birthplace. Henry started his new life at the Dragon School, which the Grand Pasha's advisers assured him was the finest preparatory school in the land. The boy left this establishment four years later, having developed a passionate love for the polo field and a thorough distaste for the classroom. He proceeded, with the minimum academic qualifications, to Eton, which the Pasha's advisers assured him was the best school in Europe. He was gratified to learn the school had been founded by his favourite king. Henry spent five years at Eton, where he added squash, golf and tennis to his loves, and applied mathematics, jazz and cross-country running to his dislikes.

On leaving school, he once again failed to make more than a passing impression on the examiners. Nevertheless, he was found a place at Balliol College, Oxford, which the Pasha's advisers assured him was the greatest University in the world. Three years at Balliol added two more loves to his life: horses and women, and three more ineradicable aversions: politics, philosophy and economics.

At the end of his time in *statu pupillari*, he totally failed to impress the examiners and went down without a degree. His father, who considered young Henry's two goals against Cambridge in the Varsity polo match a wholly satisfactory result of his University career, despatched the boy on a journey round the world to complete his education. Henry enjoyed the experience, learning more on the race course at Longchamps and in the back streets of Benghazi than he ever had acquired from his formal upbringing in England.

The Grand Pasha would have been proud of the tall, sophisticated and handsome young man who returned to England a year later showing only the slightest trace of a foreign accent, if he hadn't died before his beloved son reached Southampton. Henry, although broken-hearted, was certainly not broke, as his father had left him some twenty million in known assets, including a racing stud at Suffolk, a 100-foot yacht in Nice, and a palace in Cairo. But by far the most important of his father's bequests was the finest manservant in London, one Godfrey Barker. Barker could arrange or rearrange anything, at a moment's notice.

Henry, for the lack of something better to do, settled himself into his father's old suite at the Ritz, not troubling to read the situations vacant column in the London *Times*. Rather he embarked on a life of single-minded dedication to the pursuit of pleasure, the only career for which Eton, Oxford and inherited wealth had adequately equipped him. To do Henry justice, he had, despite a more than generous helping of charm and good looks, enough common sense to choose carefully those permitted to spend the unforgiving minute with him. He selected only old friends from school and University who, although they were without exception not as well breached as he, weren't the sort of fellows who came begging for the loan of a fiver to cover a gambling debt.

Whenever Henry was asked what was the first love of his life, he was always hard pressed to choose between horses and women, and as he found it possible to spend the day with the one and the night with the other without causing any jealousy or recrimination, he never overtaxed himself with resolving the problem. Most of his horses were fine stallions, fast, sleek, velvet-skinned, with dark eyes and firm limbs; this would have adequately described most of his women, except that they were fillies. Henry fell in and out of love with every girl in the chorus line of the London Palladium, and when the affairs had come to an end, Barker saw to it that they always received some suitable memento to ensure no scandal ensued. Henry also won every classic race on the English turf before he was thirty-five and Barker always seemed to know the right year to back his master.

Henry's life quickly fell into a routine, never dull. One month was spent in Cairo going through the motions of attending to his business, three months in the south of France with the occasional excursion to Biarritz, and for the remaining eight months he resided at the Ritz. For the four months he was out of London his magnificent suite overlooking St James's Park remained unoccupied. History does not record whether Henry left the rooms empty because he disliked the thought of unknown persons splashing in the sunken marble bath or because he simply couldn't be bothered with the fuss of signing in and out of the hotel twice a year. The Ritz management never commented on the matter to his father; why should they with the son? This programme fully accounted for Henry's year except for the odd trip to Paris when some home counties girl came a little too close to the altar. Although almost every girl who met Henry wanted to marry him, a good many would have done so even if he had been penniless. However, Henry saw absolutely no reason to be faithful to one woman. "I have a hundred horses and a hundred male friends," he would explain when asked. "Why, should I confine myself to one female?" There seemed no immediate answer to Henry's logic.

The story of Henry would have ended there had he continued life as destiny seemed content to allow, but even the Henrys of this world have the occasional hiccup.

As the years passed Henry grew into the habit of never planning ahead as experience – and his able manservant, Barker – had always led him to believe that with vast wealth you could acquire anything you desired at the last minute, and cover any contingencies that arose later. However, even Barker couldn't formulate a contingency plan in response to Mr Chamberlain's statement of 3 September, 1939, that the British people were at war with Germany. Henry felt it inconsiderate of Chamberlain to have declared war so soon after Wimbledon and the Oaks, and even more inconsiderate of the Home Office to advise him a few months later that Barker must stop serving the Grand Pasha and, until further notice, serve His Majesty the King instead.

What could poor Henry do? Now in his fortieth year he was not used to living anywhere other than the Ritz, and the Germans who had caused Wimbledon to be cancelled were also occupying the George V in Paris and the Negresco in Nice. As the weeks passed and daily an invasion seemed more certain Henry came to the distasteful conclusion that he would have to return to a neutral Cairo until the British had won the war. It never crossed Henry's mind, even for one moment, that the British might lose. After all, they had won the First World War and therefore they must win the Second. "History repeats itself" was about the only piece of wisdom he recalled clearly from three years of tutorials at Oxford.

Henry summoned the manager of the Ritz and told him that his suite was to be left unoccupied until he returned. He paid one year in advance, which he felt was more than enough time to take care of upstarts like Herr Hitler, and set off for Cairo. The manager was heard to remark later that the Grand Pasha's departure for Egypt was most ironic; he was, after all, more British than the British.

Henry spent a year at his palace in Cairo and then found he could bear his fellow countrymen no longer, so he removed himself to New York only just before it would have been possible for him to come face to face with Rommel. Once in New York, Henry bivouacked in the Pierre Hotel on Fifth Avenue, selected an American manservant called Eugene, and waited for Mr Churchill to finish the war. As if to prove his continuing support for the British, on the first of January every year he forwarded a cheque to the Ritz to cover the cost of his rooms for the next twelve months.

Henry celebrated V-J Day in Times Square with a million Americans and immediately made plans for his return to Britain. He was surprised and disappointed when the British Embassy in Washington informed him that it might be some time before he was allowed to return to the land he loved, and despite continual pressure and all the influence he could bring to bear, he was unable to board a ship for Southampton until July 1946. From the first-class deck he waved goodbye to America and

Eugene, and looked forward to England and Barker.

Once he had stepped off the ship on to English soil he headed straight for the Ritz to find his rooms exactly as he had left them. As far as Henry could see, nothing had changed except that his manservant (now the batman to a general) could not be released from the armed forces for at least another six months. Henry was determined to play his part in the war effort by surviving without him for the ensuing period, and remembering Barker's words: "Everyone knows who you are. Nothing will change," he felt confident all would be well. Indeed on the *Bonheur-du-jour* in his room at the Ritz was an invitation to dine with Lord and Lady Lympsham in their Chelsea Square home the following night. It looked as if Barker's prediction was turning out to be right: everything would be just the same. Henry penned an affirmative reply to the invitation, happy with the thought that he was going to pick up his life in England exactly where he had left off.

The following evening Henry arrived on the Chelsea Square doorstep a few minutes after eight o'clock. The Lympshams, an elderly couple who had not qualified for the war in any way, gave every appearance of not even realising that it had taken place or that Henry had been absent from the London social scene. Their table, despite rationing, was as fine as Henry remembered and, more important one of the guests present was quite unlike anyone he could ever remember. Her name, Henry learned from his host, was Victoria Campbell, and she turned out to be the daughter of another guest, General Sir Ralph Colquhoun. Lady Lympsham confided to Henry over the quails' eggs that the sad young thing had lost her husband when the allies advanced on Berlin, only a few days before the Germans had surrendered. For the first time Henry felt guilty about not having played some part in the war.

All through dinner, he could not take his eyes from young Victoria whose classical beauty was only equalled by her well-informed and lively conversation. He feared he might be staring too obviously at the slim, dark-haired girl with the high cheek bones; it was like admiring a beautiful sculpture and wanting to touch it. Her bewitching smile elicited an answering smile from all who received it. Henry did everything in his power to be the receiver and was rewarded on several occasions, aware that, for the first time in his life, he was becoming totally infatuated – and was delighted to be.

The ensuing courtship was an unusual one for Henry, in that he made no attempt to persuade Victoria to compliance. He was sympathetic and attentive, and when she had come out of mourning he approached her father and asked if he might request his daughter's hand in marriage. Henry was overjoyed when first the General agreed and later Victoria accepted. After an announcement in *The Times* they celebrated the engagement with a small dinner party at the Ritz, attended by one hundred and twenty close friends who might have been forgiven for coming to a conclusion that Attlee was exaggerating about his austerity programme. After the last guest had left Henry walked Victoria back to her father's home in Belgrave Mews, while discussing the wedding arrangements and his plans for the honeymoon.

"Everything must be perfect for you, my angel," he said, as once again he admired the way her long, dark hair curled at the shoulders. "We shall be married in St Margaret's, Westminster, and after a reception at the Ritz we will be driven to Victoria Station where you will be met by Fred, the senior porter. Fred will allow no one else to carry my bags to the last carriage of the Golden Arrow. One should always have the last carriage, my darling," explained Henry, "so that one cannot be disturbed by other travellers."

Victoria was impressed by Henry's mastery of the arrangements, especially remembering the absence of his manservant, Barker.

Henry warmed to his theme. "Once we have boarded the Golden Arrow, you will be served with China tea and some wafer-thin smoked salmon sandwiches which we can enjoy while relaxing on our journey to Dover. When we arrive at the Channel port, you will be met by Albert whom Fred will have alerted. Albert will remove the bags from our carriage, but not before everyone else has left the train. He will then escort us to the ship, where we will take sherry with the captain while our bags are being placed in cabin number three. Like my father, I always have cabin number three; it is not only the largest and most comfortable stateroom on board, but the cabin is situated in the centre of the ship, which makes it possible to enjoy a comfortable crossing even should one have the misfortune to encounter bad weather. And when we have docked in Calais you will find Pierre waiting for us. He will have organised everything for the front carriage of the Flèche d'Or."

"Such a programme must take a considerable amount of detailed planning," suggested Victoria, her hazel eyes sparkling as she listened to her future husband's description of the promised tour.

"More tradition than organisation I would say, my dear," replied Henry, smiling, as they strolled hand in hand across Hyde Park. "Although, I confess, in the past Barker has kept his eye on things should any untoward emergency arise. In any case I have *always* had the front carriage of the Flèche d'Or because it assures one of being off the train and away before anyone realises that you have actually arrived in the French capital. Other than Raymond, of course."

"Raymond?"

"Yes, Raymond, a servant *par excellence*, who adored my father, he will have organised a bottle of Veuve Cliquot '37 and a little Russian caviar for the journey. He will also have ensured that there is a couch in the railway carriage should you need to rest, my dear."

"You seem to have thought of everything, Henry darling," she said, as they entered Belgrave Mews.

"I hope you will think so, Victoria; for when you arrive in Paris which I have not had the opportunity to visit for so many years, there will be a Rolls-Royce standing by the side of the carriage, door open, and you will step out of the Flèche d'Or into the car and Maurice will drive us to the George V, arguably the finest hotel in Europe. Louis, the manager, will be on the steps of the hotel to greet you and he will conduct us to the bridal suite with its stunning view of the city. A maid will unpack for you while you retire to bathe and rest from the tiresome journey. When you are fully recovered we shall dine at Maxim's, where you will be guided to the corner table furthest from the orchestra by Marcel, the finest head waiter in the world. As you are seated, the musicians will strike up 'A Room with A View' my favourite tune, and we will then be served with the most magnificent langouste you have ever tasted, of that I can assure you."

Henry and Victoria arrived at the front door of the general's small house in Belgrave Mews. He took her hand before continuing.

"After you have dined, my dear, we shall stroll into the Madeleine where I shall buy a dozen red roses from Paulette, the most beautiful flower girl in Paris. She is almost as lovely as you." Henry sighed and concluded: "Then we shall return to the George V and spend our first night together."

Victoria's hazel eyes showed delighted anticipation. "I only wish it could be tomorrow," she said.

Henry kissed her gallantly on the cheek and said: "It will be worth waiting for, my dear, I can assure you it will be a day neither of us will ever forget."

"I'm sure of that," Victoria replied as he released her hand.

On the morning of his wedding Henry leaped out of bed and drew back the curtains with a flourish, only to be greeted by a steady drizzle.

"The rain will clear by eleven o'clock," he said out loud with immense confidence, and hummed as he shaved slowly and with care.

The weather had not improved by mid-morning. On the contrary, heavy rain was falling by the time Victoria entered the church. Henry's disappointment evaporated the instant he saw his beautiful bride; all he could think of was taking her to Paris. The ceremony over, the Grand Pasha and his wife stood outside the church, a golden couple, smiling for the press photographers as the loyal guests scattered damp rice over them. As soon as they decently could, they set off for the reception at the Ritz. Between them they managed to chat to every guest present, and they would have been away in better time had Victoria been a little quicker changing and the general's toast to the happy couple been considerably shorter. The guests crowded on to the steps of the Ritz, overflowing on to the pavement in Piccadilly to wave good-bye to the departing honeymooners, and were only sheltered from the downpour by a capacious red awning.

The general's Rolls took the Grand Pasha and his wife to the station, where the chauffeur unloaded the bags. Henry instructed him to return to the Ritz as he had everything under control. The chauffeur touched his cap and said: "I hope you and madam have a wonderful trip, sir," and left them. Henry stood on the station, looking for Fred. There was no sign of him, so he hailed a passing porter.

"Where is Fred?" inquired Henry.

"Fred who?" came the reply.

"How in heaven's name should I know?" said Henry.

"Then how in hell's name should I know?" retorted the porter.

Victoria shivered. English railway stations are not designed for the latest fashion in silk coats.

"Kindly take my bags to the end carriage of the train," said Henry.

The porter looked down at the fourteen bags. "All right," he said reluctantly.

Henry and Victoria stood patiently in the cold as the porter loaded the bags on to his trolley and trundled them off along the platform.

"Don't worry, my dear," said Henry. "A cup of Lapsang Souchong tea and some smoked salmon sandwiches and you'll feel a new girl."

"I'm just fine," said Victoria, smiling, though not quite as bewitchingly as normal, as she put her arm through her husband's. They strolled along together to the end carriage.

"Can I check your tickets, sir?" said the conductor, blocking the entrance to the last carriage.

"My what?" said Henry, his accent sounding unusually pronounced.

"Your tic . . . kets," said the conductor, conscious he was addressing a foreigner.

"In the past I have always made the arrangements on the train, my good man."

"Not nowadays you don't, sir. You'll have to go to the booking office and buy your tickets like everyone else, and you'd better be quick about it because the train is due to leave in a few minutes."

Henry stared at the conductor in disbelief. "I

assume my wife may rest on the train while I go and purchase the tickets?" he asked.

"No, I'm sorry, sir. No one is allowed to board the train unless they are in possession of a valid ticket."

"Remain here, my dear," said Henry, "and I will deal with this little problem immediately. Kindly direct me to the ticket office, porter."

"End of Platform Four, governor," said the conductor, slamming the train door annoyed at being described as a porter.

That wasn't quite what Henry had meant by "direct me". Nevertheless, he left his bride with the fourteen bags and somewhat reluctantly headed back towards the ticket office at the end of Platform Four, where he went to the front of a long line.

"There's a queue, you know, mate," someone shouted.

Henry didn't know. "I'm in a frightful hurry," he said.

"And so am I," came back the reply, "so get to the back."

Henry had been told that the British were good at standing in queues, but as he had never had to join one before that moment, he was quite unable to confirm or deny the rumour. He reluctantly walked to the back of a queue. It took some time before Henry reached the front.

"I would like to take the last carriage to Dover."

"You would like what . . . ?"

"The last carriage," repeated Henry a little more loudly.

"I am sorry, sir, but every first-class seat is sold."

"I don't want a seat," said Henry "I require the carriage."

"There are no carriages available nowadays, sir, and as I said, all the seats in first class are sold. I can still fix you up in third class."

"I don't mind what it costs," said Henry. "I must travel first class."

"I don't have a first-class seat, sir. It wouldn't matter if you could afford the whole train."

"I can," said Henry.

"I still don't have a seat left in first class," said the clerk unhelpfully.

Henry would have persisted, but several people in the queue behind him were pointing out that there were only two minutes before the train was due to leave and that they wanted to catch it even if he didn't.

"Two seats then," said Henry, unable to make himself utter the words "third class".

Two green tickets marked Dover were handed through the little grille. Henry took them and started to walk away.

"That will be seventeen and sixpence please, sir."

"Oh, yes, of course," said Henry apologetically. He fumbled in his pocket and unfolded one of the three large white five-pound notes he always carried on him.

"Don't you have anything smaller?"

"No, I do not," said Henry, who found the idea of carrying money vulgar enough without it having to be in small denominations.

The clerk handed back four pounds and a half-crown. Henry did not pick up the half-crown.

"Thank you, sir," said the startled man. It was more than his Saturday bonus.

Henry put the tickets in his pocket and quickly returned to Victoria, who was smiling defiantly against the cold wind; it was not quite the smile that had originally captivated him. Their porter had long ago disappeared and Henry couldn't see another in sight. The conductor took his tickets and clipped them.

"All aboard," he shouted, waved a green flag and blew his whistle.

Henry quickly threw all fourteen bags through the open door and pushed Victoria on to the moving train before leaping on himself. Once he had caught his breath he walked down the corridor, staring into the third class carriages. He had never seen one before. The seats were nothing more than thin worn-out cushions, and as he looked into one half-full carriage a young couple jumped in and took the last two adjacent seats. Henry searched frantically for a free carriage but he was unable even to find one with two seats together. Victoria took a single seat in a packed compartment without complaint, while Henry sat forlornly on one of the suitcases in the corridor.

"It will be different once we're in Dover," he said, without his usual self-confidence.

"I am sure it will, Henry," she replied, smiling kindly at him.

The two-hour journey seemed interminable. Passengers of all shapes and sizes squeezed past him in the corridor, treading on his Lobbs hand-made leather shoes, with the words:

"Sorry, sir."

"Sorry, guv."

"Sorry, mate."

Henry put the blame firmly on the shoulders of Clement Attlee and his ridiculous campaign for social equality, and waited for the train to reach Dover Priory Station. The moment the engine pulled in Henry leaped out of the carriage first, not last, and called for Albert at the top of his voice. Nothing happened, except a stampede of people rushed past him on their way to the ship. Eventually Henry spotted a porter and rushed over to him only to find he was already loading up his trolley with someone else's luggage. Henry sprinted to a second man and then on to a third and waved a pound note at a fourth, who came immediately and unloaded the fourteen bags.

"Where to, guv?" asked the porter amicably.

"The ship," said Henry, and returned to claim his bride. He helped Victoria down from the train and they both ran through the rain until, breathless, they reached the gangplank of the ship.

"Tickets, sir," said a young officer in a dark blue uniform at the bottom of the gangplank.

"I always have cabin number three," said Henry between breaths.

"Of course, sir," said the young man and looked at his clip board. Henry smiled confidently at Victoria.

"Mr and Mrs William West."

"I beg your pardon?" said Henry.

"You must be Mr William West."

"I am certainly not. I am the Grand Pasha of Cairo."

"Well, I'm sorry, sir, cabin number three is booked in the name of a Mr William West and family."

"I have never been treated by Captain Rogers in this cavalier fashion before," said Henry, his accent now even more pronounced. "Send for him immediately."

"Captain Rogers was killed in the war, sir. Captain Jenkins is now in command of this ship and he never leaves the bridge thirty minutes before sailing."

Henry's exasperation was turning to panic. "Do you have a free cabin?"

The young officer looked down his list. "No, sir, I'm afraid not. The last one was taken a few minutes ago."

"May I have two tickets?" asked Henry.

"Yes, sir," said the young officer. "But you'll have to buy them from the booking office on the quayside."

Henry decided that any further argument would be only time-consuming so he turned on his heel without another word, leaving his wife with the laden porter. He strode to the booking office.

"Two first-class tickets to Calais," he said firmly.

The man behind the little glass pane gave Henry a tired look. "It's all one class nowadays, sir, unless you have a cabin."

He proffered two tickets. "That will be one pound exactly."

Henry handed over a pound note, took his tickets, and hurried back to the young officer.

The porter was off-loading their suitcases on to the quayside.

"Can't you take them on board," cried Henry, "and put them in the hold?"

"No, sir, not now. Only the passengers are allowed on board after the ten-minute signal."

Victoria carried two of the smaller suitcases while Henry humped the twelve remaining ones in relays up the gangplank. He finally sat down on the deck exhausted. Every seat seemed already to be occupied. Henry couldn't make up his mind if he was cold from the rain or hot from his exertions. Victoria's smile was fixed firmly in place as she took Henry's hand.

"Don't worry about a thing, darling," she said. "Just relax and enjoy the crossing; it will be such fun being out on deck together."

The ship moved sedately out of the calm of the bay into the Dover Straits. Later that night Captain Jenkins told his wife that the twenty-five mile journey had been among the most unpleasant crossings he had ever experienced. He added that he had nearly turned back when his second officer, a veteran of two wars, was violently sick. Henry and Victoria spent most of the trip hanging over the rails getting rid of everything they had consumed at their reception. Two people had never been more happy to see land in their life than Henry and Victoria were at the first sight of the Normandy coastline. They staggered off the ship, taking the suitcases one at a time.

"Perhaps France will be different," Henry said lamely, and after a perfunctory search for Pierre he went straight to the booking office and obtained two third-class seats on the Flèche d'Or. They were at least able to sit next to each other this time, but in a carriage already occupied by six other passengers as well as a dog and a hen. The six of them left Henry in no doubt that they enjoyed the modern habit of smoking in public and the ancient custom of taking garlic in their food. He would have been sick again at any other time but there was nothing left in his stomach. Henry considered walking up and down the train searching for Raymond but feared it could only result in him losing his seat next to Victoria. He gave up trying to hold any conversation with her above the noise of the dog, the hen and the Gallic babble, and satisfied himself by looking out of the window, watching the French countryside and, for the first time in his life, noting the name of every station through which they passed.

Once they arrived at the Gare du Nord Henry made no attempt to look for Maurice and simply headed straight for the nearest taxi rank. By the time he had transferred all fourteen cases he was well down the queue. He and Victoria stood there for just over an hour, moving the cases forward inch by inch until it was their turn.

"Monsieur?"

"Do you speak English?"

"Un peu, un peu."

"Hotel George V."

"Oui, mais je ne peux pas mettre toutes les valises dans le coffre."

So Henry and Victoria sat huddled in the back

of the taxi, bruised, tired, soaked and starving, surrounded by leather suitcases, only to be bumped up and down over the cobbled stones all the way to the George V.

The hotel doorman rushed to help them as Henry offered the taxi driver a pound note.

"No take English money, monsieur."

Henry couldn't believe his ears. The doorman happily paid the taxi driver in francs and quickly pocketed the pound note. Henry was too tired even to comment. He helped Victoria up the marble steps and went over to the reception desk.

"The Grand Pasha of Cairo and his wife. The bridal suite, please."

"Oui, monsieur."

Henry smiled at Victoria.

"You 'ave your booking confirmation with you?"

"No," said Henry, "I have never needed to confirm my booking with you in the past. Before the war I . . ."

"I am sorry, sir, but the 'otel is fully booked at the moment. A conference."

"Even the bridal suite," asked Victoria.

"Yes, Madam, the chairman and his lady, you understand." He nearly winked.

Henry certainly did not understand. There had always been a room for him at the George V whenever he had wanted one in the past. Desperate, he unfolded the second of his five-pound notes and slipped it across the counter.

"Ah," said the booking clerk, "I see we still have one room unoccupied, but I fear it is not very large."

Henry waved a listless hand.

The booking clerk banged the bell on the counter in front of him with the palm of his hand, and a porter appeared immediately and escorted them to the promised room. The booking clerk had been telling the truth. Henry could only have described what they found themselves standing in as a box room. The reason that the curtains were perpetually drawn was that the view over the chimneys of Paris, was singularly unprepossessing, but that was not to be the final blow, as Henry realised, staring in disbelief at the sight of the two narrow single beds. Victoria started unpacking without a word while Henry sat despondently on the end of one of them. After Victoria had sat soaking in a bath that was the perfect size for a six-year-old, she lay down exhausted on the other bed. Neither spoke for nearly an hour.

Come on, darling, said Henry finally. 'Let's go and have dinner."

Victoria rose loyally but reluctantly and dressed for dinner while Henry sat in the bath, knees on nose, trying to wash himself before changing into evening dress. This time he phoned the front desk and ordered a taxi as well as booking a table at Maxim's.

The taxi driver did accept his pound note on this occasion, but as Henry and his bride entered the great restaurant he recognised no one and no one recognised him. A waiter led them to a small table hemmed in between two other couples just below the band. As he walked into the dining room the musicians struck up "Alexander's Rag Time Band".

They both ordered from the extensive menu and the langouste turned out to be excellent, every bit as good as Henry had promised of Maxim's, but by then neither of them had the stomach to eat a full meal and the greater part of both their dishes was left on the plate.

Henry found it hard to convince the new head waiter that the lobster had been superb and that they had purposely come to Maxim's not to eat it. Over coffee, he took Victoria's hand and tried to apologise.

"Let us end this farce," he said, "by completing my plan and going to the Madeleine and presenting you with the promised flowers. Paulette will not be in the square to greet you but there will surely be someone who can sell us roses."

Henry called for the bill and unfolded the third five-pound note (Maxim's are always happy to accept other people's currency and certainly didn't bother him with any change) and they left, walking hand in hand towards the Madeleine. For once Henry turned out to be right, for Paulette was nowhere to be seen. An old lady with a shawl over her head and a wart on the side of her nose stood in her place on the corner of the square, surrounded by the most beautiful flowers.

Henry selected a dozen of the longest stemmed red roses and then placed them in the arms of his bride. The old lady smiled at Victoria.

Victoria returned her smile.

"Dix francs, monsieur," said the old lady to Henry.

Henry fumbled in his pocket, only to discover he

had spent all his money. He looked despairingly at the old lady who raised her hands, smiled at him, and said:

"Don't worry, Henry, have them on me. For old time's sake."

A Matter of Principle

SIR Hamish Graham had many of the qualities and most of the failings that result from being born to a middle-class Scottish family. He was well educated, hard working and honest, while at the same time being narrow-minded, uncompromising and proud. Never on any occasion had he allowed hard liquor to pass his lips and he mistrusted all men who had not been born north of Hadrian's Wall, and many of those who had.

After spending his formative years at Fettes School, to which he had won a minor scholarship, and at Edinburgh University, where he obtained a second-class honours degree in engineering, he was chosen from a field of twelve to be a trainee with the international construction company, TarMac (named after its founder, J. L. McAdam, who discovered that tar when mixed with stones was the best constituent for making roads). The new trainee, through diligent work and uncompromising tactics, became the firm's youngest and most disliked project manager. By the age of thirty Graham had been appointed deputy managing director of TarMac and was already beginning to realise that he could not hope to progress much farther while he was in someone else's employ. He therefore started to consider forming his own company. When two years later the chairman of TarMac, Sir Alfred Hickman, offered Graham the opportunity to replace the retiring managing director, he resigned immediately. After all, if Sir Alfred felt he had the ability to run TarMac he must also be competent enough to start his own company.

The next day, young Hamish Graham made an appointment to see the local manager of the Bank of Scotland who was responsible for the TarMac account, and with whom he had dealt for the past ten years. Graham explained to the manager his plans for the future, submitting a full written proposal, and requesting that his overdraft facility might be extended from fifty pounds to ten thousand. Three weeks later Graham learned that his application had been viewed favourably. He remained in his lodgings in Edinburgh, while renting an office in the north of the city (or, to be more accurate, a room at ten shillings a week). He purchased a typewriter, hired a secretary and ordered some unembossed headed letter-paper. After a further month of diligent interviewing, he employed two engineers, both graduates of Aberdeen University, and five out-of-work labourers from Glasgow.

During those first few weeks on his own Graham tendered for several small road contracts in the central lowlands of Scotland, the first seven of which he failed to secure. Preparing a tender is always tricky and often expensive, so by the end of his first six months in business Graham was beginning to wonder if his sudden departure from TarMac had not been foolhardy. For the first time in his life he experienced self-doubt, but that was soon removed by the Ayrshire County Council, who accepted his tender to construct a minor road which was to join a projected school with the main highway. The road was only five hundred yards in length but the assignment took Graham's little team seven months to complete and when all the bills had been paid and all expenses taken into account Graham Construction made a net loss of £143.10s.6d.

Still, in the profit column was a small reputation which had been invisibly earned, and caused the Ayrshire Council to invite him to build the school at the end of their new road. This contract made Graham Construction a profit of £420 and added still further to his reputation. From that moment Graham Construction went from strength to strength, and as early as his third year in business he was able to declare a small pre-tax profit, and this grew steadily over the next five years. When Graham Construction was floated on the London Stock Exchange the demand for the shares was over-subscribed ten times and the newly quoted company was soon considered a blue-chip institution, a considerable achievement for Graham to have pulled off in his own lifetime. But then the City likes men who grow slowly and can be relied on not to involve themselves in unnecessary risks.

In the sixties Graham Construction built motorways, hospitals, factories, and even a power station, but the achievement the chairman took most pride in was Edinburgh's newly completed art gallery, which was the only contract that showed a deficit in the annual general report. The invisible earnings column however recorded the award of knight bachelor for the chairman.

Sir Hamish decided that the time had come for Graham Construction to expand into new fields, and looked, as generations of Scots had before him, towards the natural market of the British Empire. He built in Australia and Canada with his own finances, and in India and Africa with a subsidy from the British government. In 1963 he was named "Businessman of the Year" by *The Times* and three years later "Chairman of the Year" by *The Economist*. Sir Hamish never once altered his methods to keep pace with the changing times, and if anything grew more stubborn in the belief that his ideas of doing business were correct whatever anyone else thought; and he had a long credit column to prove he was right.

In the early seventies, when the slump hit the construction business, Graham Construction suffered the same cut in budgets and lost contracts as any of its major competitors. Sir Hamish reacted in a predictable way, by tightening his belt and paring his estimates while at the same time refusing one jot to compromise his business principles. The company therefore grew leaner and many of his more enterprising young executives left Graham Construction for firms which still believed in taking on the occasional risky contract.

Only when the slope of the profits graph started

taking on the look of a downhill slalom did Sir Hamish become worried. One night, while brooding over the company's profit-and-loss account for the previous three years, and realising that he was losing contracts even in his native Scotland, Sir Hamish reluctantly came to the conclusion that he must tender for less established work, and perhaps even consider the odd gamble.

His brightest young executive, David Heath, a stocky, middle-aged bachelor, whom he did not entirely trust – after all, the man had been educated south of the border and worse, some extraordinary place in the United States called the Wharton Business School – wanted Sir Hamish to put a toe into Mexican waters. Mexico, as Heath was not slow to point out, had discovered vast reserves of oil off their eastern coast and had overnight become rich with American dollars. The construction business in Mexico was suddenly proving most lucrative and contracts were coming up for tender with figures as high as thirty to forty million dollars attached to them. Heath urged Sir Hamish to go after one such contract that had recently been announced in a full-page advertisement in *The Economist*. The Mexican Government were issuing tender documents for a proposed ring road around their capital, Mexico City. In an article in the business section of the *Observer*, detailed arguments were put forward as to why established British companies should try to fulfil the ring road tender. Heath had offered shrewd advice on overseas contracts in the past that Sir Hamish had subsequently let slip through his fingers.

The next morning, Sir Hamish sat at his desk listening attentively to David Heath, who felt that as Graham Construction had already built the Glasgow and Edinburgh ring roads any application they made to the Mexican Government had to be taken seriously. To Heath's surprise, Sir Hamish agreed with his project manager and allowed a team of six men to travel to Mexico to obtain the tender documents and research the project.

The research team was led by David Heath, and consisted of three other engineers, a geologist and an accountant. When the team arrived in Mexico they obtained the tender documents from the Minister of Works and settled down to study them minutely. Having pinpointed the major problems they walked around Mexico City with their ears open and their mouths shut and made a list of the problems they were clearly going to encounter: the impossibility of unloading anything at Vera Cruz and then transporting the cargo to Mexico City without half of the original assignment being stolen, the lack of communications between ministries, and worst of all the attitude of the Mexicans to work. But David Heath's most positive contribution to the list was the discovery that each minister had his own outside man, and that man had better be well disposed to Graham Construction if the firm were to be even considered for the short list. Heath immediately sought out the Minister of Works' man, one Victor Perez, and took him to an extravagant lunch at the *Fonda el Refugio* where both of them nearly ended up drunk, although Heath remained sober enough to agree all of the necessary terms, conditional upon

Sir Hamish's approval. Having taken every possible precaution, Heath agreed on a tender figure with Perez which was to include the minister's percentage. Once he had completed the report for his chairman, he flew back to England with his team.

On the evening of David Heath's return, Sir Hamish retired to bed early to study his project manager's conclusions. He read the report through the night as others might read a spy story, and was left in no doubt that this was the opportunity he had been looking for to overcome the temporary setbacks Graham Construction was now suffering. Although Sir Hamish would be up against Costains, Sunleys, and John Brown, as well as many international companies, he still felt confident that any application he made must have a "fair chance". On arrival at his office the next morning Sir Hamish sent for David Heath, who was delighted by the chairman's initial response to his report.

Sir Hamish started speaking as soon as his burly project manager entered the room, not even inviting him to take a seat.

"You must contact our Embassy in Mexico City immediately and inform them of our intentions," pronounced Sir Hamish. "I may speak to the Ambassador myself," he said, intending that to be the concluding remark of the interview.

"Useless," said David Heath.

"I beg your pardon?"

"I don't wish to appear rude, sir, but it doesn't work like that any more. Britain is no longer a great power dispensing largesse to all far flung and grateful recipients."

"More's the pity," said Sir Hamish.

The project manager continued as though he had not heard the remark.

"The Mexicans now have vast wealth of their own and the United States, Japan, France and Germany keep massive embassies in Mexico City with highly professional trade delegations trying to influence every ministry."

"But surely history counts for something," said Sir Hamish. "Wouldn't they rather deal with an established British company than some upstarts from –?"

"Perhaps, sir, but in the end all that really matters is which minister is in charge of what contract and who is his outside representative."

Sir Hamish looked puzzled. "Your meaning is obscure to me, Mr Heath."

"Allow me to explain, sir. Under the present system in Mexico, each ministry has an allocation of money to spend on projects agreed to by the government. Every Secretary of State is acutely aware that his tenure of office may be very short, so he picks out a major contract for himself from the many available. It's the one way to ensure a pension for life if the government is changed overnight or the minister simply loses his job."

"Don't bandy words with me, Mr Heath. What you are suggesting is that I should bribe a government official, I have never been involved in that sort of thing in thirty years of business."

"And I wouldn't want you to start now," replied Heath. "The Mexican is far too experienced in business etiquette for anything as clumsy as that to be suggested, but while the law requires that you appoint a Mexican agent, it must make sense to try and sign up the minister's man, who in the end is the one person who can ensure that you will be awarded the contract. The system seems to work well, and as long as a minister deals only with reputable international firms and doesn't become greedy, no one complains. Fail to observe either of those two golden rules and the whole house of cards collapses. The minister ends up in Le Cumberri for thirty years and the company concerned has all its assets expropriated and is banned from any future business dealings in Mexico."

"I really cannot become involved in such shenanigans," said Sir Hamish. "I still have my shareholders to consider."

"*You* don't have to become involved," Heath rejoined. "After we have tendered for the contract you wait and see if the company has been shortlisted and then, if we have, you wait again to find out if the minister's man approaches us. I know the man, so if he does make contact we have a deal. After all, Graham Construction is a respectable international company."

"Precisely, and that's why it's against my principles," said Sir Hamish with hauteur.

"I do hope, Sir Hamish, it's also against your principles to allow the Germans and the Americans to steal the contract from under our noses."

Sir Hamish glared back at his project manager but remained silent.

"And I feel I must add, sir," said David Heath moving restlessly from foot to foot, "that the pickings in Scotland haven't exactly yielded a harvest lately."

"All right, all right, go ahead," said Sir Hamish reluctantly. "Put in a tender figure for the Mexico City ring road and be warned if I find bribery is involved, on your head be it," he added, banging his closed fist on the table.

"What tender figure have you settled on, sir?" asked the project manager. "I believe, as I stressed in my report that we should keep the amount under forty million dollars."

"Agreed," said Sir Hamish who paused for a moment and smiled to himself before saying: "Make it $39,121,110."

"Why that particular figure, sir?"

"Sentimental reasons," said Sir Hamish, without further explanation.

David Heath left, pleased that he had convinced his boss to go ahead but he feared it might in the end prove harder to overcome Sir Hamish's principles than the entire Mexican government. Nevertheless he filled in the bottom line of the tender as instructed and then had the document signed by three directors including his chairman, as required by Mexican law. He sent the tender by special messenger to be delivered at the Ministry of Buildings in Paseo de la Reforma: when tendering for a contract for over thirty-nine million dollars, one does not send the document by first-class post.

Several weeks passed before the Mexican Embassy in London contacted Sir Hamish, requesting that he travel to Mexico City for a meeting with Manuel Unichurtu, the minister concerned with the city's ring road project. Sir Hamish remained sceptical, but David Heath was jubilant, because he had already learned through another source that Graham Construction was the only tender being seriously considered at that moment, although there were one or two outstanding items still to be agreed on. David Heath knew exactly what that meant.

A week later Sir Hamish, travelling first class, and David Heath, travelling economy, flew out of Heathrow bound for Mexico International airport. On arrival they took an hour to clear customs and another thirty minutes to find a taxi to take them to the city, and then only after the driver had bargained with them for an outrageous fare. They covered the fifteen-mile journey from the airport to their hotel in just over an hour and Sir Hamish was able to observe at first hand why the Mexicans were so desperate to build a ring road. Even with the windows down the ten-year-old car was like an oven that had been left on high all night, but during the journey Sir Hamish never once loosened his collar or tie. The two men checked into their rooms, phoned the minister's secretary to inform her of their arrival, and then waited.

For two days, nothing happened.

David Heath assured his chairman that such a hold up was not an unusual course of events in Mexico as the minister was undoubtedly in meetings most of the day, and after all wasn't "*mañana*" the one Spanish word every foreigner understood?

On the afternoon of the third day, only just before Sir Hamish was threatening to return home, David Heath received a call from the minister's man, who accepted an invitation to join them both for dinner in Sir Hamish's suite that evening.

Sir Hamish put on evening dress for the occasion, despite David Heath's counselling against the idea. He even had a bottle of *Fina La Ina* sherry sent up in case the minister's man required some refreshment. The dinner table was set and the hosts were ready for seven-thirty. The minister's man did not appear at seven-thirty, or seven-forty-five, or eight o'clock or eight-fifteen, or eight-thirty. At eight-forty-nine there was a loud rap on the door, and Sir Hamish muttered an inaudible reproach as David Heath went to open it and find his contact standing there.

"Good evening, Mr Heath, I'm sorry to be late. Held up with the minister, you understand."

"Yes, of course," said David Heath. "How good of you to come, Señor Perez. May I introduce my chairman, Sir Hamish Graham?"

"How do you do, Sir Hamish? Victor Perez at your service."

Sir Hamish was dumbfounded. He simply stood and stared at the little middle-aged Mexican who had arrived for dinner dressed in a grubby white tee-shirt and Western jeans. Perez looked as if he hadn't shaved for three days and reminded Sir Hamish of those bandits he had seen in B-Movies when he was a schoolboy. He wore a heavy gold bracelet around his wrist that could have come from Cartier's and a tiger's tooth on a platinum chain around his neck that looked as if it had come from Woolworth's. Perez grinned from ear to ear, pleased with the effect he was causing.

"Good evening," replied Sir Hamish stiffly, taking a step backwards. "Would you care for a sherry?"

"No, thank you, Sir Hamish. I've grown into the habit of liking your whisky, on the rocks with a little soda."

"I'm sorry, I only have . . ."

"Don't worry, sir, I have some in my room," said David Heath, and rushed away to retrieve a bottle of Johnnie Walker he had hidden under the shirts in his top drawer. Despite this Scottish aid, the conversation before dinner among the three men was somewhat stilted, but David Heath had not come five thousand miles for an inferior hotel meal with Victor Perez, and Victor Perez in any other circumstances would not have crossed the road to meet Sir Hamish Graham even if he'd built it. Their conversation ranged from the recent visit to Mexico of Her Majesty The Queen – as Sir Hamish referred to her – to the proposed return trip of President Portillo to Britain. Dinner might have gone more smoothly if Mr Perez hadn't eaten most of the food with his hands and then proceeded to clean his fingers on the side of his jeans. The more Sir Hamish stared at him in disbelief the more the little Mexican would grin from ear to ear. After dinner David Heath thought the time had come to steer the conversation towards the real purpose of the meeting, but not before Sir Hamish had reluctantly had to call for a bottle of brandy and a box of cigars.

"We are looking for an agent to represent the Graham Construction Company in Mexico, Mr Perez, and you have been highly recommended," said Sir Hamish, sounding unconvinced by his own statement.

"Do call me Victor."

Sir Hamish bowed silently and shuddered. There was no way this man was going to be allowed to call him Hamish.

"I'd be pleased to represent you, Hamish," continued Perez, "provided that you find my terms acceptable."

"Perhaps you could enlighten us as to what those – hm, terms – might be," said Sir Hamish stiffly.

"Certainly," said the little Mexican cheerfully. "I require ten per cent of the agreed tender figure, five per cent to be paid on the day you are awarded the contract and five per cent whenever you present your completion certificates. Not a penny to be paid until you have received your fee, all my payments deposited in an account at Credit Suisse in Geneva within seven days of the National Bank of Mexico clearing your cheque."

David Heath drew in his breath sharply and stared down at the stone floor.

"But under those terms you would make nearly four million dollars," protested Sir Hamish, now red in the face. "That's over half our projected profit."

"That, as I believe you say in England, Hamish, is your problem, you fixed the tender price," said Perez, "not me. In any case, there's still enough in the deal for both of us to make a handsome profit which is surely fair as we bring half the equation to the table."

Sir Hamish was speechless as he fiddled with

his bow tie. David Heath examined his fingernails attentively.

"Think the whole thing over, Hamish," said Victor Perez, sounding unperturbed, "and let me know your decision by midday tomorrow. The outcome makes little difference to me." The Mexican rose, shook hands with Sir Hamish and left. David Heath, sweating slightly, accompanied him down in the lift. In the foyer he clasped hands damply with the Mexican.

"Good night, Victor. I'm sure everything will be all right – by midday tomorrow."

"I hope so," replied the Mexican, "for your sake." He strolled out of the foyer whistling.

Sir Hamish, a glass of water in his hand, was still seated at the dinner table when his project manager returned.

"I do not believe it is possible that that – that that man can represent the Secretary of State, represent a government minister."

"I am assured that he does," replied David Heath.

"But to part with nearly four million dollars to such an individual . . ."

"I agree with you, sir, but that is the way business is conducted out here."

"I can't believe it," said Sir Hamish. "I *won't* believe it. I want you to make an appointment for me to see the minister first thing tomorrow morning."

"He won't like that, sir. It might expose his position, and put him right out in the open in a way that could only embarrass him."

"I don't give a damn about embarrassing him. We are discussing a bribe, do I have to spell it out for you, Heath? A bribe of nearly four million dollars. Have you no principles, man?"

"Yes, sir, but I would still advise you against seeing the Secretary of State. He won't want any of your conversation with Mr Perez on the record."

"I have run this company my way for nearly thirty years, Mr Heath, and I shall be the judge of what I want on the record."

"Yes, of course, sir."

"I will see the Secretary of State first thing in the morning. Kindly arrange a meeting."

"If you insist, sir," said David Heath resignedly.

"I insist."

The project manager departed to his own room and a sleepless night. Early the next morning he delivered a handwritten, personal and private letter to the minister, who sent a car round immediately for the Scottish industrialist.

Sir Hamish was driven slowly through the noisy, exuberant, bustling crowds of the city in the minister's black Ford Galaxy with flag flying. People made way for the car respectfully. The chauffeur came to a halt outside the Ministry of Buildings and Public Works in Paseo de la Reforma and guided Sir Hamish through the long, white corridors to a waiting room. A few minutes later an assistant showed Sir Hamish through to the Secretary of State and took a seat by his side. The minister, a severe looking man who appeared to be well into his seventies, was dressed in an immaculate white suit, white shirt and blue tie. He rose, leaned over the vast expanse of green leather and offered his hand.

"Do have a seat, Sir Hamish."

"Thank you," the chairman said, feeling more at home as he took in the minister's office; on the ceiling a large propellor-like fan revolved slowly round making little difference to the stuffiness of the room, while hanging on the wall behind the minister was a signed picture of President José Lopez Portillo, in full morning dress and below the photo a plaque displaying a coat of arms.

"I see you were educated at Cambridge."

"That is correct, Sir Hamish, I was at Corpus Christi for three years."

"Then you know my country well, sir."

"I do have many happy memories of my stays in England, Sir Hamish; in fact, I still visit London as often as my leave allows."

"You must take a trip to Edinburgh some time."

"I have already done so, Sir Hamish. I attended the Festival on two occasions and now know why your city is described as the Athens of the North."

"You are well informed, Minister."

"Thank you, Sir Hamish. Now I must ask how I can help you. Your assistant's note was rather vague."

"First let me say, Minister, that my company is honoured to be considered for the city ring road project and I hope that our experience of thirty years in construction, twenty of them in the third world" – he nearly said the undeveloped countries, an expression his project manager had warned him against – "is the reason you, as Minister in charge, found us the natural choice for this contract."

"That, and your reputation for finishing a job on time at the stipulated price," replied the Secretary of State. "Only twice in your history have you returned to the principal asking for changes in the payment schedule. Once in Uganda when you were held up by Amin's pathetic demands, and the other project, if I remember rightly, was in Bolivia, an airport, when you were unavoidably delayed for six months because of an earthquake. In both cases, you completed the contract at the new price stipulated and my principal advisers think you must have lost money on both occasions." The Secretary of State mopped his brow with a silk handkerchief before continuing. "I would not wish you to think my government takes these decisions of selection lightly."

Sir Hamish was astounded by the Secretary of State's command of his brief, the more so as no prompting notes lay on the leather-topped desk in front of him. He suddenly felt guilty at the little he knew about the Secretary of State's background or history.

"Of course not, Minister. I am flattered by your personal concern, which makes me all the more determined to broach an embarrassing subject that has . . ."

"Before you say anything else, Sir Hamish, may I ask you some questions?"

"Of course, Minister."

"Do you still find the tender price of $39,121,110 acceptable in *all* the circumstances?"

"Yes, Minister."

"That amount still leaves you enough to do a worthwhile job while making a profit for your company?"

"Yes, Minister, but . . ."

"Excellent, then I think all you have to decide is whether you want to sign the contract by midday today." The minister emphasised the word midday as clearly as he could.

Sir Hamish, who had never understood the expression "a nod is as good as a wink", charged foolishly on.

"There is, nevertheless, one aspect of the contract I feel that I should discuss with you privately."

"Are you sure that would be wise, Sir Hamish?"

Sir Hamish hesitated, but only for a moment, before proceeding. Had David Heath heard the conversation that had taken place so far, he would have stood up, shaken hands with the Secretary of State, removed the top of his fountain pen and headed towards the contract – but not his employer.

"Yes, Minister, I feel I must," said Sir Hamish firmly.

"Will you kindly leave us, Miss Vieites?" said the Secretary of State.

The assistant closed her shorthand book, rose and left the room. Sir Hamish waited for the door to close before he began again.

"Yesterday I had a visit from a countryman of yours, a Mr Victor Perez, who resides here in Mexico City and claims –"

"An excellent man," said the Minister very quietly.

Still Sir Hamish charged on. "Yes, I daresay he is, Minister, but he asked to be allowed to represent Graham Construction as our agent and I wondered –"

"A common practice in Mexico, no more than is required by the law." said the Minister, swinging his chair round and staring out of the window.

"Yes, I appreciate that is the custom," said Sir Hamish now talking to the minister's back, "but if I am to part with ten per cent of the government's money I must be convinced that such a decision meets with your personal approval." Sir Hamish thought he had worded that rather well.

"Um," said the Secretary of State, measuring his words, "Victor Perez is a good man and has always been loyal to the Mexican cause. Perhaps he leaves an unfortunate impression sometimes, not out of what you would call the 'top drawer', Sir Hamish, but then we have no class barriers in Mexico." The Minister swung back to face Sir Hamish.

The Scottish industrialist flushed. "Of course not, Minister, but that, if you will forgive me, is hardly the point. Mr Perez is asking me to hand over nearly four million dollars, which is over half of my estimated profit on the project without allowing for any contingencies or mishaps that might occur later."

"You chose the tender figure, Sir Hamish. I confess I was amused by the fact you added your date of birth to the thirty-nine million."

Sir Hamish's mouth opened wide.

"I would have thought," continued the minister, "given your record over the past three years and the present situation in Britain, you were not in a position to be fussy."

The minister gazed impassively at Sir Hamish's startled face. Both started to speak at the same time. Sir Hamish swallowed his words.

"Allow me to tell you a little story about Victor Perez. When the war was at its fiercest" (the old Secretary of State was referring to the Mexican Revolution, in the same way that an American thinks of Vietnam or a Briton of Germany when they hear the word "war"), "Victor's father was one of the young men under my command who died on the battlefield at Celaya only a few days before victory was ours. He left a son born on the day of independence who never knew his father. I have the honour, Sir Hamish, to be godfather to that child. We christened him Victor."

"I can understand that you have a responsibility to an old comrade but I still feel four million is –"

"Do you? Then let me continue. Just before Victor's father died I visited him in a field hospital and he asked only that I should take care of his wife. She died in childbirth. I therefore considered my responsibility passed on to their only child."

Sir Hamish remained silent for a moment. "I appreciate your attitude, Minister, but ten per cent of one of your largest contracts?"

"One day," continued the Secretary of State, as if he had not heard Sir Hamish's comment, "Victor's father was fighting in the front line at Zacatecas and looking out across a minefield he saw a young lieutenant, lying face down in the mud with his leg nearly blown off. With no thought for his own safety, he crawled through that minefield until he reached the lieutenant and then he dragged him yard by yard back to the camp. It took him over three hours. He then carried the lieutenant to a truck and drove him to the nearest field hospital, undoubtedly saving his leg, and probably his life. So you see the government have good cause to allow Perez's son the privilege of representing them from time to time."

"I agree with you, Minister," said Sir Hamish quietly. "Quite admirable." The Secretary of State smiled for the first time. "But I still confess I cannot understand why you allow him such a large percentage."

The minister frowned. "I am afraid, Sir Hamish, if you cannot understand that, you can never hope to understand the principles we Mexicans live by."

The Secretary of State rose from behind his desk, limped to the door and showed Sir Hamish out.

The Hungarian Professor

COINCIDENCES, writers are told (usually by the critics) must be avoided, although in truth the real world is full of incidents that in themselves are unbelievable. Everyone has had an experience that if they wrote about it would appear to others as pure fiction.

The same week that the headlines in the world newspapers read "Russia invades Afghanistan, America to withdraw from Moscow Olympics" there also appeared a short obituary in *The Times* for the distinguished Professor of English at the University of Budapest. "A man who was born and died in his native Budapest and whose reputation remains assured by his brilliant translation of the works of Shakespeare into his native Hungarian. Although some linguists consider his *Coriolanus* immature they universally acknowledge his *Hamlet* to be a translation of genius."

Nearly a decade after the Hungarian Revolution I had the chance to participate in a student athletics meeting in Budapest. The competition was scheduled to last for a full week so I felt there would be an opportunity to find out a little about the country. The team flew in to Ferihegy Airport on the Sunday night and we were taken immediately to the Hotel Ifushág. (I learned later that the word meant youth in Hungarian). Having settled in, most of the team went to bed early as their opening round heats were the following day.

Breakfast the next morning comprised of milk, toast and an egg, served in three acts with long intervals between each. Those of us who were running that afternoon skipped lunch for fear that a matinee performance might cause us to miss our events completely.

Two hours before the start of the meeting, we were taken by bus to the Nép stadium and unloaded outside the dressing rooms (I always feel they should be called undressing rooms). We changed into track suits and sat around on benches anxiously waiting to be called. After what seemed to be an interminable time but was in fact only a few minutes, an official appeared and led us out on to the track. As it was the opening day of competition, the stadium was packed. When I had finished my usual warm-up of jogging, sprinting and some light callisthenics, the loudspeaker announced the start of the 100m race in three languages. I stripped off my track suit and ran over to the start. When called, I pressed my spikes against the blocks and waited nervously for the starter's pistol. Felkészülni, Kész – bang. Ten seconds later the race was over and the only virtue in coming last was that it left me six free days to investigate the Hungarian capital.

Walking around Budapest reminded me of my childhood days in Bristol just after the war, but with one noticeable difference. As well as the bombed-out buildings, there was row upon row of bullet holes in some of the walls. The revolution, although eight years past, was still much in evidence, perhaps because the nationals did not want anyone to forget. The people on the streets had lined faces, stripped of all emotion, and they shuffled rather than walked, leaving the impression of a nation of old men. If you inquired innocently why, they told you there was nothing to hurry for, or to be happy about, although they always seemed to be thoughtful with each other.

On the third day of the games, I returned to the Nép stadium to support a friend of mine who was competing in the semi-finals of the 400m hurdles which was the first event that afternoon. Having a competitor's pass, I could sit virtually anywhere in the half-empty arena. I chose to watch the race from just above the final bend, giving me a good view of the home straight. I sat down on the wooden bench without paying much attention to the people on either side of me. The race began and as my friend hit the bend crossing the seventh hurdle with only three hurdles to cover before the finishing line, I stood and cheered him heartily all the way down the home straight. He managed to come in third, ensuring himself a place in the final the next day. I sat down again and wrote out the detailed result in my programme. I was about to leave, as there were no British competitors in the hammer or the pole vault, when a voice behind me said:

"You are English?"

"Yes," I replied, turning in the direction from which the question had been put.

An elderly gentleman looked up at me. He wore a three-piece suit that must have been out of date when his father owned it, and even lacked the possible virtue that some day the style might come back into fashion. The leather patches on the elbows left me in no doubt that my questioner was a bachelor for they could only have been sewn on by a man – either that or one had to conclude he had elbows in odd places. The length of his trousers revealed that his father had been two inches taller than he. As for the man himself, he had a few strands of white hair, a walrus moustache, and ruddy cheeks. His tired blue eyes were perpetually half-closed like the shutter of a camera that has just been released. His forehead was so lined that he might have been any age between fifty and seventy. The overall impression was of a cross between a tram inspector and an out-of-work violinist.

I sat down for a second time.

"I hope you didn't mind my asking?" he added.

"Of course not," I said.

"It's just that I have so little opportunity to converse with an Englishman. So when I spot one I always grasp the nettle. Is that the right colloquial expression?"

"Yes," I said, trying to think how many Hungarian words I knew. Yes, No, Good morning, Goodbye, I am lost, Help.

"You are in the student games?"

"Were, not are," I said. "I departed somewhat rapidly on Monday."

"Because you were not rapid enough, perhaps?"

I laughed, again admiring his command of my first language.

"Why is your English so excellent?" I inquired.

"I'm afraid it's a little neglected," the old man replied. "But they still allow me to teach the subject at the University. I must confess to you that I have absolutely no interest in sport, but these occasions always afford me the opportunity to capture someone like yourself and oil the rusty machine, even if only for a few minutes." He gave me a tired smile but his eyes were now alight.

"What part of England do you hail from?" For the first time his pronouncement faltered as "hail" came out as "heel".

"Somerset," I told him.

"Ah," he said, "perhaps the most beautiful county in England." I smiled, as most foreigners never seem to travel much beyond Stratford-on-Avon or Oxford. "To drive across the Mendips," he continued, "through perpetually green hilly countryside and to stop at Cheddar to see Cough's caves, at Wells to be amused by the black swans ringing the bell on the Cathedral wall, or at Bath to admire the lifestyle of classical Rome, and then perhaps to go over the county border and on to Devon . . . Is Devon even more beautiful than Somerset, in your opinion?"

"Never," said I.

"Perhaps you are a little prejudiced," he laughed. "Now let me see if I can recall:

Of the western counties there are seven
But the most glorious is surely that of Devon.

Perhaps Hardy, like you, was prejudiced and could think only of his beloved Exmoor, the village of Tiverton and Drake's Plymouth."

"Which is *your* favourite county?" I asked.

"The North Riding of Yorkshire has always been underrated, in my opinion," replied the old man. "When people talk of Yorkshire, I suspect Leeds, Sheffield and Barnsley spring to mind. Coal mining and heavy industry. Visitors should travel and see the dales there; they will find them as different as chalk and cheese. Lincolnshire is too flat and so much of the Midlands must now be spoilt by sprawling towns. The Birminghams of this world hold no appeal for me. But in the end I come down in favour of Worcestershire and Warwickshire, quaint old English villages nestling in the Cotswolds and crowned by Stratford-upon-Avon. How I wish I could have been in England in 1959 while my countrymen were recovering from the scars of revolution. Olivier performing Coriolanus, another man who did not want to show his scars."

"I saw the performance," I said. "I went with a school party."

"Lucky boy. I translated the play into Hungarian at the age of nineteen. Reading over my work again last year made me aware I must repeat the exercise before I die."

"You have translated other Shakespeare plays?"

"All but three, I have been leaving *Hamlet* to last, and then I shall return to *Coriolanus* and start again.

As you are a student, am I permitted to ask which University you attend?"

"Oxford."

"And your College?"

"Brasenose."

"Ah. BNC. How wonderful to be a few yards away from the Bodleian, the greatest library in the world. If I had been born in England I should have wanted to spend my days at All Souls, that is just opposite BNC, is it not?"

"That's right."

The professor stopped talking while we watched the next race, the first semi-final of the 1,500 metres. The winner was Anfras Patovich, a Hungarian, and the partisan crowd went wild with delight.

"That's what I call support," I said.

"Like Manchester United when they have scored the winning goal in the Cup Final. But my fellow countrymen do not cheer because the Hungarian was first," said the old man.

"No?" I said, somewhat surprised.

"Oh, no, they cheer because he beat the Russian."

"I hadn't even noticed," I said.

"There is no reason why you should, but their presence is always in the forefront of our minds and we are rarely given the opportunity to see them beaten in public."

I tried to steer him back to a happier subject. "And before you had been elected to All Souls, which college would you have wanted to attend?"

"As an undergraduate, you mean?"

"Yes."

"Undoubtedly Magdalen is the most beautiful college. It has the distinct advantage of being situated on the River Cherwell; and in any case I confess a weakness for perpendicular architecture and a love of Oscar Wilde." The conversation was interrupted by the sound of a pistol and we watched the second semi-final of the 1,500 metres which was won by Orentas of the USSR and the crowd showed its disapproval more obviously this time, clapping in such a way that left hands passed by right without coming into contact. I found myself joining in on the side of the Hungarians. The scene made the old man lapse into a sad silence. The last race of the day was won by Tim Johnston of England and I stood and cheered unashamedly. The Hungarian crowd clapped politely.

I turned to say goodbye to the professor, who had not spoken for some time.

"How long are you staying in Budapest?" he asked. "The rest of the week. I return to England on Sunday."

"Could you spare the time to join an old man for dinner one night?"

"I should be delighted."

"How considerate of you," he said, and he wrote out his full name and address in capital letters on the back of my programme and returned it to me. "Why don't we say tomorrow at seven? And if you have any old newspapers or magazines do bring them with you," he said looking a little sheepish. "And I shall quite understand if you have to change your plans."

* * *

I spent the next morning looking over St Matthias Church and the ancient fortress, two of the buildings that showed no evidence of the revolution. I then took a short trip down the Danube before spending the afternoon supporting the swimmers at the Olympic pool. At six I left the pool and went back to my hotel. I changed into my team blazer and grey slacks, hoping I looked smart enough for my distinguished host. I locked my door, and started towards the lift and then remembered. I returned to my room to pick up the pile of newspapers and magazines I had collected from the rest of the team.

Finding the professor's home was not as easy as I had expected. After meandering around cobbled streets and waving the professor's address at several passers-by, I was finally directed to an old apartment block. I ran up the three flights of the wooden staircase in a few leaps and bounds, wondering how long the climb took the professor every day. I stopped at the door that displayed his number and knocked.

The old man answered immediately as if he had been standing there, waiting by the door. I noticed that he was wearing the same suit he had had on the previous day.

"I am sorry to be late," I said.

"No matter, my own students also find me hard to find the first time," he said, grasping my hand. He paused. "Bad to use the same word twice in the same sentence. 'Locate' would have been better, wouldn't it?"

He trotted on ahead of me, not waiting for my reply, a man obviously used to living on his own.

He led me down a small, dark corridor into his drawing room. I was shocked by its size. Three sides were covered with indifferent prints and water-colours, depicting English scenes, while the fourth wall was dominated by a large bookcase. I could spot Shakespeare, Dickens, Austen, Trollope, Hardy, Evelyn Waugh and Graham Greene. On the table was a faded copy of the *New Statesman* and I looked round to see if we were on our own, but there seemed to be no sign of a wife or child either in person or picture, and indeed the table was only set for two.

The old man turned and stared with childish delight at my pile of newspapers and magazines.

"*Punch*, *Time* and the *Observer*, a veritable feast," he declared gathering them into his arms before placing them lovingly on his bed in the corner of the room.

The professor then opened a bottle of Szürkebarát and left me to look at the pictures while he prepared the meal. He slipped away into an alcove which was so small that I had not realised the room contained a kitchenette. He continued to bombard me with questions about England, many of which I was quite unable to answer.

A few minutes later he stepped back into the room, requesting me to take a seat. "Do be seated," he said, on reflection. "I do not wish you to remove the seat. I wish you to sit on it." He put a plate in front of me which had on it a leg of something that might have been a chicken, a piece of salami and a tomato. I felt sad, not because the food was inadequate, but because he believed it to be plentiful.

After dinner, which despite my efforts to eat slowly

and hold him in conversation, did not take up much time, the old man made some coffee which tasted bitter and then filled a pipe before we continued our discussion. We talked of Shakespeare and his views on A. L. Rowse and then he turned to politics.

"Is it true," the professor asked, "that England will soon have a Labour government?"

"The opinion polls seem to indicate as much," I said.

"I suppose the British feel that Sir Alec Douglas-Home is not swinging enough for the sixties," said the professor, now puffing vigorously away at his pipe. He paused and looked up at me through the smoke. "I did not offer you a pipe as I assumed after your premature exit in the first round of the competition you would not be smoking." I smiled. "But Sir Alec," he continued, "is a man with long experience in politics and it's no bad thing for a country to be governed by an experienced gentleman."

I would have laughed out loud had the same opinion been expressed by my own tutor.

"And what of the Labour leader?" I said, forebearing to mention his name.

"Moulded in the white heat of a technological revolution," he replied. "I am not so certain. I liked Gaitskell, an intelligent and shrewd man. An untimely death. Attlee, like Sir Alec, was a gentleman. But as for Mr Wilson, I suspect that history will test his mettle – a pun which I had not intended – in that white heat and only then will we discover the truth."

I could think of no reply.

"I was considering last night after we parted," the old man continued, "the effect that Suez must have had on a nation which only ten years before had won a world war. The Americans should have backed you. Now we read in retrospect, always the historian's privilege, that at the time Prime Minister Eden was tired and ill. The truth was he didn't get the support from his closest allies when he most needed it."

"Perhaps we should have supported you in 1956."

"No, no, it was too late then for the West to shoulder Hungary's problems. Churchill understood that in 1945. He wanted to advance beyond Berlin and to free all the nations that bordered Russia. But the West had had a belly full of war by then and left Stalin to take advantage of that apathy. When Churchill coined the phrase 'the Iron Curtain', he foresaw exactly what was going to happen in the East. Amazing to think that when that great man said, 'if the British Empire should last a thousand years', it was in fact destined to survive for only twenty-five. How I wish he had still been around the corridors of power in 1956."

"Did the revolution greatly affect your life?"

"I do not complain. It is a privilege to be the Professor of English in a great University. They do not interfere with me in my department and Shakespeare is not yet considered subversive literature." He paused and took a luxuriant puff at his pipe. "And what will you do, young man, when you leave the University – as you have shown us that you cannot hope to make a living as a runner?"

"I want to be a writer."

"Then travel, travel, travel," he said. "You cannot hope to learn everything from books. You must see the world for yourself if you ever hope to paint a picture for others."

I looked up at the old clock on his mantelpiece only to realise how quickly the time had passed.

"I must leave you, I'm afraid; they expect us all to be back in the hotel by ten."

"Of course," he said smiling the English Public School mentality. "I will accompany you to Kossuth Square and then you will be able to see your hotel on the hill."

As we left the flat, I noticed that he didn't bother to lock the door. Life had left him little to lose. He led me quickly through the myriad of narrow roads that I had found so impossible to navigate earlier in the evening, chatting about this building and that, an endless fund of knowledge about his own country as well as mine. When we reached Kossuth Square he took my hand and held on to it, reluctant to let go, as lonely people often will.

"Thank you for allowing an old man to indulge himself by chattering on about his favourite subject."

"Thank you for your hospitality," I said, "and when you are next in Somerset you must come to Lympsham and meet my family."

"Lympsham? I cannot place it," he said, looking worried. "I'm not surprised. The village only has a population of twenty-two."

"Enough for two cricket teams," remarked the professor. "A game, I confess, with which I have never come to grips."

"Don't worry," I said, "neither have half the English."

"Ah, but I should like to. What is a gully, a no-ball, a night watchman? The terms have always intrigued me."

"Then remember to get in touch when you're next in England and I'll take you to Lord's and see if I can teach you something."

"How kind," he said, and then he hesitated before adding: "But I don't think we shall meet again."

"Why not?" I asked.

"Well, you see, I have never been outside Hungary in my whole life. When I was young I couldn't afford to and now I don't imagine that those in authority would allow me to see your beloved England."

He released my hand, turned and shuffled back into the shadows of the side streets of Budapest.

I read his obituary in *The Times* once again as well as the headlines about Afghanistan and its effect on the Moscow Olympics.

He was right. We never met again.

Old Love

SOME people, it is said, fall in love at first sight but that was not what happened to William Hatchard and Philippa Jameson. They hated each other from the moment they met. This mutual loathing commenced at the first tutorial of their freshmen terms. Both had come up in the early thirties with major scholarships to read English language and literature, William to Merton, Philippa to Somerville. Each had been reliably assured by their schoolteachers that they would be the star pupil of their year.

Their tutor, Simon Jakes of New College, was both bemused and amused by the ferocious competition that so quickly developed between his two brightest pupils, and he used their enmity skilfully to bring out the best in both of them without ever allowing either to indulge in outright abuse. Philippa, an attractive, slim red-head with a rather high-pitched voice, was the same height as William so she conducted as many of her arguments as possible standing in newly acquired high-heeled shoes, while William, whose deep voice had an air of authority, would always try to expound his opinions from a sitting position. The more intense their rivalry became the harder the one tried to outdo the other. By the end of their first year they were far ahead of their contemporaries while remaining neck and neck with each other. Simon Jakes told the Merton Professor of Anglo-Saxon Studies that he had never had a brighter pair up in the same year and that it wouldn't be long before they were holding their own with him.

During the long vacation both worked to a gruelling timetable, always imagining the other would be doing a little more. They stripped bare Blake, Wordsworth, Coleridge, Shelley, Byron, and only went to bed with Keats. When they returned for the second year, they found that absence had made the heart grow even more hostile; and when they were both awarded alpha plus for their essays on Beowulf, it didn't help. Simon Jakes remarked at New College high table one night that if Philippa Jameson had been born a boy some of his tutorials would undoubtedly have ended in blows.

"Why don't you separate them?" asked the Dean, sleepily.

"What, and double my work-load?" said Jakes. "They teach each other most of the time: I merely act as referee."

Occasionally the adversaries would seek his adjudication as to who was ahead of whom, and so confident was each of being the favoured pupil that one would always ask in the other's hearing. Jakes was far too canny to be drawn; instead he would remind them that the examiners would be the final arbiters. So they began their own subterfuge by referring to each other, just in earshot, as "that silly woman", and "that arrogant man". By the end of their second year they were almost unable to remain in the same room together.

In the long vacation William took a passing interest in Al Jolson and a girl called Ruby while Philippa flirted with the Charleston and a young naval lieutenant from Dartmouth. But when term started in earnest these interludes were never admitted and soon forgotten.

At the beginning of their third year they both, on Simon Jakes' advice, entered for the Charles Oldham Shakespeare prize along with every other student in the year who was considered likely to gain a First. The Charles Oldham was awarded for an essay on a set aspect of Shakespeare's work, and Philippa and William both realised that this would be the only time in their academic lives that they would be tested against each other in closed competition. Surreptitiously, they worked their separate ways through the entire Shakespearian canon, from *Henry VI* to *Henry VIII*, and kept Jakes well over his appointed tutorial hours, demanding more and more refined discussion of more and more obscure points.

The chosen theme for the prize essay that year was "Satire in Shakespeare". *Troilus and Cressida* clearly called for the most attention but both found there were nuances in virtually every one of the bard's thirty-seven plays. "Not to mention a gross of sonnets," wrote Philippa home to her father in a rare moment of self-doubt. As the year drew to a close it became obvious to all concerned that either William or Philippa had to win the prize while the other would undoubtedly come second. Nevertheless no one was willing to venture an opinion as to who the victor would be. The New College porter, an expert in these matters, opening his usual book for the Charles Oldham, made them both evens, ten to one the rest of the field.

Before the prize essay submission date was due, they both had to sit their final degree examinations. Philippa and William confronted the examination papers every morning and afternoon for two weeks with an appetite that bordered on the vulgar. It came as no surprise to anyone that they both achieved first class degrees in the final honours school. Rumour spread around the University that the two rivals had been awarded alphas in every one of their nine papers.

"I would be willing to believe that is the case," Philippa told William. "But I feel I must point out to you that there is a considerable difference between an alpha plus and an alpha minus."

"I couldn't agree with you *more*," said William. "And when you discover who has won the Charles Oldham, you will know who was awarded *less*."

With only three weeks left before the prize essay had to be handed in they both worked twelve hours a day, falling asleep over open text books, dreaming that the other was still beavering away. When the appointed hour came they met in the marble-floored entrance hall of the Examination Schools, sombre in subfusc.

"Good morning, William, I do hope your efforts will manage to secure a place in the first six."

"Thank you, Philippa. If they don't I shall look for the names C. S. Lewis, Nichol Smith, Nevil Coghill, Edmund Blunden, R. W. Chambers and H. W. Garrard ahead of me. There's certainly no one else in the field to worry about."

"I am only pleased," said Philippa, as if she had not heard his reply, "that you were not seated next to me when I wrote my essay, thus ensuring for the first time in three years that you weren't able to crib from my notes."

"The only item I have ever cribbed from you, Philippa, was the Oxford to London timetable, and that I discovered later to be out-of-date, which was in keeping with the rest of your efforts."

They both handed in their twenty-five thousand word essays to the collector's office in the Examination Schools and left without a further word, returning to their respective colleges impatiently to await the result.

William tried to relax the weekend after submitting his essay, and for the first time in three years he played some tennis, against a girl from St Anne's, failing to win a game, let alone a set. He nearly sank when he went swimming, and actually did so when punting. He was only relieved that Philippa had not been witness to any of his feeble physical efforts.

On Monday night after a resplendent dinner with the Master of Merton, he decided to take a walk along the banks of the Cherwell to clear his head before going to bed. The May evening was still light as he made his way down through the narrow confines of Merton Wall, across the meadows to the banks of the Cherwell. As he strolled along the winding path, he thought he spied his rival ahead of him under a tree reading. He considered turning back but decided she might already have spotted him, so he kept on walking.

He had not seen Philippa for three days although she had rarely been out of his thoughts: once he had won the Charles Oldham, the silly woman would have to climb down from that high horse of hers. He smiled at the thought and decided to walk nonchalantly past her. As he drew nearer, he lifted his eyes from the path in front of him to steal a quick glance in her direction, and could feel himself reddening in anticipation of her inevitable well-timed insult. Nothing happened so he looked more carefully, only to discover on closer inspection that she was not reading: her head was bowed in her hands and she appeared to be sobbing quietly. He slowed his progress to observe, not the formidable rival who had for three years dogged his every step, but a forlorn and lonely creature who looked somewhat helpless.

William's first reaction was to think that the winner of the prize essay competition had been leaked to her and that he had indeed achieved his victory. On reflection, he realised that could not be the case: the examiners would only have received the essays that morning and as all the assessors read each submission the results could not possibly be forthcoming until at least the end of the week. Philippa did not look up when he reached her side – he was even unsure whether she was aware of his presence. As he stopped to gaze at his adversary William could not help noticing how her long red hair curled just as it touched the shoulder. He sat down beside her but still she did not stir.

"What's the matter?" he asked. "Is there anything I can do?"

She raised her head, revealing a face flushed from crying.

"No, nothing William, except leave me alone. You deprive me of solitude without affording me company."

William was pleased that he immediately recognised the little literary allusion. "What's the matter, Madame de Sévigné?" he asked, more out of curiosity than concern, torn between sympathy and catching her with her guard down.

It seemed a long time before she replied.

"My father died this morning," she said finally, as if speaking to herself.

It struck William as strange that after three years of seeing Philippa almost every day he knew nothing about her home life.

"And your mother?" he said.

"She died when I was three. I don't even remember her. My father is –." She paused. "Was a parish priest and brought me up, sacrificing everything he had to get me to Oxford, even the family silver. I wanted so much to win the Charles Oldham for him."

William put his arm tentatively on Philippa's shoulder.

"Don't be absurd. When you win the prize, they'll pronounce you the star pupil of the decade. After all, you will have had to beat me to achieve the distinction."

She tried to laugh. "Of course I wanted to beat you, William, but only for my father."

"How did he die?"

"Cancer, only he never let me know. He asked me not to go home before the summer term as he felt the break might interfere with my finals and the Charles Oldham. While all the time he must have been keeping me away because he knew if I saw the state he was in that would have been the end of my completing any serious work."

"Where do you live?" asked William, again surprised that he did not know.

"Brockenhurst. In Hampshire. I'm going back there tomorrow morning. The funeral's on Wednesday."

"May I take you?" asked William.

Philippa looked up and was aware of a softness in her adversary's eyes that she had not seen before. "That would be kind, William."

"Come on then, you silly woman," he said. "I'll walk you back to your college."

"Last time you called me 'silly woman' you meant it."

William found it natural that they should hold hands as they walked along the river bank. Neither spoke until they reached Somerville.

"What time shall I pick you up?" he asked, not letting go of her hand.

"I didn't know you had a car."

"My father presented me with an old MG when I was awarded a first. I have been longing to find some excuse to show the damn thing off to you. It has a press button start, you know."

"Obviously he didn't want to risk waiting to give you the car on the Charles Oldham results." William laughed more heartily than the little dig merited.

"Sorry," she said. "Put it down to habit. I shall look forward to seeing if you drive as appallingly as you write, in which case the journey may never come to any conclusion. I'll be ready for you at ten."

On the journey down to Hampshire, Philippa talked about her father's work as a parish priest and inquired after William's family. They stopped for lunch at a pub in Winchester. Rabbit stew and mashed potatoes.

"The first meal we've had together," said William.

No sardonic reply came flying back; Philippa simply smiled.

After lunch they travelled on to the village of Brockenhurst. William brought his car to an uncertain halt on the gravel outside the vicarage. An elderly maid, dressed in black, answered the door, surprised to see Miss Philippa with a man. Philippa introduced Annie to William and asked her to make up the spare room.

"I'm so glad you've found yourself such a nice young man," remarked Annie later. "Have you known him long?"

Philippa smiled. "No, we met for the first time yesterday."

Philippa cooked William dinner, which they ate by a fire he had made up in the front room. Although hardly a word passed between them for three hours, neither was bored. Philippa began to notice the way William's untidy fair hair fell over his forehead and thought how distinguished he would look in old age.

The next morning, she walked into the church on William's arm and stood bravely through the funeral. When the service was over William took her back to the vicarage, crowded with the many friends the parson had made.

"You mustn't think ill of us," said Mr Crump, the vicar's warden, to Philippa. "You were everything to your father and we were all under strict instructions not to let you know about his illness in case it should interfere with the Charles Oldham. That is the name of the prize, isn't it?"

"Yes," said Philippa. "But that all seems so unimportant now."

"She will win the prize in her father's memory," said William.

Philippa turned and looked at him, realising for the first time that he actually wanted her to win the Charles Oldham.

They stayed that night at the vicarage and drove back to Oxford on the Thursday. On the Friday morning at ten o'clock William returned to Philippa's college and asked the porter if he could speak to Miss Jameson.

"Would you be kind enough to wait in the Horsebox, sir," said the porter as he showed William into a little room at the back of the lodge and then scurried off to find Miss Jameson. They returned together a few minutes later.

"What on earth are you doing here?"

"Come to take you to Stratford."

"But I haven't even had time to unpack the things I brought back from Brockenhurst."

"Just do as you are told for once; I'll give you fifteen minutes."

"Of course," she said. "Who am I to disobey the next winner of the Charles Oldham? I shall even allow you to come up to my room for one minute and help me unpack."

The porter's eyebrows nudged the edge of his cap but he remained silent, in deference to Miss Jameson's recent bereavement. Again it surprised William to think that he had never been to Philippa's room during their three years. He had climbed the walls of all the women's colleges to be with a variety of girls of varying stupidity but never with Philippa. He sat down on the end of the bed.

"Not there, you thoughtless creature. The maid has only just made it. Men are all the same, you never sit in chairs."

"I shall one day," said William. "The chair of English Language and Literature."

"Not as long as I'm at this University, you won't," she said, as she disappeared into the bathroom.

"Good intentions are one thing but talent is quite another," he shouted at her retreating back, privately pleased that her competitive streak seemed to be returning.

Fifteen minutes later she came out of the bathroom in a yellow flowered dress with a neat white collar and matching cuffs. William thought she might even be wearing a touch of make-up.

"It will do our reputations no good to be seen together," she said.

"I've thought about that," said William. "If asked, I shall say you're my charity."

"Your charity?"

"Yes, this year I'm supporting distressed orphans."

Philippa signed out of college until midnight and the two scholars travelled down to Stratford, stopping off at Broadway for lunch. In the afternoon they rowed on the River Avon. William warned Philippa of his last disastrous outing in a punt. She admitted that she had already heard of the exhibition he had made of himself, but they arrived safely back at the shore: perhaps because Philippa took over the rowing. They went to see John Gielgud playing Romeo and dined at the Dirty Duck. Philippa was even quite rude to William during the meal.

They started their journey home just after eleven and Philippa fell into a half sleep as they could hardly hear each other above the noise of the car engine. It must have been about twenty-five miles outside of Oxford that the MG came to a halt.

"I thought," said William, "that when the petrol gauge showed empty there was at least another gallon left in the tank."

"You're obviously wrong, and not for the first time, and because of such foresight you'll have to walk to the nearest garage all by yourself – you needn't imagine that I'm going to keep you company. I intend to stay put, right here in the warmth."

"But there isn't a garage between here and Oxford," protested William.

"Then you'll have to carry me. I am far too fragile to walk."

"I wouldn't be able to manage fifty yards after that sumptuous dinner and all that wine."

"It is no small mystery to me, William, how you could have managed a first class honours degree in English when you can't even read a petrol gauge."

"There's only one thing for it," said William. "We'll have to wait for the first bus in the morning."

Philippa clambered into the back seat and did not speak to him again before falling asleep. William donned his hat, scarf and gloves, crossed his arms for warmth, and touched the tangled red mane of Philippa's hair as she slept. He then took off his coat and placed it so that it covered her.

Philippa woke first, a little after six, and groaned as she tried to stretch her aching limbs. She then shook William awake to ask him why his father hadn't been considerate enough to buy him a car with a comfortable back seat.

"But this is the niftiest thing going," said William, gingerly kneading his neck muscles before putting his coat back on.

"But it isn't going, and won't without petrol," she replied getting out of the car to stretch her legs.

"But I only let it run out for one reason," said William following her to the front of the car.

Philippa waited for a feeble punch line and was not disappointed.

"My father told me if I spent the night with a barmaid then I should simply order an extra pint of beer, but if I spent the night with the vicar's daughter, I would have to marry her."

Philippa laughed. William, tired, unshaven, and encumbered by his heavy coat, struggled to get down on one knee.

"What are you doing, William?"

"What do you think I'm doing, you silly woman. I am going to ask you to marry me."

"An invitation I am happy to decline, William. If I accepted such a proposal I might end up spending the rest of my life stranded on the road between Oxford and Stratford."

"Will you marry me if I win the Charles Oldham?"

"As there is absolutely no fear of that happening I can safely say, yes. Now do get off your knee, William, before someone mistakes you for a straying stork."

The first bus arrived at five-past-seven that Saturday morning and took Philippa and William back to Oxford. Philippa went to her rooms for a long hot bath while William filled a petrol can and returned to his deserted MG. Having completed the task, he drove straight to Somerville and once again asked if he could see Miss Jameson. She came down a few minutes later.

"What you again?" she said. "Am I not in enough trouble already?"

"Why so?"

"Because I was out after midnight, unaccompanied."

"You were accompanied."

"Yes, and that's what's worrying them."

"Did you tell them we spent the night together?"

"No, I did not. I don't mind our contemporaries thinking I'm promiscuous, but I have strong objections to their believing that I have no taste. Now kindly go away, as I am contemplating the horror of your winning the Charles Oldham and my having to spend the rest of my life with you."

"You know I'm bound to win, so why don't you come live with me now?"

"I realise that it has become fashionable to sleep with just anyone nowadays, William, but if this is to be my last weekend of freedom I intend to savour it, especially as I may have to consider committing suicide."

"I love you."

"For the last time, William, go away. And if you haven't won the Charles Oldham don't ever show your face in Somerville again."

William left, desperate to know the result of the prize essay competition. Had he realised how much Philippa wanted him to win he might have slept that night.

On Monday morning they both arrived early in the Examination Schools and stood waiting impatiently without speaking to each other, jostled by the other undergraduates of their year who had also been entered for the prize. On the stroke of ten the chairman of the examiners, in full academic dress, walking at tortoise-like pace, arrived in the great hall and with a considerable pretence at indifference pinned a notice to the board. All the undergraduates who had entered for the prize rushed forward except for William and Philippa who stood alone, aware that it was now too late to influence a result they were both dreading.

A girl shot out from the mêlée around the notice board and ran over to Philippa.

"Well done, Phil. You've won."

Tears came to Philippa's eyes as she turned towards William.

"May I add my congratulations," he said quickly, "you obviously deserved the prize."

"I wanted to say something to you on Saturday."

"You did, you said if I lost I must never show my face in Somerville again."

"No, I wanted to say: I do love nothing in the world so well as you; is not that strange?"

He looked at her silently for a long moment. It was impossible to improve upon Beatrices's reply.

"As strange as the thing I know not," he said softly.

A college friend slapped-him on the shoulder, took his hand and shook it vigorously. *Proxime accessit* was obviously impressive in some people's eyes, if not in William's.

"Well done, William."

"Second place is not worthy of praise," said William disdainfully.

"But you won, Billy boy."

Philippa and William stared at each other.

"What do you mean?" said William.

"Exactly what I said. You've won the Charles Oldham."

Philippa and William ran to the board and studied the notice.

Charles Oldham Memorial Prize
The examiners felt unable on this occasion to award the prize to one person and have therefore decided that it should be shared by

They gazed at the notice board in silence for some moments. Finally, Philippa bit her lip and said in a small voice:

"Well, you didn't do too badly, considering the competition. I'm prepared to honour my undertaking but by this light I take thee for pity."

William needed no prompting. "I would not deny you, but by this good day I yield upon great persuasion, for I was told you were in a consumption."

And to the delight of their peers and the amazement of the retreating don, they embraced under the notice board.

Rumour had it that from that moment on they were never apart for more than a few hours.

The marriage took place a month later in Philippa's family church at Brockenhurst. "Well, when you think about it," said William's room-mate, "who else could she have married?" The contentious couple started their honeymoon in Athens arguing about the relative significance of Doric and Ionic architecture of which neither knew any more than they had covertly conned from a half-crown tourist guide. They sailed on to Istanbul, where William prostrated himself at the front of every mosque he could find while Philippa stood on her own at the back fuming at the Turks' treatment of women.

"The Turks are a shrewd race," declared William, "so quick to appreciate real worth."

"Then why don't you embrace the Moslim religion, William, and I need only be in your presence once a year."

"The misfortune of birth, a misplaced loyalty and the signing of an unfortunate contract dictate that I spend the rest of my life with you."

Back at Oxford, with junior research fellowships at their respective colleges, they settled down to serious creative work. William embarked upon a massive study of word usage in Marlowe and, in his spare moments, taught himself statistics to assist his findings. Philippa chose as her subject the influence of the Reformation on seventeenth-century English writers and was soon drawn beyond literature into art and music. She bought herself a spinet and took to playing Dowland and Gibbons in the evening.

"For Christ's sake," said William, exasperated by the tinny sound, "you won't deduce their religious convictions from their key signatures."

"More informative than ifs and ands, my dear," she said, imperturbably, "and at night so much more relaxing than pots and pans."

Three years later, with well-received D. Phils, they moved on, inexorably in tandem, to college teaching fellowships. As the long shadow of fascism fell across Europe, they read, wrote, criticised and coached by quiet firesides in unchanging quadrangles.

"A rather dull Schools year for me," said William, "but I still managed five firsts from a field of eleven."

"An even duller one for me," said Philippa, "but

somehow I squeezed three firsts out of six, and you won't have to invoke the binomial theorem, William, to work out that it's an arithmetical victory for me."

"The chairman of the examiners tells me," said William, "that a greater part of what your pupils say is no more than a recitation from memory."

"He told me," she retorted, "that yours have to make it up as they go along."

When they dined together in college the guest list was always quickly filled, and as soon as grace had been said, the sharpness of their dialogue would flash across the candelabra.

"I hear a rumour, Philippa, that the college doesn't feel able to renew your fellowship at the end of the year?"

"I fear you speak the truth, William," she replied. "They decided they couldn't renew mine at the same time as offering me yours."

"Do you think they will ever make you a Fellow of the British Academy, William?"

"I must say, with some considerable disappointment, never."

"I am sorry to hear that; why not?"

"Because when they did invite me, I informed the President that I would prefer to wait to be elected at the same time as my wife."

Some non-University guests sitting in high table for the first time took their verbal battles seriously; others could only be envious of such love.

One Fellow uncharitably suggested they rehearsed their lines before coming to dinner for fear it might be thought they were getting on well together.

During their early years as young dons, they became acknowledged as the leaders in their respective fields. Like magnets, they attracted the brightest undergraduates while apparently remaining poles apart themselves.

"Dr Hatchard will be delivering half these lectures," Philippa announced at the start of the Michaelmas Term of their joint lecture course on Arthurian legend. "But I can assure you it will not be the better half. You would be wise always to check which Dr Hatchard is lecturing."

When Philippa was invited to give a series of lectures at Yale, William took a sabbatical so that he could be with her.

On the ship crossing the Atlantic, Philippa said, "Let's at least be thankful the journey is by sea, my dear, so we can't run out of petrol."

"Rather let us thank God," replied William, "that the ship has an engine because you would even take the wind out of Cunard's sails."

The only sadness in their lives was that Philippa could bear William no children, but if anything it drew the two closer together. Philippa lavished quasi-maternal affection on her tutorial pupils and allowed herself only the wry comment that she was spared the probability of producing a child with William's looks and William's brains.

At the outbreak of war William's expertise with handling words made a move into cipher-breaking inevitable. He was recruited by an anonymous gentleman who visited them at home with a briefcase chained to his wrist. Philippa listened shamelessly at the keyhole while they discussed the problems they had come up against and burst into the room and demanded to be recruited as well.

"Do you realise that I can complete *The Times* crossword puzzle in half the time my husband can?"

The anonymous man was only thankful that he wasn't chained to Philippa. He drafted them both to the Admiralty section to deal with enciphered wireless messages to and from German submarines.

The German signal manual was a four-letter code book and each message was reciphered, the substitution table changing daily. William taught Philippa how to evaluate letter frequencies and she applied her new knowledge to modern German texts, coming up with a frequency analysis that was soon used by every code-breaking department in the Commonwealth.

Even so breaking the ciphers and building up the master signal book was a colossal task which took them the best part of two years.

"I never knew your ifs and ands could be so informative," she said admiringly of her own work.

When the allies invaded Europe husband and wife could together, often break ciphers with no more than half a dozen lines of encoded text to go on.

"They're an illiterate lot," grumbled William. "They don't encipher their umlauts. They deserve to be misunderstood."

"How can you give an opinion when you never dot your i's William?"

"Because, I consider the dot is redundant and I hope to be responsible for removing it from the English language."

"Is that to be your major contribution to the scholarship, William, if so I am bound to ask how anyone reading the work of most of our undergraduates' essays would be able to tell the difference between and I and an i."

"A feeble argument my dear, that if it had any conviction would demand that you put a dot on top of an n so as to be sure it wasn't mistaken for an h."

"Keep working away at your theories, William, because I intend to spend my energy removing more than the dot and the I from Hitler."

In May 1945 they dined privately with the Prime Minister and Mrs Churchill at Number Ten Downing Street.

"What did the Prime Minister mean when he said to me he could never understand what you were up to?" asked Philippa in the taxi to Paddington Station.

"The same as when he said to me he knew exactly what you were capable of, I suppose," said William.

When the Merton Professor of English retired in the early nineteen-fifties the whole University waited to see which Doctor Hatchard would be appointed to the chair.

"If Council invite you to take the chair," said William, putting his hand through his greying hair, "it will be because they are going to make me Vice-Chancellor."

"The only way you could ever be invited to hold a position so far beyond your ability would be nepotism, which would mean I was already Vice-Chancellor."

The General Board, after several hours' discussion of the problem, offered two chairs and appointed William and Philippa full professors on the same day.

When the Vice-Chancellor was asked why precedent had been broken he replied: "Simple; if I hadn't given them both a chair, one of them would have been after my job."

That night, after a celebration dinner when they were walking home together along the banks of the Isis across Christ Church Meadows, in the midst of a particularly heated argument about the quality of the last volume of Proust's monumental works, a policeman, noticing the affray, ran over to them and asked:

"Is everything all right, madam?"

"No, it is not," William interjected, "this woman has been attacking me for over thirty years and to date the police have done deplorably little to protect me."

In the late fifties Harold Macmillan invited Philippa to join the board of the IBA.

"I suppose you'll become what's known as a telly don," said William, "and as the average mental age of those who watch the box is seven you should feel quite at home."

"Agreed," said Philippa. "Twenty years of living with you has made me fully qualified to deal with infants."

The chairman of the BBC wrote to William a few weeks later inviting him to join the Board of Governors.

"Are you to replace 'Hancock's Half Hour' or

'Dick Barton, Special Agent'?" Philippa inquired.

"I am to give a series of twelve lectures."

"On what subject, pray?"

"Genius."

Philippa flicked through the *Radio Times*. "I see that 'Genius' is to be viewed at two o'clock on a Sunday morning, which is understandable, as it's when you are at your most brilliant."

When William was awarded an honorary doctorate at Princeton, Philippa attended the ceremony and sat proudly in the front row.

"I tried to secure a place at the back," she explained, "but it was filled with sleeping students who had obviously never heard of you."

"If that's the case, Philippa, I am only surprised you didn't mistake them for one of your tutorial lectures."

As the years passed many anecdotes, only some of which were apocryphal, passed into the Oxford fabric. Everyone in the English school knew the stories about the "fighting Hatchards". How they spent their first night together. How they jointly won the Charles Oldham. How Phil would complete *The Times* crossword before Bill had finished shaving. How they were both appointed to professorial chairs on the same day, and worked longer hours than any of their contemporaries as if they still had something to prove, if only to each other. It seemed almost required by the laws of symmetry that they should always be judged equals. Until it was announced in the New Year's Honours that Philippa had been made a Dame of the British Empire.

"At least our dear Queen has worked out which

one of us is truly worthy of recognition," she said over the college dessert.

"Our dear Queen," said William, selecting the Madeira, "knows only too well how little competition there is in the women's colleges: sometimes one must encourage weaker candidates in the hope that it might inspire some real talent lower down."

After that, whenever they attended a public function together, Philippa would have the MC announce them as Professor William and Dame Philippa Hatchard. She looked forward to many happy years of starting every official occasion one up on her husband, but her triumph lasted for only six months as William received a knighthood in the Queen's Birthday Honours. Philippa feigned surprise at the dear Queen's uncharacteristic lapse of judgment and forthwith insisted on their being introduced in public as Sir William and Dame Philippa Hatchard.

"Understandable," said William. "The Queen had to make you a Dame first in order that no one should mistake you for a lady. When I married you, Philippa, you were a young fellow, and now I find I'm living with an old Dame."

"It's no wonder," said Philippa, "that your poor pupils can't make up their minds whether you're homosexual or you simply have a mother fixation. Be thankful that I did not accept Girton's invitation: then you would have been married to a mistress."

"I always have been, you silly woman."

As the years passed, they never let up their pretended belief in the other's mental feebleness.

Philippa's books, "works of considerable distinction" she insisted, were published by Oxford University Press while William's "works of monumental significance" he declared, were printed at the presses of Cambridge University.

The tally of newly appointed professors of English they had taught as undergraduates soon reached double figures.

"If you will count polytechnics, I shall have to throw in Maguire's readership in Kenya," said William.

"You did not teach the Professor of English at Nairobi," said Philippa. "I did. You taught the Head of State, which may well account for why the University is so highly thought of while the country is in such disarray."

In the early sixties they conducted a battle of letters in the TLS on the works of Philip Sidney without ever discussing the subject in each other's presence. In the end the editor said the correspondence must stop and adjudicated a draw.

They both declared him an idiot.

If there was one act that annoyed William in old age about Philippa, it was her continued determination each morning to complete *The Times* crossword before he arrived at the breakfast table. For a time, William ordered two copies of the paper until Philippa filled them both in while explaining to him it was a waste of money.

One particular morning in June at the end of their final academic year before retirement, William came down to breakfast to find only one space in the crossword left for him to complete. He studied the clue: "Skelton reported that this landed in the soup." He immediately filled in the eight little boxes.

Philippa looked over his shoulder. "There's no such word, you arrogant man," she said firmly. "You made it up to annoy me." She placed in front of him a very hard boiled egg.

"Of course there is, you silly woman; look whym-wham up in the dictionary."

Philippa checked in the *Oxford Shorter* among the cookery books in the kitchen, and trumpeted her delight that it was nowhere to be found.

"My dear Dame Philippa," said William, as if he were addressing a particularly stupid pupil, "you surely cannot imagine because you are old and your hair has become very white that you are a sage. You must understand that the Shorter Oxford Dictionary was cobbled together for simpletons whose command of the English language stretches to no more than one hundred thousand words. When I go to college this morning I shall confirm the existence of the word in the OED on my desk. Need I remind you that the OED is a serious work which, with over five hundred thousand words, was designed for scholars like myself?"

"Rubbish," said Philippa. "When I am proved right, you will repeat this story word for word, including your offensive non-word, at Somerville's Gaudy Feast."

"And you, my dear, will read the Collected Works of John Skelton and eat humble pie as your first course."

"We'll ask old Onions along to adjudicate."

"Agreed."

"Agreed."

With that, Sir William picked up his paper, kissed his wife on the cheek and said with an exaggerated sigh, "It's at times like this that I wished I'd lost the Charles Oldham."

"You did, my dear. It was in the days when it wasn't fashionable to admit a woman had won anything."

"You won me."

"Yes, you arrogant man, but I was led to believe you were one of those prizes one could return at the end of the year. And now I find I shall have to keep you, even in retirement."

"Let us leave it to the Oxford English Dictionary, my dear, to decide the issue the Charles Oldham examiners were unable to determine," and with that he departed for his college.

"There's no such word," Philippa muttered as he closed the front door.

Heart attacks are known to be rarer among women than men. When Dame Philippa suffered hers in the kitchen that morning she collapsed on the floor calling hoarsely for William, but he was already out of earshot. It was the cleaning woman who found Dame Philippa on the kitchen floor and ran to fetch someone in authority. The Bursar's first reaction was that she was probably pretending that Sir William had hit her with a frying pan but nevertheless she hurried over to the Hatchards' house in Little Jericho just in case. The Bursar checked Dame Philippa's pulse and called for the college doctor and then the Principal. Both arrived within minutes.

The Principal and the Bursar stood waiting by the side of their illustrious academic colleague but they already knew what the doctor was going to say.

"She's dead," he confirmed. "It must have been very sudden and with the minimum of pain." He checked his watch; the time was nine-forty-seven. He covered his patient with a blanket and called for an ambulance. He had taken care of Dame Philippa for over thirty years and he had told her so often to slow down that he might as well have made a gramophone record of it for all the notice she took.

"Who will tell Sir William?" asked the Principal. The three of them looked at each other.

"I will," said the doctor.

It's a short walk from Little Jericho to Radcliffe Square. It was a long walk from Little Jericho to Radcliffe Square for the doctor that day. He never relished telling anyone of the death of a spouse but this one was going to be the unhappiest of his career.

When he knocked on the professor's door, Sir William bade him enter. The great man was sitting at his desk poring over the Oxford Dictionary, humming to himself.

"I told her, but she wouldn't listen, the silly woman," he was saying to himself and then he turned and saw the doctor standing silently in the doorway. "Doctor, you must be my guest at Somerville's Gaudy next Thursday week where Dame Philippa will be eating humble pie. It will be nothing less than game, set, match and championship for me. A vindication of thirty years' scholarship."

The doctor did not smile, nor did he stir. Sir William walked over to him and gazed at his old friend intently. No words were necessary. The doctor said only, "I'm more sorry than I am able to express," and he left Sir William to his private grief.

Sir William's colleagues all knew within the hour. College lunch that day was spent in a silence broken only by the Senior Tutor inquiring of the Master if some food should be taken up to the Merton professor.

"I think not," said the Master. Nothing more was said

Professors, Fellows and students alike crossed the front quadrangle in silence and when they gathered for dinner that evening still no one felt like conversation. At the end of the meal the Senior Tutor suggested once again that something should be taken up to Sir William. This time the Master nodded his agreement and a light meal was prepared by the college chef. The Master and the Senior Tutor climbed the worn stone steps to Sir William's room and while one held the tray the other gently knocked on the door. There was no reply, so the Master, used to William's ways, pushed the door ajar and looked in.

The old man lay motionless on the wooden floor in a pool of blood, a small pistol by his side. The two men walked in and stared down. In his right hand, William was holding the Collected Works of John Skelton. The book was opened at *The Tunnyng of Elynour Rummyng*, and the word "whymwham" was underlined.

a 1529, Skelton, *E. Rummyng* 75

After the Sarasyns gyse,
Woth a whym wham,
Knyt with a trym tram,
Upon her brayne pan.

Sir William, in his neat hand, had written a note in the margin: "Forgive me, but I had to let her know."

"Know what, I wonder?" said the Master softly to himself as he attempted to remove the book from Sir William's hand, but the fingers were already stiff and cold around it.

Legend has it that they were never apart for more than a few hours.

THE END

JEFFREY ARCHER

A TWIST IN THE TALE

To Henry and Suzanne

AUTHOR'S NOTE

Of these twelve short stories, gathered in my travels from Tokyo to Trumpington, ten are based on known incidents – some embellished with considerable licence. Only two are totally the result of my own imagination.

I would like to thank all those people who allowed me to learn some of their innermost secrets.

J.A.
September 1988

Contents

A TWIST IN THE TALE

The Perfect Murder

IF I hadn't changed my mind that night I would never have found out the truth.

I couldn't believe that Carla had slept with another man, that she had lied about her love for me – and that I might be second or even third in her affections.

Carla had phoned me at the office during the day, something I had told her not to do, but since I also warned her never to call me at home she hadn't been left with a lot of choice. As it turned out, all she had wanted to let me know was that she wouldn't be able to make it for what the French so decorously call a "*cinq à sept*". She had to visit her sister in Fulham who had been taken ill, she explained.

I was disappointed. It had been another depressing day, and now I was being asked to forgo the one thing that would have made it bearable.

"I thought you didn't get on well with your sister," I said tartly.

There was no immediate reply from the other end. Eventually Carla asked, "Shall we make it next Tuesday, the usual time?"

"I don't know if that's convenient," I said. "I'll call you on Monday when I know what my plans are." I put down the receiver.

Wearily, I phoned my wife to let her know I was on the way home – something I usually did from the phone box outside Carla's flat. It was a trick I often used to make Elizabeth feel she knew where I was every moment of the day.

Most of the office staff had already left for the night so I gathered together some papers I could work on at home. Since the new company had taken us over six months ago, the management had not only sacked my Number Two in the accounts department but expected me to cover his work as well as my own. I was hardly in a position to complain, since my new boss made it abundantly clear that if I didn't like the arrangement I should feel free to seek employment elsewhere. I might have, too, but I couldn't think of many firms that would readily take on a man who had reached that magic age somewhere between the sought-after and the available.

As I drove out of the office car park and joined the evening rush hour I began to regret having been so sharp with Carla. After all, the role of the other woman was hardly one she delighted in. The feeling of guilt persisted, so that when I reached the corner of Sloane Square, I jumped out of my car and ran across the road.

"A dozen roses," I said, fumbling with my wallet.

A man who must have made his profit from lovers selected twelve unopened buds without comment. My choice didn't show a great deal of imagination but at least Carla would know I'd tried.

I drove on towards her flat, hoping she had not yet left for her sister's, that perhaps we might even find time for a quick drink. Then I remembered that I had already told my wife I was on the way home. A few minutes' delay could be explained by a traffic jam, but that lame excuse could hardly cover my staying on for a drink.

When I arrived at Carla's home I had the usual trouble finding a parking space, until I spotted a gap that would just take a Rover opposite the paper shop. I stopped and would have backed into the space had I not noticed a man coming out of the entrance to her block of flats. I wouldn't have given it a second thought if Carla hadn't followed him a moment later. She stood there in the doorway, wearing a loose blue housecoat. She leaned forward to give her departing visitor a kiss that could hardly have been described as sisterly. As she closed the door I drove my car round the corner and double-parked.

I watched the man in my rear-view mirror as he crossed the road, went into the newsagent and a few moments later reappeared with an evening paper and what looked like a packet of cigarettes. He walked to his car, a blue BMW, stopped to remove a parking ticket from his windscreen and appeared to curse. How long had the BMW been there? I even began to wonder if he had been with Carla when she phoned to tell me not to come round.

The man climbed into the BMW, fastened his seat belt and lit a cigarette before driving off. I took his parking meter space in part-payment for my woman. I didn't consider it a fair exchange. I checked up and down the street, as I always did, before getting out and walking over to the block of flats. It was already dark and no one gave me a second glance. I pressed the bell marked 'Moorland'.

When Carla opened the front door I was greeted with a huge smile which quickly turned into a frown, then just as quickly back to a smile. The first smile must have been meant for the BMW man. I often wondered why she wouldn't give me a front-door key. I stared into those blue eyes that had first captivated me so many months ago. Despite her smile, those eyes now revealed a coldness I had never seen before.

She turned to re-open the door and let me into her ground-floor flat. I noticed that under her housecoat she was wearing the wine-red negligee I had given her for Christmas. Once inside the flat I found myself checking round the room I knew so well. On the glass table in the centre of the room stood the 'Snoopy' coffee mug I usually drank from, empty. By its side was Carla's mug, also empty, and a dozen roses arranged in a vase. The buds were just beginning to open.

I have always been quick to chide and the sight of the flowers made it impossible for me to hide my anger.

"And who was the man who just left?" I asked.

"An insurance broker," she replied, removing the mugs from the table.

"And what was he insuring?" I asked. "Your love-life?"

"Why do you automatically assume he's my lover?" Her voice had begun to rise.

"Do you usually have coffee with an insurance broker in your negligee? Come to think of it, *my* negligee."

"I'll have coffee with whom I damn well please," she said, "and wearing what I damn well please, especially when you are on your way home to your wife."

"But I had wanted to come to you –"

"And then return to your wife. In any case, you're always telling me I should lead my own life and not rely on you," she added, an argument Carla often fell back on when she had something to hide.

"You know it's not that easy."

"I know it's easy enough for you to jump into bed with me whenever it suits you. That's all I'm good for, isn't it?"

"That's not fair."

"Not fair? Weren't you hoping for your usual at six so you could still be home at seven in time for supper with Elizabeth?"

"I haven't made love to my wife in years!" I shouted.

"We only have your word for that," she spat out with scorn.

"I have been utterly faithful to you."

"Which means I always have to be to you, I suppose?"

"Stop behaving like a whore."

Carla's eyes flashed as she leaped forward and slapped me across the face with all the strength she could muster.

I was still slightly off-balance when she raised her arm a second time, but as her hand came swinging towards me I blocked it and was even able to push her back against the mantelpiece. She recovered quickly and came flying at me again.

In a moment of uncontrolled fury, just as she was about to launch herself on me, I clenched my fist and took a swing at her. I caught her on the side of the chin, and she wheeled back from the impact. I watched her put an arm out to break her fall. But before she had the chance to leap back up and retaliate, I turned and strode out, slamming the flat door behind me.

I ran down the hall, out on to the street, jumped into my car and drove off quickly. I couldn't have been with her for more than ten minutes. Although I felt like murdering her at the time I regretted having hit her long before I reached home. Twice I nearly turned back. Everything she had complained about was fair and I wondered if I dared phone her from home. Although Carla and I had only been lovers for a few months, she must have known how much I cared.

If Elizabeth had intended to comment on my being late, she changed her mind the moment I handed her the roses. She began to arrange them in a vase while I poured myself a large whisky. I waited for her to say something as I rarely drank before dinner but she seemed preoccupied with the flowers. Although I had already made up my mind to phone Carla and try to make amends, I decided I couldn't do it from home. In any case, if I waited until the morning when I was back in the office, she might by then have calmed down a little.

I woke early the next day and lay in bed, considering what form my apology should take. I decided to invite her to lunch at the little French bistro she liked so much, half way between my office and hers. Carla always appreciated seeing me in the middle of the day, when she knew it couldn't be for sex. After I had shaved and dressed I joined Elizabeth for breakfast, and seeing there was nothing interesting on the front page, I turned to the financial section. The company's shares had fallen again, following City forecasts of poor interim profits. Millions would undoubtedly be wiped off our share value following such a bad piece of publicity. I already knew that when it came to publishing the annual accounts it would be a miracle if the company didn't declare a loss.

After gulping down a second cup of coffee I kissed my wife on the cheek and made for the car. It was then that I decided to drop a note through Carla's letterbox rather than cope with the embarrassment of a phone call.

"Forgive me," I wrote. "Marcel's, one o'clock. *Sole Véronique* on a Friday. Love, Casaneva." I rarely wrote to Carla, and when I did I only ever signed it with her chosen nickname.

I took a short detour so that I could pass her home but was held up by a traffic jam. As I approached the flat I could see that the hold-up was being caused by some sort of accident. It had to be quite a serious one because there was an ambulance blocking the other side of the road and delaying the flow of oncoming vehicles. A traffic warden was trying to help but she was only slowing things down even more. It was obvious that it was going to be impossible to park anywhere near Carla's flat, so I resigned myself to phoning her from the office. I did not relish the prospect.

I felt a sinking feeling moments later when I saw that the ambulance was parked only a few yards from the front door to her block of flats. I knew I was being irrational but I began to fear the worst. I tried to convince myself it was probably a road accident and had nothing to do with Carla.

It was then that I spotted the police car tucked in behind the ambulance.

As I drew level with the two vehicles I saw that Carla's front door was wide open. A man in a long white coat came scurrying out and opened the back of the ambulance. I stopped my car to observe more carefully what was going on, hoping the man behind me would not become impatient. Drivers coming from the other direction raised a hand to thank me for allowing them to pass. I thought I could let a dozen or so through before anyone would start to complain. The traffic warden helped by urging them on.

Then a stretcher appeared at the end of the hall. Two uniformed orderlies carried a shrouded body out on to the road and placed it in the back of the ambulance. I was unable to see the face because it was covered by the sheet, but a third man, who could only have been a detective, walked immediately behind the stretcher. He was carrying a plastic bag, inside which I could make out a red garment that I feared was the negligee I had given Carla.

I vomited my breakfast all over the passenger seat, my head finally resting on the steering wheel.

A moment later they closed the ambulance door, a siren started up and the traffic warden began waving me on. The ambulance moved quickly off and the man behind me started to press his horn. He was, after all, only an innocent bysitter. I lurched forward and later couldn't recall any part of my journey to the office.

Once I had reached the office car park I cleared up the mess on the passenger seat as best I could and left a window open before taking a lift to the washroom on the seventh floor. I tore my lunch invitation to Carla into little pieces and flushed them down the lavatory. I walked into my room on the twelfth floor a little after eight thirty, to find the managing director pacing up and down in front of my desk, obviously waiting for me. I had quite forgotten that it was Friday and he always expected the latest completed figures to be ready for his consideration.

This Friday it turned out he also wanted the projected accounts for the months of May, June and July. I promised they would be on his desk by midday. The one thing I needed was a clear morning and I was not going to be allowed it.

Every time the phone rang, the door opened or anyone even spoke to me, my heart missed a beat – I assumed it could only be the police. By midday I had finished some sort of report for the managing director, but I knew he would find it neither adequate nor accurate. As soon as I had deposited the papers with his secretary, I left for an early lunch. I realised I wouldn't be able to eat anything, but at least I could get hold of the first edition of the

Standard and search for any news they might have picked up about Carla's death.

I sat in the corner of my local pub where I knew I couldn't be seen from behind the bar. A tomato juice by my side, I began slowly to turn the pages of the paper.

She hadn't made page one. She hadn't made the second, third or fourth page. And on page five she rated only a tiny paragraph. "Miss Carla Moorland, aged 31, was found dead at her home in Pimlico earlier this morning." I remember thinking at the time they hadn't even got her age right. "Detective Inspector Simmons, who has been put in charge of the case, said that an investigation was being carried out and they were awaiting the pathologist's report but to date they had no reason to suspect foul play."

After that piece of news I even managed a little soup and a roll. Once I had read the report a second time I made my way back to the office car park and sat in my car. I wound down the other front window to allow more fresh air in before turning on the *World At One* on the radio. Carla didn't even get a mention. In the age of pump shotguns, drugs, Aids and gold bullion robberies the death of a thirty-two-year-old industrial personal assistant had passed unnoticed by the BBC.

I returned to my office to find on my desk a memo containing a series of questions that had been fired back from the managing director, leaving me in no doubt as to how he felt about my report. I was able to deal with nearly all his queries and return the answers to his secretary before I left the office that night, despite spending most of the afternoon trying to convince myself that whatever had caused Carla's death must have happened after I left and could not possibly have been connected with my hitting her. But that red negligee kept returning to my thoughts. Was there any way they could trace it back to me? I had bought it at Harrods – an extravagance, but I felt certain it couldn't be unique and it was still the only serious present I'd ever given her. But the note that was attached – had Carla destroyed it? Would they discover who Casaneva was?

I drove directly home that evening, aware that I would never again be able to travel down the road Carla had lived in. I listened to the end of the *PM* programme on my car radio and as soon as I reached home switched on the six o'clock news. I turned to Channel Four at seven and back to the BBC at nine. I returned to ITV at ten and even ended up watching *Newsnight*.

Carla's death, in their combined editorial opinion, must have been less important than a Third-Division football result between Reading and Walsall. Elizabeth continued reading her latest library book, oblivious to my possible peril.

I slept fitfully that night, and as soon as I heard the papers pushed through the letterbox the next morning I ran downstairs to check the headlines.

"DUKAKIS NOMINATED AS CANDIDATE" stared up at me from the front page of *The Times*.

I found myself wondering, irrelevantly, if he would ever be President. "President Dukakis" didn't sound quite right to me.

I picked up my wife's *Daily Express* and the

three-word headline filled the top of the page: "LOVERS' TIFF MURDER".

My legs gave way and I fell to my knees. I must have made a strange sight, crumpled up on the floor trying to read that opening paragraph. I couldn't make out the words of the second paragraph without my spectacles. I stumbled back upstairs with the papers and grabbed the glasses from the table on my side of the bed. Elizabeth was still sleeping soundly. Even so, I locked myself in the bathroom where I could read the story slowly and without fear of interruption.

> Police are now treating as murder the death of a beautiful Pimlico secretary, Carla Moorland, 32, who was found dead in her flat early yesterday morning. Detective Inspector Simmons of Scotland Yard, who is in charge of the case, initially considered Carla Moorland's death to be due to natural causes, but an X-ray has revealed a broken jaw which could have been caused in a fight.
>
> An inquest will be held on April 19th.
>
> Miss Moorland's daily, Maria Lucia (48), said – exclusively to the *Express* – that her employer had been with a man friend when she had left the flat at five o'clock on the night in question. Another witness, Mrs Rita Johnson, who lives in the adjoining block of flats, stated she had seen a man leaving Miss Moorland's flat at around six, before entering the newsagents opposite and later driving away. Mrs Johnson added that she couldn't be sure of the make of the car but it might have been a Rover . . .

"Oh, my God," I exclaimed in such a loud voice that I was afraid it might have woken Elizabeth. I shaved and showered quickly, trying to think as I went along. I was dressed and ready to leave for work even before my wife had woken. I kissed her on the cheek but she only turned over, so I scribbled a note and left it on her side of the bed, explaining that I had to spend the morning in the office as I had an important report to complete.

On my journey to work I rehearsed exactly what I was going to say. I went over it again and again. I arrived on the twelfth floor a little before eight and left my door wide open so I would be aware of the slightest intrusion. I felt confident that I had a clear fifteen, even twenty minutes before anyone else could be expected to arrive.

Once again I went over exactly what I needed to say. I found the number in the L–R directory and scribbled it down on a pad in front of me before writing five headings in block capitals, something I always did before a board meeting.

BUS STOP
COAT
NO. 19
BMW
TICKET

Then I dialled the number.

I took off my watch and placed it in front of me. I had read somewhere that the location of a telephone call can be traced in about three minutes.

A woman's voice said, "Scotland Yard."

"Inspector Simmons, please," was all I volunteered.

"Can I tell him who's calling?"

"No, I would prefer not to give my name."

"Yes, of course, sir," she said, evidently used to such callers.

Another ringing tone. My mouth went dry as a man's voice announced "Simmons" and I heard the detective speak for the first time. I was taken aback to find that a man with so English a name could have such a strong Glaswegian accent.

"Can I help you?" he asked.

"No, but I think I can help you," I said in a quiet tone which I pitched considerably lower than my natural speaking voice.

"How can you help me, sir?"

"Are you the officer in charge of the Carla-whatever-her-name-is case?"

"Yes, I am. But how can you help?" he repeated.

The second hand showed one minute had already passed.

"I saw a man leaving her flat that night."

"Where were you at the time?"

"At the bus stop on the same side of the road."

"Can you give me a description of the man?" Simmons's tone was every bit as casual as my own.

"Tall. I'd say five eleven, six foot. Well built. Wore one of those posh City coats – you know, the black ones with a velvet collar."

"How can you be so sure about the coat?" the detective asked.

"It was so cold standing out there waiting for the No. 19 that I wished it had been me who was wearing it."

"Do you remember anything in particular that happened after he left the flat?"

"Only that he went into the paper shop opposite before getting into his car and driving away."

"Yes, we know that much," said the Detective Inspector. "I don't suppose you recall what make of car it was?"

Two minutes had now passed and I began to watch the second hand more closely.

"I think it was a BMW," I said.

"Do you remember the colour by any chance?"

"No, it was too dark for that." I paused. "But I saw him tear a parking ticket off the windscreen, so it shouldn't be too hard for you to trace him."

"And at what time did all this take place?"

"Around six fifteen to six thirty, Inspector," I said.

"And can you tell me . . . ?"

Two minutes fifty-eight seconds. I put the phone back on the hook. My whole body broke out in a sweat.

"Good to see you in the office on a Saturday morning," said the managing director grimly as he passed my door. "Soon as you're finished whatever you're doing I'd like a word with you."

I left my desk and followed him along the corridor into his office. For the next hour he went over my projected figures, but however hard I tried I couldn't concentrate. It wasn't long before he stopped trying to disguise his impatience.

"Have you got something else on your mind?" he asked as he closed his file. "You seem preoccupied."

"No," I insisted, "just been doing a lot of overtime lately," and stood up to leave.

Once I had returned to my office, I burnt the piece of paper with the five headings and left to go home. In the first edition of the afternoon paper, the "Lovers' Tiff" story had been moved back to page seven. They had nothing new to report.

The rest of Saturday seemed interminable but my wife's *Sunday Express* finally brought me some relief.

"Following up information received in the Carla Moorland 'Lovers' Tiff' murder, a man is helping the police with their inquiries." The commonplace expressions I had read so often in the past suddenly took on a real meaning.

I scoured the other Sunday papers, listened to every news bulletin and watched each news item on television. When my wife became curious I explained that there was a rumour in the office that the company might be taken over again, which meant I could lose my job.

By Monday morning the *Daily Express* had named the man in "The Lovers' Tiff murder" as Paul Menzies (51), an insurance broker from Sutton. His wife was at a hospital in Epsom under sedation while he was being held in the cells of Brixton Prison under arrest. I began to wonder if Mr Menzies had told Carla the truth about *his* wife and what *his* nickname might be. I poured myself a strong black coffee and left for the office.

Later that morning, Menzies appeared before the magistrates at the Horseferry Road court, charged with the murder of Carla Moorland. The police had been successful in opposing bail, the *Standard* reassured me.

* * *

It takes six months, I was to discover, for a case of this gravity to reach the Old Bailey. Paul Menzies passed those months on remand in Brixton Prison. I spent the same period fearful of every telephone call, every knock on the door, every unexpected visitor. Each one created its own nightmare. Innocent people have no idea how many such incidents occur every day. I went about my job as best I could, often wondering if Menzies knew of my relationship with Carla, if he knew my name or if he even knew of my existence.

It must have been a couple of months before the trial was due to begin that the company held its annual general meeting. It had taken some considerable creative accountancy on my part to produce a set of figures that showed us managing any profit at all. We certainly didn't pay our shareholders a dividend that year.

I came away from the meeting relieved, almost elated. Six months had passed since Carla's death and not one incident had occurred during that period to suggest that anyone suspected I had even known her, let alone been the cause of her death. I still felt guilty about Carla, even missed her, but after six months I was now able to go for a whole day without fear entering my mind. Strangely, I felt no guilt about Menzies's plight. After all, it was he who had become the instrument that was going to keep me from a lifetime spent in prison. So when the blow came it had double the impact.

It was on August 26th – I shall never forget it – that I received a letter which made me realise it might be necessary to follow every word of the trial.

However much I tried to convince myself I should explain why I couldn't do it, I knew I wouldn't be able to resist it.

That same morning, a Friday – I suppose these things always happen on a Friday – I was called in for what I assumed was to be a routine weekly meeting with the managing director, only to be informed that the company no longer needed me.

"Frankly, in the last few months your work has gone from bad to worse," I was told.

I didn't feel able to disagree with him.

"And you have left me with no choice but to replace you."

A polite way of saying, "You're sacked."

"Your desk will be cleared by five this evening," the managing director continued, "when you will receive a cheque from the accounts department for £17,500."

I raised an eyebrow.

"Six months' compensation, as stipulated in your contract when we took over the company," he explained.

When the managing director stretched out his hand it was not to wish me luck, but to ask for the keys of my Rover.

I remember my first thought when he informed me of his decision: at least I would be able to attend every day of the trial without any hassle.

Elizabeth took the news of my sacking badly but only asked what plans I had for finding a new job. During the next month I pretended to look for a position in another company but realised I couldn't hope to settle down to anything until the case was over.

On the morning of the trial all the popular papers had colourful background pieces. The *Daily Express* even displayed on its front page a flattering picture of Carla in a swimsuit on the beach at Marbella: I wondered how much her sister in Fulham had been paid for that particular item. Alongside it was a profile photo of Paul Menzies which made him look as if he were already a convict.

I was amongst the first to be told in which court at the Old Bailey the case of the Crown v. Menzies would be tried. A uniformed policeman gave me detailed directions and along with several others I made my way to Court No. 4.

Once I had reached the courtroom I filed in and made sure that I sat on the end of my row. I looked round thinking everyone would stare at me, but to my relief no one showed the slightest interest.

I had a good view of the defendant as he stood in the dock. Menzies was a frail man who looked as if he had recently lost a lot of weight; fifty-one, the newspapers had said, but he looked nearer seventy. I began to wonder how much I must have aged over the past few months.

Menzies wore a smart, dark blue suit that hung loosely on him, a clean shirt and what I thought must be a regimental tie. His grey thinning hair was swept straight back; a small silver moustache gave him a military air. He certainly didn't look like a murderer or much of a catch as a lover, but anyone glancing towards me would probably have come to the same conclusion. I searched around the sea of faces for Mrs Menzies but no one in the court fitted the newspaper description of her.

We all rose when Mr Justice Buchanan came in.

"The Crown v. Menzies," the clerk of the court read out.

The judge leaned forward to tell Menzies that he could be seated and then turned slowly towards the jury box.

He explained that, although there had been considerable press interest in the case, their opinion was all that mattered because they alone would be asked to decide if the prisoner were guilty or not guilty of murder. He also advised the jury against reading any newspaper articles concerning the trial or listening to anyone else's views, especially those who had not been present in court: such people, he said, were always the first to have an immutable opinion on what the verdict should be. He went on to remind the jury how important it was to concentrate on the evidence because a man's life was at stake. I found myself nodding in agreement.

I glanced round the court hoping there was nobody there who would recognise me. Menzies's eyes remained fixed firmly on the judge, who was turning back to face the prosecuting counsel.

Even as Sir Humphrey Mountcliff rose from his place on the bench I was thankful he was against Menzies and not me. A man of dominating height with a high forehead and silver grey hair, he commanded the court not only with his physical presence but with a voice that was never less than authoritative.

To a silent assembly he spent the rest of the morning setting out the case for the prosecution. His eyes rarely left the jury box except occasionally to peer down at his notes.

He reconstructed the events as he imagined

they had happened that evening in April.

The opening address lasted two and a half hours, shorter than I'd expected. The judge then suggested a break for lunch and asked us all to be back in our places by ten past two.

After lunch Sir Humphrey called his first witness, Detective Inspector Simmons. I was unable to look directly at the policeman while he presented his evidence. Each reply he gave was as if he were addressing me personally. I wondered if he suspected all along that there was another man. Simmons gave a highly professional account of himself as he described in detail how they had found the body and later traced Menzies through two witnesses and the damning parking ticket. By the time Sir Humphrey sat down few people in that court could have felt that Simmons had arrested the wrong man.

Menzies's defence counsel, who rose to cross-examine the Detective Inspector, could not have been in greater contrast to Sir Humphrey. Mr Robert Scott, QC, was short and stocky, with thick bushy eyebrows. He spoke slowly and without inflection. I was happy to observe that one member of the jury was having difficulty in staying awake.

For the next twenty minutes Scott took the Detective Inspector painstakingly back over his evidence but was unable to make Simmons retract anything substantial. As the Inspector stepped out of the witness box I felt confident enough to look him straight in the eye.

The next witness was a Home Office pathologist, Dr Anthony Mallins, who, after answering a few preliminary questions to establish his professional status, moved on to answer an inquiry from Sir Humphrey that took everyone by surprise. The pathologist informed the court that there was clear evidence to suggest that Miss Moorland had had sexual intercourse shortly before her death.

"How can you be so certain, Dr Mallins?"

"Because I found traces of blood group B on the deceased's upper thigh, while Miss Moorland was later found to be blood group O. There were also traces of seminal fluid on the negligee she was wearing at the time of her death."

"Are these common blood groups?" Sir Humphrey asked.

"Blood group O is common," Dr Mallins admitted. "Group B, however, is fairly unusual."

"And what would you say was the cause of her death?" Sir Humphrey asked.

"A blow or blows to the head, which caused a broken jaw, and lacerations at the base of the skull which may have been delivered by a blunt instrument."

I wanted to stand up and say, "I can tell you which!" when Sir Humphrey said, "Thank you, Dr Mallins. No more questions. Please wait there."

Mr Scott treated the doctor with far more respect than he had Inspector Simmons, despite Mallins being the defendant's witness.

"Could the blow on the back of Miss Moorland's head have been caused by a fall?" he asked.

The doctor hesitated. "Possibly," he agreed. "But that wouldn't explain the broken jaw."

Mr Scott ignored the comment and pressed on.

"What percentage of people in Britain are blood group B?"

"About five, six per cent," volunteered the doctor.

"Two and a half million people," said Mr Scott, and waited for the figure to sink in before he suddenly changed tack.

But as hard as he tried he could not shift the pathologist on the time of death or on the fact that sexual intercourse must have taken place around the hours his client had been with Carla.

When Mr Scott sat down the judge asked Sir Humphrey if he wished to re-examine.

"I do, my Lord. Dr Mallins, you told the court that Miss Moorland suffered from a broken jaw and lacerations on the back of her head. Could the lacerations have been caused by falling on to a blunt object after the jaw had been broken?"

"I must object, my Lord," said Mr Scott, rising with unusual speed. "This is a leading question."

Mr Justice Buchanan leaned forward and peered down at the doctor. "I agree, Mr Scott, but I would like to know if Dr Mallins found blood group O, Miss Moorland's blood group, on any other object in the room?"

"Yes, my Lord," replied the doctor. "On the edge of the glass table in the centre of the room."

"Thank you, Dr Mallins," said Sir Humphrey. "No more questions."

Sir Humphrey's next witness was Mrs Rita Johnson, the lady who claimed she had seen everything.

"Mrs Johnson, on the evening of April 7th, did you see a man leave the block of flats where Miss Moorland lived?" Sir Humphrey asked.

"Yes, I did."

"At about what time was that?"

"A few minutes after six."

"Please tell the court what happened next."

"He walked across the road, removed a parking ticket, got into his car and drove away."

"Do you see that man in the court today?"

"Yes," she said firmly, pointing to Menzies, who at this suggestion shook his head vigorously.

"No more questions."

Mr Scott rose slowly again.

"What did you say was the make of the car the man got into?"

"I can't be sure," Mrs Johnson said, "but I think it was a BMW."

"Not a Rover as you first told the police the following morning?"

The witness did not reply.

"And did you actually see the man in question remove a parking ticket from the car windscreen?" Mr Scott asked.

"I think so, sir, but it all happened so quickly."

"I'm sure it did," said Mr Scott. "In fact, I suggest to you that it happened so quickly that you've got the wrong man and the wrong car."

"No, sir," she replied, but without the same conviction with which she had delivered her earlier replies.

Sir Humphrey did not re-examine Mrs Johnson. I realised that he wanted her evidence to be forgotten by the jury as quickly as possible. As it was, when she left the witness box she also left everyone in court in considerable doubt.

Carla's daily, Maria Lucia, was far more convincing. She stated unequivocally that she had seen

Menzies in the living room of the flat that afternoon when she arrived a little before five. However, she had, she admitted, never seen him before that day.

"But isn't it true," asked Sir Humphrey, "that you usually only work in the mornings?"

"Yes," she replied. "Although Miss Moorland was in the habit of bringing work home on a Thursday afternoon so it was convenient for me to come in and collect my wages."

"And how was Miss Moorland dressed that afternoon?" asked Sir Humphrey.

"In her blue morning coat," replied the daily.

"Is this how she usually dressed on a Thursday afternoon?"

"No, sir, but I assumed she was going to have a bath before going out that evening."

"But when you left the flat was she still with Mr Menzies?"

"Yes, sir."

"Do you remember anything else she was wearing that day?"

"Yes, sir. Underneath the morning coat she wore a red negligee."

My negligee was duly produced and Maria Lucia identified it. At this point I stared directly at the witness but she showed not a flicker of recognition. I thanked all the gods in the Pantheon that I had never once been to visit Carla in the morning.

"Please wait there," were Sir Humphrey's final words to Miss Lucia.

Mr Scott rose to cross-examine.

"Miss Lucia, you have told the court that the purpose of the visit was to collect your wages. How long were you at the flat on this occasion?"

"I did a little clearing up in the kitchen and ironed a blouse, perhaps twenty minutes."

"Did you see Miss Moorland during this time?"

"Yes, I went into the drawing room to ask if she would like some more coffee but she said no."

"Was Mr Menzies with her at the time?"

"Yes, he was."

"Were you at any time aware of a quarrel between the two of them or even raised voices?"

"No, sir."

"When you saw them together did Miss Moorland show any signs of distress or need of help?"

"No, sir."

"Then what happened?"

"Miss Moorland joined me in the kitchen a few minutes later, gave me my wages and I let myself out."

"When you were alone in the kitchen with Miss Moorland, did she give any sign of being afraid of her guest?"

"No, sir."

"No more questions, my Lord."

Sir Humphrey did not re-examine Maria Lucia and informed the judge that he had completed the case for the prosecution. Mr Justice Buchanan nodded and said he felt that was enough for the day; but I wasn't convinced it was enough to convict Menzies.

When I got home that night Elizabeth did not ask me where I had been, and I did not volunteer any information. I spent the evening pretending to go over job applications.

* * *

The following morning I had a late breakfast and read the papers before returning to my place at the end of a row in Court No. 4, only a few moments before the judge made his entrance.

Mr Justice Buchanan, having sat down, adjusted his wig before calling on Mr Scott to open the case for the defence. Mr Scott, QC, was once again slow to rise – a man paid by the hour, I thought uncharitably. He started by promising the court that his opening address would be brief, and he then remained on his feet for the next two and a half hours.

He began the case for the defence by going over in detail the relevant parts, as he saw them, of Menzies's past. He assured us all that those who wished to dissect it later would only find an unblemished record. Paul Menzies was a happily married man who lived in Sutton with his wife and three children, Polly, aged twenty-one, Michael, nineteen, and Sally, sixteen. Two of the children were now at university and the youngest had just completed her GCSE. Doctors had advised Mrs Menzies not to attend the trial, following her recent release from hospital. I noticed two of the women on the jury smile sympathetically.

Mr Menzies, Mr Scott continued, had been with the same firm of insurance brokers in the City of London for the past six years and, although he had not been promoted, he was a much respected member of the staff. He was a pillar of his local community, having served with the Territorial Army and on the committee of the local camera club. He had once even stood for the Sutton council. He could hardly be described as a serious candidate as a murderer.

Mr Scott then went on to the actual day of the killing and confirmed that Mr Menzies had an appointment with Miss Moorland on the afternoon in question, but in a strictly professional capacity with the sole purpose of helping her with a personal insurance plan. There could have been no other reason to visit Miss Moorland during office hours. He did not have sexual intercourse with her and he certainly did not murder her.

The defendant had left his client a few minutes after six. He understood she had intended to change before going out to dinner with her sister in Fulham. He had arranged to see her the following Wednesday at his office for the purpose of drawing up the completed policy. The defence, Mr Scott went on, would later produce a diary entry that would establish the truth of this statement.

The charge against the accused was, he submitted, based almost completely on circumstantial evidence. He felt confident that, when the trial reached its conclusion, the jury would be left with no choice but to release his client back into the bosom of his loving family. "You must end this nightmare," Mr Scott concluded. "It has gone on far too long for an innocent man."

At this point the judge suggested a break for lunch. During the meal I was unable to concentrate or even take in what was being said around me. The majority of those who had an opinion to give now seemed convinced that Menzies was innocent.

As soon as we returned, at ten past two, Mr Scott called his first witness: the defendant himself.

Paul Menzies left the dock and walked slowly over to the witness box. He took a copy of the New

Testament in his right hand and haltingly read the words of the oath, from a card which he held in his left.

Every eye was fixed on him while Mr Scott began to guide his client carefully through the minefield of evidence.

Menzies became progressively more confident in his delivery as the day wore on, and when at four thirty the judge told the court, "That's enough for today," I was convinced that he would get off, even if only by a majority verdict.

I spent a fitful night before returning to my place on the third day fearing the worst. Would Menzies be released and would they then start looking for me?

Mr Scott opened the third morning as gently as he had begun the second, but he repeated so many questions from the previous day that it became obvious he was only steadying his client in preparation for prosecuting counsel. Before he finally sat down he asked Menzies for a third time, "Did you ever have sexual intercourse with Miss Moorland?"

"No, sir. I had only met her for the first time that day," Menzies replied firmly.

"And did you murder Miss Moorland?"

"Certainly not, sir," said Menzies, his voice now strong and confident.

Mr Scott resumed his place, a look of quiet satisfaction on his face.

In fairness to Menzies, very little which takes place in normal life could have prepared anyone for cross-examination by Sir Humphrey Mountcliff. I could not have asked for a better advocate.

"I'd like to start, if I may, Mr Menzies," he began, "with what your counsel seems to set great store by as proof of your innocence."

Menzies's thin lips remained in a firm straight line.

"The pertinent entry in your diary which suggests that you made a second appointment to see Miss Moorland, the murdered woman" – three words Sir Humphrey was to repeat again and again during his cross-examination – "for the Wednesday after she had been killed."

"Yes, sir," said Menzies.

"This entry was made – correct me if I'm wrong – following your Thursday meeting at Miss Moorland's flat."

"Yes, sir," said Menzies, obviously tutored not to add anything that might later help prosecuting counsel.

"So when did you make that entry?" Sir Humphrey asked.

"On the Friday morning."

"After Miss Moorland had been killed?"

"Yes, but I didn't know."

"Do you carry a diary on you, Mr Menzies?"

"Yes, but only a small pocket diary, not my large desk one."

"Do you have it with you today?"

"I do."

"May I be allowed to see it?"

Reluctantly Menzies took a small green diary out of his jacket pocket and handed it over to the clerk of the court, who in turn passed it on to Sir Humphrey. Sir Humphrey began to leaf through the pages.

"I see that there is no entry for your appointment with Miss Moorland for the afternoon on which she was murdered?"

"No, sir," said Menzies. "I put office appointments only in my desk diary, personal appointments are restricted to my pocket diary."

"I understand," said Sir Humphrey. He paused and looked up. "But isn't it strange, Mr Menzies, that you agreed to an appointment with a client to discuss further business and you then trusted it to memory, when you so easily could have put it in the diary you carry around with you all the time before transferring it?"

"I might have written it down on a slip of paper at the time, but as I explained that's a personal diary."

"Is it?" said Sir Humphrey as he flicked back a few more pages. "Who is David Paterson?" he asked.

Menzies looked as if he were trying to place him.

"Mr David Paterson, 112 City Road, 11.30, January 9th this year," Sir Humphrey read out to the court. Menzies looked anxious. "We could subpoena Mr Paterson if you can't recall the meeting," said Sir Humphrey helpfully.

"He's a client of my firm," said Menzies in a quiet voice.

"A client of your firm," Sir Humphrey repeated slowly. "I wonder how many of those I could find if I went through your diary at a more leisurely pace?" Menzies bowed his head as Sir Humphrey passed the diary back to the clerk, having made his point.

"Now I should like to turn to some more important questions . . ."

"Not until after lunch, Sir Humphrey," the

judge intervened. "It's nearly one and I think we'll take a break now."

"As you wish, my Lord," came back the courteous reply.

I left the court in a more optimistic mood, even though I couldn't wait to discover what could be more important than that diary. Sir Humphrey's emphasis on little lies, although they did not prove Menzies was a murderer, did show he was hiding something. I became anxious that during the break Mr Scott might advise Menzies to admit to his affair with Carla, and thus make the rest of his story appear more credible. To my relief, over the meal I learned that under English law Menzies could not consult his counsel while he was still in the witness box. I noticed when we returned to court that Mr Scott's smile had disappeared.

Sir Humphrey rose to continue his cross-examination.

"You have stated under oath, Mr Menzies, that you are a happily married man."

"I am, sir," said the defendant with feeling.

"Was your first marriage as happy, Mr Menzies?" asked Sir Humphrey casually. The defendant's cheeks drained of their colour. I quickly looked over towards Mr Scott who could not mask that this was information with which he had not been entrusted.

"Take your time before you answer," said Sir Humphrey.

All eyes turned to the man in the witness box.

"No," said Menzies and quickly added, "but I was very young at the time. It was many years ago and all a ghastly mistake."

"All a ghastly mistake?" repeated Sir Humphrey, looking straight at the jury. "And how did that marriage end?"

"In divorce," Menzies said quite simply.

"And what were the grounds for that divorce?"

"Cruelty," said Menzies, "but . . ."

"But . . . would you like me to read out to the jury what your first wife swore under oath in court that day?"

Menzies stood there shaking. He knew that "No" would damn him and "Yes" would hang him.

"Well, as you seem unable to advise us I will, with your permission, my Lord, read the statement made before Mr Justice Rodger on June 9th, 1961, at the Swindon County Court by the first Mrs Menzies." Sir Humphrey cleared his throat. "'He used to hit me again and again, and it became so bad that I had to run away for fear he might one day kill me.'" Sir Humphrey emphasised the last five words.

"She was exaggerating," shouted Menzies from the witness box.

"How unfortunate that poor Miss Carla Moorland cannot be with us today to let us know if your story about her is also an exaggeration."

"I object, my Lord," said Mr Scott. "Sir Humphrey is harassing the witness."

"I agree," said the judge. "Tread more carefully in future, Sir Humphrey."

"I apologise, my Lord," said Sir Humphrey, sounding singularly unapologetic. He closed the file to which he had been referring and replaced it on the desk in front of him before taking up a new one. He opened it slowly, making sure all in the court were following every movement before he extracted a single sheet of paper.

"How many mistresses have you had since you were married to the second Mrs Menzies?"

"Objection, my Lord. How can this be relevant?"

"My Lord, it is relevant, I respectfully suggest. I intend to show that this was not a business relationship that Mr Menzies was conducting with Miss Moorland but a highly personal one."

"The question can be put to the defendant," ruled the judge.

Menzies said nothing as Sir Humphrey held up the sheet of paper in front of him and studied it.

"Take your time because I want the exact number," Sir Humphrey said, looking over the top of his glasses.

The seconds ticked on as we all waited.

"Hm – three, I think," Menzies said eventually in a voice that just carried. The gentlemen of the press began scribbling furiously.

"Three," said Sir Humphrey, staring at his piece of paper in disbelief.

"Well, perhaps four."

"And was the fourth Miss Carla Moorland?" Sir Humphrey asked. "Because you had sexual intercourse with her that evening, didn't you?"

"No, I did not," said Menzies, but by this time few in that courtroom could have believed him.

"Very well then," continued Sir Humphrey, as he placed the piece of paper on the bench in front of him. "But before I return to your relationship with

Miss Moorland, let us discover the truth about the other four."

I stared at the piece of paper from which Sir Humphrey had been reading. From where I was seated I could see that there was nothing written on it at all. A blank white sheet lay before him.

I was finding it hard to keep a grin off my face. Menzies's adulterous background was an unexpected bonus for me and the press – and I couldn't help wondering how Carla would have reacted if she had known about it.

Sir Humphrey spent the rest of the day making Menzies relate the details of his previous relationships with the four mistresses. The court was agog and the journalists continued to scribble away, knowing they were about to have a field day. When the court rose Mr Scott's eyes were closed.

I drove home that night feeling not a little pleased with myself; like a man who had just completed a good day's work.

On entering the courtroom the following morning I noticed people were beginning to acknowledge other regulars and nod. I found myself falling into the same pattern and greeted people silently as I took my regular position on the end of the bench.

Sir Humphrey spent the morning going over some of Menzies's other misdemeanours. We discovered that he had served in the Territorial Army for only five months and left after a misunderstanding with his commanding officer over how many hours he should have been spending on exercises during weekends and how much he had claimed in expenses for those hours. We also learned that his attempts to get on the local council sprung more from anger at being refused planning permission to build on a piece of land adjoining his house than from an altruistic desire to serve his fellow men. To be fair, Sir Humphrey could have made the Archangel Gabriel look like a soccer hooligan; but his trump card was still to come.

"Mr Menzies, I should now like to return to your version of what happened on the night Miss Moorland was killed."

"Yes," sighed Menzies in a tired voice.

"When you visit a client to discuss one of your policies, how long would you say such a consultation usually lasts?"

"Usually half an hour, an hour at the most," said Menzies.

"And how long did the consultation with Miss Moorland take?"

"A good hour," said Menzies.

"And you left her, if I remember your evidence correctly, a little after six o'clock."

"That is correct."

"And what time was your appointment?"

"At five o'clock, as was shown clearly in my desk diary," said Menzies.

"Well, Mr Menzies, if you arrived at about five to keep your appointment with Miss Moorland and left a little after six, how did you manage to get a parking fine?"

"I didn't have any small change for the meter at the time," said Menzies confidently. "As I was already a couple of minutes late, I just risked it."

"You just risked it," repeated Sir Humphrey slowly. "You are obviously a man who takes risks, Mr Menzies. I wonder if you would be good enough to look at the parking ticket in question."

The clerk handed it up to Menzies.

"Would you read out to the court the hour and minute that the traffic warden has written in the little boxes to show when the offence occurred."

Once again Menzies took a long time to reply.

"Four sixteen to four thirty," he said eventually.

"I didn't hear that," said the judge.

"Would you be kind enough to repeat what you said for the judge?" Sir Humphrey asked.

Menzies repeated the damning figures.

"So now we have established that you were in fact with Miss Moorland some time before four sixteen, and not, as I suggest you later wrote in your diary, five o'clock. That was just another lie, wasn't it?"

"No," said Menzies. "I must have arrived a little earlier than I realised."

"At least an hour earlier, it seems. And I also suggest to you that you arrived at that early hour because your interest in Carla Moorland was not simply professional?"

"That's not true."

"Then it wasn't your intention that she should become your mistress?"

Menzies hesitated long enough for Sir Humphrey to answer his own question. "Because the business part of your meeting finished in the usual half hour, did it not, Mr Menzies?" He waited for a response but still none was forthcoming.

"What is your blood group, Mr Menzies?"

"I have no idea."

Sir Humphrey without warning changed tack: "Have you heard of DNA, by any chance?"

"No," came back the puzzled reply.

"Deoxyribonucleic acid is a proven technique that shows genetic information can be unique to every individual. Blood or semen samples can be matched. Semen, Mr Menzies, is as unique as any fingerprint. With such a sample we would know immediately if you raped Miss Moorland."

"I didn't rape her," Menzies said indignantly.

"Nevertheless sexual intercourse did take place, didn't it?" said Sir Humphrey quietly.

Menzies remained silent.

"Shall I recall the Home Office pathologist and ask him to carry out a DNA test?"

Menzies still made no reply.

"And check your blood group?" Sir Humphrey paused. "I will ask you once again, Mr Menzies. Did sexual intercourse between you and the murdered woman take place that Thursday afternoon?"

"Yes, sir," said Menzies in a whisper.

"Yes, sir," repeated Sir Humphrey so that the whole court could hear it.

"But it wasn't rape," Menzies shouted back at Sir Humphrey.

"Wasn't it?" said Sir Humphrey.

"And I swear I didn't kill her."

I must have been the only person in that courtroom who knew he was telling the truth. All Sir Humphrey said was, "No more questions, my Lord."

Mr Scott tried manfully to resurrect his client's credibility during re-examination but the fact that Menzies had been caught lying about his relationship with Carla made everything he had said previously appear doubtful.

If only Menzies had told the truth about being

Carla's lover, his story might well have been accepted. I wondered why he had gone through the charade – in order to protect his wife? Whatever the motive, it had only ended by making him appear guilty of a crime he hadn't committed.

I went home that night and ate the largest meal I had had for several days.

The following morning Mr Scott called two more witnesses. The first turned out to be the vicar of St Peter's, Sutton, who was there as a character witness to prove what a pillar of the community Menzies was. After Sir Humphrey had finished his cross-examination the vicar ended up looking like a rather kind, unworldly old man, whose knowledge of Menzies was based on the latter's occasional attendance at Sunday matins.

The second was Menzies's superior at the company they both worked for in the City. He was a far more impressive figure but he was unable to confirm that Miss Moorland had ever been a client of the company.

Mr Scott put up no more witnesses and informed Mr Justice Buchanan that he had completed the case for the defence. The judge nodded and, turning to Sir Humphrey, told him he would not be required to begin his final address until the following morning.

That heralded the signal for the court to rise.

Another long evening and an even longer night had to be endured by Menzies and myself. As on every other day during the trial, I made sure I was in my place the next morning before the judge entered.

Sir Humphrey's closing speech was masterful.

Every little untruth was logged so that one began to accept that very little of Menzies's testimony could be relied on.

"We will never know for certain," said Sir Humphrey, "for what reason poor young Carla Moorland was murdered. Refusal to succumb to Menzies's advances? A fit of temper which ended with a blow that caused her to fall and later die alone? But there are, however, some things, members of the jury, of which we can be quite certain.

"We can be certain that Menzies was with the murdered woman that day before the hour of four sixteen because of the evidence of the damning parking ticket.

"We can be certain that he left a little after six because we have a witness who saw him drive away, and he does not himself deny this evidence.

"And we can be certain that he wrote a false entry in his diary to make you believe he had a business appointment with the murdered woman at five, rather than a personal assignation some time before.

"And we can now be certain that he lied about having sexual intercourse with Miss Moorland a short time before she was killed, though we cannot be certain if intercourse took place before or after her jaw had been broken." Sir Humphrey's eyes rested on the jury before he continued.

"We can, finally, establish, beyond reasonable doubt, from the pathologist's report, the time of death and that, therefore, Menzies was the last person who could possibly have seen Carla Moorland alive.

"Therefore no one else could have killed Carla

Moorland – for do not forget Inspector Simmons's evidence – and if you accept that, you can be in no doubt that only Menzies could have been responsible for her death. And how damning you must have found it that he tried to hide the existence of a first wife who had left him on the grounds of his cruelty, and the four mistresses who left him we know not why or how. Only one less than Bluebeard," Sir Humphrey added with feeling.

"For the sake of every young girl who lives on her own in our capital, you must carry out your duty, however painful that duty might be. And find Menzies guilty of murder."

When Sir Humphrey sat down I wanted to applaud.

The judge sent us away for another break. Voices all around me were now damning Menzies. I listened contentedly without offering an opinion. I knew that if the jury convicted Menzies the file would be closed and no eyes would ever be turned in my direction. I was seated in my place before the judge appeared at ten past two. He called on Mr Scott.

Menzies's counsel put up a spirited defence of his client, pointing out that almost all the evidence that Sir Humphrey had come up with had been circumstantial, and that it was even possible someone else could have visited Carla Moorland after his client had left that night. Mr Scott's bushy eyebrows seemed almost to have a life of their own as he energetically emphasised that it was the prosecution's responsibility to prove their case beyond reasonable doubt and not his to disprove it, and that, in his opinion, his learned friend, Sir Humphrey, had failed to do so.

During his summing-up Scott avoided any mention of diary entries, parking tickets, past mistresses, sexual intercourse or questions of his client's role in the community. A latecomer listening only to the closing speeches might have been forgiven for thinking the two learned gentlemen were summarising different cases.

Mr Scott's expression became grim as he turned to face the jury for his summation. "The twelve of you," he said, "hold the fate of my client in your hands. You must, therefore, be certain, I repeat, certain beyond reasonable doubt that Paul Menzies could have committed such an evil crime as murder.

"This is not a trial about Mr Menzies's lifestyle, his position in the community or even his sexual habits. If adultery were a crime I feel confident Mr Menzies would not be the only person in this courtroom to be in the dock today." He paused as his eyes swept up and down the jury.

"For this reason I feel confident that you will find it in your hearts to release my client from the torment he has been put through during the last seven months. He has surely been shown to be an innocent man deserving of your compassion."

Mr Scott sank down on the bench having, I felt, given his client a glimmer of hope.

The judge told us that he would not begin his own summing-up until Monday morning.

The weekend seemed interminable to me. By Monday I had convinced myself that enough members of the jury would feel there just had not been sufficient evidence to convict.

As soon as the trial was under way the judge

began by explaining once again that it was the jury alone who must make the ultimate decision. It was not his job to let them know how he felt, but only to advise them on the law.

He went back over all the evidence, trying to put it in perspective, but he never gave as much as a hint as to his own opinions. When he had completed his summing-up late that afternoon he sent the jury away to consider their verdict.

I waited with nearly as much anxiety as Menzies must have done while I listened to others giving their opinion as the minutes ticked by in that little room. Then, four hours later, a note was sent up to the judge.

He immediately asked the jury to return to their places while the press flooded back into the courtroom, making it look like the House of Commons on Budget Day. The clerk dutifully handed up the note to Mr Justice Buchanan. He opened it and read what only twelve other people in the courtroom could have known.

He handed it back to the clerk who then read the note to a silent court.

Mr Justice Buchanan frowned before asking if there were any chance of a unanimous verdict being reached if he allowed more time. Once he had learned that it was proving impossible he reluctantly nodded his agreement to a majority verdict.

The jury disappeared downstairs again to continue their deliberations, and did not return to their places for another three hours. I could sense the tension in the court as neighbours sought to give opinions to each other in noisy whispers. The clerk called for silence as the judge waited for everyone to settle before he instructed the clerk to proceed.

When the clerk rose, I could hear the person next to me breathing.

"Would the Foreman please stand?"

I rose from my place.

"Have you reached a verdict on which at least ten of you are agreed?"

"We have, sir."

"Do you find the defendant, Paul Menzies, guilty or not guilty?"

"Guilty," I replied.

Clean Sweep Ignatius

FEW showed much interest when Ignatius Agarbi was appointed Nigeria's Minister of Finance. After all, the cynics pointed out, he was the seventeenth person to hold the office in seventeen years.

In Ignatius's first major policy statement to Parliament he promised to end graft and corruption in public life and warned the electorate that no one holding an official position could feel safe unless he led a blameless life. He ended his maiden speech with the words, "I intend to clear out Nigeria's Augean stables."

Such was the impact of the minister's speech that it failed to get a mention in the Lagos *Daily Times*. Perhaps the editor considered that, since the paper had covered the speeches of the previous sixteen ministers *in extenso*, his readers might feel they had heard it all before.

Ignatius, however, was not to be disheartened by the lack of confidence shown in him, and set about his new task with vigour and determination. Within days of his appointment he had caused a minor official at the Ministry of Trade to be jailed for falsifying documents relating to the import of grain. The next to feel the bristles of Ignatius's new broom was a leading Lebanese financier, who was deported without trial for breach of the exchange control regulations. A month later came an event which even Ignatius considered a personal coup: the arrest of the Inspector General of Police for accepting bribes – a perk the citizens of Lagos had in the past considered went with the job. When four months later the Police Chief was sentenced to eighteen months in jail, the new Finance Minister finally made the front page of the Lagos *Daily Times*. A leader on the centre page dubbed him "Clean Sweep Ignatius", the new broom every guilty man feared. Ignatius's reputation as Mr Clean continued to grow as arrest followed arrest and unfounded rumours began circulating in the capital that even General Otobi, the Head of State, was under investigation by his own Finance Minister.

Ignatius alone now checked, vetted and authorised all foreign contracts worth over one hundred million dollars. And although every decision he made was meticulously scrutinised by his enemies, not a breath of scandal ever became associated with his name.

When Ignatius began his second year of office as Minister of Finance even the cynics began to acknowledge his achievements. It was about this time that General Otobi felt confident enough to call Ignatius in for an unscheduled consultation.

The Head of State welcomed the Minister to Dodan Barracks and ushered him to a comfortable chair in his study overlooking the parade ground.

"Ignatius, I have just finished going over the latest budget report and I am alarmed by your conclusion that the Exchequer is still losing millions of dollars each year in bribes paid to go-betweens by foreign companies. Have you any idea into whose pockets this money is falling? That's what I want to know."

Ignatius sat bolt upright, his eyes never leaving the Head of State.

"I suspect a great percentage of the money is ending up in private Swiss bank accounts but I am at present unable to prove it."

"Then I will give you whatever added authority you require to do so," said General Otobi. "You can use any means you consider necessary to ferret out these villains. Start by investigating every member of my Cabinet, past and present. And show no fear or favour in your endeavours, no matter what their rank or connections."

"For such a task to have any chance of success I would need a special letter of authority signed by you, General . . ."

"Then it will be on your desk by six o'clock this evening," said the Head of State.

"And the rank of Ambassador Plenipotentiary whenever I travel abroad."

"Granted."

"Thank you," said Ignatius, rising from his chair on the assumption that the audience was over.

"You may also need this," said the General as they walked towards the door. The Head of State handed Ignatius a small automatic pistol. "Because I suspect by now that you have almost as many enemies as I."

Ignatius took the pistol from the soldier awkwardly, put it in his pocket and mumbled his thanks.

Without another word passing between the two men, Ignatius left his leader and was driven back to his Ministry.

Without the knowledge of the Governor of the Central Bank of Nigeria, and unhindered by any senior civil servants, Ignatius enthusiastically set about his new task. He researched alone at night, and by day discussed his findings with no one. Three months later he was ready to pounce.

The Minister selected the month of August to make an unscheduled visit abroad, as it was the time when most Nigerians went on holiday, and his absence would therefore not be worthy of comment.

He asked his Permanent Secretary to book him, his wife and their two children on a flight to Orlando, and to be certain that the tickets were charged to his personal account.

On their arrival in Florida, the family checked into the local Marriott Hotel. Ignatius then informed his wife, without warning or explanation, that he would be spending a few days in New York on business before rejoining them for the rest of the holiday. The following morning he left his family to the mysteries of Disney World while he took a flight to New York. It was a short taxi ride from LaGuardia to Kennedy, where, after a change of clothes and the purchase of a return tourist ticket for cash, he boarded a Swissair flight for Geneva unobserved.

Once he had arrived, Ignatius booked into an inconspicuous hotel, retired to bed and slept soundly for eight hours. Over breakfast the following morning he studied the list of banks he had so carefully drawn up after completing his research in Nigeria: each name was written out boldly in his own hand. Ignatius decided to start with Gerber et Cie whose building, he observed from the hotel bedroom, took up half the Avenue de Parchine. He checked the telephone number with the concierge before placing a call. The chairman agreed to see him at twelve o'clock.

Carrying only a battered briefcase, Ignatius arrived at the bank a few minutes before the appointed hour – an unusual occurrence for a Nigerian, thought the young man dressed in a smart grey suit, white shirt and grey silk tie, who was waiting in the marble hall to greet him. He bowed to the Minister, introducing himself as the chairman's personal assistant, and explained that he would accompany Ignatius to the chairman's office. The young executive led the Minister to a waiting lift and neither man uttered another word until they had reached the eleventh floor. A gentle tap on the chairman's door elicited "*Entrez*," which the young man obeyed.

"The Nigerian Minister of Finance, sir."

The chairman rose from behind his desk and stepped forward to greet his guest. Ignatius could not help noticing that he too wore a grey suit, white shirt and grey silk tie.

"Good morning, Minister," the chairman said. "Won't you have a seat?" He ushered Ignatius towards a low glass table surrounded by comfortable chairs on the far side of the room. "I have ordered coffee for both of us if that is acceptable."

Ignatius nodded, placed the battered briefcase on the floor by the side of his chair and stared out of the large plate-glass window. He made some small-talk about the splendid view of the magnificent fountain while a girl served all three men with coffee.

Once the young woman had left the room Ignatius got down to business.

"My Head of State has requested that I visit your bank with a rather unusual request," he began. Not a flicker of surprise appeared on the face of the chairman or his young assistant. "He has honoured me with the task of discovering which Nigerian citizens hold numbered accounts with your bank."

On learning this piece of information only the chairman's lips moved. "I am not at liberty to disclose –"

"Allow me to put my case," said the Minister, raising a white palm. "First, let me assure you that I come with the absolute authority of my government." Without another word, Ignatius extracted an envelope from his inside pocket with a flourish. He handed it to the chairman who removed the letter inside and read it slowly.

Once he had finished reading, the banker cleared his throat. "This document, I fear, sir, carries no validity in my country." He replaced it in the envelope and handed it back to Ignatius. "I am, of course," continued the chairman, "not for one moment doubting that you have the full backing of your Head of State, both as a Minister and an Ambassador, but that does not change the bank's rule of confidentiality in such matters. There are no circumstances in which we would release the names of any of our account holders without their authority. I'm sorry to be of so little help, but those are, and will always remain, the bank rules." The chairman rose to his feet, as he considered the meeting was now at an end; but he had not bargained for Clean Sweep Ignatius.

"My Head of State," said Ignatius, softening his tone perceptibly, "has authorised me to approach your bank to act as the intermediary for all future transactions between my country and Switzerland."

"We are flattered by your confidence in us, Minister," replied the chairman, who remained standing. "However, I feel sure that you will understand that it cannot alter our attitude to our customers' confidentiality."

Ignatius remained unperturbed.

"Then I am sorry to inform you, Mr Gerber, that our Ambassador in Geneva will be instructed to make an official communiqué to the Swiss Foreign Office about the lack of co-operation your bank has shown concerning requests for information about our nationals." He waited for his words to sink in. "You could avoid such embarrassment, of course, by simply letting me know the names of my countrymen who hold accounts with Gerber et Cie and the amounts involved. I can assure you we would not reveal the source of our information."

"You are most welcome to lodge such a communiqué, sir, and I feel sure that our Minister will explain to your Ambassador in the most courteous of diplomatic language that the Foreign Ministry does not have the authority under Swiss law to demand such disclosures."

"If that is the case, I shall instruct my own

Ministry of Trade to halt all future dealings in Nigeria with any Swiss nationals until these names are revealed."

"That is your privilege, Minister," replied the chairman, unmoved.

"And we may also have to reconsider every contract currently being negotiated by your countrymen in Nigeria. And in addition I shall personally see to it that no penalty clauses are honoured."

"Would you not consider such action a little precipitate?"

"Let me assure you, Mr Gerber, that I would not lose one moment of sleep over such a decision," said Ignatius. "Even if my efforts to discover those names were to bring your country to its knees I would not be moved."

"So be it, Minister," replied the chairman. "However, it still does not alter the policy or the attitude of this bank to confidentiality."

"If that remains the case, sir, this very day I shall give instructions to our Ambassador to close our Embassy in Geneva and I shall declare your Ambassador in Lagos *persona non grata*."

For the first time the chairman raised his eyebrows.

"Furthermore," continued Ignatius, "I will hold a conference in London which will leave the world's press in no doubt of my Head of State's displeasure with the conduct of this bank. After such publicity I feel confident you will find that many of your customers would prefer to close their accounts, while others who have in the past considered you a safe haven may find it necessary to look elsewhere."

The Minister waited but still the chairman did not respond.

"Then you leave me no choice," said Ignatius, rising from his seat.

The chairman stretched out his arm, assuming that at last the Minister was leaving, only to watch with horror as Ignatius placed a hand in his jacket pocket and removed a small pistol. The two Swiss bankers froze as the Nigerian Minister of Finance stepped forward and pressed the muzzle against the chairman's temple.

"I need those names, Mr Gerber, and by now you must realise I will stop at nothing. If you don't supply them immediately I'm going to blow your brains out. Do you understand?"

The chairman gave a slight nod, beads of sweat appearing on his forehead. "And he will be next," said Ignatius, gesturing towards the young assistant, who stood speechless and paralysed a few paces away.

"Get me the names of every Nigerian who holds an account in this bank," Ignatius said quietly, looking towards the young man, "or I'll blow your chairman's brains all over his soft pile carpet. Immediately, do you hear me?" he added sharply.

The young man looked towards the chairman, who was now trembling but said quite clearly, "*Non, Pierre, jamais.*"

"*D'accord,*" replied the assistant in a whisper.

"You can't say I didn't give you every chance." Ignatius pulled back the hammer. The sweat was now pouring down the chairman's face and the young man had to turn his eyes away as he waited in terror for the pistol shot.

"Excellent," said Ignatius, as he removed the gun from the chairman's head and returned to his seat. Both the bankers were still trembling and quite unable to speak.

The Minister picked up the battered briefcase by the side of his chair and placed it on the glass table in front of him. He pressed back the clasps and the lid flicked up.

The two bankers stared down at the neatly packed rows of hundred-dollar bills. Every inch of the briefcase had been taken up. The chairman quickly estimated that it probably amounted to around five million dollars.

"I wonder, sir," said Ignatius, "how I go about opening an account with your bank?"

A la Carte

ARTHUR Hapgood was demobbed on November 3rd, 1946. Within a month he was back at his old workplace on the shop-floor of the Triumph factory on the outskirts of Coventry.

The five years spent in the Sherwood Foresters, four of them as a quartermaster seconded to a tank regiment, only underlined Arthur's likely post-war fate, despite having hoped to find more rewarding work once the war was over. However, on returning to England he quickly discovered that in a "land fit for heroes" jobs were not that easy to come by, and although he did not want to go back to the work he had done for five years before war had been declared, that of fitting wheels on cars, he reluctantly, after four weeks on the dole, went to see his former works' manager at Triumph.

"The job's yours if you want it, Arthur," the works' manager assured him.

"And the future?"

"The car's no longer a toy for the eccentric rich or even just a necessity for the businessman," the works' manager replied. "In fact," he continued, "management are preparing for the 'two-car family'."

"So they'll need even more wheels to be put on cars," said Arthur forlornly.

"That's the ticket."

Arthur signed on within the hour and it was only a matter of days before he was back into his old routine. After all, he often reminded his wife, it didn't take a degree in engineering to screw four knobs on to a wheel a hundred times a shift.

Arthur soon accepted the fact that he would have to settle for second best. However, second best was not what he planned for his son.

Mark had celebrated his fifth birthday before his father had even set eyes on him, but from the moment Arthur returned home he lavished everything he could on the boy.

Arthur was determined that Mark was not going to end up working on the shop-floor of a car factory for the rest of his life. He put in hours of overtime to earn enough money to ensure that the boy could have extra tuition in maths, general science and English. He felt well rewarded when the boy passed his eleven-plus and won a place at King Henry VIII Grammar School, and that pride did not falter when Mark went on to pass five O-levels and two years later added two A-levels.

Arthur tried not to show his disappointment when, on Mark's eighteenth birthday, the boy informed him that he did not want to go to university.

"What kind of career *are* you hoping to take up then, lad?" Arthur enquired.

"I've filled in an application form to join you on the shop-floor just as soon as I leave school."

"But why would you –"

"Why not? Most of my friends who're leaving this term have already been accepted by Triumph, and they can't wait to get started."

"You must be out of your mind."

"Come off it, Dad. The pay's good and you've shown that there's always plenty of extra money to be picked up with overtime. And I don't mind hard work."

"Do you think I spent all those years making sure you got a first-class education just to let you end up like me, putting wheels on cars for the rest of your life?" Arthur shouted.

"That's not the whole job and you know it, Dad."

"You go there over my dead body," said his father. "I don't care what your friends end up doing, I only care about you. You could be a solicitor, an accountant, an army officer, even a schoolmaster. Why should you want to end up at a car factory?"

"It's better paid than schoolmastering for a start," said Mark. "My French master once told me that he wasn't as well off as you."

"That's not the point, lad –"

"The point is, Dad, I can't be expected to spend the rest of my life doing a job I don't enjoy just to satisfy one of your fantasies."

"Well, I'm not going to allow you to waste the rest of your life," said Arthur, getting up from the breakfast table. "The first thing I'm going to do when I get in to work this morning is see that your application is turned down."

"That isn't fair, Dad. I have the right to –"

But his father had already left the room, and did not utter another word to the boy before leaving for the factory.

For over a week father and son didn't speak to each other. It was Mark's mother who was left to come up with the compromise. Mark could apply for any job that met with his father's approval and as long as he completed a year at that job he could, if he still wanted to, reapply to work at the factory. His father for his part would not then put any obstacle in his son's way.

Arthur nodded. Mark also reluctantly agreed to the solution.

"But only if you complete the full year," Arthur warned solemnly.

During those last days of the summer holiday Arthur came up with several suggestions for Mark to consider, but the boy showed no enthusiasm for any of them. Mark's mother became quite anxious that her son would end up with no job at all until, while helping her slice potatoes for dinner one night, Mark confided that he thought hotel management seemed the least unattractive proposition he had considered so far.

"At least you'd have a roof over your head and be regularly fed," his mother said.

"Bet they don't cook as well as you, Mum," said Mark as he placed the sliced potatoes on the top of the Lancashire hot-pot. "Still, it's only a year."

During the next month Mark attended several

interviews at hotels around the country without success. It was then that his father discovered that his old company sergeant was head porter at the Savoy: immediately Arthur started to pull a few strings.

"If the boy's any good," Arthur's old comrade-in-arms assured him over a pint, "he could end up as a head porter, even a hotel manager." Arthur seemed well satisfied, even though Mark was still assuring his friends that he would be joining them a year to the day.

On September 1st, 1959, Arthur and Mark Hapgood travelled together by bus to Coventry station. Arthur shook hands with the boy and promised him, "Your mother and I will make sure it's a special Christmas this year when they give you your first leave. And don't worry – you'll be in good hands with 'Sarge'. He'll teach you a thing or two. Just remember to keep your nose clean."

Mark said nothing and returned a thin smile as he boarded the train. "You'll never regret it . . ." were the last words Mark heard his father say as the train pulled out of the station.

Mark regretted it from the moment he set foot in the hotel.

As a junior porter he started his day at six in the morning and ended at six in the evening. He was entitled to a fifteen-minute mid-morning break, a forty-five-minute lunch break and another fifteen-minute break around mid-afternoon. After the first month had passed he could not recall when he had been granted all three breaks on the same day, and he quickly learned that there was no one to whom he could protest. His duties consisted of carrying guests' cases up to their rooms, then lugging them back down again the moment they wanted to leave. With an average of three hundred people staying in the hotel each night the process was endless. The pay turned out to be half what his friends were getting back home and as he had to hand over all his tips to the head porter, however much overtime Mark put in, he never saw an extra penny. On the only occasion he dared to mention it to the head porter he was met with the words, "Your time will come, lad."

It did not worry Mark that his uniform didn't fit or that his room was six foot by six foot and overlooked Charing Cross Station, or even that he didn't get a share of the tips; but it did worry him that there was nothing he could do to please the head porter – however clean he kept his nose.

Sergeant Crann, who considered the Savoy nothing more than an extension of his old platoon, didn't have a lot of time for young men under his command who hadn't done their national service.

"But I wasn't *eligible* to do national service," insisted Mark. "No one born after 1939 was called up."

"Don't make excuses, lad."

"It's not an excuse, Sarge. It's the truth."

"And don't call me 'Sarge'. I'm 'Sergeant Crann' to you, and don't you forget it."

"Yes, Sergeant Crann."

At the end of each day Mark would return to his little box-room with its small bed, small chair and tiny chest of drawers, and collapse exhausted. The only picture in the room – of the Laughing Cavalier

– was on the calendar that hung above Mark's bed. The date of September 1st, 1960, was circled in red to remind him when he would be allowed to re-join his friends at the factory back home. Each night before falling asleep he would cross out the offending day like a prisoner making scratch marks on a wall.

At Christmas Mark returned home for a four-day break, and when his mother saw the general state of the boy she tried to talk his father into allowing Mark to give up the job early, but Arthur remained implacable.

"We made an agreement. I can't be expected to get him a job at the factory if he isn't responsible enough to keep to his part of a bargain."

During the holiday Mark waited for his friends outside the factory gate until their shift had ended and listened to their stories of weekends spent watching football, drinking at the pub and dancing to the Everly Brothers. They all sympathised with his problem and looked forward to him joining them in September. "It's only a few more months," one of them reminded him cheerfully.

Far too quickly, Mark was on the journey back to London, where he continued unwillingly to hump cases up and down the hotel corridors for month after month.

Once the English rain had subsided the usual influx of American tourists began. Mark liked the Americans, who treated him as an equal and often tipped him a shilling when others would have given him only sixpence. But whatever the amount Mark received Sergeant Crann would still pocket it with the inevitable, "Your time will come, lad."

One such American for whom Mark ran around diligently every day during his fortnight's stay ended up presenting the boy with a ten-bob note as he left the front entrance of the hotel.

Mark said, "Thank you, sir," and turned round to see Sergeant Crann standing in his path.

"Hand it over," said Crann as soon as the American visitor was well out of earshot.

"I was going to the moment I saw you," said Mark, passing the note to his superior.

"Not thinking of pocketing what's rightfully mine, was you?"

"No, I wasn't," said Mark. "Though God knows I earned it."

"Your time will come, lad," said Sergeant Crann without much thought.

"Not while someone as mean as you is in charge," replied Mark sharply.

"What was that you said?" asked the head porter, veering round.

"You heard me the first time, Sarge."

The clip across the ear took Mark by surprise.

"You, lad, have just lost your job. Nobody, but nobody, talks to me like that." Sergeant Crann turned and set off smartly in the direction of the manager's office.

The hotel manager, Gerald Drummond, listened to the head porter's version of events before asking Mark to report to his office immediately. "You realise I have been left with no choice but to sack you," were his first words once the door was closed.

Mark looked up at the tall, elegant man in his long, black coat, white collar and black tie. "Am I allowed to tell you what actually happened, sir?" he asked.

Mr Drummond nodded, then listened without interruption as Mark gave his version of what had taken place that morning, and also disclosed the agreement he had entered into with his father. "Please let me complete my final ten weeks," Mark ended, "or my father will only say I haven't kept my end of our bargain."

"I haven't got another job vacant at the moment," protested the manager. "Unless you're willing to peel potatoes for ten weeks."

"Anything," said Mark.

"Then report to the kitchen at six tomorrow morning. I'll tell the third chef to expect you. Only if you think the head porter is a martinet just wait until you meet Jacques, our *maître chef de cuisine*. He won't clip your ear, he'll cut it off."

Mark didn't care. He felt confident that for just ten weeks he could face anything, and at five thirty the following morning he exchanged his dark blue uniform for a white top and blue and white check trousers before reporting for his new duties. To his surprise the kitchen took up almost the entire basement of the hotel, and was even more of a bustle than the lobby had been.

The third chef put him in the corner of the kitchen, next to a mountain of potatoes, a bowl of cold water and a sharp knife. Mark peeled through breakfast, lunch and dinner, and fell asleep on his bed that night without even enough energy left to cross a day off his calendar.

For the first week he never actually saw the fabled Jacques. With seventy people working in the kitchens Mark felt confident he could pass his whole period there without anyone being aware of him.

Each morning at six he would start peeling, then hand over the potatoes to a gangling youth called Terry who in turn would dice or cut them according to the third chef's instructions for the dish of the day. Monday sauté, Tuesday mashed, Wednesday French-fried, Thursday sliced, Friday roast, Saturday croquette . . . Mark quickly worked out a routine which kept him well ahead of Terry and therefore out of any trouble.

Having watched Terry do his job for over a week Mark felt sure he could have shown the young apprentice how to lighten his workload quite simply, but he decided to keep his mouth closed: opening it might only get him into more trouble, and he was certain the manager wouldn't give him a second chance.

Mark soon discovered that Terry always fell badly behind on Tuesday's shepherd's pie and Thursday's Lancashire hot-pot. From time to time the third chef would come across to complain and he would glance over at Mark to be sure that it wasn't him who was holding the process up. Mark made certain that he always had a spare tub of peeled potatoes by his side so that he escaped censure.

It was on the first Thursday morning in August (Lancashire hot-pot) that Terry sliced off the top of his forefinger. Blood spurted all over the sliced potatoes and on to the wooden table as the lad began yelling hysterically.

"Get him out of here!" Mark heard the *maître chef*

de cuisine bellow above the noise of the kitchen as he stormed towards them.

"And you," he said, pointing at Mark, "clean up mess and start slicing rest of potatoes. I 'ave eight hundred hungry customers still expecting to feed."

"Me?" said Mark in disbelief. "But –"

"Yes, you. You couldn't do worse job than idiot who calls himself trainee chef and cuts off finger." The chef marched away, leaving Mark to move reluctantly across to the table where Terry had been working. He felt disinclined to argue while the calendar was there to remind him that he was down to his last twenty-five days.

Mark set about a task he had carried out for his mother many times. The clean, neat cuts were delivered with a skill Terry would never learn to master. By the end of the day, although exhausted, Mark did not feel quite as tired as he had in the past.

At eleven that night the *maître chef de cuisine* threw off his hat and barged out of the swing doors, a sign to everyone else they could also leave the kitchen once everything that was their responsibility had been cleared up. A few seconds later the door swung back open and the chef burst in. He stared round the kitchen as everyone waited to see what he would do next. Having found what he was looking for, he headed straight for Mark.

"Oh, my God," thought Mark. "He's going to kill me."

"How is your name?" the chef demanded.

"Mark Hapgood, sir," he managed to splutter out.

"You waste on 'tatoes, Mark Hapgood," said the

chef. "You start on vegetables in morning. Report at seven. If that *crétin* with half finger ever returns, put him to peeling 'tatoes."

The chef turned on his heel even before Mark had the chance to reply. He dreaded the thought of having to spend three weeks in the middle of the kitchens, never once out of the *maître chef de cuisine*'s sight, but he accepted there was no alternative.

The next morning Mark arrived at six for fear of being late and spent an hour watching the fresh vegetables being unloaded from Covent Garden market. The hotel's supply manager checked every case carefully, rejecting several before he signed a chit to show the hotel had received over three thousand pounds' worth of vegetables. An average day, he assured Mark.

The *maître chef de cuisine* appeared a few minutes before seven thirty, checked the menus and told Mark to score the Brussels sprouts, trim the French beans and remove the coarse outer leaves of the cabbages.

"But I don't know how," Mark replied honestly. He could feel the other trainees in the kitchen edging away from him.

"Then I teach you," roared the chef. "Perhaps only thing you learn is if hope to be good chef, you able to do everyone's job in kitchen, even 'tato peeler's."

"But I'm hoping to be a . . ." Mark began and then thought better of it. The chef seemed not to have heard Mark as he took his place beside the new recruit. Everyone in the kitchen stared as the chef began to show Mark the basic skills of cutting, dicing and slicing.

"And remember other idiot's finger," the chef said on completing the lesson and passing the razor-sharp knife back to Mark. "Yours can be next."

Mark started gingerly dicing the carrots, then the Brussels sprouts, removing the outer layer before cutting a firm cross in the stalk. Next he moved on to trimming and slicing the beans. Once again he found it fairly easy to keep ahead of the chef's requirements.

At the end of each day, after the head chef had left, Mark stayed on to sharpen all his knives in preparation for the following morning, and would not leave his work area until it was spotless.

On the sixth day, after a curt nod from the chef, Mark realised he must be doing something half-right. By the following Saturday he felt he had mastered the simple skills of vegetable preparation and found himself becoming fascinated by what the chef himself was up to. Although Jacques rarely addressed anyone as he marched round the acre of kitchen except to grunt his approval or disapproval – the latter more commonly – Mark quickly learned to anticipate his needs. Within a short space of time he began to feel that he was part of a team – even though he was only too aware of being the novice recruit.

On the deputy chef's day off the following week Mark was allowed to arrange the cooked vegetables in their bowls and spent some time making each dish look attractive as well as edible. The chef not only noticed but actually muttered his greatest accolade – "*Bon.*"

During his last three weeks at the Savoy Mark

did not even look at the calendar above his bed.

One Thursday morning a message came down from the under-manager that Mark was to report to his office as soon as was convenient. Mark had quite forgotten that it was August 31st – his last day. He cut ten lemons into quarters, then finished preparing the forty plates of thinly sliced smoked salmon that would complete the first course for a wedding lunch. He looked with pride at his efforts before folding up his apron and leaving to collect his papers and final wage packet.

"Where you think you're going?" asked the chef, looking up.

"I'm off," said Mark. "Back to Coventry."

"See you Monday then. You deserve day off."

"No, I'm going home for good," said Mark.

The chef stopped checking the cuts of rare beef that would make up the second course of the wedding feast.

"Going?" he repeated as if he didn't understand the word.

"Yes. I've finished my year and now I'm off home to work."

"I hope you found first-class hotel," said the chef with genuine interest.

"I'm not going to work in a hotel."

"A restaurant, perhaps?"

"No, I'm going to get a job at Triumph."

The chef looked puzzled for a moment, unsure if it was his English or whether the boy was mocking him.

"What is – Triumph?"

"A place where they manufacture cars."

"You will manufacture cars?"

"Not a whole car, but I will put the wheels on."

"You put cars on wheels?" the chef said in disbelief.

"No," laughed Mark. "Wheels on cars."

The chef still looked uncertain.

"So you will be cooking for the car workers?"

"No. As I explained, I'm going to put the wheels on the cars," said Mark slowly, enunciating each word.

"That not possible."

"Oh yes it is," responded Mark. "And I've waited a whole year to prove it."

"If I offered you job as commis chef, you change mind?" asked the chef quietly.

"Why would you do that?"

"Because you 'ave talent in those fingers. In time I think you become chef, perhaps even good chef."

"No, thanks. I'm off to Coventry to join my mates."

The head chef shrugged. "*Tant pis*," he said, and without a second glance returned to the carcass of beef. He glanced over at the plates of smoked salmon. "A wasted talent," he added after the swing door had closed behind his potential protégé.

Mark locked his room, threw the calendar in the wastepaper basket and returned to the hotel to hand in his kitchen clothes to the housekeeper. The final action he took was to return his room key to the under-manager.

"Your wage packet, your cards and your PAYE. Oh, and the chef has phoned up to say he would be happy to give you a reference," said the under-manager. "Can't pretend that happens every day."

"Won't need that where I'm going," said Mark. "But thanks all the same."

He started off for the station at a brisk pace, his small battered suitcase swinging by his side, only to find that each step took a little longer. When he arrived at Euston he made his way to Platform 7 and began walking up and down, occasionally staring at the great clock above the booking hall. He watched first one train and then another pull out of the station bound for Coventry. He was aware of the station becoming dark as shadows filtered through the glass awning on to the public concourse. Suddenly he turned and walked off at an even brisker pace. If he hurried he could still be back in time to help chef prepare dinner that night.

Mark trained under Jacques le Renneu for five years. Vegetables were followed by sauces, fish by poultry, meats by pâtisserie. After eight years at the Savoy he was appointed second chef, and had learned so much from his mentor that regular patrons could no longer be sure when it was the *maître chef de cuisine*'s day off. Two years later Mark became a master chef, and when in 1971 Jacques was offered the opportunity to return to Paris and take over the kitchens of the George Cinq – an establishment that is to Paris what Harrods is to London – Jacques agreed, but only on condition that Mark accompanied him.

"It is wrong direction from Coventry," Jacques warned him, "and in any case they sure to offer you my job at the Savoy."

"I'd better come along otherwise those Frogs will never get a decent meal."

"Those Frogs," said Jacques, "will always know when it's my day off."

"Yes, and book in even greater numbers," suggested Mark, laughing.

It was not to be long before Parisians were flocking to the George Cinq, not to rest their weary heads but to relish the cooking of the two-chef team.

When Jacques celebrated his sixty-fifth birthday the great hotel did not have to look far to appoint his successor.

"The first Englishman ever to be *maître chef de cuisine* at the George Cinq," said Jacques, raising a glass of champagne at his farewell banquet. "Who would believe it? Of course, you will have to change your name to Marc to hold down such a position."

"Neither will ever happen," said Mark.

"Oh yes it will, because I 'ave recommended you."

"Then I shall turn it down."

"Going to put cars on wheels, *peut-être*?" asked Jacques mockingly.

"No, but I have found a little restaurant on the Left Bank. With my savings alone I can't quite afford the lease, but with your help . . ."

Chez Jacques opened on the rue du Plaisir on the Left Bank on May 1st, 1982, and it was not long before those customers who had taken the George Cinq for granted transferred their allegiance.

Mark's reputation spread as the two chefs pioneered "nouvelle cuisine", and soon the only way anyone could be guaranteed a table at the restaurant in under three weeks was to be a film star or a Cabinet Minister.

The day Michelin gave Chez Jacques their third

star Mark, with Jacques's blessing, decided to open a second restaurant. The press and customers then quarrelled amongst themselves as to which was the finer establishment. The booking sheets showed clearly the public felt there was no difference.

When in October 1986 Jacques died, at the age of seventy-one, the restaurant critics wrote confidently that standards were bound to fall. A year later the same journalists had to admit that one of the five great chefs of France had come from a town in the British Midlands they could not even pronounce.

Jacques's death only made Mark yearn more for his homeland, and when he read in the *Daily Telegraph* of a new development to be built in Covent Garden he called the site agent to ask for more details.

Mark's third restaurant was opened in the heart of London on February 11th, 1987.

Over the years Mark Hapgood often travelled back to Coventry to see his parents. His father had retired long since but Mark was still unable to persuade either parent to take the trip to Paris and sample his culinary efforts. But now he had opened in the country's capital he hoped to tempt them.

"We don't need to go up to London," said his mother, laying the table. "You always cook for us whenever you come home, and we read of your successes in the papers. In any case, your father isn't so good on his legs nowadays."

"What do you call this, son?" his father asked a few minutes later as noisette of lamb surrounded by baby carrots was placed in front of him.

"Nouvelle cuisine."

"And people pay good money for it?"

Mark laughed and the following day prepared his father's favourite Lancashire hot-pot.

"Now that's a real meal," said Arthur after his third helping. "And I'll tell you something for nothing, lad. You cook it almost as well as your mother."

A year later Michelin announced the restaurants throughout the world that had been awarded their coveted third star. *The Times* let its readers know on its front page that Chez Jacques was the first English restaurant ever to be so honoured.

To celebrate the award Mark's parents finally agreed to make the journey down to London, though not until Mark had sent a telegram saying he was reconsidering that job at British Leyland. He sent a car to fetch his parents and had them installed in a suite at the Savoy. That evening he reserved the most popular table at Chez Jacques in their name.

Vegetable soup followed by steak and kidney pie with a plate of bread and butter pudding to end on were not the table d'hôte that night, but they were served for the special guests on Table 17.

Under the influence of the finest wine, Arthur was soon chatting happily to anyone who would listen and couldn't resist reminding the head waiter that it was his son who owned the restaurant.

"Don't be silly, Arthur," said his wife. "He already knows that."

"Nice couple, your parents," the head waiter confided to his boss after he had served them with their coffee and supplied Arthur with a cigar.

"What did your old man do before he retired? Banker, lawyer, schoolmaster?"

"Oh no, nothing like that," said Mark quietly. "He spent the whole of his working life putting wheels on cars."

"But why would he waste his time doing that?" asked the waiter incredulously.

"Because he wasn't lucky enough to have a father like mine," Mark replied.

Not
The Real Thing

GERALD Haskins and Walter Ramsbottom had been eating cornflakes for over a year.

"I'll swap you my MC and DSO for your VC," said Walter, on the way to school one morning.

"Never," said Gerald. "In any case, it takes ten packet tops to get a VC and you only need two for an MC or a DSO."

Gerald went on collecting packet tops until he had every medal displayed on the back of the packet.

Walter never got the VC.

Angela Bradbury thought they were both silly.

"They're only replicas," she continually reminded them, "not the real thing, and *I* am only interested in the real thing," she told them haughtily.

Neither Gerald nor Walter cared for Angela's opinion at the time, both boys still being more interested in medals than the views of the opposite sex.

Kellogg's offer of free medals ended on January

1st, 1950, just at the time when Gerald had managed to complete the set.

Walter gave up eating cornflakes.

Children of the Fifties were then given the opportunity to discover the world of Meccano. Meccano demanded eating even more cornflakes and within a year Gerald had collected a large enough set to build bridges, pontoons, cranes and even an office block.

Gerald's family nobly went on munching cornflakes, but when he told them he wanted to build a whole town – Kellogg's positively final offer – it took nearly all his friends in the fifth form at Hull Grammar School to assist him in consuming enough breakfast cereal to complete his ambition.

Walter Ramsbottom refused to be of assistance.

Angela Bradbury's help was never sought.

All three continued on their separate ways.

Two years later, when Gerald Haskins won a place at Durham University, no one was surprised that he chose to read engineering and listed as his main hobby collecting medals.

Walter Ramsbottom joined his father in the family jewellery business and started courting Angela Bradbury.

It was during the spring holiday in Gerald's second year at Durham that he came across Walter and Angela again. They were sitting in the same row at a Bach quintet concert in Hull Town Hall. Walter told him in the interval that they had just become engaged but had not yet settled on a date for the wedding.

Gerald hadn't seen Angela for over a year but

this time he did listen to her opinions, because like Walter he fell in love with her.

He replaced eating cornflakes with continually inviting Angela out to dinner in an effort to win her away from his old rival.

Gerald notched up another victory when Angela returned her engagement ring to Walter a few days before Christmas.

Walter spread it around that Gerald only wanted to marry Angela because her father was chairman of the Hull City Amenities Committee and he was hoping to get a job with the council after he'd taken his degree at Durham. When the invitations for the wedding were sent out, Walter was not on the guest list.

Mr and Mrs Haskins travelled to Multavia for their honeymoon, partly because they couldn't afford Nice and didn't want to go to Cleethorpes. In any case, the local travel agent was making a special offer for those considering a visit to the tiny kingdom that was sandwiched between Austria and Czechoslovakia.

When the newly married couple arrived at their hotel in Teske, the capital, they discovered why the terms had been so reasonable.

Multavia was, in 1959, going through an identity crisis as it attempted to adjust to yet another treaty drawn up by a Dutch lawyer in Geneva, written in French, but with the Russians and Americans in mind. However, thanks to King Alfons III, their shrewd and popular monarch, the kingdom continued to enjoy uninterrupted grants from the West and non-disruptive visits from the East.

The capital of Multavia, the Haskins were quickly to discover, had an average temperature of 92°F in June, no rainfall and the remains of a sewerage system that had been indiscriminately bombed by both sides between 1939 and 1944. Angela actually found herself holding her nose as she walked through the cobbled streets. The People's Hotel claimed to have forty-five rooms, but what the brochure did not point out was that only three of them had bathrooms and none of those had bath plugs. Then there was the food, or lack of it; for the first time in his life Gerald lost weight.

The honeymoon couple were also to discover that Multavia boasted no monuments, art galleries, theatres or opera houses worthy of the name and the outlying country was flatter and less interesting than the fens of Cambridgeshire. The kingdom had no coastline and the only river, the Plotz, flowed from Germany and on into Russia, thus ensuring that none of the locals trusted it.

By the end of their honeymoon the Haskins were only too pleased to find that Multavia did not boast a national airline. BOAC got them home safely, and that would have been the end of Gerald's experience of Multavia had it not been for those sewers – or the lack of them.

Once the Haskins had returned to Hull, Gerald took up his appointment as an assistant in the engineering department of the city council. His first job was as a third engineer with special responsibility for the city's sewerage. Most ambitious young men would have treated such an appointment as nothing more than a step on life's ladder. Gerald however did not. He quickly made contact with all the leading sewerage companies, their advisers as well as his opposite numbers throughout the county.

Two years later he was able to put in front of his father-in-law's committee a paper showing how the council could save a considerable amount of the ratepayers' money by redeveloping its sewerage system.

The committee were impressed and decided to carry out Mr Haskins's recommendation, and at the same time appointed him second engineer.

That was the first occasion Walter Ramsbottom stood for the council; he wasn't elected.

When, three years later, the network of little tunnels and waterways had been completed, Gerald's diligence was rewarded by his appointment as deputy borough engineer. In the same year his father-in-law became Mayor and Walter Ramsbottom became a councillor.

Councils up and down the country were now acknowledging Gerald as a man whose opinion should be sought if they had any anxieties about their sewerage system. This provoked an irreverent round of jokes at every Rotary Club dinner Gerald attended, but they nevertheless still hailed him as the leading authority in his field, or drain.

When in 1966 the Borough of Halifax considered putting out to tender the building of a new sewerage system they first consulted Gerald Haskins – Yorkshire being the one place on earth where a prophet is with honour in his own country.

After spending a day in Halifax with the town council's senior engineer and realising how much had to be spent on the new system, Gerald remarked to his wife, not for the first time, "Where there's muck there's brass." But it was Angela who was shrewd enough to work out just how much of that brass her husband could get hold of with the minimum of risk. During the next few days Gerald considered his wife's proposition and when he returned to Halifax the following week it was not to visit the council chambers but the Midland Bank. Gerald did not select the Midland by chance; the manager of the bank was also chairman of the planning committee on the Halifax borough council.

A deal that suited both sides was struck between the two Yorkshiremen, and with the bank's blessing Gerald resigned his position as deputy borough engineer and formed a private company. When he presented his tender, in competition with several large organisations from London, no one was surprised that Haskins of Hull was selected unanimously by the planning committee to carry out the job.

Three years later Halifax had a fine new sewerage system and the Midland Bank was delighted to be holding Haskins of Hull's company account.

Over the next fifteen years Chester, Runcorn, Huddersfield, Darlington, Macclesfield and York were jointly and severally grateful for the services rendered to them by Gerald Haskins, of Haskins & Co plc.

Haskins & Co (International) plc then began contract work in Dubai, Lagos and Rio de Janeiro. In 1983 Gerald received the Queen's Award for Industry from a grateful government, and a year later he was made a Commander of the British Empire by a grateful monarch.

The investiture took place at Buckingham Palace in the same year as King Alfons III of Multavia died and was succeeded by his son King Alfons IV. The newly crowned King decided something had finally to be done about the drainage problems of Teske. It had been his father's dying wish that his people should not go on suffering those unseemly smells, and King Alfons IV did not intend to bequeath the problem to *his* son.

After much begging and borrowing from the West, and much visiting and talking with the East, the newly anointed monarch decided to invite tenders for a new sewerage system in the kingdom's capital.

The tender document supplying several pages of details and listing the problems facing any engineer who wished to tackle the problem arrived with a thud on most of the boardroom tables of the world's major engineering companies. Once the paperwork had been seriously scrutinised and the realistic opportunity for a profit considered, King Alfons IV received only a few replies. Nevertheless, the King was able to sit up all night considering the merits of the three interested companies that had been short-listed. Kings are also human, and when Alfons discovered that Gerald had chosen Multavia for his honeymoon some twenty-five years before it tipped the balance. By the time Alfons IV fell asleep that morning he had decided to accept Haskins & Co (International) plc's tender.

And thus Gerald Haskins made his second visit to Multavia, this time accompanied by a site manager, three draughtsmen and eleven engineers. Gerald had a private audience with the King and assured him the job would be completed on time and for the price specified. He also told the King how much he was enjoying his second visit to his country. However, when he returned to England he assured his wife that there was still little in Multavia that could be described as entertainment before or after the hour of seven.

A few years later and after some considerable haggling over the increase in the cost of materials, Teske ended up with one of the finest sewerage systems in Central Europe. The King was delighted – although he continued to grumble about how Haskins & Co had over-run the original contract price. The words "contingency payment" had to be explained to the monarch several times, who realised that the extra two hundred and forty thousand pounds would in turn have to be explained to the East and "borrowed" from the West. After many veiled threats and "without prejudice" solicitors' letters, Haskins & Co received the final payment but not until the King had been given a further grant from the British government, a payment which involved the Midland Bank, Sloane Street, transferring a sum of money to the Midland Bank, High Street, Hull, without Multavia ever getting their hands on it. This was after all, Gerald explained to his wife, how most overseas aid was distributed.

Thus the story of Gerald Haskins and the drainage problems of Teske might have ended, had not the

British Foreign Secretary decided to pay a visit to the kingdom of Multavia.

The original purpose of the Foreign Secretary's European trip was to take in Warsaw and Prague, in order to see how *glasnost* and *perestroika* were working in those countries. But when the Foreign Office discovered how much aid had been allocated to Multavia and after they explained to their minister its role as a buffer state, the Foreign Secretary decided to accept King Alfons's long-standing invitation to visit the tiny kingdom. Such excursions to smaller countries by British Foreign Secretaries usually take place in airport lounges, a habit the British picked up from Henry Kissinger, and later Comrade Gorbachev; but not on this occasion. It was felt Multavia warranted a full day.

As the hotels had improved only slightly since the time of Gerald's honeymoon, the Foreign Secretary was invited to lodge at the palace. He was asked by the King to undertake only two official engagements during his brief stay: the opening of the capital's new sewerage system, and a formal banquet.

Once the Foreign Secretary had agreed to these requests the King invited Gerald and his wife to be present at the opening ceremony – at their own expense. When the day of the opening came the Foreign Secretary delivered the appropriate speech for the occasion. He first praised Gerald Haskins on a remarkable piece of work in the great tradition of British engineering, then commended Multavia for her shrewd common sense in awarding the contract to a British company in the first place. The Foreign Secretary omitted to mention the fact that the

British government had ended up underwriting the entire project. Gerald, however, was touched by the minister's words and said as much to the Foreign Secretary after the latter had pulled the lever that opened the first sluice gate.

That evening in the palace there was a banquet for over three hundred guests, including the ambassadorial corps and several leading British businessmen. There followed the usual interminable speeches about "historic links", Multavia's role in Anglo-Soviet affairs and the "special relationship" with Britain's own royal family.

The highlight of the evening, however, came after the speeches when the King made two investitures. The first was the award of the Order of the Peacock (Second Class) to the Foreign Secretary. "The highest award a commoner can receive," the King explained to the assembled audience, "as the Order of the Peacock (First Class) is reserved for royalty and heads of state."

The King then announced a second investiture. The Order of the Peacock (Third Class) was to be awarded to Gerald Haskins, CBE, for his work on the drainage system of Teske. Gerald was surprised and delighted as he was conducted from his place on the top table to join the King, who leaned forward to put a large gold chain encrusted with gems of various colours and sizes over his visitor's head. Gerald took two respectful paces backwards and bowed low, as the Foreign Secretary looked up from his seat and smiled encouragingly at him.

Gerald was the last foreign guest to leave the banquet that night. Angela, who had left on her own over two hours before, had already fallen asleep by the time Gerald returned to their hotel room. He placed the chain on the bed, undressed, put on his pyjamas, checked his wife was still asleep and then placed the chain back over his head to rest on his shoulders.

Gerald stood and looked at himself in the bathroom mirror for several minutes. He could not wait to return home.

The moment Gerald got back to Hull he dictated a letter to the Foreign Office. He requested permission to be allowed to wear his new award on those occasions when it stipulated on the bottom right-hand corner of invitation cards that decorations and medals should be worn. The Foreign Office duly referred the matter to the Palace where the Queen, a distant cousin of King Alfons IV, agreed to the request.

The next official occasion at which Gerald was given the opportunity to sport the Order of the Peacock was the Mayor-making ceremony held in the chamber of Hull's City Hall, which was to be preceded by dinner at the Guildhall.

Gerald returned especially from Lagos for the occasion and even before changing into his dinner jacket couldn't resist a glance at the Order of the Peacock (Third Class). He opened the box that held his prize possession and stared down in disbelief: the gold had become tarnished and one of the stones looked as if it were coming loose. Mrs Haskins stopped dressing in order to steal a glance at the order. "It's not gold," she declared with a simplicity that would have stopped the IMF in their tracks.

Gerald offered no comment and quickly fixed the

loose stone back in place with Araldite but he had to admit to himself that the craftmanship didn't bear careful scrutiny. Neither of them mentioned the subject again on their journey to Hull's City Hall.

Some of the guests during the Mayor's dinner that night at the Guildhall enquired after the history of the Order of the Peacock (Third Class), and although it gave Gerald some considerable satisfaction to explain how he had come by the distinction and indeed the Queen's permission to wear it on official occasions, he felt one or two of his colleagues had been less than awed by the tarnished peacock. Gerald also considered it was somewhat unfortunate that they had ended up on the same table as Walter Ramsbottom, now the Deputy Mayor.

"I suppose it would be hard to put a true value on it," said Walter, staring disdainfully at the chain.

"It certainly would," said Gerald firmly.

"I didn't mean a monetary value," said the jeweller with a smirk. "That would be only too easy to ascertain. I meant a sentimental value, of course."

"Of course," said Gerald. "And are you expecting to be the Mayor next year?" he asked, trying to change the subject.

"It is the tradition," said Walter, "that the Deputy succeeds the Mayor if he doesn't do a second year. And be assured, Gerald, that I shall see to it that you are placed on the top table for that occasion." Walter paused. "The Mayor's chain, you know, is fourteen-carat gold."

Gerald left the banquet early that evening determined to do something about the Order of the

Peacock before it was Walter's turn to be Mayor.

None of Gerald's friends would have described him as an extravagant man and even his wife was surprised at the whim of vanity that was to follow. At nine o'clock the next morning Gerald rang his office to say he would not be in to work that day. He then travelled by train to London to visit Bond Street in general and a famed jeweller in particular.

The door of the Bond Street shop was opened for Gerald by a sergeant from the Corps of Commissionaires. Once he had stepped inside Gerald explained his problem to the tall, thin gentleman in a black suit who had come forward to welcome him. He was then led to a circular glass counter in the middle of the shop floor.

"Our Mr Pullinger will be with you in a moment," he was assured. Moments later Asprey's fine-gems expert arrived and happily agreed to Gerald's request to value the Order of the Peacock (Third Class). Mr Pullinger placed the chain on a black velvet cushion before closely studying the stones through a small eye glass.

After a cursory glance he frowned with the disappointment of a man who has won third prize at a shooting range on Blackpool pier.

"So what's it worth?" asked Gerald bluntly after several minutes had elapsed.

"Hard to put a value on something so intricately" – Pullinger hesitated – "unusual."

"The stones are glass and the gold's brass, that's what you're trying to say, isn't it, lad?"

Mr Pullinger gave a look that indicated that he could not have put it more succinctly himself.

"You might possibly be able to get a few hundred pounds from someone who collects such objects, but . . ."

"Oh, no," said Gerald, quite offended. "I have no interest in selling it. My purpose in coming up to London was to find out if you can *copy* it."

"Copy it?" said the expert in disbelief.

"Aye," said Gerald. "First, I want every stone to be the correct gem according to its colour. Second, I expect a setting that would impress a duchess. And third, I require the finest craftsman put to work on it in nothing less than eighteen-carat gold."

The expert from Asprey's, despite years of dealing with Arab clients, was unable to conceal his surprise.

"It would not be cheap," he uttered *sotto voce*: the word "cheap" was one of which Asprey's clearly disapproved.

"I never doubted that for one moment," said Gerald. "But you must understand that this is a once-in-a-lifetime honour for me. Now when could I hope to have an estimate?"

"A month, six weeks at the most," replied the expert.

Gerald left the plush carpet of Asprey's for the sewers of Nigeria. When a little over a month later he flew back to London, he travelled in to the West End for his second meeting with Mr Pullinger.

The jeweller had not forgotten Gerald Haskins and his strange request, and he quickly produced from his order book a neatly folded piece of paper. Gerald unfolded it and read the tender slowly. Requirement for customer's request: twelve diamonds, seven amethysts, three rubies and a sapphire, all to be of the most perfect colour and of the highest quality. A peacock to be sculpted in ivory and painted by a craftsman. The entire chain then to be moulded in the finest eighteen-carat gold. The bottom line read: "Two hundred and eleven thousand pounds – exclusive of VAT."

Gerald, who would have thought nothing of haggling over an estimate of a few thousand pounds for roofing material or the hire of heavy equipment, or even a schedule of payments, simply asked, "When will I be able to collect it?"

"One could not be certain how long it might take to put together such a fine piece," said Mr Pullinger. "Finding stones of a perfect match and colour will, I fear, take a little time." He paused. "I am also hoping that our senior craftsman will be free to work on this particular commission. He has been rather taken up lately with gifts for the Queen's forthcoming visit to Saudi Arabia so I don't think it could be ready before the end of March."

Well in time for next year's Mayor's banquet, thought Gerald. Councillor Ramsbottom would not be able to mock him this time. Fourteen-carat gold, had he said?

Lagos and Rio de Janeiro both had their sewers down and running long before Gerald was able to return to Asprey's. And he only set his eyes on the unique prize a few weeks before Mayor-making day.

When Mr Pullinger first showed his client the finished work the Yorkshireman gasped with delight. The Order was so magnificent that Gerald found it necessary to purchase a string of pearls from Asprey's to ensure a silent wife.

On his return to Hull he waited until after dinner to open the green leather box from Asprey's and surprise her with the new Order. "Fit for a monarch, lass," he assured his wife but Angela seemed preoccupied with her pearls.

After Angela had left to wash up, her husband continued to stare for some time at the beautiful jewels so expertly crafted and superbly cut before he finally closed the box. The next morning he reluctantly took the piece round to the bank and explained that it must be kept safely locked in the vaults as he would only be requiring to take it out once, perhaps twice, a year. He couldn't resist showing the object of his delight to the bank manager, Mr Sedgley.

"You'll be wearing it for Mayor-making day, no doubt?" Mr Sedgley enquired.

"If I'm invited," said Gerald.

"Oh, I feel sure Ramsbottom will want all his old friends to witness the ceremony. Especially you, I suspect," he added without explanation.

Gerald read the news item in the Court Circular of *The Times* to his wife over breakfast: "It has been announced from Buckingham Palace that King Alfons IV of Multavia will make a state visit to Britain between April 7th and 11th."

"I wonder if we will have an opportunity to meet the King again," said Angela.

Gerald offered no opinion.

In fact Mr and Mrs Gerald Haskins received two

invitations connected with King Alfons's official visit, one to dine with the King at Claridge's – Multavia's London Embassy not being large enough to cater for such an occasion – and the second arriving a day later by special delivery from Buckingham Palace.

Gerald was delighted. The Peacock, it seemed, was going to get three outings in one month, as their visit to the Palace was ten days before Walter Ramsbottom would be installed as Mayor.

The state dinner at Claridge's was memorable and although there were several hundred other guests Gerald still managed to catch a moment with his host, King Alfons IV who, he found to his pleasure, could not take his eyes off the Order of the Peacock (Third Class).

The trip to Buckingham Palace a week later was Gerald and Angela's second, following Gerald's investiture in 1984 as a Commander of the British Empire. It took Gerald almost as long to dress for the state occasion as it did his wife. He took some time fiddling with his collar to be sure that his CBE could be seen to its full advantage while the Order of the Peacock still rested squarely on his shoulders. Gerald had asked his tailor to sew little loops into his tailcoat so that the Order did not have to be continually readjusted.

When the Haskins arrived at Buckingham Palace they followed a throng of bemedalled men and tiara'd ladies through to the state dining room where a footman handed out seating cards to each of the guests. Gerald unfolded his to find an arrow pointing to his name. He took his wife by the arm and guided her to their places.

He noticed that Angela's head kept turning whenever she saw a tiara.

Although they were seated some distance away from Her Majesty at an offshoot of the main table, there was still a minor royal on Gerald's left and the Minister of Agriculture on his right. He was more than satisfied. In fact the whole evening went far too quickly, and Gerald was already beginning to feel that Mayor-making day would be something of an anti-climax. Nevertheless, Gerald imagined a scene where Councillor Ramsbottom was admiring the Order of the Peacock (Third Class), while he was telling him about the dinner at the Palace.

After two loyal toasts and two national anthems the Queen rose to her feet. She spoke warmly of Multavia as she addressed her three hundred guests, and affectionately of her distant cousin the King. Her Majesty added that she hoped to visit his kingdom at some time in the near future. This was greeted with considerable applause. She then concluded her speech by saying it was her intention to make two investitures.

The Queen created King Alfons IV a Knight Commander of the Royal Victorian Order (KCVO), and then Multavia's Ambassador to the Court of St James a Commander of the same order (CVO), both being personal orders of the monarch. A box of royal blue was opened by the Court Chamberlain and the awards placed over the recipients' shoulders. As soon as the Queen had completed her formal duties, King Alfons rose to make his reply.

"Your Majesty," he continued after the usual formalities and thanks had been completed. "I also would like to make two awards. The first is to an Englishman who has given great service to my country through his expertise and diligence" – the King then glanced in Gerald's direction – "a man," he continued, "who completed a feat of sanitary engineering that any nation on earth could be proud of and indeed, Your Majesty, it was opened by your own Foreign Secretary. We in the capital of Teske will remain in his debt for generations to come. We therefore bestow on Mr Gerald Haskins, CBE, the Order of the Peacock (Second Class)."

Gerald couldn't believe his ears.

Tumultuous applause greeted a surprised Gerald as he made his way up towards their Majesties. He came to a standstill behind the throned chairs somewhere between the Queen of England and the King of Multavia. The King smiled at the new recipient of the Order of the Peacock (Second Class) as the two men shook hands. But before bestowing the new honour upon him, King Alfons leaned forward and with some difficulty removed from Gerald's shoulders his Order of the Peacock (Third Class).

"You won't be needing this any longer," the King whispered in Gerald's ear.

Gerald watched in horror as his prize possession disappeared into a red leather box held open by the King's private secretary, who stood poised behind his sovereign. Gerald continued to stare at the private secretary, who was either a diplomat of the highest order or had not been privy to the King's plan, for his face showed no sign of anything untoward. Once Gerald's magnificent prize had been safely removed, the box snapped closed like a safe of which Gerald had not been told the combination.

Gerald wanted to protest, but remained speechless.

King Alfons then removed from another box the Order of the Peacock (Second Class) and placed it over Gerald's shoulders. Gerald, staring at the indifferent coloured glass stones, hesitated for a few moments before stumbling a pace back, bowing, and then returning to his place in the great dining room. He did not hear the waves of applause that accompanied him; his only thought was how he could possibly retrieve his lost chain immediately the speeches were over. He slumped down in the chair next to his wife.

"And now," continued the King, "I wish to present a decoration that has not been bestowed on anyone since my late father's death. The Order of the Peacock (First Class), which it gives me special delight to bestow on Her Majesty Queen Elizabeth II."

The Queen rose from her place as the King's private secretary once again stepped forward. In his hands was held the same red leather case that had snapped shut so firmly on Gerald's unique possession. The case was re-opened and the King removed the magnificent Order from the box and placed it on the shoulders of the Queen. The jewels sparkled in the candlelight and the guests gasped at the sheer magnificence of the piece.

Gerald was the only person in the room who knew its true value.

"Well, you always said it was fit for a monarch," his wife remarked as she touched her string of pearls.

"Aye," said Gerald. "But what's Ramsbottom going to say when he sees this?" he added sadly, fingering the Order of the Peacock (Second Class). "He'll know it's not the real thing."

"I don't see it matters that much," said Angela.

"What do you mean, lass?" asked Gerald. "I'll be the laughing stock of Hull on Mayor-making day."

"You should start reading the evening papers, Gerald, and stop looking in mirrors and then you'd know Walter isn't going to be Mayor this year."

"Not going to be Mayor?" repeated Gerald.

"No. The present Mayor has opted to do a second term so Walter won't be Mayor until next year."

"Is that right?" said Gerald with a smile.

"And if you're thinking what I think you're thinking, Gerald Haskins, this time it's going to cost you a tiara."

Just Good Friends

I woke up before him feeling slightly randy but I knew there was nothing I could do about it.

I blinked and my eyes immediately accustomed themselves to the half light. I raised my head and gazed at the large expanse of motionless white flesh lying next to me. If only he took as much exercise as I did he wouldn't have that spare tyre, I thought unsympathetically.

Roger stirred restlessly and even turned over to face me, but I knew he would not be fully awake until the alarm on his side of the bed started ringing. I pondered for a moment whether I could go back to sleep again or should get up and find myself some breakfast before he woke. In the end I settled for just lying still on my side day-dreaming, but making sure I didn't disturb him. When he did eventually open his eyes I planned to pretend I was still asleep – that way he would end up getting breakfast for me. I began to go over the things that needed to be done after he had left for the office. As long as I was at home ready to greet him when he returned from work, he didn't seem to mind what I got up to during the day.

A gentle rumble emanated from his side of the bed. Roger's snoring never disturbed me. My affection for him was unbounded, and I only wished I could find the words to let him know. In truth, he was the first man I had really appreciated. As I gazed at his unshaven face I was reminded that it hadn't been his looks which had attracted me in the pub that night.

I had first come across Roger in the Cat and Whistle, a public house situated on the corner of Mafeking Road. You might say it was our local. He used to come in around eight, order a pint of mild and take it to a small table in the corner of the room just beyond the dartboard. Mostly he would sit alone, watching the darts being thrown towards double top but more often settling in one or five, if they managed to land on the board at all. He never played the game himself, and I often wondered, from my vantage point behind the bar, if he were fearful of relinquishing his favourite seat or just had no interest in the sport.

Then things suddenly changed for Roger – for the better, was no doubt how he saw it – when one evening in early spring a blonde named Madeleine, wearing an imitation fur coat and drinking double gin and its, perched on the stool beside him. I had never seen her in the pub before but she was obviously known locally, and loose bar talk led me to believe it couldn't last. You see, word was about that she was looking for someone whose horizons stretched beyond the Cat and Whistle.

In fact the affair – if that's what it ever came to –

lasted for only twenty days. I know because I counted every one of them. Then one night voices were raised and heads turned as she left the small stool just as suddenly as she had come. His tired eyes watched her walk to a vacant place at the corner of the bar, but he didn't show any surprise at her departure and made no attempt to pursue her.

Her exit was my cue to enter. I almost leapt from behind the bar and, moving as quickly as dignity allowed, was seconds later sitting on the vacant stool beside him. He didn't comment and certainly made no attempt to offer me a drink, but the one glance he shot in my direction did not suggest he found me an unacceptable replacement. I looked around to see if anyone else had plans to usurp my position. The men standing round the dartboard didn't seem to care. Treble seventeen, twelve and a five kept them more than occupied. I glanced towards the bar to check if the boss had noticed my absence, but he was busy taking orders. I saw Madeleine was already sipping a glass of champagne from the pub's only bottle, purchased by a stranger whose stylish double-breasted blazer and striped bow tie convinced me she wouldn't be bothering with Roger any longer. She looked well set for at least another twenty days.

I looked up at Roger – I had known his name for some time, although I had never addressed him as such and I couldn't be sure that he was aware of mine. I began to flutter my eyelashes in a rather exaggerated way. I felt a little stupid but at least it elicited a gentle smile. He leaned over and touched my cheek, his hands surprisingly gentle. Neither of us felt the need to speak. We were both lonely and it seemed unnecessary to explain why. We sat in silence, he occasionally sipping his beer, I from time to time rearranging my legs, while a few feet from us the darts pursued their undetermined course.

When the publican cried, "Last orders," Roger downed the remains of his beer while the dart players completed what had to be their final game.

No one commented when we left together and I was surprised that Roger made no protest as I accompanied him back to his little semi-detached. I already knew exactly where he lived because I had seen him on several occasions standing at the bus queue in Dobson Street in a silent line of reluctant morning passengers. Once I even positioned myself on a nearby wall in order to study his features more carefully. It was an anonymous, almost commonplace face but he had the warmest eyes and the kindest smile I had observed in any man.

My only anxiety was that he didn't seem aware of my existence, just constantly preoccupied, his eyes each evening and his thoughts each morning only for Madeleine. How I envied that girl. She had everything I wanted – except a decent fur coat, the only thing my mother had left me. In truth, I have no right to be catty about Madeleine, as her past couldn't have been more murky than mine.

All that had taken place well over a year ago and, to prove my total devotion to Roger, I have never entered the Cat and Whistle since. He seemed to have forgotten Madeleine because he never once spoke of her in front of me. An unusual man, he didn't question me about any of my past relationships either.

Perhaps he should have. I would have liked him to know the truth about my life before we'd met, though it all seems irrelevant now. You see, I had been the youngest in a family of four so I always came last in line. I had never known my father, and I arrived home one night to discover that my mother had run off with another man. Tracy, one of my sisters, warned me not to expect her back. She turned out to be right, for I have never seen my mother since that day. It's awful to have to admit, if only to oneself, that one's mother is a tramp.

Now an orphan, I began to drift, often trying to stay one step ahead of the law – not so easy when you haven't always got somewhere to put your head down. I can't even recall how I ended up with Derek – if that was his real name. Derek, whose dark sensual looks would have attracted any susceptible female, told me that he had been on a merchant steamer for the past three years. When he made love to me I was ready to believe anything. I explained to him that all I wanted was a warm home, regular food and perhaps in time a family of my own. He ensured that one of my wishes was fulfilled, because a few weeks after he left me I ended up with twins, two girls. Derek never set eyes on them: he had returned to sea even before I could tell him I was pregnant. He hadn't needed to promise me the earth; he was so good-looking he must have known I would have been his just for a night on the tiles.

I tried to bring up the girls decently, but the authorities caught up with me this time and I lost them both. I wonder where they are now? God knows. I only hope they've ended up in a good home. At least they inherited Derek's irresistible looks, which can only help them through life. It's just one more thing Roger will never know about. His unquestioning trust only makes me feel more guilty, and now I never seem able to find a way of letting him know the truth.

After Derek had gone back to sea I was on my own for almost a year before getting part-time work at the Cat and Whistle. The publican was so mean that he wouldn't have even provided food and drink for me, if I hadn't kept to my part of the bargain.

Roger used to come in about once, perhaps twice a week before he met the blonde with the shabby fur coat. After that it was every night until she upped and left him.

I knew he was perfect for me the first time I heard him order a pint of mild. A pint of mild – I can't think of a better description of Roger. In those early days the barmaids used to flirt openly with him, but he didn't show any interest. Until Madeleine latched on to him I wasn't even sure that it was women he preferred. Perhaps in the end it was my androgynous looks that appealed to him.

I think I must have been the only one in that pub who was looking for something more permanent.

And so Roger allowed me to spend the night with him. I remember that he slipped into the bathroom to undress while I rested on what I assumed would be my side of the bed. Since that night he has never once asked me to leave, let alone tried to kick me out. It's an easy-going relationship. I've never known him raise his voice or scold me unfairly. Forgive the cliché, but for once I have fallen on my feet.

Brr. Brr. Brr. That damned alarm. I wished I could have buried it. The noise would go on and on until at last Roger decided to stir himself. I once tried to stretch across him and put a stop to its infernal ringing, only ending up knocking the contraption on to the floor, which annoyed him even more than the ringing. Never again, I concluded. Eventually a long arm emerged from under the blanket and a palm dropped on to the top of the clock and the awful din subsided. I'm a light sleeper – the slightest movement stirs me. If only he had asked me I could have woken him far more gently each morning. After all, my methods are every bit as reliable as any man-made contraption.

Half awake, Roger gave me a brief cuddle before kneading my back, always guaranteed to elicit a smile. Then he yawned, stretched and declared as he did every morning, "Must hurry along or I'll be late for the office." I suppose some females would have been annoyed by the predictability of our morning routine – but not this lady. It was all part of a life that made me feel secure in the belief that at last I had found something worthwhile.

Roger managed to get his feet into the wrong slippers – always a fifty-fifty chance – before lumbering towards the bathroom. He emerged fifteen minutes later, as he always did, looking only slightly better than he had when he entered. I've learned to live with what some would have called his foibles, while he has learned to accept my mania for cleanliness and a need to feel secure.

"Get up, lazy-bones," he remonstrated but then only smiled when I re-settled myself, refusing to leave the warm hollow that had been left by his body.

"I suppose you expect me to get your breakfast before I go to work?" he added as he made his way downstairs. I didn't bother to reply. I knew that in a few moments' time he would be opening the front door, picking up the morning newspaper, any mail, and our regular pint of milk. Reliable as ever, he would put on the kettle, then head for the pantry, fill a bowl with my favourite breakfast food and add my portion of the milk, leaving himself just enough for two cups of coffee.

I could anticipate almost to the second when breakfast would be ready. First I would hear the kettle boil, a few moments later the milk would be poured, then finally there would be the sound of a chair being pulled up. That was the signal I needed to confirm it was time for me to join him.

I stretched my legs slowly, noticing my nails needed some attention. I had already decided against a proper wash until after he had left for the office. I could hear the sound of the chair being scraped along the kitchen lino. I felt so happy that I literally jumped off the bed before making my way towards the open door. A few seconds later I was downstairs. Although he had already taken his first mouthful of cornflakes he stopped eating the moment he saw me.

"Good of you to join me," he said, a grin spreading over his face.

I padded over towards him and looked up expectantly. He bent down and pushed my bowl towards me. I began to lap up the milk happily, my tail swishing from side to side.

It's a myth that we only swish our tails when we're angry.

The Steal

CHRISTOPHER and Margaret Roberts always spent their summer holiday as far away from England as they could possibly afford. However, as Christopher was the classics master at St Cuthbert's, a small preparatory school just north of Yeovil, and Margaret was the school matron, their experience of four of the five continents was largely confined to periodicals such as the *National Geographic Magazine* and *Time*.

The Roberts' annual holiday each August was nevertheless sacrosanct and they spent eleven months of the year saving, planning and preparing for their one extravagant luxury. The following eleven months were then spent passing on their discoveries to the "offspring": the Roberts, without children of their own, looked on all the pupils of St Cuthbert's as "offspring".

During the long evenings when the "offspring" were meant to be asleep in their dormitories, the Roberts would pore over maps, analyse expert opinion and then finally come up with a shortlist to consider. In recent expeditions they had been as far afield as Norway, Northern Italy and Yugoslavia, ending up the previous year exploring Achilles' island, Skyros, off the east coast of Greece.

"It has to be Turkey this year," said Christopher after much soul-searching. A week later Margaret came to the same conclusion, and so they were able to move on to Phase Two. Every book on Turkey in the local library was borrowed, consulted, re-borrowed and re-consulted. Every brochure obtainable from the Turkish Embassy or local travel agents received the same relentless scrutiny.

By the first day of the summer term, charter tickets had been paid for, a car hired, accommodation booked and everything that could be insured comprehensively covered. Their plans lacked only one final detail.

"So what will be our 'steal' this year?" asked Christopher.

"A carpet," Margaret said, without hesitation. "It has to be. For over a thousand years Turkey has produced the most sought-after carpets in the world. We'd be foolish to consider anything else."

"How much shall we spend on it?"

"Five hundred pounds," said Margaret, feeling very extravagant.

Having agreed, they once again swapped memories about the "steals" they had made over the years. In Norway, it had been a whale's tooth carved in the shape of a galleon by a local artist who soon after had been taken up by Steuben. In Tuscany, it had been a ceramic bowl found in a small village where they cast and fired them to be sold in Rome at exorbitant prices: a small blemish which only an expert would have noticed made it a "steal". Just outside Skopje the Roberts had visited a local glass factory and acquired a water jug moments after it had been blown in front of their eyes, and in Skyros they had picked up their greatest triumph to date, a fragment of an urn they discovered near an old excavation site. The Roberts reported their find immediately to the authorities, but the Greek officials had not considered the fragment important enough to prevent it being exported to St Cuthbert's.

On returning to England Christopher couldn't resist just checking with the senior classics don at his old *alma mater*. He confirmed the piece was probably twelfth century. This latest "steal" now stood, carefully mounted, on their drawing room mantelpiece.

"Yes, a carpet would be perfect," Margaret mused. "The trouble is, everyone goes to Turkey with the idea of picking up a carpet on the cheap. So to find a really good one. . . ."

She knelt and began to measure the small space in front of their drawing room fireplace.

"Seven by three should do it," she said.

Within a few days of term ending, the Roberts travelled by bus to Heathrow. The journey took a little longer than by rail but at half the cost. "Money saved is money that can be spent on the carpet," Margaret reminded her husband.

"Agreed, Matron," said Christopher, laughing.

On arrival at Heathrow they checked their baggage on to the charter flight, selected two non-smoking seats and, finding they had time to spare, decided to watch other planes taking off to even more exotic places.

It was Christopher who first spotted the two passengers dashing across the tarmac, obviously late.

"Look," he said, pointing at the running couple. His wife studied the overweight pair, still brown from a previous holiday, as they lumbered up the steps to their plane.

"Mr and Mrs Kendall-Hume," Margaret said in disbelief. After hesitating for a moment, she added, "I wouldn't want to be uncharitable about any of the offspring, but I do find young Malcolm Kendall-Hume a . . ." She paused.

"'Spoilt little brat'?" suggested her husband.

"Quite," said Margaret. "I can't begin to think what his parents must be like."

"Very successful, if the boy's stories are to be believed," said Christopher. "A string of second-hand garages from Birmingham to Bristol."

"Thank God they're not on our flight."

"Bermuda or the Bahamas would be my guess," suggested Christopher.

A voice emanating from the loudspeaker gave Margaret no chance to offer her opinion.

"Olympic Airways Flight 172 to Istanbul is now boarding at Gate No. 37."

"That's us," said Christopher happily as they began their long route-march to their departure gate.

They were the first passengers to board, and once shown to their seats they settled down to study the guidebooks of Turkey and their three files of research.

"We must be sure to see Diana's Temple when we visit Ephesus," said Christopher, as the plane taxied out on to the runway.

"Not forgetting that at that time we shall be only a few kilometres away from the purported last home of the Virgin Mary," added Margaret.

"Taken with a pinch of salt by serious historians," Christopher remarked as if addressing a member of the Lower Fourth, but his wife was too engrossed in her book to notice. They both continued to study on their own before Christopher asked what his wife was reading.

"*Carpets – Fact and Fiction* by Abdul Verizoglu – seventeenth edition," she said, confident that any errors would have been eradicated in the previous sixteen. "It's most informative. The finest examples, it seems, are from Hereke and are woven in silk and are sometimes worked on by up to twenty young women, even children, at a time."

"Why young?" pondered Christopher. "You'd have thought experience would have been essential for such a delicate task."

"Apparently not," said Margaret. "Herekes are woven by those with young eyes which can discern intricate patterns sometimes no larger than a pinpoint and with up to nine hundred knots a square inch. Such a carpet," continued Margaret, "can cost as much as fifteen, even twenty, thousand pounds."

"And at the other end of the scale? Carpets woven in old leftover wool by old leftover women?" suggested Christopher, answering his own question.

"No doubt," said Margaret. "But even for our humble purse there are some simple guidelines to follow."

Christopher leaned over so that he could be sure

to take in every word above the roar of the engines.

"The muted reds and blues with a green base are considered classic and are much admired by Turkish collectors, but one should avoid the bright yellows and oranges," read his wife aloud. "And never consider a carpet that displays animals, birds or fishes, as they are produced only to satisfy Western tastes."

"Don't they like animals?"

"I don't think that's the point," said Margaret. "The Sunni Muslims, who are the country's religious rulers, don't approve of graven images. But if we search diligently round the bazaars we should still be able to come across a bargain for a few hundred pounds."

"What a wonderful excuse to spend all day in the bazaars."

Margaret smiled, before continuing. "But listen. It's most important to bargain. The opening price the dealer offers is likely to be double what he expects to get and treble what the carpet is worth." She looked up from her book. "If there's any bargaining to be done it will have to be carried out by you, my dear. They're not used to that sort of thing at Marks & Spencer."

Christopher smiled.

"And finally," continued his wife, turning a page of her book, "if the dealer offers you coffee you should accept. It means he expects the process to go on for some time as he enjoys the bargaining as much as the sale."

"If that's the case they had better have a very large pot percolating for us," said Christopher as he closed his eyes and began to contemplate the pleasures that awaited him. Margaret only closed her books on carpets when the plane touched down at Istanbul airport, and at once opened file Number One, entitled "Pre-Turkey".

"A shuttle bus should be waiting for us at the north side of the terminal. It will take us on to the local flight," she assured her husband as she carefully wound her watch forward two hours.

The Roberts were soon following the stream of passengers heading in the direction of passport control. The first people they saw in front of them were the same middle-aged couple they had assumed were destined for more exotic shores.

"Wonder where they're heading," said Christopher.

"Istanbul Hilton, I expect," said Margaret as they climbed into a vehicle that had been declared redundant by the Glasgow Corporation Bus Company some twenty years before. It spluttered out black exhaust fumes as it revved up before heading off in the direction of the local THY flight.

The Roberts soon forgot all about Mr and Mrs Kendall-Hume once they looked out of the little aeroplane windows to admire the west coast of Turkey highlighted by the setting sun. The plane landed in the port of Izmir just as the shimmering red ball disappeared behind the highest hill. Another bus, even older than the earlier one, ensured that the Roberts reached their little guest house just in time for late supper.

Their room was tiny but clean and the owner much in the same mould. He greeted them both with exaggerated gesturing and a brilliant smile which augured well for the next twenty-one days.

Early the following morning, the Roberts checked over their detailed plans for Day One in file Number Two. They were first to collect the rented Fiat that had already been paid for in England, before driving off into the hills to the ancient Byzantine fortress at Selcuk in the morning, to be followed by the Temple of Diana in the afternoon if they still had time.

After breakfast had been cleared away and they had cleaned their teeth, the Roberts left the guest house a few minutes before nine. Armed with their hire car form and guidebook, they headed off for Beyazik's Garage where their promised car awaited them. They strolled down the cobbled streets past the little white houses, enjoying the sea breeze until they reached the bay. Christopher spotted the sign for Beyazik's Garage when it was still a hundred yards ahead of them.

As they passed the magnificent yachts moored alongside the harbour, they tested each other on the nationality of each flag, feeling not unlike the "offspring" completing a geography test.

"Italian, French, Liberian, Panamanian, German. There aren't many British boats," said Christopher, sounding unusually patriotic, the way he always did, Margaret reflected, the moment they were abroad.

She stared at the rows of gleaming hulls lined up like buses in Piccadilly during the rush hour; some of the boats were even bigger than buses. "I wonder what kind of people can possibly afford such luxury?" she asked, not expecting a reply.

"Mr and Mrs Roberts, isn't it?" shouted a voice from behind them. They both turned to see a now-familiar figure dressed in a white shirt and white shorts, wearing a hat that made him look not unlike the "Bird's Eye" captain, waving at them from the bow of one of the bigger yachts.

"Climb on board, me hearties," Mr Kendall-Hume declared enthusiastically, more in the manner of a command than an invitation.

Reluctantly the Roberts walked the gang-plank.

"Look who's here," their host shouted down a large hole in the middle of the deck. A moment later Mrs Kendall-Hume appeared from below, dressed in a diaphanous orange sarong and a matching bikini top. "It's Mr and Mrs Roberts – you remember, from Malcolm's school."

Kendall-Hume turned back to face the dismayed couple. "I don't remember your first names, but this is Melody and I'm Ray."

"Christopher and Margaret," the schoolmaster admitted as handshakes were exchanged.

"What about a drink? Gin, vodka or . . . ?"

"Oh, no," said Margaret. "Thank you very much, we'll both have an orange juice."

"Suit yourselves," said Ray Kendall-Hume. "You must stay for lunch."

"But we couldn't impose . . ."

"I insist," said Mr Kendall-Hume. "After all, we're on holiday. By the way, we'll be going over to the other side of the bay for lunch. There's one hell of a beach there, and it will give you a chance to sunbathe and swim in peace."

"How considerate of you," said Christopher.

"And where's young Malcolm?" asked Margaret.

"He's on a scouting holiday in Scotland. Doesn't like to mess about in boats the way we do."

For the first time he could recall Christopher felt some admiration for the boy. A moment later the engine started thunderously.

On the trip across the bay, Ray Kendall-Hume expounded his theories about "having to get away from it all". "Nothing like a yacht to ensure your privacy and not having to mix with the *hoi polloi.*" He only wanted the simple things in life: the sun, the sea and an infinite supply of good food and drink.

The Roberts could have asked for nothing less. By the end of the day they were both suffering from a mild bout of sunstroke and were also feeling a little seasick. Despite white pills, red pills and yellow pills, liberally supplied by Melody, when they finally got back to their room that night they were unable to sleep.

Avoiding the Kendall-Humes over the next twenty days did not prove easy. Beyazik's, the garage where their little hire car awaited them each morning and to which it had to be returned each night, could only be reached via the quayside where the Kendall-Humes' motor yacht was moored like an insuperable barrier at a gymkhana. Hardly a day passed that the Roberts did not have to spend some part of their precious time bobbing up and down on Turkey's choppy coastal waters, eating oily food and discussing how large a carpet would be needed to fill the Kendall-Humes' front room.

However, they still managed to complete a large part of their programme and determinedly set aside the whole of the last day of the holiday in their quest for a carpet. As they did not need Beyazik's car to go into town, they felt confident that for that day at least they could safely avoid their tormentors.

On the final morning they rose a little later than planned and after breakfast strolled down the tiny cobbled path together, Christopher in possession of the seventeenth edition of *Carpets – Fact and Fiction*, Margaret with a tape measure and five hundred pounds in travellers' cheques.

Once the schoolmaster and his wife had reached the bazaar they began to look around a myriad of little shops, wondering where they should begin their adventure. Fez-topped men tried to entice them to enter their tiny emporiums but the Roberts spent the first hour simply taking in the atmosphere.

"I'm ready to start the search now," shouted Margaret above the babble of voices around her.

"Then we've found you just in time," said the one voice they thought they had escaped.

"We were just about to –"

"Then follow me."

The Roberts' hearts sank as they were led by Ray Kendall-Hume out of the bazaar and back towards the town.

"Take my advice, and you'll end up with one hell of a bargain," Kendall-Hume assured them both. "I've picked up some real beauties in my time from every corner of the globe at prices you wouldn't believe. I am happy to let you take full advantage of my expertise at no extra charge."

"I don't know how you could stand the noise and smell of that bazaar," said Melody, obviously glad to be back among the familiar signs of Gucci, Lacoste and Saint Laurent.

"We rather like . . ."

"Rescued in the nick of time," said Ray Kendall-Hume. "And the place I'm told you have to start and finish at if you want to purchase a serious carpet is Osman's."

Margaret recalled the name from her carpet book: "Only to be visited if money is no object and you know exactly what you are looking for." The vital last morning was to be wasted, she reflected as she pushed open the large glass doors of Osman's to enter a ground-floor area the size of a tennis court. The room was covered in carpets on the floor, the walls, the windowsills, and even the tables. Anywhere a carpet could be laid out, a carpet was there to be seen. Although the Roberts realised immediately that nothing on show could possibly be in their price range, the sheer beauty of the display entranced them.

Margaret walked slowly round the room, mentally measuring the small carpets so she could anticipate the sort of thing they might look for once they had escaped.

A tall, elegant man, hands raised as if in prayer and dressed immaculately in a tailored worsted suit that could have been made in Savile Row, advanced to greet them.

"Good morning, sir," he said to Mr Kendall-Hume, selecting the serious spender without difficulty. "Can I be of assistance?"

"You certainly can," replied Kendall-Hume. "I want to be shown your finest carpets, but I do not intend to pay your finest prices."

The dealer smiled politely and clapped his hands. Six small carpets were brought in by three assistants who rolled them out in the centre of the room. Margaret fell in love with a muted green-based carpet with a pattern of tiny red squares woven around the borders. The pattern was so intricate she could not take her eyes off it. She measured the carpet out of interest: seven by three exactly.

"You have excellent taste, madam," said the dealer. Margaret, colouring slightly, quickly stood up, took a pace backwards and hid the tape measure behind her back.

"How do you feel about that lot, pet?" asked Kendall-Hume, sweeping a hand across the six carpets.

"None of them are big enough," Melody replied, giving them only a fleeting glance.

The dealer clapped his hands a second time and the exhibits were rolled up and taken away. Four larger ones soon replaced them.

"Would you care for some coffee?" the dealer asked Mr Kendall-Hume as the new carpets lay unfurled at their feet.

"Haven't the time," said Kendall-Hume shortly. "Here to buy a carpet. If I want a coffee, I can always go to a coffee shop," he said with a chuckle. Melody smiled her complicity.

"Well, I would like some coffee," declared Margaret, determined to rebel at some point on the holiday.

"Delighted, madam," said the dealer, and one of the assistants disappeared to carry out her wishes while the Kendall-Humes studied the new carpets.

The coffee arrived a few moments later. She thanked the young assistant and began to sip the thick black liquid slowly. Delicious, she thought, and smiled her acknowledgment to the dealer.

"Still not large enough," Mrs Kendall-Hume insisted. The dealer gave a slight sigh and clapped his hands yet again. Once more the assistants began to roll up the rejected goods. He then addressed one of his staff in Turkish. The assistant looked doubtfully at his mentor but the dealer gave a firm nod and waved him away. The assistant returned a little later with a small platoon of lesser assistants carrying two carpets, both of which when unfolded took up most of the shop floor. Margaret liked them even less than the ones she had just been shown, but as her opinion was not sought she did not offer it.

"That's more like it," said Ray Kendall-Hume. "Just about the right size for the lounge, wouldn't you say, Melody?"

"Perfect," his wife replied, making no attempt to measure either of the carpets.

"I'm glad we agree," said Ray Kendall-Hume. "But which one, my pet? The faded red and blue, or the bright yellow and orange?"

"The yellow and orange one," said Melody without hesitation. "I like the pattern of brightly coloured birds running round the outside." Christopher thought he saw the dealer wince.

"So now all we have left to do is agree on a price," said Kendall-Hume. "You'd better sit down, pet, as this may take a while."

"I hope not," said Mrs Kendall-Hume, resolutely standing. The Roberts remained mute.

"Unfortunately, sir," began the dealer, "your wife has selected one of the finest carpets in our collection and so I fear there can be little room for any re-adjustment."

"How much?" said Kendall-Hume.

"You see, sir, this carpet was woven in Demirdji, in the province of Izmir, by over a hundred seamstresses and it took them more than a year to complete."

"Don't give me that baloney," said Kendall-Hume, winking at Christopher. "Just tell me how much I'm expected to pay."

"I feel it my duty to point out, sir, that this carpet shouldn't be here at all," said the Turk plaintively. "It was originally made for an Arab prince who failed to complete the transaction when the price of oil collapsed."

"But he must have agreed on a price at the time?"

"I cannot reveal the exact figure, sir. It embarrasses me to mention it."

"It wouldn't embarrass me," said Kendall-Hume. "Come on, what's the price?" he insisted.

"Which currency would you prefer to trade in?" the Turk asked.

"Pounds."

The dealer removed a slim calculator from his jacket pocket, programmed some numbers into it, then looked unhappily towards the Kendall-Humes.

Christopher and Margaret remained silent, like schoolchildren fearing the headmaster might ask them a question to which they could not possibly know the answer.

"Come on, come on, how much were you hoping to sting me for?"

"I think you must prepare yourself for a shock, sir," said the dealer.

"How much?" repeated Kendall-Hume, impatiently.

"Twenty-five thousand."

"Pounds?"

"Pounds."

"You must be joking," said Kendall-Hume, walking round the carpet and ending up standing next to Margaret. "You're about to find out why I'm considered the scourge of the East Midlands car trade," he whispered to her. "I wouldn't pay more than fifteen thousand for that carpet." He turned back to face the dealer. "Even if my life depended on it."

"Then I fear your time has been wasted, sir," the Turk replied. "For this is a carpet intended only for the *cognoscenti*. Perhaps madam might reconsider the red and blue?"

"Certainly not," said Kendall-Hume. "The colour's all faded. Can't you see? You obviously left it in the window too long, and the sun has got at it. No, you'll have to reconsider your price if you want the orange and yellow one to end up in the home of a connoisseur."

The dealer sighed as his fingers tapped the calculator again.

While the transaction continued, Melody looked on vacantly, occasionally gazing out of the window towards the bay.

"I could not drop a penny below twenty-three thousand pounds."

"I'd be willing to go as high as eighteen thousand," said Kendall-Hume, "but not a penny more."

The Roberts watched the dealer tap the numbers into the calculator.

"That would not even cover the cost of what I paid for it myself," he said sadly, staring down at the little glowing figures.

"You're pushing me, but don't push me too far. Nineteen thousand," said Mr Kendall-Hume. "That's my final offer."

"Twenty thousand pounds is the lowest figure I could consider," replied the dealer. "A give-away price on my mother's grave."

Kendall-Hume took out his wallet and placed it on the table by the side of the dealer.

"Nineteen thousand pounds and you've got yourself a deal," he said.

"But how will I feed my children?" asked the dealer, his arms raised above his head.

"The same way I feed mine," said Kendall-Hume, laughing. "By making a fair profit."

The dealer paused as if re-considering, then said, "I can't do it, sir. I'm sorry. We must show you some other carpets." The assistants came forward on cue.

"No, that's the one I want," said Mrs Kendall-Hume. "Don't quarrel over a thousand pounds, pet."

"Take my word for it, madam," the dealer said, turning towards Mrs Kendall-Hume. "My family would starve if we only did business with customers like your husband."

"Okay, you get the twenty thousand, but on one condition."

"Condition?"

"My receipt must show that the bill was for ten thousand pounds. Otherwise I'll only end up paying the difference in customs duty."

The dealer bowed low as if to indicate he did not find the request an unusual one.

Mr Kendall-Hume opened his wallet and withdrew ten thousand pounds in travellers' cheques and ten thousand pounds in cash.

"As you can see," he said, grinning, "I came prepared." He removed another five thousand pounds and, waving it at the dealer, added, "and I would have been willing to pay far more."

The dealer shrugged. "You drive a hard bargain, sir. But you will not hear me complain now the deal has been struck."

The vast carpet was folded, wrapped and a receipt for ten thousand pounds made out while the travellers' cheques and cash were paid over.

The Roberts had not uttered a word for twenty minutes. When they saw the cash change hands it crossed Margaret's mind that it was more money than the two of them earned in a year.

"Time to get back to the yacht," said Kendall-Hume. "Do join us for lunch if you choose a carpet in time."

"Thank you," said the Roberts in unison. They waited until the Kendall-Humes were out of sight, two assistants bearing the orange and yellow carpet in their wake, before they thanked the dealer for the coffee and in turn began to make their move towards the door.

"What sort of carpet were you looking for?" asked the dealer.

"I fear your prices are way beyond us," said Christopher politely. "But thank you."

"Well, let me at least find out. Have you or your wife seen a carpet you liked?"

"Yes," replied Margaret, "the small carpet, but . . ."

"Ah, yes," said the dealer. "I remember madam's eyes when she saw the Hereke."

He left them, to return a few moments later with the little soft-toned, green-based carpet with the tiny red squares that the Kendall-Humes had so firmly rejected. Not waiting for assistance he rolled it out himself for the Roberts in inspect more carefully.

Margaret thought it looked even more magnificent the second time and feared that she could never hope to find its equal in the few hours left to them.

"Perfect," she admitted, quite unashamedly.

"Then we have only the price to discuss," said the dealer kindly. "How much were you wanting to spend, madam?"

"We had planned to spend three hundred pounds," said Christopher, jumping in. Margaret was unable to hide her surprise.

"But we agreed –" she began.

"Thank you, my dear, I think I should deal with this matter."

The dealer smiled and returned to the bargaining.

"I would have to charge you six hundred pounds," he said. "Anything less would be robbery."

"Four hundred pounds is my final offer," said

Christopher, trying to sound in control.

"Five hundred pounds would have to be my bottom price," said the dealer.

"I'll take it!" cried Christopher.

An assistant began waving his arms and talking to the dealer noisily in his native tongue. The owner raised a hand to dismiss the young man's protests, while the Roberts looked on anxiously.

"My son," explained the dealer, "is not happy with the arrangement, but I am delighted that the little carpet will reside in the home of a couple who will so obviously appreciate its true worth."

"Thank you," said Christopher quietly.

"Will you also require a bill of a different price?"

"No, thank you," said Christopher, handing over ten fifty-pound notes and then waiting until the carpet was wrapped and he was presented with the correct receipt.

As he watched the Roberts leave his shop clinging on to their purchase, the dealer smiled to himself.

When they arrived at the quayside, the Kendall-Humes' boat was already half way across the bay heading towards the quiet beach. The Roberts sighed their combined relief and returned to the bazaar for lunch.

It was while they were waiting for their baggage to appear on the carousel at Heathrow Airport that Christopher felt a tap on his shoulder. He turned round to face a beaming Ray Kendall-Hume.

"I wonder if you could do me a favour, old boy?"

"I will if I can," said Christopher, who still

had not fully recovered from their last encounter.

"It's simple enough," said Kendall-Hume. "The old girl and I have brought back far too many presents and I wondered if you could take one of them through customs. Otherwise we're likely to be held up all night."

Melody, standing behind an already laden trolley, smiled at the two men benignly.

"You would still have to pay any duty that was due on it," said Christopher firmly.

"I wouldn't dream of doing otherwise," said Kendall-Hume, struggling with a massive package before pushing it on the Roberts' trolley. Christopher wanted to protest as Kendall-Hume peeled off two thousand pounds and handed the money and the receipt over to the schoolmaster.

"What do we do if they claim your carpet is worth a lot more than ten thousand pounds?" asked Margaret anxiously, coming to stand by her husband's side.

"Pay the difference and I'll refund you immediately. But I assure you it's most unlikely to arise."

"I hope you're right."

"Of course I'm right," said Kendall-Hume. "Don't worry, I've done this sort of thing before. And I won't forget your help when it comes to the next school appeal," he added, leaving them with the huge parcel.

Once Christopher and Margaret had located their own bags, they collected the second trolley and took their place in the red "Something to Declare" queue.

"Are you in possession of any items over five

hundred pounds in value?" asked the young customs official politely.

"Yes," said Christopher. "We purchased two carpets when we were on holiday in Turkey." He handed over the two bills.

The customs official studied the receipts carefully, then asked if he might be allowed to see the carpets for himself.

"Certainly," said Christopher, and began the task of undoing the larger package while Margaret worked on the smaller one.

"I shall need to have these looked at by an expert," said the official once the parcels were unwrapped. "It shouldn't take more than a few minutes." The carpets were soon taken away.

The "few minutes" turned out to be over fifteen and Christopher and Margaret were soon regretting their decision to assist the Kendall-Humes, whatever the needs of the school appeal. They began to indulge in irrelevant small-talk that wouldn't have fooled the most amateur of sleuths.

At last the customs official returned.

"I wonder if you would be kind enough to have a word with my colleague in private?" he asked.

"Is that really necessary?" asked Christopher, reddening.

"I'm afraid so, sir."

"We shouldn't have agreed to it in the first place," whispered Margaret. "We've never been in any trouble with the authorities before."

"Don't fret, dear. It will be all over in a few minutes, you'll see," said Christopher, not sure that he believed his own words. They followed the young man out through the back and into a small room.

"Good afternoon, sir," said a white-haired man with several gold rings around the cuff of his sleeve. "I am sorry to have kept you waiting but we have had your carpets looked at by our expert and he feels sure a mistake must have been made."

Christopher wanted to protest but he couldn't get a word out.

"A mistake?" managed Margaret.

"Yes, madam. The bills you presented don't make any sense to him."

"Don't make any sense?"

"No, madam," said the senior customs officer. "I repeat, we feel certain a mistake has been made."

"What kind of mistake?" asked Christopher, at last finding his voice.

"Well, you have come forward and declared two carpets, one at a price of ten thousand pounds and one at a price of five hundred pounds, according to these receipts."

"Yes?"

"Every year hundreds of people return to England with Turkish carpets, so we have some experience in these matters. Our adviser feels certain that the bills have been incorrectly made out."

"I don't begin to understand . . ." said Christopher.

"Well," explained the senior officer, "the large carpet, we are assured, has been spun with a crude distaff and has only two hundred ghiordes, or knots, per square inch. Despite its size we estimate it to be valued around five thousand pounds. The small carpet, on the other hand, we estimate to have nine hundred knots per square inch and is a fine example of a silk hand-woven traditional

Hereke and undoubtedly would have been a bargain at five hundred pounds. As both carpets come from the same shop, we assume it must be a clerical error."

The Roberts remained speechless.

"It doesn't make any difference to the duty you will have to pay, but we felt sure you would want to know, for insurance purposes."

Still the Roberts said nothing.

"As you're allowed five hundred pounds before paying any duty, the excise will still be two thousand pounds."

Christopher quickly handed over the Kendall-Humes' wad of notes. The senior officer counted them while his junior carefully re-wrapped the two carpets.

"Thank you," said Christopher, as they were handed back the parcels and a receipt for the two thousand pounds.

The Roberts quickly bundled the large package on to its trolley before wheeling it through the concourse and on to the pavement outside where the Kendall-Humes impatiently awaited them.

"You were in there a long time," said Kendall-Hume. "Any problems?"

"No, they were just assessing the value of the carpets."

"Any extra charge?" Kendall-Hume asked apprehensively.

"No, your two thousand pounds covered everything," said Christopher, passing over the receipt.

"Then we got away with it, old fellow. Well done. One hell of a bargain to add to my collection." Kendall-Hume turned to bundle the large package into the boot of his Mercedes before locking it and taking his place behind the steering wheel. "Well done," he repeated through the open window, as the car drove off. "I won't forget the school appeal."

The Roberts stood and watched as the silver grey car joined a line of traffic leaving the airport.

"Why didn't you tell Mr Kendall-Hume the real value of his carpet?" asked Margaret once they were seated in the bus.

"I did give it some considerable thought but I came to the conclusion that the *truth* was the last thing Kendall-Hume wanted to be told."

"But don't you feel any guilt? After all, we've stolen –"

"Not at all, my dear. We haven't stolen anything. But we did get one hell of a 'steal'."

Colonel Bullfrog

THERE is one cathedral in England that has never found it necessary to launch a national appeal.

When the Colonel woke he found himself tied to a stake where the ambush had taken place. He could feel a numb sensation in his leg. The last thing he could recall was the bayonet entering his thigh. All he was aware of now were ants crawling up the leg on an endless march towards the wound.

It would have been better to have remained unconscious, he decided.

Then someone undid the knots and he collapsed head first into the mud. It would be better still to be dead, he concluded. The Colonel somehow got to his knees and crawled over to the stake next to him. Tied to it was a corporal who must have been dead for several hours. Ants were crawling into his mouth. The Colonel tore off a strip from the man's shirt, washed it in a large puddle nearby and cleaned the wound in his leg as best he could before binding it tightly.

That was February 17th, 1943, a date that would be etched on the Colonel's memory for the rest of his life.

That same morning the Japanese received orders that the newly captured Allied prisoners were to be moved at dawn. Many were to die on the march and even more had perished before the trek began. Colonel Richard Moore was determined not to be counted among them.

Twenty-nine days later, one hundred and seventeen of the original seven hundred and thirty-two Allied troops reached Tonchan. Any man whose travels had previously not taken him beyond Rome could hardly have been prepared for such an experience as Tonchan. This heavily guarded prisoner-of-war camp, some three hundred miles north of Singapore and hidden in the deepest equatorial jungle, offered no possibility of freedom. Anyone who contemplated escape could not hope to survive in the jungle for more than a few days, while those who remained discovered the odds were not a lot shorter.

When the Colonel first arrived, Major Sakata, the camp commandant, informed him that he was the senior ranking officer and would therefore be held responsible for the welfare of all Allied troops.

Colonel Moore had stared down at the Japanese officer. Sakata must have been a foot shorter than himself but after that twenty-eight-day march the British soldier couldn't have weighed much more than the diminutive Major.

Moore's first act on leaving the commandant's office was to call together all the Allied officers. He discovered there was a good cross-section from

Britain, Australia, New Zealand and America but few could have been described as fit. Men were dying daily from malaria, dysentery and malnutrition. He was suddenly aware what the expression "dying like flies" meant.

The Colonel learned from his staff officers that for the previous two years of the camp's existence they had been ordered to build bamboo huts for the Japanese officers. These had had to be completed before they had been allowed to start on a hospital for their own men and only recently huts for themselves. Many prisoners had died during those two years, not from illness but from the atrocities some Japanese perpetrated on a daily basis. Major Sakata, known because of his skinny arms as "Chopsticks", was, however, not considered to be the villain. His second-in-command, Lieutenant Takasaki (the Undertaker), and Sergeant Ayut (the Pig) were of a different mould and to be avoided at all cost, his men warned him.

It took the Colonel only a few days to discover why.

He decided his first task was to try to raise the battered morale of his troops. As there was no padre among those officers who had been captured he began each day by conducting a short service of prayer. Once the service was over the men would start work on the railway that ran alongside the camp. Each arduous day consisted of laying tracks to help Japanese soldiers get to the front more quickly so they could in turn kill and capture more Allied troops. Any prisoner suspected of undermining this work was found guilty of sabotage and put to death without trial. Lieutenant Takasaki considered taking an unscheduled five-minute break to be sabotage.

At lunch prisoners were allowed twenty minutes off to share a bowl of rice – usually with maggots – and, if they were lucky, a mug of water. Although the men returned to the camp each night exhausted, the Colonel still set about organising squads to be responsible for the cleanliness of their huts and the state of the latrines.

After only a few months, the Colonel was able to organise a football match between the British and the Americans, and following its success even set up a camp league. But he was even more delighted when the men turned up for karate lessons under Sergeant Hawke, a thick-set Australian, who had a Black Belt and for good measure also played the mouth-organ. The tiny instrument had survived the march through the jungle but everyone assumed it would be discovered before long and confiscated.

Each day Moore renewed his determination not to allow the Japanese to believe for one moment that the Allies were beaten – despite the fact that while he was at Tonchan he lost another twenty pounds in weight, and at least one man under his command every day.

To the Colonel's surprise the camp commandant, despite the Japanese national belief that any soldier who allowed himself to be captured ought to be treated as a deserter, did not place too many unnecessary obstacles in his path.

"You are like the British Bullfrog," Major Sakata suggested one evening as he watched the Colonel carving cricket bails out of bamboo. It was one of the rare occasions when the Colonel managed a smile.

His real problems continued to come from Lieutenant Takasaki and his henchmen, who considered captured Allied prisoners fit only to be considered as traitors. Takasaki was always careful how he treated the Colonel personally, but felt no such reservations when dealing with the other ranks, with the result that Allied soldiers often ended up with their meagre rations confiscated, a rifle butt in the stomach, or even left bound to a tree for days on end.

Whenever the Colonel made an official complaint to the commandant, Major Sakata listened sympathetically and even made an effort to weed out the main offenders. Moore's happiest moment at Tonchan was to witness the Undertaker and the Pig boarding the train for the front line. No one attempted to sabotage that journey. The commandant replaced them with Sergeant Akida and Corporal Sushi, known by the prisoners almost affectionately as "Sweet and Sour Pork". However, the Japanese High Command sent a new Number Two to the camp, a Lieutenant Osawa, who quickly became known as "The Devil" since he perpetrated atrocities that made the Undertaker and the Pig look like church fête organisers.

As the months passed the Colonel and the commandant's mutual respect grew. Sakata even confided to his English prisoner that he had requested that he be sent to the front line and join the real war. "And if," the Major added, "the High Command grants my request, there will be only two NCOs I would want to accompany me."

Colonel Moore knew the Major had Sweet and Sour Pork in mind, and was fearful what might become of his men if the only three Japanese he could work with were posted back to active duties to leave Lieutenant Osawa in command of the camp.

Colonel Moore realised that something quite extraordinary must have taken place for Major Sakata to come to his hut, because he had never done so before. The Colonel put his bowl of rice back down on the table and asked the three Allied officers who were sharing breakfast with him to wait outside.

The Major stood to attention and saluted.

The Colonel pushed himself to his full six feet, returned the salute and stared down into Sakata's eyes.

"The war is over," said the Japanese officer. For a brief moment Moore feared the worst. "Japan has surrendered unconditionally. You, sir," Sakata said quietly, "are now in command of the camp."

The Colonel immediately ordered all Japanese officers to be placed under arrest in the commandant's quarters. While his orders were being carried out he personally went in search of The Devil. Moore marched across the parade ground and headed towards the officers' quarters. He located the second-in-command's hut, walked up the steps and threw open Osawa's door. The sight that met the new commandant's eyes was one he would never forget. The Colonel had read of ceremonial hara-kiri without any real idea of what the final act consisted. Lieutenant Osawa must have cut himself a hundred times before he eventually died. The blood, the stench and the sight of the mutilated body would have caused a Gurkha to be sick. Only the head was there to confirm that the remains had once belonged to a human being.

The Colonel ordered Osawa to be buried outside the gates of the camp.

When the surrender of Japan was finally signed on board the US *Missouri* in Tokyo Bay, all at Tonchan PoW camp listened to the ceremony on the single camp radio. Colonel Moore then called a full parade on the camp square. For the first time in two and a half years he wore his dress uniform which made him look like a pierrot who had turned up at a formal party. He accepted the Japanese flag of surrender from Major Sakata on behalf of the Allies, then made the defeated enemy raise the American and British flags to the sound of both national anthems played in turn by Sergeant Hawke on his mouth-organ.

The Colonel then held a short service of thanksgiving which he conducted in the presence of all the Allied and Japanese soldiers.

Once command had changed hands Colonel Moore waited as week followed pointless week for news that he would be sent home. Many of his men had been given their orders to start the ten-thousand-mile journey back to England via Bangkok and Calcutta, but no such orders came for the Colonel and he waited in vain to be sent his repatriation papers.

Then, in January 1946, a smartly dressed young

Guards officer arrived at the camp with orders to see the Colonel. He was conducted to the commandant's office and saluted before shaking hands. Richard Moore stared at the young captain who, from his healthy complexion, had obviously arrived in the Far East long after the Japanese had surrendered. The captain handed over a letter to the Colonel.

"Home at last," said the older man breezily, as he ripped open the envelope, only to discover that it would be years before he could hope to exchange the paddy fields of Tonchan for the green fields of Lincolnshire.

The letter requested that the Colonel travel to Tokyo and represent Britain on the forthcoming war tribunal which was to be conducted in the Japanese capital. Captain Ross of the Coldstream Guards would take over his command at Tonchan.

The tribunal was to consist of twelve officers under the chairmanship of General Matthew Tomkins. Moore was to be the sole British representative and was to report directly to the General, "as soon as you find it convenient". Further details would be supplied to him on his arrival in Tokyo. The letter ended: "If for any reason you should require my help in your deliberations, do not hesitate to contact me personally." There followed the signature of Clement Attlee.

Staff officers are not in the habit of disobeying Prime Ministers, so the Colonel resigned himself to a prolonged stay in Japan.

It took several months to set up the tribunal and during that time Colonel Moore continued supervising the return of British troops to their homeland. The paperwork was endless and some of the men under his command were so frail that he found it necessary to build them up spiritually as well as physically before he could put them on boats to their various destinations. Some died long after the declaration of surrender had been ratified.

During this period of waiting, Colonel Moore used Major Sakata and the two NCOs in whom he had placed so much trust, Sergeant Akida and Corporal Sushi, as his liaison officers. This sudden change of command did not affect the relationship between the two senior officers, although Sakata admitted to the Colonel that he wished he had been killed in the defence of his country and not left to witness its humiliations. The Colonel found the Japanese remained well-disciplined while they waited to learn their fate, and most of them assumed death was the natural consequence of defeat.

The war tribunal held its first plenary session in Tokyo on April 19th, 1946. General Tomkins took over the fifth floor of the old Imperial Courthouse in the Ginza quarter of Tokyo – one of the few buildings that had survived the war intact. Tomkins, a squat, short-tempered man who was described by his own staff officer as a "pen-pusher from the Pentagon", arrived in Tokyo only a week before he began his first deliberations. The only rat-a-tat-tat this General had ever heard, the staff officer freely admitted to Colonel Moore, had come from the typewriter in his secretary's office. However, when it came to those on trial the General was in no doubt as to where the guilt lay and how the guilty should be punished.

"Hang every one of the little slit-eyed, yellow bastards," turned out to be one of Tomkins's favourite expressions.

Seated round a table in an old courtroom, the twelve-man tribunal conducted their deliberations. It was clear from the opening session that the General had no intention of considering "extenuating circumstances", "past record" or "humanitarian grounds". As the Colonel listened to Tomkins's views he began to fear for the lives of any innocent member of the armed forces who was brought in front of the General.

The Colonel quickly identified four Americans from the tribunal who, like himself, did not always concur with the General's sweeping judgments. Two were lawyers and the other two had been fighting soldiers recently involved in combat duty. The five men began to work together to counteract the General's most prejudiced decisions. During the following weeks they were able to persuade one or two others around the table to commute the sentences of hanging to life imprisonment for several Japanese who had been condemned for crimes they could not possibly have committed.

As each such case was debated, General Tomkins left the five men in no doubt as to his contempt for their views. "Goddam Nip sympathisers," he often suggested, and not always under his breath. As the General still held sway over the twelve-man tribunal, the Colonel's successes turned out to be few in number.

When the time came to determine the fate of

those who had been in command of the PoW camp at Tonchan the General demanded mass hanging for every Japanese officer involved without even the pretence of a proper trial. He showed no surprise when the usual five tribunal members raised their voices in protest. Colonel Moore spoke eloquently of having been a prisoner at Tonchan and petitioned in the defence of Major Sakata, Sergeant Akida and Corporal Sushi. He attempted to explain why hanging them would in its own way be as barbaric as any atrocity carried out by the Japanese. He insisted their sentence should be commuted to life imprisonment. The General yawned throughout the Colonel's remarks and, once Moore had completed his case, made no attempt to justify his position but simply called for a vote. To the General's surprise, the result was six-all; an American lawyer who previously had sided with the General raised his hand to join the Colonel's five. Without hesitation the General threw his casting vote in favour of the gallows. Tomkins leered down the table at Moore and said, "Time for lunch, I think, gentlemen. I don't know about you but I'm famished. And no one can say that this time we didn't give the little yellow bastards a fair hearing."

Colonel Moore rose from his place and without offering an opinion left the room.

He ran down the steps of the courthouse and instructed his driver to take him to British HQ in the centre of the city as quickly as possible. The short journey took them some time because of the mêlée of people that were always thronging the streets night and day. Once the Colonel arrived at his office he asked his secretary to place a call through to England. While she was carrying out his order Moore went to his green cabinet and thumbed through several files until he reached the one marked "Personal". He opened it and fished out the letter. He wanted to be certain that he had remembered the sentence accurately . . .

"If for any reason you should require my help in your deliberations, do not hesitate to contact me personally."

"He's coming to the phone, sir," the secretary said nervously. The Colonel walked over to the phone and waited. He found himself standing to attention when he heard the gentle, cultivated voice ask, "Is that you, Colonel?" It took Richard Moore less than ten minutes to explain the problem he faced and obtain the authority he needed.

Immediately he had completed his conversation he returned to the tribunal headquarters. He marched straight back into the conference room just as General Tomkins was settling down in his chair to start the afternoon proceedings.

The Colonel was the first to rise from his place when the General declared the tribunal to be in session. "I wonder if I might be allowed to open with a statement?" he requested.

"Be my guest," said Tomkins. "But make it brief. We've got a lot more of these Japs to get through yet."

Colonel Moore looked around the table at the other eleven men.

"Gentlemen," he began. "I hereby resign my position as the British representative on this commission."

General Tomkins was unable to stifle a smile.

"I do it," the Colonel continued, "reluctantly, but with the backing of my Prime Minister, to whom I spoke only a few moments ago." At this piece of information Tomkins's smile was replaced by a frown. "I shall be returning to England in order to make a full report to Mr Attlee and the British Cabinet on the manner in which this tribunal is being conducted."

"Now look here, sonny," began the General. "You can't –"

"I can, sir, and I will. Unlike you, I am unwilling to have the blood of innocent soldiers on my hands for the rest of my life."

"Now look here, sonny," the General repeated. "Let's at least talk this through before you do anything you might regret."

There was no break for the rest of that day, and by late afternoon Major Sakata, Sergeant Akida and Corporal Sushi had had their sentences commuted to life imprisonment.

Within a month, General Tomkins had been recalled by the Pentagon to be replaced by a distinguished American marine who had been decorated in combat during the First World War.

In the weeks that followed the new appointment the death sentences of two hundred and twenty-nine Japanese prisoners of war were commuted.

Colonel Moore returned to Lincolnshire on November 11th, 1948, having had enough of the realities of war and the hypocrisies of peace.

Just under two years later Richard Moore took holy orders and became a parish priest in the sleepy hamlet of Weddlebeach, in Suffolk. He enjoyed his calling and although he rarely mentioned his war-time experiences to his parishioners he often thought of his days in Japan.

"Blessed are the peacemakers for they shall . . ." the vicar began his sermon from the pulpit one Palm Sunday morning in the early 1960s, but he failed to complete the sentence.

His parishioners looked up anxiously only to see that a broad smile had spread across the vicar's face as he gazed down at someone seated in the third row.

The man he was staring at bowed his head in embarrassment and the vicar quickly continued with his sermon.

When the service was over Richard Moore waited by the east door to be sure his eyes had not deceived him. When they met face to face for the first time in fifteen years both men bowed and then shook hands.

The priest was delighted to learn over lunch that day back at the vicarage that Chopsticks Sakata had been released from prison after only five years, following the Allies' agreement with the newly installed Japanese government to release all prisoners who had not committed capital crimes. When the Colonel enquired after "Sweet and Sour Pork" the Major admitted that he had lost touch with Sergeant Akida (Sweet) but that Corporal Sushi (Sour) and he were working for the same electronics company. "And whenever we meet," he assured the priest, "we talk of the honourable man who saved our lives, 'the British Bullfrog'."

* * *

Over the years, the priest and his Japanese friend progressed in their chosen professions and regularly corresponded with each other. In 1971 Ari Sakata was put in charge of a large electronics factory in Osaka while eighteen months later Richard Moore became the Very Revd Richard Moore, Dean of Lincoln Cathedral.

"I read in the London *Times* that your cathedral is appealing for a new roof," wrote Sakata from his homeland in 1975.

"Nothing unusual about that," the Dean explained in his letter of reply. "There isn't a cathedral in England that doesn't suffer from dry rot or bomb damage. The former I fear is terminal; the latter at least has the chance of a cure."

A few weeks later the Dean received a cheque for ten thousand pounds from a not-unknown Japanese electronics company.

When in 1979 the Very Revd Richard Moore was appointed to the bishopric of Taunton, the new managing director of the largest electronics company in Japan flew over to attend his enthronement.

"I see you have another roof problem," commented Ari Sakata as he gazed up at the scaffolding surrounding the pulpit. "How much will it cost this time?"

"At least twenty-five thousand pounds a year," replied the Bishop without thought. "Just to make sure the roof doesn't fall in on the congregation during my sterner sermons." He sighed as he passed the evidence of reconstruction all around him. "As soon as I've settled into my new job I intend to launch a proper appeal to ensure my successor doesn't have to worry about the roof ever again."

The managing director nodded his understanding. A week later a cheque for twenty-five thousand pounds arrived on the churchman's desk.

The Bishop tried hard to express his grateful thanks. He knew he must never allow Chopsticks to feel that by his generosity he might have done the wrong thing as this would only insult his friend and undoubtedly end their relationship. Rewrite after rewrite was drafted to ensure that the final version of the long hand-written letter would have passed muster with the Foreign Office mandarin in charge of the Japanese desk. Finally the letter was posted.

As the years passed Richard Moore became fearful of writing to his old friend more than once a year as each letter elicited an even larger cheque. And, when towards the end of 1986 he did write, he made no reference to the Dean and Chapter's decision to designate 1988 as the cathedral's appeal year. Nor did he mention his own failing health, lest the old Japanese gentleman should feel in some way responsible, as his doctor had warned him that he could never expect to recover fully from those experiences at Tonchan.

The Bishop set about forming his appeal committee in January 1987. The Prince of Wales became the patron and the Lord Lieutenant of the county its chairman. In his opening address to the members of the appeal committee the Bishop instructed them that it was their duty to raise not less than three million pounds during 1988. Some apprehensive looks appeared on the faces around the table.

On August 11th, 1987, the Bishop of Taunton was umpiring a village cricket match when he suddenly collapsed from a heart attack. "See that the appeal brochures are printed in time for the next meeting," were his final words to the captain of the local team.

Bishop Moore's memorial service was held in Taunton Cathedral and conducted by the Archbishop of Canterbury. Not a seat could be found in the cathedral that day, and so many crowded into every pew that the west door was left open. Those who arrived late had to listen to the Archbishop's address relayed over loudspeakers placed around the market square.

Casual onlookers must have been puzzled by the presence of several elderly Japanese gentlemen dotted around the congregation.

When the service came to an end the Archbishop held a private meeting in the vestry of the cathedral with the chairman of the largest electronics company in the world.

"You must be Mr Sakata," said the Archbishop, warmly shaking the hand of a man who stepped forward from the small cluster of Japanese who were in attendance. "Thank you for taking the trouble to write and let me know that you would be coming. I am delighted to meet you at last. The Bishop always spoke of you with great affection and as a close friend – 'Chopsticks', if I remember."

Mr Sakata bowed low.

"And I also know that he always considered himself in your personal debt for such generosity over so many years."

"No, no, not me," replied the former Major. "I,

like my dear friend the late Bishop, am representative of higher authority."

The Archbishop looked puzzled.

"You see, sir," continued Mr Sakata, "I am only the chairman of the company. May I have the honour of introducing my President?"

Mr Sakata took a pace backwards to allow an even smaller figure, whom the Archbishop had originally assumed to be part of Mr Sakata's entourage, to step forward.

The President bowed low and, still without speaking, passed an envelope to the Archbishop.

"May I be allowed to open it?" the church leader asked, unaware of the Japanese custom of waiting until the giver has departed.

The little man bowed again.

The Archbishop slit open the envelope and removed a cheque for three million pounds.

"The late Bishop must have been a very close friend," was all he could think of saying.

"No, sir," the President replied. "I did not have that privilege."

"Then he must have done something incredible to be deserving of such a munificent gesture."

"He performed an act of honour over forty years ago and now I try inadequately to repay it."

"Then he would surely have remembered you," said the Archbishop.

"Is possible he would remember me but if so only as the sour half of 'Sweet and Sour Pork'."

There is one cathedral in England that has never found it necessary to launch a national appeal.

Checkmate

AS she entered the room every eye turned towards her.

When admiring a girl some men start with her head and work down. I start with the ankles and work up.

She wore black high-heeled velvet shoes and a tight-fitting black dress that stopped high enough above the knees to reveal the most perfectly tapering legs. As my eyes continued their upward sweep they paused to take in her narrow waist and slim athletic figure. But it was the oval face that I found captivating, slightly pouting lips and the largest blue eyes I've ever seen, crowned with a head of thick, black, short-cut hair that literally shone with lustre. Her entrance was all the more breathtaking because of the surroundings she had chosen. Heads would have turned at a diplomatic reception, a society cocktail party, even a charity ball, but at a chess tournament . . .

I followed her every movement, patronisingly unable to accept she could be a player. She walked slowly over to the club secretary's table and signed in to prove me wrong. She was handed a number to indicate her challenger for the opening match. Anyone who had not yet been allocated an opponent waited to see if she would take her place opposite their side of the board.

The player checked the number she had been given and made her way towards an elderly man who was seated in the far corner of the room, a former captain of the club now past his best.

As the club's new captain I had been responsible for instigating these round-robin matches. We meet on the last Friday of the month in a large club-like room on top of the Mason's Arms in the High Street. The landlord sees to it that thirty tables are set out for us and that food and drink are readily available. Three or four other clubs in the district send half a dozen opponents to play a couple of blitz games, giving us a chance to face rivals we would not normally play. The rules for the matches are simple enough – one minute on the clock is the maximum allowed for each move, so a game rarely lasts for more than an hour, and if a pawn hasn't been captured in thirty moves the game is automatically declared a draw. A short break for a drink between games, paid for by the loser, ensures that everyone has the chance to challenge two opponents during the evening.

A thin man wearing half-moon spectacles and a dark blue three-piece suit made his way over towards my board. We smiled and shook hands. My guess would have been a solicitor, but I was wrong as he turned out to be an accountant working for a stationery supplier in Woking.

I found it hard to concentrate on my opponent's well-rehearsed Moscow opening as my eyes kept leaving the board and wandering over to the girl in the black dress. On the one occasion our eyes did meet she gave me an enigmatic smile, but although I tried again I was unable to elicit the same response a second time. Despite being preoccupied I still managed to defeat the accountant, who seemed unaware that there were several ways out of a seven-pawn attack.

At the half-time break three other members of the club had offered her a drink before I even reached the bar. I knew I could not hope to play my second match against the girl as I would be expected to challenge one of the visiting team captains. In fact she ended up playing the accountant.

I defeated my new opponent in a little over forty minutes and, as a solicitous host, began to take an interest in the other matches that were still being played. I set out on a circuitous route that ensured I ended up at her table. I could see that the accountant already had the better of her and within moments of my arrival she had lost both her queen and the game.

I introduced myself and found that just shaking hands with her was a sexual experience. Weaving our way through the tables we strolled over to the bar together. Her name, she told me, was Amanda Curzon. I ordered Amanda the glass of red wine she requested and a half-pint of beer for myself. I began by commiserating with her over the defeat.

"How did you get on against him?" she asked.

"Just managed to beat him," I said. "But it was very close. How did your first game with our old captain turn out?"

"Stalemate," said Amanda. "But I think he was just being courteous."

"Last time I played him it ended up in stalemate," I told her.

She smiled. "Perhaps we ought to have a game some time?"

"I'll look forward to that," I said, as she finished her drink.

"Well, I must be off," she announced suddenly. "Have to catch the last train to Hounslow."

"Allow me to drive you," I said gallantly. "It's the least the host captain can be expected to do."

"But surely it's miles out of your way?"

"Not at all," I lied, Hounslow being about twenty minutes beyond my flat. I gulped down the last drop of my beer and helped Amanda on with her coat. Before leaving I thanked the landlord for the efficient organisation of the evening.

We then strolled into the car park. I opened the passenger door of my Scirocco to allow Amanda to climb in.

"A slight improvement on London Transport," she said as I slid into my side of the car. I smiled and headed out on the road northwards. That black dress that I described earlier goes even higher up the legs when a girl sits back in a Scirocco. It didn't seem to embarrass her.

"It's still very early," I ventured after a few inconsequential remarks about the club evening. "Have you time to drop in for a drink?"

"It would have to be a quick one," she replied, looking at her watch. "I've a busy day ahead of me tomorrow."

"Of course," I said, chatting on, hoping she

wouldn't notice a detour that could hardly be described as on the way to Hounslow.

"Do you work in town?" I asked.

"Yes. I'm a receptionist for a firm of estate agents in Berkeley Square."

"I'm surprised you're not a model."

"I used to be," she replied without further explanation. She seemed quite oblivious to the route I was taking as she chatted on about her holiday plans for Ibiza. Once we had arrived at my place I parked the car and led Amanda through my front gate and up to the flat. In the hall I helped her off with her coat before taking her through to the front room.

"What would you like to drink?" I asked.

"I'll stick to wine, if you've a bottle already open," she replied, as she walked slowly round, taking in the unusually tidy room. My mother must have dropped by during the morning, I thought gratefully.

"It's only a bachelor pad," I said, emphasising the word "bachelor" before going into the kitchen. To my relief I found there was an unopened bottle of wine in the larder. I joined Amanda with the bottle and two glasses a few moments later, to find her studying my chess board and fingering the delicate ivory pieces that were set out for a game I was playing by post.

"What a beautiful set," she volunteered as I handed her a glass of wine. "Where did you find it?"

"Mexico," I told her, not explaining that I had won it in a tournament while on holiday there. "I was only sorry we didn't have the chance to have a game ourselves."

She checked her watch. "Time for a quick one," she said, taking a seat behind the little white pieces.

I quickly took my place opposite her. She smiled, picked up a white and a black bishop and hid them behind her back. Her dress became even tighter and emphasised the shape of her breasts. She then placed both clenched fists in front of me. I touched her right hand and she turned it over and opened it to reveal a white bishop.

"Is there to be a wager of any kind?" I asked lightheartedly. She checked inside her evening bag.

"I only have a few pounds on me," she said.

"I'd be willing to play for lower stakes."

"What do you have in mind?" she asked.

"What can you offer?"

"What would you like?"

"Ten pounds if you win."

"And if I lose?"

"You take something off."

I regretted the words the moment I had said them and waited for her to slap my face and leave but she said simply, "There's not much harm in that if we only play one game."

I nodded my agreement and stared down at the board.

She wasn't a bad player – what the pros call a *patzer* – though her Roux opening was somewhat orthodox. I managed to make the game last twenty minutes while sacrificing several pieces without making it look too obvious. When I said "Checkmate", she kicked off both her shoes and laughed.

"Care for another drink?" I asked, not feeling too hopeful. "After all, it's not yet eleven."

"All right. Just a small one and then I must be off."

I went to the kitchen, returned a moment later clutching the bottle, and refilled her glass.

"I only wanted half a glass," she said, frowning.

"I was lucky to win," I said, ignoring her remark, "after your bishop captured my knight. Extremely close-run thing."

"Perhaps," she replied.

"Care for another game?" I ventured.

She hesitated.

"Double or quits?"

"What do you mean?"

"Twenty pounds or another garment?"

"Neither of us is going to lose much tonight, are we?"

She pulled up her chair as I turned the board round and we both began to put the ivory pieces back in place.

The second game took a little longer as I made a silly mistake early on, castling on my queen's side, and it took several moves to recover. However, I still managed to finish the game off in under thirty minutes and even found time to refill Amanda's glass when she wasn't looking.

She smiled at me as she hitched her dress up high enough to allow me to see the tops of her stockings. She undid the suspenders and slowly peeled the stockings off before dropping them on my side of the table.

"I nearly beat you that time," she said.

"Almost," I replied. "Want another chance to get even? Let's say fifty pounds this time," I suggested, trying to make the offer sound magnanimous.

"The stakes are getting higher for both of us," she replied as she reset the board. I began to wonder what might be going through her mind. Whatever it was, she foolishly sacrificed both her rooks early on and the game was over in a matter of minutes.

Once again she lifted her dress but this time well above her waist. My eyes were glued to her thighs as she undid the black suspender belt and held it high above my head before letting it drop and join her stockings on my side of the table.

"Once I had lost the second rook," she said, "I was never in with a chance."

"I agree. It would therefore only be fair to allow you one more chance," I said, quickly re-setting the board. "After all," I added, "you could win one hundred pounds this time." She smiled.

"I really ought to be going home," she said as she moved her queen's pawn two squares forward. She smiled that enigmatic smile again as I countered with my bishop's pawn.

It was the best game she had played all evening and her use of the Warsaw gambit kept me at the board for over thirty minutes. In fact I damn nearly lost early on because I found it hard to concentrate properly on her defence strategy. A couple of times Amanda chuckled when she thought she had got the better of me, but it became obvious she had not seen Karpov play the Sicilian defence and win from a seemingly impossible position.

"Checkmate," I finally declared.

"Damn," she said, and standing up turned her back on me. "You'll have to give me a hand." Trembling, I leaned over and slowly pulled the zip down until it reached the small of her back. Once again I wanted to touch the smooth, creamy skin. She swung round to face me, shrugged gracefully and the dress fell to the ground as if a statue were being unveiled. She leaned forward and brushed the side of my cheek with her hand, which had much the same effect as an electric shock. I emptied the last of the bottle of wine into her glass and left for the kitchen with the excuse of needing to refill my own. When I returned she hadn't moved. A gauzy black bra and pair of panties were now the only garments that I still hoped to see removed.

"I don't suppose you'd play one more game?" I asked, trying not to sound desperate.

"It's time you took me home," she said with a giggle.

I passed her another glass of wine. "Just one more," I begged. "But this time it must be for both garments."

She laughed. "Certainly not," she said. "I couldn't afford to lose."

"It would have to be the last game," I agreed. "But two hundred pounds this time and we play for both garments." I waited, hoping the size of the wager would tempt her. "The odds must surely be on your side. After all, you've nearly won three times."

She sipped her drink as if considering the proposition. "All right," she said. "One last fling."

Neither of us voiced our feeling as to what was certain to happen if she lost.

I could not stop myself trembling as I set the board up once again. I cleared my mind, hoping she hadn't noticed that I had drunk only one glass of wine all night. I was determined to finish this one off quickly.

I moved my queen's pawn one square forward. She retaliated, pushing her king's pawn up two squares. I knew exactly what my next move needed to be and because of it the game only lasted eleven minutes.

I have never been so comprehensively beaten in my life. Amanda was in a totally different class to me. She anticipated my every move and had gambits I had never encountered or even read of before.

It was her turn to say "Checkmate", which she delivered with the same enigmatic smile as before, adding, "You did say the odds were on my side this time."

I lowered my head in disbelief. When I looked up again, she had already slipped that beautiful black dress back on, and was stuffing her stockings and suspenders into her evening bag. A moment later she put on her shoes.

I took out my cheque book, filled in the name "Amanda Curzon" and added the figure "£200", the date and my signature. While I was doing this she replaced the little ivory pieces on the exact squares on which they had been when she had first entered the room.

She bent over and kissed me gently on the cheek. "Thank you," she said as she placed the cheque in her handbag. "We must play again some time." I was still staring at the re-set board in disbelief when I heard the front door close behind her.

"Wait a minute," I said, rushing to the door. "How will you get home?"

I was just in time to see her running down the

steps and towards the open door of a BMW. She climbed in, allowing me one more look at those long tapering legs. She smiled as the car door was closed behind her.

The accountant strolled round to the driver's side, got in, revved up the engine and drove the champion home.

The Wine Taster

THE WINE TASTER

THE first occasion I met Sefton Hamilton was in late August last year when my wife and I were dining with Henry and Suzanne Kennedy at their home in Warwick Square.

Hamilton was one of those unfortunate men who have inherited immense wealth but not a lot more. He was able quickly to convince us that he had little time to read and no time to attend the theatre or opera. However, this did not prevent him from holding opinions on every subject from Shaw to Pavarotti, from Gorbachev to Picasso. He remained puzzled, for instance, as to what the unemployed had to complain about when their dole packet was only just less than what he was currently paying the labourers on his estate. In any case, they only spent it on bingo and drinking, he assured us.

Drinking brings me to the other dinner guest that night – Freddie Barker, the President of the Wine Society, who sat opposite my wife and unlike Hamilton hardly uttered a word. Henry had assured me over the phone that Barker had not only managed to get the Society back on to a proper financial footing but was also acknowledged as a leading authority on his subject. I looked forward to picking up useful bits of inside knowledge. Whenever Barker was allowed to get a word in edgeways, he showed enough knowledge of the topic under discussion to convince me that he would be fascinating if only Hamilton would remain silent long enough for him to speak.

While our hostess produced as a starter a spinach soufflé that melted in the mouth, Henry moved round the table pouring each of us a glass of wine.

Barker sniffed his appreciatively. "Appropriate in bicentennial year that we should be drinking an Australian Chablis of such fine vintage. I feel sure their whites will soon be making the French look to their laurels."

"Australian?" said Hamilton in disbelief as he put down his glass. "How could a nation of beer-swiggers begin to understand the first thing about producing a half decent wine?"

"I think you'll find," began Barker, "that the Australians –"

"Bicentennial indeed," Hamilton continued. "Let's face it, they're only celebrating two hundred years of parole." No one laughed except Hamilton. "I'd still pack the rest of our criminals off there, given half a chance."

No one doubted him.

Hamilton sipped the wine tentatively, like a man who fears he is about to be poisoned, then began to explain why, in his considered view, judges were far too lenient with petty criminals. I found myself concentrating more on the food than the incessant flow of my neighbour's views.

I always enjoy Beef Wellington, and Suzanne can produce a pastry that doesn't flake when cut and meat that's so tender that once one has finished a first helping, Oliver Twist comes to mind. It certainly helped me to endure Hamilton's pontificating. Barker managed to pass an appreciative comment to Henry on the quality of the claret between Hamilton's opinions on the chances of Paddy Ashdown reviving the Liberal Party and the role of Arthur Scargill in the trade union movement, allowing no one the chance to reply.

"I don't allow my staff to belong to any union," Hamilton declared, gulping down his drink. "I run a closed shop." He laughed once more at his own joke and held his empty glass high in the air as if it would be filled by magic. In fact it was filled by Henry with a discretion that shamed Hamilton – not that he noticed. In the brief pause that followed, my wife suggested that perhaps the trade union movement had been born out of a response to a genuine social need.

"Balderdash, madam," said Hamilton. "With great respect, the trade unions have been the single most important factor in the decline of Britain as we know it. They've no interest in anybody but themselves. You only have to look at Ron Todd and the whole Ford fiasco to understand that."

Suzanne began to clear the plates away and I noticed she took the opportunity to nudge Henry, who quickly changed the subject.

Moments later a raspberry meringue glazed with a thick sauce appeared. It seemed a pity to cut such a creation but Suzanne carefully divided six generous helpings like a nanny feeding her charges while

Henry uncorked a 1981 Sauternes. Barker literally licked his lips in anticipation.

"And another thing," Hamilton was saying. "The Prime Minister has got far too many Wets in her Cabinet for my liking."

"With whom would you replace them?" asked Barker innocently.

Herod would have had little trouble in convincing the list of gentlemen Hamilton proffered that the slaughter of the innocents was merely an extension of the child care programme.

Once again I became more interested in Suzanne's culinary efforts, especially as she had allowed me an indulgence: Cheddar was to be served as the final course. I knew the moment I tasted it that it had been purchased from the Alvis Brothers' farm in Keynsham; we all have to be knowledgeable about something, and Cheddar is my speciality.

To accompany the cheese, Henry supplied a port which was to be the highlight of the evening. "Sandeman 1970," he said in an aside to Barker as he poured the first drops into the expert's glass.

"Yes, of course," said Barker, holding it to his nose. "I would have known it anywhere. Typical Sandeman warmth but with real body. I hope you've laid some down, Henry," he added. "You'll enjoy it even more in your old age."

"Think you're a bit of an authority on wines, do you?" said Hamilton, the first question he had asked all evening.

"Not exactly," began Barker, "but I –"

"You're all a bunch of humbugs, the lot of you,"

interrupted Hamilton. "You sniff and you swirl, you taste and you spit, then you spout a whole lot of gobbledegook and expect us to swallow it. Body and warmth be damned. You can't take me in that easily."

"No one was trying to," said Barker with feeling.

"You've been keen to put one over on us all evening," replied Hamilton, "with your 'Yes, of course, I'd have known it anywhere' routine. Come on, admit it."

"I didn't mean to suggest –" added Barker.

"I'll prove it, if you like," said Hamilton.

The five of us stared at the ungracious guest and, for the first time that evening, I wondered what could possibly be coming next.

"I have heard it said," continued Hamilton, "that Sefton Hall boasts one of the finest wine cellars in England. It was laid down by my father and his father before him, though I confess I haven't found the time to continue the tradition." Barker nodded in belief. "But my butler knows exactly what I like. I therefore invite you, sir, to join me for lunch on the Saturday after next, when I will produce four wines of the finest vintage for your consideration. And I offer you a wager," he added, looking straight at Barker. "Five hundred pounds to fifty a bottle – tempting odds, I'm sure you'll agree – that you will be unable to name any one of them." He stared belligerently at the distinguished President of the Wine Society.

"The sum is so large that I could not consider –"

"Unwilling to take up the challenge, eh, Barker? Then you are, sir, a coward as well as a humbug."

After the embarrassing pause that followed, Barker replied, "As you wish, sir. It appears I am left with no choice but to accept your challenge."

A satisfied grin appeared on the other man's face. "You must come along as a witness, Henry," he said, turning to our host. "And why don't you bring along that author johnny?" he added, pointing at me. "Then he'll really have something to write about for a change."

From Hamilton's manner it was obvious that the feelings of our wives were not to be taken into consideration. Mary gave me a wry smile.

Henry looked anxiously towards me, but I was quite content to be an observer of this unfolding drama. I nodded my assent.

"Good," said Hamilton, rising from his place, his napkin still tucked under his collar. "I look forward to seeing the three of you at Sefton Hall on Saturday week. Shall we say twelve thirty?" He bowed to Suzanne.

"I won't be able to join you, I'm afraid," she said, clearing up any lingering doubt she might have been included in the invitation. "I always have lunch with my mother on Saturdays."

Hamilton waved a hand to signify that it did not concern him one way or the other.

After the strange guest had left we sat in silence for some moments before Henry volunteered a statement. "I'm sorry about all that," he began. "His mother and my aunt are old friends and she's asked me on several occasions to have him over to dinner. It seems no one else will."

"Don't worry," said Barker eventually. "I'll do my best not to let you down. And in return for such excellent hospitality perhaps both of you would be kind enough to leave Saturday evening free? There is," he explained, "an inn near Sefton Hall I have wanted to visit for some time: the Hamilton Arms. The food, I'm assured, is more than adequate but the wine list is . . ." he hesitated, "considered by experts to be exceptional."

Henry and I both checked our diaries and readily accepted his invitation.

I thought a great deal about Sefton Hamilton during the next ten days and awaited our lunch with a mixture of apprehension and anticipation. On the Saturday morning Henry drove the three of us down to Sefton Park and we arrived a little after twelve thirty. Actually we passed through the massive wrought-iron gates at twelve thirty precisely, but did not reach the front door of the house until twelve thirty-seven.

The great oak door was opened before we had a chance to knock by a tall elegant man in a tail coat, wing collar and black tie. He informed us that he was Adams, the butler. He then escorted us to the morning room, where we were greeted by a large log fire. Above it hung a picture of a disapproving man who I presumed was Sefton Hamilton's grandfather. On the other walls was a massive tapestry of the Battle of Waterloo and an enormous oil of the Crimean War. Antique furniture littered the room and the one sculpture on display was of a Greek figure throwing a discus. Looking around, I reflected that only the telephone belonged to the present century.

Sefton Hamilton entered the room as a gale

might hit an unhappy seaside town. Immediately he stood with his back to the fire, blocking any heat we might have been appreciating.

"Whisky!" he bellowed as Adams appeared once again. "Barker?"

"Not for me," said Barker with a thin smile.

"Ah," said Hamilton. "Want to keep your taste buds at their most sensitive, eh?"

Barker did not reply. Before we went into lunch we learned that the estate was seven thousand acres in size and had some of the finest shooting outside of Scotland. The Hall had one hundred and twelve rooms, one or two of which Hamilton had not visited since he was a child. The roof itself, he assured us finally, was an acre and a half, a statistic that will long remain in my memory as it is the same size as my garden.

The longcase clock in the corner of the room struck one. "Time for the contest to begin," declared Hamilton, and marched out of the room like a general who assumes his troops will follow him without question. We did, all the way down thirty yards of corridor to the dining room. The four of us then took our places around a seventeenth-century oak table that could comfortably have seated twenty.

Adorning the centre of the table were two Georgian decanters and two unlabelled bottles. The first bottle was filled with a clear white wine, the first decanter with a red, the second bottle with a richer white and the second decanter with a tawny red substance. In front of the four wines were four white cards. By each lay a slim bundle of fifty-pound notes.

Hamilton took his place in the large chair at the top of the table while Barker and I sat opposite each other in the centre, facing the wine, leaving Henry to occupy the final place at the far end of the table.

The butler stood one pace behind his master's chair. He nodded and four footmen appeared, bearing the first course. A fish and prawn terrine was placed in front of each of us. Adams received a nod from his master before he picked up the first bottle and began to fill Barker's glass. Barker waited for the butler to go round the table and fill the other three glasses before he began his ritual.

First he swirled the wine round while at the same time studying it carefully. Then he sniffed it. He hesitated and a surprised look came over his face. He took a sip.

"Um," he said eventually. "I confess, quite a challenge." He sniffed it again just to be sure. Then he looked up and gave a smile of satisfaction. Hamilton stared at him, his mouth slightly open, although he remained unusually silent.

Barker took one more sip. "Montagny Tête de Cuvée 1985," he declared with the confidence of an expert, "bottled by Louis Latour." We all looked towards Hamilton who, in contrast, displayed an unhappy frown.

"You're right," said Hamilton. "It was bottled by Latour. But that's about as clever as telling us that Heinz bottle tomato sauce. And as my father died in 1984 I can assure you, sir, you are mistaken." He looked round at his butler to confirm the statement. Adams's face remained inscrutable. Barker turned over the card. It read: "Chevalier Montrachet Les Demorselles 1983". He stared at the card, obviously unable to believe his eyes.

"One down and three to go," Hamilton declared, oblivious to Barker's reaction. The footmen reappeared and took away the fish plates, to replace them a few moments later with lightly cooked grouse. While its accompaniments were being served Barker did not speak. He just stared at the other three decanters, not even hearing his host inform Henry who his guests were to be for the first shoot of the season the following week. I remember that the names corresponded roughly with the ones Hamilton had suggested for his ideal Cabinet.

Barker nibbled at the grouse as he waited for Adams to fill a glass from the first decanter. He had not finished his terrine after the opening failure, only taking the occasional sip of water.

"As Adams and I spent a considerable part of our morning selecting the wines for this little challenge, let us hope you can do better this time," said Hamilton, unable to hide his satisfaction. Barker once again began to swirl the wine round. He seemed to take longer this time, sniffing it several times before putting his glass to his lips and finally sipping from it.

A smile of instant recognition appeared on his face and he did not hesitate. "Château la Louvière 1978."

"This time you have the correct year, sir, but you have insulted the wine."

Immediately Barker turned the card over and read it out incredulously: Château Lafite 1978. Even I knew that to be one of the finest clarets one might ever hope to taste. Barker lapsed into a deep silence and continued to nibble at his food.

Hamilton appeared to be enjoying the wine almost as much as the half-time score. "One hundred pounds to me, nothing to the President of the Wine Society," he reminded us. Embarrassed, Henry and I tried to keep the conversation going until the third course had been served – a lemon and lime soufflé which could not compare in presentation or subtlety with any of Suzanne's offerings.

"Shall we move on to my third challenge?" asked Hamilton crisply.

Once again, Adams picked up a decanter and began to pour the wine. I was surprised to see that he spilled a little as he filled Barker's glass.

"Clumsy oaf," barked Hamilton.

"I do apologise, sir," said Adams. He removed the spilled drop from the wooden table with a napkin. As he did so he stared at Barker with a desperate look that I felt sure had nothing to do with the spilling of the wine. However, he remained mute as he continued to circle the table.

Once again Barker went through his ritual, the swirling, the sniffing and finally the tasting. This time he took even longer. Hamilton became impatient and drummed the great Jacobean table with his podgy fingers.

"It's a Sauternes," began Barker.

"Any half-wit could tell you that," said Hamilton. "I want to know the year and the vintage."

His guest hesitated.

"Château Guiraud 1976," he said flatly.

"At least you are consistent," said Hamilton. "You're always wrong."

Barker flicked over the card.

"Château d'Yquem 1980," he said in disbelief. It

was a vintage that I had only seen at the bottom of wine lists in expensive restaurants and had never had the privilege of tasting. It puzzled me greatly that Barker could have been wrong about the Mona Lisa of wines.

Barker quickly turned towards Hamilton to protest and must have seen Adams standing behind his master, all six foot three of the man trembling, at exactly the same time I did. I wanted Hamilton to leave the room so I could ask Adams what was making him so fearful, but the owner of Sefton Hall was now in full cry.

Meanwhile Barker gazed at the butler for a moment more and, sensing his discomfort, lowered his eyes and contributed nothing else to the conversation until the port was poured some twenty minutes later.

"Your last chance to avoid complete humiliation," said Hamilton.

A cheese board, displaying several varieties, was brought round and each guest selected his choice – I stuck to a Cheddar that I could have told Hamilton had not been made in Somerset. Meanwhile the port was poured by the butler, who was now as white as a sheet. I began to wonder if he was going to faint, but somehow he managed to fill all four glasses before returning to stand a pace behind his master's chair. Hamilton noticed nothing untoward.

Barker drank the port, not bothering with any of his previous preliminaries.

"Taylors," he began.

"Agreed," said Hamilton. "But as there are only three decent suppliers of port in the world, the year can be all that matters – as you, in your exalted position, must be well aware, Mr Barker."

Freddie nodded his agreement. "Nineteen seventy-five," he said firmly, then quickly flicked the card over.

"Taylors 1927", I read upside-down.

Once again Barker turned sharply towards his host, who was rocking with laughter. The butler stared back at his master's guest with haunted eyes. Barker hesitated only for a moment before removing a cheque book from his inside pocket. He filled in the name "Sefton Hamilton" and the figure of £200. He signed it and wordlessly passed the cheque along the table to his host.

"That was only half the bargain," said Hamilton, enjoying every moment of his triumph.

Barker rose, paused and said, "I am a humbug."

"You are indeed, sir," said Hamilton.

After spending three of the most unpleasant hours of my life, I managed to escape with Henry and Freddie Barker a little after four o'clock. As Henry drove away from Sefton Hall neither of us uttered a word. Perhaps we both felt that Barker should be allowed the first comment.

"I fear, gentlemen," he said eventually, "I shall not be good company for the next few hours, and so I will, with your permission, take a brisk walk and join you both for dinner at the Hamilton Arms around seven thirty. I have booked a table for eight o'clock." Without another word, Barker signalled that Henry should bring the car to a halt and we watched as he climbed out and headed off down a country lane. Henry did not drive on until his friend was well out of sight.

My sympathies were entirely with Barker, although I remained puzzled by the whole affair. How could the President of the Wine Society make such basic mistakes? After all, I could read one page of Dickens and know it wasn't Graham Greene.

Like Dr Watson, I felt I required a fuller explanation.

Barker found us sitting round the fire in the private bar at the Hamilton Arms a little after seven thirty that night. Following his exercise, he appeared in far better spirits. He chatted about nothing consequential and didn't once mention what had taken place at lunchtime.

It must have been a few minutes later, when I turned to check the old clock above the door, that I saw Hamilton's butler seated at the bar in earnest conversation with the innkeeper. I would have thought nothing of it had I not noticed the same terrified look that I had witnessed earlier in the afternoon as he pointed in our direction. The innkeeper appeared equally anxious, as if he had been found guilty of serving half-measures by a customs and excise officer.

He picked up some menus and walked over to our table.

"We've no need for those," said Barker. "Your reputation goes before you. We are in your hands. Whatever you suggest we will happily consume."

"Thank you, sir," he said and passed our host the wine list.

Barker studied the contents inside the leather-bound covers for some time before a large smile appeared on his face. "I think you had better select the wines as well," he said, "as I have a feeling you know the sort of thing I would expect."

"Of course, sir," said the innkeeper as Freddie passed back the wine list leaving me totally mystified, remembering that this was Barker's first visit to the inn.

The innkeeper left for the kitchens while we chatted away and didn't reappear for some fifteen minutes.

"Your table is ready, gentlemen," he said, and we followed him into an adjoining dining room. There were only a dozen tables but as ours was the last to be filled there was no doubting the inn's popularity.

The innkeeper had selected a light supper of consommé, followed by thin slices of duck, almost as if he had known that we would be unable to handle another heavy meal after our lunch at the Hall.

I was also surprised to find that all the wines he had chosen were served in decanters and I assumed that the innkeeper must therefore have selected the house wines. As each was poured and consumed I admit that, to my untutored palate, they seemed far superior to those which I had drunk at Sefton Hall earlier that day. Barker certainly seemed to linger over every mouthful and on one occasion said appreciatively, "This is the real McCoy."

At the end of the evening when our table had been cleared we sat back and enjoyed a magnificent port and smoked cigars.

It was at this point that Henry mentioned Hamilton for the first time.

"Are you going to let us into the mystery of what really happened at lunch today?" he asked.

"I'm still not altogether sure myself," came back Barker's reply, "but I am certain of one thing: Mr Hamilton's father was a man who knew his wines, while his son doesn't."

I would have pressed Barker further on the subject if the innkeeper had not arrived by his side at that moment.

"An excellent meal," Barker declared. "And as for the wine – quite exceptional."

"You are kind, sir," said the innkeeper, as he handed him the bill.

My curiosity got the better of me, I'm sorry to admit, and I glanced at the bottom of the slim strip of paper. I couldn't believe my eyes – the bill came to two hundred pounds.

To my surprise, Barker only commented, "Very reasonable, considering." He wrote out a cheque and passed it over to the innkeeper. "I have only tasted Château d'Yquem 1980 once before today," he added, "and Taylors 1927 never."

The innkeeper smiled. "I hope you enjoyed them both, sir. I feel sure you wouldn't have wanted to see them wasted on a humbug."

Barker nodded his agreement.

I watched as the innkeeper left the dining room and returned to his place behind the bar.

He passed the cheque over to Adams the butler, who studied it for a moment, smiled and then tore it into little pieces.

A Chapter of Accidents

A CHAPTER OF ACCIDENTS

WE first met Patrick Travers on our annual winter holiday to Verbier. We were waiting at the ski lift that first Saturday morning when a man who must have been in his early forties stood aside to allow Caroline to take his place, so that we could travel up together. He explained that he had already completed two runs that morning and didn't mind waiting. I thanked him and thought nothing more of it.

As soon as we reach the top my wife and I always go our separate ways, she to the A-slope to join Marcel, who only instructs advanced skiers – she has been skiing since the age of seven – I to the B-slope and any instructor who is available – I took up skiing at the age of forty-one – and frankly the B-slope is still too advanced for me though I don't dare admit as much, especially to Caroline. We always meet up again at the ski lift after completing our different runs.

That evening we bumped into Travers at the hotel bar. Since he seemed to be on his own we invited him to join us for dinner. He proved to be an amusing companion and we passed a pleasant enough evening together. He flirted politely with my wife without ever overstepping the mark and she appeared to be flattered by his attentions. Over the years I have become used to men being attracted to Caroline and I never need reminding how lucky I am. During dinner we learned that Travers was a merchant banker with an office in the City and a flat in Eaton Square. He had come to Verbier every year since he had been taken on a school trip in the late Fifties, he told us. He still prided himself on being the first on the ski lift every morning, almost always beating the local blades up and down.

Travers appeared to be genuinely interested in the fact that I ran a small West End art gallery; as it turned out, he was something of a collector himself, specialising in minor Impressionists. He promised he would drop by and see my next exhibition when he was back in London.

I assured him that he would be most welcome but never gave it a second thought. In fact I only saw Travers a couple of times over the rest of the holiday, once talking to the wife of a friend of mine who owned a gallery that specialises in oriental rugs, and later I noticed him following Caroline expertly down the treacherous A-slope.

It was six weeks later, and some minutes before I could place him that night at my gallery. I had to rack that part of one's memory which recalls names, a skill politicians rely on every day.

"Good to see you, Edward," he said. "I saw the write-up you got in the *Independent* and remembered your kind invitation to the private view."

"Glad you could make it, Patrick," I replied, remembering just in time.

"I'm not a champagne man myself," he told me, "but I'll travel a long way to see a Vuillard."

"You think highly of him?"

"Oh yes. I would compare him favourably with Pissarro and Bonnard, and he still remains one of the most underrated of the Impressionists."

"I agree," I replied. "But my gallery has felt that way about Vuillard for some considerable time."

"How much is 'The Lady at the Window'?" he asked.

"Eighty thousand pounds," I said quietly.

"It reminds me of a picture of his in the Metropolitan," he said, as he studied the reproduction in the catalogue.

I was impressed, and told Travers that the Vuillard in New York had been painted within a month of the one he so admired.

He nodded. "And the small nude?"

"Forty-seven thousand," I told him.

"Mrs Hensell, the wife of his dealer and Vuillard's second mistress, if I'm not mistaken. The French are always so much more civilised about these things than we are. But my favourite painting in this exhibition," he continued, "compares surely with the finest of his work." He turned to face the large oil of a young girl playing a piano, her mother bending to turn a page of the score.

"Magnificent," he said. "Dare I ask how much?"

"Three hundred and seventy thousand pounds," I said, wondering if such a price tag put it out of Travers's bracket.

"What a super party, Edward," said a voice from behind my shoulder.

"Percy!" I cried, turning round. "I thought you said you wouldn't be able to make it."

"Yes I did, old fellow, but I decided I couldn't sit at home alone all the time, so I've come to drown my sorrows in champagne."

"Quite right too," I said. "Sorry to hear about Diana," I added as Percy moved on. When I turned back to continue my conversation with Patrick Travers he was nowhere to be seen. I searched around the room and spotted him standing in the far corner of the gallery chatting to my wife, a glass of champagne in his hand. She was wearing an off-the-shoulder green dress that I considered a little too modern. Travers's eyes seemed to be glued to a spot a few inches below the shoulders. I would have thought nothing of it had he spoken to anyone else that evening.

The next occasion on which I saw Travers was about a week later on returning from the bank with some petty cash. Once again he was standing in front of the Vuillard oil of mother and daughter at the piano.

"Good morning, Patrick," I said as I joined him.

"I can't seem to get that picture out of my mind," he declared, as he continued to stare at the two figures.

"Understandably."

"I don't suppose you would allow me to live with them for a week or two until I can finally make up my mind? Naturally I would be quite happy to leave a deposit."

"Of course," I said. "I would require a bank

reference as well and the deposit would be twenty-five thousand pounds."

He agreed to both requests without hesitation so I asked him where he would like the picture delivered. He handed me a card which revealed his address in Eaton Square. The following morning his bankers confirmed that three hundred and seventy thousand pounds would not be a problem for their client.

Within twenty-four hours the Vuillard had been taken round to his home and hung in the dining room on the ground floor. He phoned back in the afternoon to thank me and asked if Caroline and I would care to join him for dinner; he wanted, he said, a second opinion on how the painting looked.

With three hundred and seventy thousand pounds at stake I didn't feel it was an invitation I could reasonably turn down, and in any case Caroline seemed eager to accept, explaining that she was interested to see what his house was like.

We dined with Travers the following Thursday. We turned out to be the only guests, and I remember being surprised that there wasn't a Mrs Travers or at least a resident girlfriend. He was a thoughtful host and the meal he had arranged was superb. However, I considered at the time that he seemed a little too solicitous with Caroline, although she certainly gave the impression of enjoying his undivided attention. At one point I began to wonder if either of them would have noticed if I had disappeared into thin air.

When we left Eaton Square that night Travers told me that he had almost made up his mind about the picture, which made me feel the evening had served at least some purpose.

Six days later the painting was returned to the gallery with a note attached explaining that he no longer cared for it. Travers did not elaborate on his reasons, but simply ended by saying that he hoped to drop by some time and reconsider the other Vuillards. Disappointed, I returned his deposit, but realised that customers often do come back, sometimes months, even years later.

But Travers never did.

It was about a month later that I learned why he would never return. I was lunching at the large centre table at my club, as in most all-male establishments the table reserved for members who drift in on their own. Percy Fellows was the next to enter the dining room so he took a seat opposite me. I hadn't seen him to talk to since the private view of the Vuillard exhibition and we hadn't really had much of a conversation then. Percy was one of the most respected antique dealers in England and I had once even done a successful barter with him, a Charles II writing desk in exchange for a Dutch landscape by Utrillo.

I repeated how sorry I was to learn about Diana.

"It was always going to end in divorce," he explained. "She was in and out of every bedroom in London. I was beginning to look a complete cuckold, and that bloody man Travers was the last straw."

"Travers?" I said, not understanding.

"Patrick Travers, the man named in my divorce petition. Ever come across him?"

"I know the name," I said hesitantly, wanting to

hear more before I admitted to our slight acquaintanceship.

"Funny," he said. "Could have sworn I saw him at the private view."

"But what do you mean, he was the last straw?" I asked, trying to take his mind off the opening.

"Met the bloody fellow at Ascot, didn't we? Joined us for lunch, happily drank my champagne, ate my strawberries and cream and then before the week was out had bedded my wife. But that's not the half of it."

"The half of it?"

"The man had the nerve to come round to my shop and put down a large deposit on a Georgian table. Then he invites the two of us round to dinner to see how it looks. After he's had enough time to make love to Diana he returns them both slightly soiled. You don't look too well, old fellow," said Percy suddenly. "Something wrong with the food? Never been the same since Harry left for the Carlton. I've written to the wine committee about it several times but –"

"No, I'm fine," I said. "I just need a little fresh air. Please excuse me, Percy."

It was on the walk back from my club that I decided I would have to do something about Mr Travers.

The next morning I waited for the mail to arrive and checked any envelopes addressed to Caroline. Nothing seemed untoward but then I decided that Travers wouldn't have been foolish enough to commit anything to paper. I also began to eavesdrop on her telephone conversations, but he was not among the callers, at least not while I was at home. I even checked the mileometer on her Mini to see if she had driven any long distances, but then Eaton Square isn't all that far. It's often what you don't do that gives the game away, I decided: we didn't make love for a fortnight, and she didn't comment.

I continued to watch Caroline more carefully over the next fortnight but it became obvious to me that Travers must have tired of her about the same time as he had returned the Vuillard. This only made me more angry.

I then formed a plan of revenge that seemed quite extraordinary to me at the time and I assumed that in a matter of days I would get over it, even forget it. But I didn't. If anything, the idea grew into an obsession. I began to convince myself that it was my bounden duty to do away with Travers before he besmirched any more of my friends.

I have never in my life knowingly broken the law. Parking fines annoy me, dropped litter offends me and I pay my VAT on the same day the frightful buff envelope drops through the letterbox.

Nevertheless once I'd decided what had to be done I set about my task meticulously. At first I had considered shooting Travers until I discovered how hard it is to get a gun licence and that if I did the job properly, he would end up feeling very little pain, which wasn't what I had planned for him; then poisoning crossed my mind – but that requires a witnessed prescription and I still wouldn't be able to watch the long slow death I desired. Then strangling, which I decided would necessitate too much courage – and in any case he was a bigger man than me so *I* might end up being the one who was strangled. Then drowning, which could take years to get the man near any water and then I might not be able to hang around to make sure he went under for the third time. I even gave some thought to running over the damned man, but dropped that idea when I realised opportunity would be almost nil and besides, I wouldn't be left any time to check if he was dead. I was quickly becoming aware just how hard it is to kill someone – and get away with it.

I sat awake at night reading the biographies of murderers, but as they had all been caught and found guilty that didn't fill me with much confidence. I turned to detective novels which always seemed to allow for a degree of coincidence, luck and surprise that I was unwilling to risk, until I came across a rewarding line from Conan Doyle: "Any intended victim who has a regular routine immediately makes himself more vulnerable". And then I recalled one routine of which Travers was particularly proud. It required a further six-month wait on my part but that also gave me more time to perfect my plan. I used the enforced wait well because whenever Caroline was away for more than twenty-four hours, I booked in for a skiing lesson on the dry slope at Harrow.

I found it surprisingly easy to discover when Travers would be returning to Verbier, and I was able to organise the winter holiday so that our paths would cross for only three days, a period of time quite sufficient for me to commit my first crime.

Caroline and I arrived in Verbier on the second Friday in January. She had commented on the state of my nerves more than once over the Christmas period, and hoped the holiday would help me relax. I could hardly explain to her that it was the thought of the holiday that was making me so tense. It didn't help when she asked me on the plane to Switzerland if I thought Travers might be there this year.

On the first morning after our arrival we took the ski lift up at about ten thirty and, once we had reached the top, Caroline duly reported to Marcel. As she departed with him for the A-slope I returned to the B-slope to work on my own. As always we agreed to meet back at the ski lift or, if we missed each other, at least for lunch.

During the days that followed I went over and over the plan I had perfected in my mind and practised so diligently at Harrow until I felt sure it was foolproof. By the end of the first week I had convinced myself I was ready.

The night before Travers was due to arrive I was the last to leave the slopes. Even Caroline commented on how much my skiing had improved and she suggested to Marcel that I was ready for the A-slope with its sharper bends and steeper inclines.

"Next year, perhaps," I told her, trying to make light of it, and returned to the B-slope.

During the final morning I skied over the first mile of the course again and again, and became so preoccupied with my work that I quite forgot to join Caroline for lunch.

In the afternoon I checked and rechecked the placing of every red flag marking the run, and once

I was convinced the last skier had left the slope for the evening I collected about thirty of the flags and replaced them at intervals I had carefully worked out. My final task was to check the prepared patch before building a large mound of snow some twenty paces above the chosen spot. Once my preparations were complete I skied slowly down the mountain in the fading light.

"Are you trying to win an Olympic gold medal or something?" Caroline asked me when I eventually got back to our room. I closed the bathroom door so she couldn't expect a reply.

Travers checked in to the hotel an hour later.

I waited until the early evening before I joined him at the bar for a drink. He seemed a little nervous when he first saw me, but I quickly put him at ease. His old self-confidence soon returned, which only made me more determined to carry out my plan. I left him at the bar a few minutes before Caroline came down for dinner so that she would not see the two of us together. Innocent surprise would be necessary once the deed had been done.

"Unlike you to eat so little, especially as you missed your lunch," Caroline commented as we left the dining room that night.

I made no comment as we passed Travers seated at the bar, his hand on the knee of another innocent middle-aged woman.

I did not sleep for one second that night and I crept out of bed just before six the next morning, careful not to wake Caroline. Everything was laid out on the bathroom floor just as I had left it the night before. A few moments later I was dressed and ready. I walked down the back stairs of the hotel, avoiding the lift, and crept out by the "fire exit", realising for the first time what a thief must feel like. I had a woollen cap pulled well down over my ears and a pair of snow goggles covering my eyes: not even Caroline would have recognised me.

I arrived at the bottom of the ski lift forty minutes before it was due to open. As I stood alone behind the little shed that housed the electrical machinery to work the lift I realised that everything now depended on Travers's sticking to his routine. I wasn't sure I could go through with it if my plan had to be moved on to the following day. As I waited, I stamped my feet in the freshly fallen snow, and slapped my arms around my chest to keep warm. Every few moments I kept peering round the corner of the building in the hope that I would see him striding towards me. At last a speck appeared at the bottom of the hill by the side of the road, a pair of skis resting on the man's shoulders. But what if it didn't turn out to be Travers?

I stepped out from behind the shed a few moments later to join the warmly wrapped man. It *was* Travers and he could not hide his surprise at seeing me standing there. I started up a casual conversation about being unable to sleep, and how I thought I might as well put in a few runs before the rush began. Now all I needed was the ski lift to start up on time. A few minutes after seven an engineer arrived and the vast oily mechanism cranked into action.

We were the first two to take our places on those little seats before heading up and over the deep ravine. I kept turning back to check there was still no one else in sight.

"I usually manage to complete a full run even before the second person arrives," Travers told me when the lift had reached its highest point. I looked back again to be sure we were now well out of sight of the engineer working the lift, then peered down some two hundred feet and wondered what it would be like to land head first in the ravine. I began to feel dizzy and wished I hadn't looked down.

The ski lift jerked slowly on up the icy wire until we finally reached the landing point.

"Damn," I said, as we jumped off our little seats. "Marcel isn't here."

"Never is at this time," said Travers, making off towards the advanced slope. "Far too early for him."

"I don't suppose you would come down with me?" I said, calling after Travers.

He stopped and looked back suspiciously.

"Caroline thinks I'm ready to join you," I explained, "but I'm not so sure and would value a second opinion. I've broken my own record for the B-slope several times, but I wouldn't want to make a fool of myself in front of my wife."

"Well, I –"

"I'd ask Marcel if he were here. And in any case you're the best skier I know."

"Well, if you –" he began.

"Just the once, then you can spend the rest of your holiday on the A-slope. You could even treat the run as a warm-up."

"Might make a change, I suppose," he said.

"Just the once," I repeated. "That's all I'll need. Then you'll be able to tell me if I'm good enough."

"Shall we make a race of it?" he said, taking me

by surprise just as I began clamping on my skis. I couldn't complain; all the books on murder had warned me to be prepared for the unexpected. "That's one way we can find out if you're ready," he added cockily.

"If you insist. Don't forget, I'm older and less experienced than you," I reminded him. I checked my skis quickly because I knew I had to start off in front of him.

"But you know the B-course backwards," he retorted. " I've never even seen it before."

"I'll agree to a race, but only if you'll consider a wager," I replied.

For the first time I could see I had caught his interest. "How much?" he asked.

"Oh, nothing so vulgar as money," I said. "The winner gets to tell Caroline the truth."

"The truth?" he said, looking puzzled.

"Yes," I replied, and shot off down the hill before he could respond. I got a good start as I skied in and out of the red flags, but looking back over my shoulder I could see he had recovered quickly and was already chasing hard after me. I realised that it was vital for me to stay in front of him for the first third of the course, but I could already feel him cutting down my lead.

After half a mile of swerving and driving he shouted, "You'll have to go a lot faster than that if you hope to beat me." His arrogant boast only pushed me to stay ahead but I kept the lead only because of my advantage of knowing every twist and turn during that first mile. Once I was sure that I would reach the vital newly marked route before he could I began to relax. After all, I had practised over the next two hundred metres fifty times a day for the last ten days, but I was only too aware that this time was the only one that mattered.

I glanced over my shoulder to see he was now about thirty metres behind me. I began to slow slightly as we approached the prepared ice patch, hoping he wouldn't notice or would think I'd lost my nerve. I held back even more when I reached the top of the patch until I could almost feel the sound of his breathing. Then, quite suddenly, the moment before I would have hit the ice I ploughed my skis and came to a complete halt in the mound of snow I had built the previous night. Travers sailed past me at about forty miles an hour, and seconds later flew high into the air over the ravine with a scream I will never forget. I couldn't get myself to look over the edge as I knew he must have broken every bone in his body the moment he hit the snow some hundred feet below.

I carefully levelled the mound of snow that had saved my life and then clambered back up the mountain as fast as I could go, gathering the thirty flags that had heralded my false route. Then I skied from side to side replacing them in their correct positions on the B-slope, some one hundred metres above my carefully prepared ice patch. Once each one was back in place I skied on down the hill, feeling like an Olympic champion. When I reached the base of the slope I pulled up my hood to cover my head and didn't remove my snow goggles. I unstrapped my skis and walked casually towards the hotel. I re-entered the building by the rear door and was back in bed by seven forty.

I tried to control my breathing but it was some

time before my pulse had returned to normal. Caroline woke a few minutes later, turned over and put her arms round me.

"Ugh," she said, "you're frozen. Have you been sleeping without the covers on?"

I laughed. "You must have pulled them off during the night."

"Go and have a hot bath."

After I had had a quick bath we made love and I dressed a second time, double-checking that I had left no clues of my early flight before going down to breakfast.

As Caroline was pouring my second cup of coffee, I heard the ambulance siren at first coming from the town and then later returning.

"Hope it wasn't a bad accident," my wife said, as she continued to pour her coffee.

"What?" I said, a little too loudly, glancing up from the previous day's *Times*.

"The siren, silly. There must have been an accident on the mountain. Probably Travers," she said.

"Travers?" I said, even more loudly.

"Patrick Travers. I saw him at the bar last night. I didn't mention it to you because I know you don't care for him."

"But why Travers?" I asked nervously.

"Doesn't he always claim he's the first on the slope every morning? Even beats the instructors up to the top."

"Does he?" I said.

"You must remember. We were going up for the first time the day we met him when he was already on his third run."

"Was he?"

"You are being dim this morning, Edward. Did you get out of bed the wrong side?" she asked, laughing.

I didn't reply.

"Well, I only hope it *is* Travers," Caroline added, sipping her coffee. "I never did like the man."

"Why not?" I asked, somewhat taken aback.

"He once made a pass at me," she said casually.

I stared across at her, unable to speak.

"Aren't you going to ask what happened?"

"I'm so stunned I don't know what to say," I replied.

"He was all over me at the gallery that night and then invited me out to lunch after we had dinner with him. I told him to get lost," Caroline said. She touched me gently on the hand. "I've never mentioned it to you before because I thought it might have been the reason he returned the Vuillard, and that only made me feel guilty."

"But it's me who should feel guilty," I said, fumbling with a piece of toast.

"Oh, no, darling, you're not guilty of anything. In any case, if I ever decided to be unfaithful it wouldn't be with a lounge lizard like that. Good heavens no. Diana had already warned me what to expect from him. Not my style at all."

I sat there thinking of Travers on his way to a morgue, or even worse, still buried under the snow, knowing there was nothing I could do about it.

"You know, I think the time really has come for you to tackle the A-slope," Caroline said as we finished breakfast. "Your skiing has improved beyond words."

"Yes," I replied, more than a little preoccupied.

I hardly spoke another word as we made our way together to the foot of the mountain.

"Are you all right, darling?" Caroline asked as we travelled up side by side on the lift.

"Fine," I said, unable to look down into the ravine as we reached the highest point. Was Travers still down there, or already in the morgue?

"Stop looking like a frightened child. After all the work you've put in this week you're more than ready to join me," she said reassuringly.

I smiled weakly. When we reached the top, I jumped off the ski lift just a moment too early, and knew immediately I took my second step that I had sprained an ankle.

I received no sympathy from Caroline. She was convinced I was putting it on in order to avoid attempting the advanced run. She swept past me and sped on down the mountain while I returned in ignominy via the lift. When I reached the bottom I glanced towards the engineer but he didn't give me a second look. I hobbled over to the First Aid post and checked in. Caroline joined me a few minutes later.

I explained to her that the duty orderly thought it might be a fracture and it had been suggested I report to the hospital immediately.

Caroline frowned, removed her skis and went off to find a taxi to take us to the hospital. It wasn't a long journey but it was one the taxi driver evidently had done many times before from the way he took the slippery bends.

"I ought to be able to dine out on this for about a

year," Caroline promised me as we entered the double doors of the hospital.

"Would you be kind enough to wait outside, madam?" asked a male orderly as I was ushered into the X-ray room.

"Yes, but will I ever see my poor husband again?" she mocked as the door was closed in front of her.

I entered a room full of sophisticated machinery presided over by an expensively dressed doctor. I told him what I thought was wrong with me and he lifted the offending foot gently up on to an X-ray machine. Moments later he was studying the large negative.

"There's no fracture there," he assured me, pointing to the bone. "But if you are still in any pain it might be wise for me to bind the ankle up tightly." The doctor then pinned my X-ray next to five others hanging from a rail.

"Am I the sixth person already today?" I asked, looking up at the row of X-rays.

"No, no," he said, laughing. "The other five are all the same man. I think he must have tried to fly over the ravine, the fool."

"Over the ravine?"

"Yes, showing off, I suspect," he said as he began to bind my ankle. "We get one every year but this poor fellow broke both his legs and an arm, and will have a nasty scar on his face to remind him of his stupidity. Lucky to be alive in my opinion."

"Lucky to be alive?" I repeated weakly.

"Yes, but only because he didn't know what he was doing. My fourteen-year-old skis over that ravine and can land like a seagull on water. He, on the other hand," the doctor pointed to the X-rays, "won't be skiing again this holiday. In fact, he won't be walking for at least six months."

"Really?" I said.

"And as for you," he added, after he finished binding me up, "just rest the ankle in ice every three hours and change the bandage once a day. You should be back on the slopes again in a couple of days, three at the most."

"We're flying back this evening," I told him as I gingerly got to my feet.

"Good timing," he said, smiling.

I hobbled happily out of the X-ray room to find Caroline head down in *Elle*.

"You look pleased with yourself," she said, looking up.

"I am. It turns out to be nothing worse than two broken legs, a broken arm and a scar on the face."

"How stupid of me," said Caroline, "I thought it was a simple sprain."

"Not me," I told her. "Travers – the accident this morning, you remember? The ambulance. Still, they assure me he'll live," I added.

"Pity," she said, linking her arm through mine. "After all the trouble you took, I was rather hoping you'd succeed."

The Loophole

"THAT isn't the version I heard," said Philip.

One of the club members seated at the bar glanced round at the sound of raised voices, but when he saw who was involved only smiled and continued his conversation.

The Haslemere Golf Club was fairly crowded that Saturday morning. And just before lunch it was often difficult to find a seat in the spacious clubhouse.

Two of the members had already ordered their second round and settled themselves in the alcove overlooking the first hole long before the room began to fill up. Philip Masters and Michael Gilmour had finished their Saturday morning game earlier than usual and now seemed engrossed in conversation.

"And what did you hear?" asked Michael Gilmour quietly, but in a voice that carried.

"That you weren't altogether blameless in the matter."

"I most certainly was," said Michael. "What are you suggesting?"

"I'm not suggesting anything," said Philip. "But don't forget, you can't fool me. I employed you myself once and I've known you for far too long to accept everything you say at face value."

"I wasn't trying to fool anyone," said Michael. "It's common knowledge that I lost my job. I've never suggested otherwise."

"Agreed. But what isn't common knowledge is *how* you lost your job and why you haven't been able to find a new one."

"I haven't been able to find a new one for the simple reason jobs aren't that easy to come by at the moment. And by the way, it's not my fault you're a success story and a bloody millionaire."

"And it's not my fault that you're penniless and always out of work. The truth is that jobs are easy enough to come by for someone who can supply references from his last employer."

"Just what are you hinting at?" said Michael.

"I'm not hinting at anything."

Several members had stopped taking part in the conversation in front of them as they tried to listen to the one going on behind them.

"What I am saying," Philip continued, "is that no one will employ you for the simple reason that you can't find anyone who will supply you with a reference – and everybody knows it."

Everybody didn't know it, which explained why most people in the room were now trying to find out.

"I was made redundant," insisted Michael.

"In your case redundant was just a euphemism for sacked. No one pretended otherwise at the time."

"I was made redundant," repeated Michael, "for the simple reason that the company profits turned out to be a little disappointing this year."

"A little disappointing? That's rich. They were non-existent."

"Simply because we lost one or two of our major accounts to rivals."

"Rivals who, I'm informed, were only too happy to pay for a little inside information."

By now most members of the club had cut short their own conversations as they leaned, twisted, turned and bent in an effort to capture every word coming from the two men seated in the window alcove of the club room.

"The loss of those accounts was fully explained in the report to shareholders at this year's AGM," said Michael.

"But was it explained to those same shareholders how a former employee could afford to buy a new car only a matter of days after being sacked?" pursued Philip. "A second car, I might add." Philip took a sip of his tomato juice.

"It wasn't a new car," said Michael defensively. "It was a second-hand Mini and I bought it with part of my redundancy pay when I had to return the company car. And in any case, you know Carol needs her own car for the job at the bank."

"Frankly, I am amazed Carol has stuck it for so long as she has after all you've put her through."

"All I've put her through; what are you implying?" asked Michael.

"I am not *implying* anything," Philip retorted. "But the fact is that a certain young woman who shall remain nameless" – this piece of information seemed to disappoint most eavesdroppers – "also became redundant at about the same time, not to mention pregnant."

The barman had not been asked for a drink for nearly seven minutes, and by now there were few members still affecting not to be listening to the altercation between the two men. Some were even staring in open disbelief.

"But I hardly knew her," protested Michael.

"As I said, that's not the version I heard. And what's more I'm told the child bears a striking resemblance –"

"That's going too far –"

"Only if you have nothing to hide," said Philip grimly.

"You know I've nothing to hide."

"Not even the blonde hairs Carol found all over the back seat of the new Mini. The girl at work was a blonde, wasn't she?"

"Yes, but those hairs came from a golden retriever."

"You don't have a golden retriever."

"I know, but the dog belonged to the last owner."

"That bitch didn't belong to the last owner, and I refuse to believe Carol fell for that old chestnut."

"She believed it because it was the truth."

"The truth, I fear, is something you lost contact with a long time ago. You were sacked, first because you couldn't keep your hands off anything in a skirt under forty, and second, because you couldn't keep your fingers out of the till. I ought to know. Don't forget I had to get rid of you for the same reasons."

Michael jumped up, his cheeks almost the colour of Philip's tomato juice. He raised his clenched fist and was about to take a swing at Philip when Colonel Mather, the club president, appeared at his side.

"Good morning, sir," said Philip calmly, rising for the Colonel.

"Good morning, Philip," the Colonel barked. "Don't you think this little misunderstanding has gone quite far enough?"

"Little misunderstanding?" protested Michael. "Didn't you hear what he's been saying about me?"

"Every word, unfortunately, like any other member present," said the Colonel. Turning back to Philip, he added, "Perhaps you two should shake hands like good fellows and call it a day."

"Shake hands with that philandering, double-crossing shyster? Never," said Philip. "I tell you, Colonel, he's not fit to be a member of this club, and I can assure you that you've only heard half the story."

Before the Colonel could attempt another round of diplomacy Michael sprang on Philip and it took three men younger than the club president to prise them apart. The Colonel immediately ordered both men off the premises, warning them that their conduct would be reported to the house committee at its next monthly meeting. And until that meeting had taken place, they were both suspended.

The club secretary, Jeremy Howard, escorted the two men off the premises and watched Philip get into his Rolls-Royce and drive sedately down the drive and out through the gates. He had to wait on the steps of the club for several minutes before Michael departed in his Mini. He appeared to be sitting in the front seat writing something. When he had eventually passed through the club gates, the secretary turned on his heels and made his way back to the bar. What they did to each other after they left the grounds was none of his business.

Back in the clubhouse, the secretary found that the conversation had not returned to the likely winner of the President's Putter, the seeding of the Ladies' Handicap Cup, or who might be prevailed upon to sponsor the Youth Tournament that year.

"They seemed in a jolly enough mood when I passed them on the sixteenth hole earlier this morning," the club captain informed the Colonel.

The Colonel admitted to being mystified. He had known both men since the day they joined the club nearly fifteen years before. They weren't bad lads, he assured the captain; in fact he rather liked them. They had played a round of golf every Saturday morning for as long as anyone could remember, and never a cross word had been known to pass between them.

"Pity," said the Colonel. "I was hoping to ask Masters to sponsor the Youth Tournament this year."

"Good idea, but I can't see you pulling that off now."

"I can't imagine what they thought they were up to."

"Can it simply be that Philip is such a success story and Michael has fallen on hard times?" suggested the captain.

"No, there's more to it than that," replied the

Colonel. "This morning's little episode requires a fuller explanation," he added sagely.

Everyone in the club was aware that Philip Masters had built up his own business from scratch after he had left his first job as a kitchen salesman. "Ready-Fit Kitchens" had started in a shed at the end of Philip's garden and ended up in a factory on the other side of town which employed over three hundred people. After Ready-Fit went public the financial press speculated that Philip's shares alone had to be worth a couple of million. When five years later the company was taken over by the John Lewis Partnership, it became public knowledge that Philip had walked away from the deal with a cheque for seventeen million pounds and a five-year service contract that would have pleased a pop star. Some of the windfall had been spent on a magnificent Georgian house in sixty acres of woodland just outside Haslemere: he could even see the golf course from his bedroom. Philip had been married for over twenty years and his wife Sally was chairman of the regional branch of the Save the Children Fund and a JP. Their son had just won a place at St Anne's College, Oxford.

Michael was the boy's godfather.

Michael Gilmour could not have been a greater contrast. On leaving school, where Philip had been his closest friend, he had drifted from job to job. He started out as a trainee with Watneys, but lasted only a few months before moving on to work as a rep with a publishing company. Like Philip, he married his childhood sweetheart, Carol West, the daughter of a local doctor.

When their own daughter was born, Carol

complained about the hours Michael spent away from home so he left publishing and signed on as a distribution manager with a local soft drinks firm. He lasted for a couple of years until his deputy was promoted over him as area manager, at which decision Michael left in a huff. After his first spell on the dole, Michael joined a grain-packing company, but found he was allergic to corn and, having been supplied with a medical certificate to prove it, collected his first redundancy cheque. He then joined Philip as a Ready-Fit Kitchens rep but left without explanation within a month of the company being taken over. Another spell of unemployment followed before he took up the job of sales manager with a company that made microwave ovens. He seemed to have settled down at last until, without warning, he was made redundant. It was true that the company profits had been halved that year, while the company directors were sorry to see Michael go – or that was how it was expressed in their in-house magazine.

Carol was unable to hide her distress when Michael was made redundant for the fourth time. They could have done with the extra cash now that their daughter had been offered a place at art school.

Philip was the girl's godfather.

"What are you going to do about it?" asked Carol anxiously, when Michael had told her what had taken place at the club.

"There's only one thing I can do," he replied. "After all, I have my reputation to consider. I shall sue the bastard."

"That's a terrible way to talk about your oldest friend. And anyway we can't afford to go to law," said Carol. "Philip's a millionaire and we're penniless."

"Can't be helped," said Michael. "I'll have to go through with it, even if it means selling up everything."

"And even if the rest of your family has to suffer along with you?"

"None of us will suffer when he ends up paying my costs plus massive damages."

"But you could *lose*," said Carol. "Then we would end up with nothing – worse than nothing."

"That's not possible," said Michael. "He made the mistake of saying all those things in front of witnesses. There must have been over fifty members in the clubhouse this morning, including the president of the club and the editor of the local paper, and they couldn't have failed to hear every word."

Carol remained unconvinced, and she was relieved that during the next few days Michael didn't mention Philip's name once. She hoped that her husband had come to his senses and the whole affair was best forgotten.

But then the *Haslemere Chronicle* decided to print its version of the quarrel between Michael and Philip. Under the headline "Fight breaks out at golf club" came a carefully worded account of what had taken place on the previous Saturday. The editor of the *Haslemere Chronicle* knew only too well that the conversation itself was unprintable unless he also wanted to be sued, but he managed to include enough innuendo in the article to give a full flavour of what had happened that morning.

"That's the final straw," said Michael, when he finished reading the article for a third time. Carol realised that nothing she could say or do was going to stop her husband now.

The following Monday, Michael contacted a local solicitor, Reginald Lomax, who had been at school with them both. Armed with the article, Michael briefed Lomax on the conversation that the *Chronicle* had felt injudicious to publish in any great detail. Michael also gave Lomax his own detailed account of what had happened at the club that morning, and handed him four pages of handwritten notes to back his claims up.

Lomax studied the notes carefully.

"When did you write these?"

"In my car, immediately after we were suspended."

"That was circumspect of you," said Lomax. "Most circumspect." He stared quizzically at his client over the top of his half-moon spectacles. Michael made no comment. "Of course you must be aware that the law is an expensive pastime," Lomax continued. "Suing for slander will not come cheap, and even with evidence as strong as this" – he tapped the notes in front of him – "you could still lose. Slander depends so much on what other people remember or, more important, will admit to remembering."

"I'm well aware of that," said Michael. "But I'm determined to go through with it. There were over fifty people in the club within earshot that morning."

"So be it," said Lomax. "Then I shall require five thousand pounds in advance as a contingency fee to cover all the immediate costs and the preparations for a court case." For the first time Michael looked hesitant.

"Returnable, of course, but only if you win the case."

Michael removed his cheque book and wrote out a figure which, he reflected, would only just be covered by the remainder of his redundancy pay.

The writ for slander against Philip Masters was issued the next morning by Lomax, Davis and Lomax.

A week later the writ was accepted by another firm of solicitors in the same town, actually in the same building.

Back at the club, debate on the rights and wrongs of Gilmour v. Masters did not subside as the weeks passed.

Club members whispered furtively among themselves whether they might be called to give evidence at the trial. Several had already received letters from Lomax, Davis and Lomax requesting statements about what they could recall being said by the two men that morning. A good many pleaded amnesia or deafness but a few turned in graphic accounts of the quarrel. Encouraged, Michael pressed on, much to Carol's dismay.

One morning about a month later, after Carol had left for the bank, Michael Gilmour received a call from Reginald Lomax. The defendant's solicitors, he was informed, had requested a "without prejudice" consultation.

"Surely you're not surprised by that after all the evidence we've collected?" Michael replied.

"It's only a consultation," Lomax reminded him.

"Consultation or no consultation I won't settle for less than one hundred thousand pounds."

"Well, I don't even know that they –" began Lomax.

"I do, and I also know that for the last eleven weeks I haven't been able to even get an interview for a job because of that bastard," Michael said with contempt. "Nothing less than one hundred thousand pounds, do you hear me?"

"I think you are being a trifle optimistic, in the circumstances," said Lomax. "But I'll call you and let you know the other side's response as soon as the meeting has taken place."

Michael told Carol the good news that evening, but like Reginald Lomax she was sceptical. The ringing of the phone interrupted their discussion on the subject. Michael, with Carol standing by his side, listened carefully to Lomax's report. Philip, it seemed, was willing to settle for twenty-five thousand pounds and had agreed to paying both sides' costs.

Carol nodded her grateful acceptance, but Michael only repeated that Lomax was to hold out for nothing less than one hundred thousand. "Can't you see that Philip's already worked out what it's going to cost him if this case ends up in court? And he knows only too well that I won't give in."

Carol and Lomax remained unconvinced. "It's much more touch and go than you realise," the solicitor told him. "A High Court jury might consider the words were only meant as banter."

"Banter? But what about the fight that followed the banter?" said Michael.

"Started by you," Lomax pointed out. "Twenty-five thousand is a good figure in the circumstances," he added.

Michael refused to budge, and ended the conversation by repeating his demand for one hundred thousand pounds.

Two weeks passed before the other side offered fifty thousand in exchange for a quick settlement. This time Lomax was not surprised when Michael rejected the offer out of hand. "Quick settlement be damned. I've told you I won't consider less than a hundred thousand." Lomax knew by now that any plea for prudence was going to fall on deaf ears.

It took three more weeks and several more phone calls between solicitors before the other side accepted that they were going to have to pay the full one hundred thousand pounds. Reginald Lomax rang Michael to inform him of the news late one evening, trying to make it sound as if he had scored a personal triumph. He assured Michael that the necessary papers could be drawn up immediately and the settlement signed in a matter of days.

"Naturally all your costs will be covered," he added.

"Naturally," said Michael.

"So all that is left for you to do now is agree on a statement."

A short statement was penned and, with the agreement of both sides, issued to the *Haslemere Chronicle*. The paper printed the contents the following Friday on its front page. "The writ for slander between Gilmour and Masters," the

Chronicle reported, "has been withdrawn with the agreement of both sides but only after a substantial out-of-court settlement by the defendant. Philip Masters has withdrawn unreservedly what was said at the club that morning and has given an unconditional apology; he has also made a promise that he will never repeat the words used again. Mr Masters has paid the plaintiff's costs in full."

Philip wrote to the Colonel the same day, admitting perhaps he had had a little too much to drink on the morning in question. He regretted his impetuous outburst, apologised and assured the club's president it would never happen again.

Carol was the only one who seemed to be saddened by the outcome.

"What's the matter, darling?" asked Michael. "We've won, and what's more it's solved our financial problems."

"I know," said Carol, "but is it worth losing your closest friend for one hundred thousand pounds?"

On the following Saturday morning Michael was pleased to find an envelope among his morning post with the Golf Club crest on the flap. He opened it nervously and pulled out a single sheet of paper. It read:

Dear Mr Gilmour,

At the monthly committee meeting held last Wednesday Colonel Mather raised the matter of your behaviour in the clubhouse on the morning of Saturday, April 16th.

It was decided to minute the complaints of several members, but on this occasion only to issue a severe reprimand to you both. Should a similar incident occur in the future, loss of membership would be automatic.

The temporary suspension issued by Colonel Mather on April 16th is now lifted.

Yours sincerely,

Jeremy Howard

Jeremy Howard (Secretary)

"I'm off to do the shopping," shouted Carol from the top of the stairs. "What are your plans for the morning?"

"I'm going to have a round of golf," said Michael, folding up the letter.

"Good idea," said Carol to herself as she wondered whom Michael would find to play against in the future.

Quite a few members noticed Michael and Philip teeing up at the first hole that Saturday morning. The club captain commented to the Colonel that he was glad to observe that the quarrel had been sorted out to everyone's satisfaction.

"Not to mine," said the Colonel under his breath. "You can't get drunk on tomato juice."

"I wonder what the devil they can be talking about?" the club captain said as he stared at them both through the bay windows. The Colonel raised his binoculars to take a closer look at the two men.

"How could you possibly miss a four-foot putt, dummy?" asked Michael when they had reached the first green. "You must be drunk again."

"As you well know," replied Philip, "I never drink before dinner, and I therefore suggest that your allegation that I am drunk again is nothing less than slander."

"Yes, but where are your witnesses?" said Michael as they moved up on to the second tee. "I had over fifty, don't forget."

Both men laughed.

Their conversation ranged over many subjects as they played the first eight holes, never once touching on their past quarrel until they reached the ninth green, the farthest point from the club-house. They both checked to see there was no one within earshot. The nearest player was still putting out some two hundred yards behind them on the eighth hole. It was then that Michael removed a bulky brown envelope from his golf bag and handed it over to Philip.

"Thank you," said Philip, dropping the package into his own golf bag as he removed a putter. "As neat a little operation as I've been involved in for a long time," Philip added as he addressed the ball.

"I end up with forty thousand pounds," said Michael grinning, "while you lose nothing at all."

"Only because I pay tax at the highest rate and can therefore claim the loss as a legitimate business expense," said Philip, "and I wouldn't have been able to do that if I hadn't once employed you."

"And I, as a successful litigant, need pay no tax at all on damages received in a civil case."

"A loophole that even this Chancellor hasn't caught on to," said Philip.

"Even though it went to Reggie Lomax, I was sorry about the solicitors' fees," added Michael.

"No problem, old fellow. They're also one hundred per cent claimable against tax. So as you see, I didn't lose a penny and you ended up with forty thousand pounds tax free."

"And nobody the wiser," said Michael, laughing.

The Colonel put his binoculars back into their case.

"Had your eye on this year's winner of the President's Putter, Colonel?" asked the club captain.

"No," the Colonel replied. "The certain sponsor of this year's Youth Tournament."

Christina Rosenthal

THE rabbi knew he couldn't hope to begin on his sermon until he'd read the letter. He had been sitting at his desk in front of a blank sheet of paper for over an hour and still couldn't come up with a first sentence. Lately he had been unable to concentrate on a task he had carried out every Friday evening for the last thirty years. They must have realised by now that he was no longer up to it. He took the letter out of the envelope and slowly unfolded the pages. Then he pushed his half-moon spectacles up the bridge of his nose and started to read.

My dear Father,

"Jew boy! Jew boy! Jew boy!" were the first words I ever heard her say as I ran past her on the first lap of the race. She was standing behind the railing at the beginning of the home straight, hands cupped around her lips to be sure I couldn't miss the chant. She must have come from another school because I didn't recognise her, but it only took a fleeting glance to see that it was Greg Reynolds who was standing by her side.

After five years of having to tolerate his snide comments

and bullying at school all I wanted to retaliate with was, "Nazi, Nazi, Nazi," but you had always taught me to rise above such provocation.

I tried to put them both out of my mind as I moved into the second lap. I had dreamed for years of winning the mile in the West Mount High School championships, and I was determined not to let them do anything to stop me.

As I came into the back straight a second time I took a more careful look at her. She was standing amid a cluster of friends who were wearing the scarves of Marianapolis Convent. She must have been about sixteen, and as slim as a willow. I wonder if you would have chastised me had I only shouted, "No breasts, no breasts, no breasts," in the hope it might at least provoke the boy standing next to her into a fight. Then I would have been able to tell you truthfully that he had thrown the first punch but the moment you had learned that it was Greg Reynolds you would have realised how little provocation I needed.

As I reached the back straight I once again prepared myself for the chants. Chanting at track meetings had become fashionable in the late 1950s when "Zat-o-pek, Zat-o-pek, Zat-o-pek" had been roared in adulation across running stadiums around the world for the great Czech champion. Not for me was there to be the shout of "Ros-en-thal, Ros-en-thal, Ros-en-thal" as I came into earshot.

"Jew boy! Jew boy! Jew boy!" she said, sounding like a gramophone record that had got stuck. Her friend Greg, who would nowadays be described as a preppie, began laughing. I knew he had put her up to it, and how I would like to have removed that smug grin from his face. I reached the half-mile mark in two minutes seventeen seconds, comfortably inside the pace necessary to break the school record, and I felt that was the best way to put the taunting girl and that

fascist Reynolds in their place. I couldn't help thinking at the time how unfair it all was. I was a real Canadian, born and bred in this country, while she was just an immigrant. After all, you, Father, had escaped from Hamburg in 1937 and started with nothing. Her parents did not land on these shores until 1949, by which time you were a respected figure in the community.

I gritted my teeth and tried to concentrate. Zatopek had written in his autobiography that no runner can afford to lose his concentration during a race. When I reached the penultimate bend the inevitable chanting began again, but this time it only made me speed up and even more determined to break that record. Once I was back in the safety of the home straight I could hear some of my friends roaring, "Come on, Benjamin, you can do it," and the timekeeper called out, "Three twenty-three, three twenty-four, three twenty-five" as I passed the bell to begin the last lap.

I knew that the record – four thirty-two – was now well within my grasp and all those dark nights of winter training suddenly seemed worthwhile. As I reached the back straight I took the lead, and even felt that I could face the girl again. I summoned up my strength for one last effort. A quick glance over my shoulder confirmed I was already yards in front of any of my rivals, so it was only me against the clock. Then I heard the chanting, but this time it was even louder than before, "Jew boy! Jew boy! Jew boy!" It was louder because the two of them were now working in unison, and just as I came round the bend Reynolds raised his arm in a flagrant Nazi salute.

If I had only carried on for another twenty yards I would have reached the safety of the home straight and the cheers of my friends, the cup and the record. But they had made me so angry that I could no longer control myself.

I shot off the track and ran across the grass over the

long-jump pit and straight towards them. At least my crazy decision stopped their chanting because Reynolds lowered his arm and just stood there staring pathetically at me from behind the small railing that surrounded the outer perimeter of the track. I leaped right over it and landed in front of my adversary. With all the energy I had saved for the final straight I took an almighty swing at him. My fist landed an inch below his left eye and he buckled and fell to the ground by her side. Quickly she knelt down and, staring up, gave me a look of such hatred that no words could have matched it. Once I was sure Greg wasn't going to get up, I walked slowly back on to the track as the last of the runners were coming round the final bend.

"Last again, Jew boy," I heard her shout as I jogged down the home straight, so far behind the others that they didn't even bother to record my time.

How often since have you quoted me those words: "Still have I borne it with a patient shrug, for sufferance is the badge of all our tribe". Of course you were right, but I was only seventeen then, and even after I had learned the truth about Christina's father I still couldn't understand how anyone who had come from a defeated Germany, a Germany condemned by the rest of the world for its treatment of the Jews, could still behave in such a manner. And in those days I really believed her family were Nazis, but I remember you patiently explaining to me that her father had been an admiral in the German navy, and had won an Iron Cross for sinking Allied ships. Do you remember me asking how could you tolerate such a man, let alone allow him to settle down in our country?

You went on to assure me that Admiral von Braumer, who came from an old Roman Catholic family and probably despised the Nazis as much as we did, had acquitted himself honourably as an officer and a gentleman throughout his life as a German sailor. But I still couldn't accept your attitude, or didn't want to.

It didn't help, Father, that you always saw the other man's point of view, and even though Mother had died prematurely because of those bastards you could still find it in you to forgive.

If you had been born a Christian, you would have been a saint.

The rabbi put the letter down and rubbed his tired eyes before he turned over another page written in that fine script that he had taught his only son so many years before. Benjamin had always learned quickly, everything from the Hebrew scriptures to a complicated algebraic equation. The old man had even begun to hope the boy might become a rabbi.

Do you remember my asking you that evening why people couldn't understand that the world had changed? Didn't the girl realise that she was no better than we were? I shall never forget your reply. She is, you said, far better than us, if the only way you can prove your superiority is to punch her friend in the face.

I returned to my room angered by your weakness. It was to be many years before I understood your strength.

When I wasn't pounding round that track I rarely had time for anything other than working for a scholarship to McGill, so it came as a surprise that her path crossed mine again so soon.

It must have been about a week later that I saw her at the local swimming pool. She was standing at the deep end, just under the diving board, when I came in. Her long fair hair was dancing on her shoulders, her bright eyes eagerly taking in everything going on around her. Greg was by her side. I was pleased to notice a deep purple patch remained under his left eye for all to see. I also remember chuckling to myself because she really did have the flattest chest I had ever seen on a sixteen-year-old girl, though I have to confess she had fantastic legs. Perhaps she's a freak, I thought. I turned to go in to the changing room – a split second before I hit the water. When I came up for breath there was no sign of who had pushed me in, just a group of grinning but innocent faces. I didn't need a law degree to work out who it must have been, but as you constantly reminded me, Father, without evidence there is no proof . . . I wouldn't have minded that much about being pushed into the pool if I hadn't been wearing my best suit – in truth, my only suit with long trousers, the one I wore on days I was going to the synagogue.

I climbed out of the water but didn't waste any time looking round for him. I knew Greg would be a long way off by then. I walked home through the back streets, avoiding taking the bus in case someone saw me and told you what a state I was in. As soon as I got home I crept past your study and on upstairs to my room, changing before you had the chance to discover what had taken place.

Old Isaac Cohen gave me a disapproving look when I turned up at the synagogue an hour later wearing a blazer and jeans.

I took the suit to the cleaners the next morning. It cost me three weeks' pocket money to be sure that you were never aware of what had happened at the swimming pool that day.

The rabbi picked up the picture of his seventeen-year-old son in that synagogue suit. He well remembered Benjamin turning up to his service in a blazer and jeans and Isaac Cohen's outspoken reprimand. The rabbi was thankful that Mr Atkins, the swimming instructor, had phoned to warn him of what had taken place that afternoon so at least he didn't add to Mr Cohen's harsh words. He continued gazing at the photograph for a long time before he returned to the letter.

The next occasion I saw Christina – by now I had found out her name – was at the end-of-term dance held in the school gymnasium. I thought I looked pretty cool in my neatly pressed suit until I saw Greg standing by her side in a smart new dinner jacket. I remember wondering at the time if I would ever be able to afford a dinner jacket. Greg had been offered a place at McGill and was announcing the fact to everyone who cared to listen, which made me all the more determined to win a scholarship there the following year.

I stared at Christina. She was wearing a long red dress that completely covered those beautiful legs. A thin gold belt emphasised her tiny waist and the only jewellery she wore was a simple gold necklace. I knew if I waited a moment longer I wouldn't have the courage to go through with it. I clenched my fists, walked over to where they were sitting, and as you had always taught me, Father, bowed slightly before I asked, "May I have the pleasure of this dance?"

She stared into my eyes. I swear if she had told me to go out and kill a thousand men before I dared ask her again I would have done it.

She didn't even speak, but Greg leaned over her shoulder and said, "Why don't you go and find yourself a nice Jewish girl?" I thought I saw her scowl at his remark, but I only blushed like someone who's been caught with their hands in the cookie jar. I didn't dance with anyone that night. I walked straight out of the gymnasium and ran home.

I was convinced then that I hated her.

That last week of term I broke the school record for the

mile. You were there to watch me but, thank heavens, she wasn't. That was the holiday we drove over to Ottawa to spend our summer vacation with Aunt Rebecca. I was told by a school friend that Christina had spent hers in Vancouver with a German family. At least Greg had not gone with her, the friend assured me.

You went on reminding me of the importance of a good education, but you didn't need to, because every time I saw Greg it made me more determined to win that scholarship.

I worked even harder in the summer of '65 when you explained that, for a Canadian, a place at McGill was like going to Harvard or Oxford and would clear a path for the rest of my days.

For the first time in my life running took second place.

Although I didn't see much of Christina that term she was often in my mind. A classmate told me that she and Greg were no longer seeing each other, but could give me no reason for this sudden change of heart. At the time I had a so-called girlfriend who always sat on the other side of the synagogue – Naomi Goldblatz, you remember her – but it was she who dated me.

As my exams drew nearer, I was grateful that you always found time to go over my essays and tests after I had finished them. What you couldn't know was that I inevitably returned to my own room to do them a third time. Often I would fall asleep at my desk. When I woke I would turn over the page and read on.

Even you, Father, who have not an ounce of vanity in you, found it hard to disguise from your congregation the pride you took in my eight straight "A's" and the award of a top scholarship to McGill. I wondered if Christina was aware of it. She must have been. My name was painted up on the Honours Board in fresh gold leaf the following week, so someone would have told her.

* * *

It must have been three months later when I was in my first term at McGill that I saw her next. Do you remember taking me to St Joan *at the Centaur Theatre? There she was, seated a few rows in front of us with her parents and a sophomore called Bob Richards. The admiral and his wife looked strait-laced and very stern but not unsympathetic. In the interval I watched her laughing and joking with them: she had obviously enjoyed herself. I hardly saw* St Joan, *and although I couldn't take my eyes off Christina she never once noticed me. I just wanted to be on the stage playing the Dauphin so she would have to look up at me.*

When the curtain came down she and Bob Richards left her parents and headed for the exit. I followed the two of them out of the foyer and into the car park, and watched them get into a Thunderbird. A Thunderbird! I remember thinking I might one day be able to afford a dinner jacket, but never a Thunderbird.

From that moment she was in my thoughts whenever I trained, wherever I worked and even when I slept. I found out everything I could about Bob Richards and discovered that he was liked by all who knew him.

For the first time in my life I hated being a Jew.

When I next saw Christina I dreaded what might happen. It was the start of the mile against the University of Vancouver and as a freshman I had been lucky to be selected for McGill. When I came out on to the track to warm up I saw her sitting in the third row of the stand alongside Richards. They were holding hands.

I was last off when the starter's gun fired but as we went into the back straight moved up into fifth position. It was the largest crowd I had ever run in front of, and when I reached the home straight I waited for the chant "Jew boy! Jew boy! Jew boy!" but nothing happened. I wondered if she had failed to notice that I was in the race. But she had noticed because as I came round the bend I could hear her voice clearly. "Come on, Benjamin, you've got to win!" she shouted.

I wanted to look back to make sure it was Christina who had called those words; it would be another quarter of a mile before I could pass her again. By the time I did so I had moved up into third place, and I could hear her clearly: "Come on, Benjamin, you can do it!"

I immediately took the lead because all I wanted to do was get back to her. I charged on without thought of who was behind me, and by the time I passed her the third time I was several yards ahead of the field. "You're going to win!" she shouted as I ran on to reach the bell in three minutes eight seconds, eleven seconds faster than I had ever done before. I remember thinking that they ought to put something in those training manuals about love being worth two to three seconds a lap.

I watched her all the way down the back straight and when I came into the final bend for the last time the crowd rose to their feet. I turned to search for her. She was jumping up and down shouting, "Look out! Look out!" which I didn't understand until I was overtaken on the inside by the Vancouver Number One string who the coach had warned me was renowned for his strong finish. I staggered over the line a few yards behind him in second place but went on running until I was safely inside the changing room. I sat alone by my locker. Four minutes seventeen, someone told me: six seconds faster than I had ever run before. It didn't help. I stood in the shower for a long time, trying to work out what could possibly have changed her attitude.

When I walked back on to the track only the ground staff were still around. I took one last look at the finishing line before I strolled over to the Forsyth Library. I felt unable to face the usual team get-together, so I tried to settle down to write an essay on the property rights of married women.

The library was almost empty that Saturday evening and I was well into my third page when I heard a voice say, "I hope I'm not interrupting you but you didn't come to Joe's." I looked up to see Christina standing on the other side of the table. Father, I didn't know what to say. I just stared up at the beautiful creature in her fashionable blue mini-skirt and tight-fitting sweater that emphasised the most perfect breasts, and said nothing.

"I was the one who shouted 'Jew boy' when you were still at High School. I've felt ashamed about it ever since. I wanted to apologise to you on the night of the prom dance but couldn't summon up the courage with Greg standing there." I nodded my understanding – I couldn't think of any words that seemed appropriate. "I never spoke to him again," she said. "But I don't suppose you even remember Greg."

I just smiled. "Care for coffee?" I asked, trying to sound as if I wouldn't mind if she replied, "I'm sorry, I must get back to Bob."

"I'd like that very much," she said.

I took her to the library coffee shop, which was about all I could afford at the time. She never bothered to explain what had happened to Bob Richards, and I never asked.

Christina seemed to know so much about me that I felt embarrassed. She asked me to forgive her for what she had shouted on the track that day two years before. She made no excuses, placed the blame on no one else, just asked to be forgiven.

Christina told me she was hoping to join me at McGill in September, to major in German. "Bit of a cheek," she admitted, "as it is *my native tongue."*

We spent the rest of that summer in each other's company. We saw St Joan *again, and even queued for a film called* Dr No *that was all the craze at the time. We worked together, we ate together, we played together, but we slept alone.*

I said little about Christina to you at the time, but I'd bet you knew already how much I loved her; I could never hide anything from you. And after all your teaching of forgiveness and understanding you could hardly disapprove.

The rabbi paused. His heart ached because he knew so much of what was still to come although he could not have foretold what would happen in the end. He had never thought he would live to regret his Orthodox upbringing but when Mrs Goldblatz first told him about Christina he had been unable to mask his disapproval. It will pass, given time, he told her. So much for wisdom.

Whenever I went to Christina's home I was always treated with courtesy but her family were unable to hide their disapproval. They uttered words they didn't believe in an attempt to show that they were not anti-semitic, and whenever I brought up the subject with Christina she told me I was over-reacting. We both knew I wasn't. They quite simply thought I was unworthy of their daughter. They were right, but it had nothing to do with my being Jewish.

I shall never forget the first time we made love. It was the day that Christina learned she had won a place at McGill.

We had gone to my room at three o'clock to change for a game of tennis. I took her in my arms for what I thought would be a brief moment and we didn't part until the next morning. Nothing had been planned. But how could it have been, when it was the first time for both of us?

I told her I would marry her – don't all men the first time? – only I meant it.

Then a few weeks later she missed her period. I begged

her not to panic, and we both waited for another month because she was fearful of going to see any doctor in Montreal.

If I had told you everything then, Father, perhaps my life would have taken a different course. But I didn't, and have only myself to blame.

I began to plan for a marriage that neither Christina's family nor you could possibly have found acceptable, but we didn't care. Love knows no parents, and certainly no religion. When she missed her second period I agreed Christina should tell her mother. I asked her if she would like me to be with her at the time, but she simply shook her head, and explained that she felt she had to face them on her own.

"I'll wait here until you return," I promised.

She smiled. "I'll be back even before you've had the time to change your mind about marrying me."

I sat in my room at McGill all that afternoon reading and pacing – mostly pacing – but she never came back, and I didn't go in search of her until it was dark. I crept round to her home, all the while trying to convince myself there must be some simple explanation as to why she hadn't returned.

When I reached her road I could see a light on in her bedroom but nowhere else in the house so I thought she must be alone. I marched through the gate and up to the front porch, knocked on the door and waited.

Her father answered the door.

"What do you want?" he asked, his eyes never leaving me for a moment.

"I love your daughter," I told him, "and I want to marry her."

"She will never marry a Jew," he said simply and closed the door. I remember that he didn't slam it; he just closed it, which made it somehow even worse.

I stood outside in the road staring up at her room for over an hour until the light went out. Then I walked home. I recall there was a light drizzle that night and few people were on the streets. I tried to work out what I should do next, although the situation seemed hopeless to me. I went to bed that night hoping for a miracle. I had forgotten that miracles are for Christians, not Jews.

By the next morning I had worked out a plan. I phoned Christina's home at eight and nearly put the phone down when I heard the voice at the other end.

"Mrs von Braumer," she said.

"Is Christina there?" I asked in a whisper.

"No, she's not," came back the controlled impersonal reply.

"When are you expecting her back?" I asked.

"Not for some time," she said, and then the phone went dead.

"Not for some time" turned out to be over a year. I wrote, telephoned, asked friends from school and university but could never find out where they had taken her.

Then one day, unannounced, she returned to Montreal accompanied by a husband and my child. I learned the bitter details from that font of all knowledge, Naomi Goldblatz, who had already seen all three of them.

I received a short note from Christina about a week later begging me not to make any attempt to contact her.

I had just begun my last year at McGill and like some eighteenth-century gentleman I honoured her wish to the letter and turned all my energies to the final exams. She still continued to preoccupy my thoughts and I considered myself lucky at the end of the year to be offered a place at Harvard Law School.

I left Montreal for Boston on September 12th, 1968.

You must have wondered why I never came home once

during those three years. I knew of your disapproval. Thanks to Mrs Goldblatz everyone was aware who the father of Christina's child was and I felt an enforced absence might make life a little easier for you.

The rabbi paused as he remembered Mrs Goldblatz letting him know what she had considered was "only her duty".

"You're an interfering old busybody," he had told her. By the following Saturday she had moved to another synagogue and let everyone in the town know why.

He was more angry with himself than with Benjamin. He should have visited Harvard to let his son know that his love for him had not changed. So much for his powers of forgiveness.

He took up the letter once again.

Throughout those years at law school I had plenty of friends of both sexes, but Christina was rarely out of my mind for more than a few hours at a time. I wrote over forty letters to her while I was in Boston, but didn't post one of them. I even phoned, but it was never her voice that answered. If it had been, I'm not even sure I would have said anything. I just wanted to hear her.

Were you ever curious about the women in my life? I had affairs with bright girls from Radcliffe who were reading law, history or science, and once with a shop assistant who never read anything. Can you imagine, in the very act of making love, always thinking of another woman? I seemed to be doing my work on autopilot, and even my passion for running became reduced to an hour's jogging a day.

Long before the end of my last year, leading law firms in New York, Chicago and Toronto were turning up to interview us. The Harvard tom-toms can be relied on to beat across the world, but even I was surprised by a visit from the senior partner of Graham Douglas & Wilkins of Toronto. It's not a firm known for its Jewish partners, but I liked the idea of their letterhead one day reading "Graham Douglas Wilkins & Rosenthal". Even her father would surely have been impressed by that.

At least if I lived and worked in Toronto, I convinced myself, it would be far enough away for me to forget her, and perhaps with luck find someone else I could feel that way about.

Graham Douglas & Wilkins found me a spacious apartment overlooking the park and started me off at a handsome salary. In return I worked all the hours God – whoever's God – made. If I thought they had pushed me at McGill or Harvard, Father, it turned out to be no more than a dry run for the real world. I didn't complain. The work was exciting, and the rewards beyond my expectation. Only now that I could afford a Thunderbird I didn't want one.

New girlfriends came, and went as soon as they talked of marriage. The Jewish ones usually raised the subject within a week, the Gentiles, I found, waited a little longer. I even began living with one of them, Rebecca Wertz, but that too ended – on a Thursday.

I was driving to the office that morning – it must have been a little after eight, which was late for me – when I saw Christina on the other side of the busy highway, a barrier separating us. She was standing at a bus stop holding the hand of a little boy, who must have been about five – my son.

The heavy morning traffic allowed me a little longer to stare in disbelief. I found that I wanted to look at them both at once. She wore a long lightweight coat that showed she had not lost her figure. Her face was serene and only reminded me why she was rarely out of my thoughts. Her son

– our son – was wrapped up in an oversize duffle coat and his head was covered by a baseball hat that informed me that he supported the Toronto Dolphins. Sadly, it really stopped me seeing what he looked like. You can't be in Toronto, I remember thinking, you're meant to be in Montreal. I watched them both in my side-mirror as they climbed on to a bus. That particular Thursday I must have been an appalling counsellor to every client who sought my advice.

For the next week I passed by that bus stop every morning within minutes of the time I had seen them standing there but never saw them again. I began to wonder if I had imagined the whole scene. Then I spotted Christina again when I was returning across the city, having visited a client. She was on her own and I braked hard as I watched her entering a shop on Bloor Street. This time I double-parked the car and walked quickly across the road feeling like a sleazy private detective who spends his life peeping through keyholes.

What I saw took me by surprise – not to find her in a beautiful dress shop, but to discover it was where she worked.

The moment I saw that she was serving a customer I hurried back to my car. Once I had reached my office I asked my secretary if she knew of a shop called "Willing's".

My secretary laughed. "You must pronounce it the German way, the W becomes a V," she explained, "thus 'Villing's'. If you were married you would know that it's the most expensive dress shop in town," she added.

"Do you know anything else about the place?" I asked, trying to sound casual.

"Not a lot," she said. "Only that it is owned by a wealthy German lady called Mrs Klaus Willing whom they often write about in the women's magazines."

I didn't need to ask my secretary any more questions and I won't trouble you, Father, with my detective work. But, armed with those snippets of information, it didn't take me long to discover where Christina lived, that her husband was an overseas director with BMW, and that they only had the one child.

The old rabbi breathed deeply as he glanced up at the clock on his desk, more out of habit than any desire to know the time. He paused for a moment before returning to the letter. He had been so proud of his lawyer son then; why hadn't he made the first step towards a reconciliation? How he would have liked to have seen his grandson.

My ultimate decision did not require an acute legal mind, just a little common sense – although a lawyer who advises himself undoubtedly has a fool for a client. Contact, I decided, had to be direct and a letter was the only method I felt Christina would find acceptable.

I wrote a simple message that Monday morning, then rewrote it several times before I telephoned "Fleet Deliveries" and asked them to hand it to her in person at the shop. When the young man left with the letter I wanted to follow him, just to be certain he had given it to the right person. I can still repeat it word for word.

Dear Christina,

You must know I live and work in Toronto. Can we meet? I will wait for you in the lounge of the Royal York Hotel every evening between six and seven this week. If you don't come be assured I will never trouble you again.

Benjamin

I arrived that evening nearly thirty minutes early. I remember taking a seat in a large impersonal lounge just off the main hall and ordering coffee.

"Will anyone be joining you, sir?" the waiter asked.

"I can't be sure," I told him. No one did join me, but I still hung around until seven forty.

By Thursday the waiter had stopped asking if anyone would be joining me as I sat alone and allowed yet another cup of coffee to grow cold. Every few minutes I checked my watch. Each time a woman with blonde hair entered the lounge my heart leaped but it was never the woman I hoped for.

It was just before seven on Friday that I finally saw Christina standing in the doorway. She wore a smart blue suit buttoned up almost to the neck and a white blouse that made her look as if she were on her way to a business conference. Her long fair hair was pulled back behind her ears to give an impression of severity, but however hard she tried she could not be other than beautiful. I stood and raised my arm. She walked quickly over and took the seat beside me. We didn't kiss or shake hands and for some time didn't even speak.

"Thank you for coming," I said.

"I shouldn't have, it was foolish."

Some time passed before either of us spoke again.

"Can I pour you a coffee?" I asked.

"Yes, thank you."

"Black?"

"Yes."

"You haven't changed."

How banal it all would have sounded to anyone eavesdropping.

She sipped her coffee.

I should have taken her in my arms right then but I had no way of knowing that that was what she wanted. For several minutes we talked of inconsequential matters, always avoiding each other's eyes, until I suddenly said, "Do you realise that I still love you?"

Tears filled her eyes as she replied, "Of course I do. And I still feel the same about you now as I did the day we parted. And don't forget I have to see you every day, through Nicholas."

She leaned forward and spoke almost in a whisper. She told me about the meeting with her parents that had taken place more than five years before as if we had not been parted in between. Her father had shown no anger when he learned she was pregnant but the family still left for Vancouver the following morning. There they had stayed with the Willings, a family also from Munich, who were old friends of the von Braumers. Their son, Klaus, had always been besotted with Christina and didn't care about her being pregnant, or even the fact she felt nothing for him. He was confident that, given time, it would all work out for the best.

It didn't, because it couldn't. Christina had always known it would never work, however hard Klaus tried. They even left Montreal in an attempt to make a go of it. Klaus bought her the shop in Toronto and every luxury that money could afford, but it made no difference. Their marriage was an obvious sham. Yet they could not bring themselves to distress their families further with a divorce so they had led separate lives from the beginning.

As soon as Christina finished her story I touched her cheek and she took my hand and kissed it. From that moment on we saw each other every spare moment that could be stolen, day or night. It was the happiest year of my life, and I was unable to hide from anyone how I felt.

Our affair – for that's how the gossips were describing it – inevitably became public. However discreet we tried to be,

Toronto, I quickly discovered, is a very small place, full of people who took pleasure in informing those whom we also loved that we had been seen together regularly, even leaving my home in the early hours.

Then quite suddenly we were left with no choice in the matter: Christina told me she was pregnant again. Only this time it held no fears for either of us.

Once she had told Klaus the settlement went through as quickly as the best divorce lawyer at Graham Douglas & Wilkins could negotiate. We were married only a few days after the final papers were signed. We both regretted that Christina's parents felt unable to attend the wedding but I couldn't understand why you didn't come.

The rabbi still could not believe his own intolerance and short-sightedness. The demands on an Orthodox Jew should be waived if it meant losing one's only child. He had searched the Talmud in vain for any passage that would allow him to break his lifelong vows. In vain.

The only sad part of the divorce settlement was that Klaus was given custody of our child. He also demanded, in exchange for a quick divorce, that I not be allowed to see Nicholas before his twenty-first birthday, and that he should not be told that I was his real father. At the time it seemed a hard price to pay, even for such happiness. We both knew that we had been left with no choice but to accept his terms.

I used to wonder how each day could be so much better than the last. If I was apart from Christina for more than a few hours I always missed her. If the firm sent me out of town on business for a night I would phone her two, three, perhaps four times, and if it was for more than a night then she came with me. I remember you once describing your love for my mother and wondering at the time if I could ever hope to achieve such happiness.

We began to make plans for the birth of our child. William, if it was a boy – her choice; Deborah, if it was a girl – mine. I painted the spare room pink, assuming I had already won.

Christina had to stop me buying too many baby clothes, but I warned her that it didn't matter as we were going to have a dozen more children. Jews, I reminded her, believed in dynasties.

She attended her exercise classes regularly, dieted carefully, rested sensibly. I told her she was doing far more than was required of a mother, even of my daughter. I asked if I could be present when our child was born and her gynaecologist seemed reluctant at first, but then agreed. By the time the ninth month came the hospital must have thought from the amount of fuss I was making they were preparing for the birth of a royal prince.

I drove Christina into Women's College Hospital on the way to work last Tuesday. Although I went on to the office I found it impossible to concentrate. The hospital rang in the afternoon to say they thought the child would be born early that evening: obviously Deborah did not wish to disrupt the working hours of Graham Douglas & Wilkins. However, I still arrived at the hospital far too early. I sat on the end of Christina's bed until her contractions started coming every minute and then to my surprise they asked me to leave. They needed to rupture her membranes, a nurse explained. I asked her to remind the midwife that I wanted to be present to witness the birth.

I went out into the corridor and began pacing up and down, the way expectant fathers do in B-movies. Christina's gynaecologist arrived about half an hour later and gave me a huge smile. I noticed a cigar in his top pocket, obviously reserved for expectant fathers. "It's about to happen," was all he said.

A second doctor whom I had never seen before arrived a few minutes later and went quickly into her room. He only gave me a nod. I felt like a man in the dock waiting to hear the jury's verdict.

It must have been at least another fifteen minutes before I saw the unit being rushed down the corridor by a team of three young interns. They didn't even give me so much as a second glance as they disappeared into Christina's room.

I heard the screams that suddenly gave way to the plaintive cry of a new-born child. I thanked my God and hers. When the doctor came out of her room I remember noticing that the cigar had disappeared.

"It's a girl," he said quietly. I was overjoyed. "No need to repaint the bedroom immediately" flashed through my mind.

"Can I see Christina now?" I asked.

He took me by the arm and led me across the corridor and into his office.

"Would you like to sit down?" he asked. "I'm afraid I have some sad news."

"Is she all right?"

"I am sorry, so very sorry, to tell you that your wife is dead."

At first I didn't believe him, I refused to believe him. Why? Why? I wanted to scream.

"We did warn her," he added.

"Warn her? Warn her of what?"

"That her blood pressure might not stand up to it a second time."

Christina had never told me what the doctor went on to explain – that the birth of our first child had been complicated, and that the doctors had advised her against becoming pregnant again.

"Why hadn't she told me?" I demanded. Then I realised why. She had risked everything for me – foolish, selfish, thoughtless me – and I had ended up killing the one person I loved.

They allowed me to hold Deborah in my arms for just a moment before they put her into an incubator and told me it would be another twenty-four hours before she came off the danger list.

You will never know how much it meant to me, Father, that you came to the hospital so quickly. Christina's parents arrived later that evening. They were magnificent. He begged for my forgiveness – begged for my *forgiveness. It could never have happened, he kept repeating, if he hadn't been so stupid and prejudiced.*

His wife took my hand and asked if she might be allowed to see Deborah from time to time. Of course I agreed. They left just before midnight. I sat, walked, slept in that corridor for the next twenty-four hours until they told me that my daughter was off the danger list. She would have to remain in the hospital for a few more days, they explained, but she was now managing to suck milk from a bottle.

Christina's father kindly took over the funeral arrangements.

You must have wondered why I didn't appear and I owe you an explanation. I thought I would just drop into the hospital on my way to the funeral so that I could spend a few moments with Deborah. I had already transferred my love.

The doctor couldn't get the words out. It took a brave man to tell me that her heart had stopped beating a few minutes before my arrival. Even the senior surgeon was in tears. When I left the hospital the corridors were empty.

I want you to know, Father, that I love you with all my

heart, but I have no desire to spend the rest of my life without Christina or Deborah.

I only ask to be buried beside my wife and daughter and to be remembered as their husband and father. That way unthinking people might learn from our love. And when you finish this letter, remember only that I had such total happiness when I was with her that death holds no fears for me.

Your son,
Benjamin.

The old rabbi placed the letter down on the table in front of him. He had read it every day for the last ten years.